## Praise for Samantha Shannon

"An impressive new voice for fantasy literature." —*USA Today*

"A great imagination at work." —*People*

"Shannon is likely on the brink of literary stardom." —*New York magazine*

## More praise for *The Mime Order*

"Propulsive." —*Kirkus Reviews*

"Shannon has continued to build on this imagined world with intricacy." —*The Washington Post*

"Full of the action, turns, and surprising revelations that readers have come to expect from Shannon." —*Library Journal*

"With a unique plot, impeccable world-building and important character connections, *The Mime Order* outshines its predecessor . . . An intelligent, adventurous read." —*Deseret News*

"Shannon's world-building is original and intriguing, especially the complex, almost mythic voyant underground." —*Publishers Weekly*

"At its best The Bone Season was a triumphant blend of Orwellian dystopia and China Miéville nonconformity . . . [and] hinted at a Rowling scope of imagination . . . The central, gripping whodunit plot of [*The Mime Order*] . . . will certainly make everyone crave book three." —*The Independent*

By the Same Author

*The Bone Season*

# The Mime Order

Samantha Shannon

B L O O M S B U R Y
NEW YORK · LONDON · OXFORD · NEW DELHI · SYDNEY

Bloomsbury USA
An imprint of Bloomsbury Publishing Plc

| 1385 Broadway | 50 Bedford Square |
| New York | London |
| NY 10018 | WC1B 3DP |
| USA | UK |

www.bloomsbury.com

BLOOMSBURY and the Diana logo are trademarks of Bloomsbury Publishing Plc

First published 2015
This paperback edition published 2016

ISBN: HB: 978-1-62040-893-3
ePub: 978-1-62040-894-0
PB: 978-1-62040-895-7

**Library of Congress Cataloging-in-Publication Data has been applied for.**

2 4 6 8 10 9 7 5 3 1

Typeset by Hewer Text UK Ltd, Edinburgh
Printed and bound in USA by Berryville Graphics Inc., Berryville, Virginia

To find out more about our authors and books visit www.bloomsbury.com.
Here you will find extracts, author interviews, details of forthcoming events,
and the option to sign up for our newsletters.

Bloomsbury books may be purchased for business or promotional use.
For information on bulk purchases please contact Macmillan Corporate and
Premium Sales Department at specialmarkets@macmillan.com.

*For the fighters—*
*and the writers*

*Mimes, in the form of God on high,*
*Mutter and mumble low,*
*And hither and thither fly—*
*Mere puppets they, who come and go*
*At bidding of vast formless things*

Edgar Allan Poe

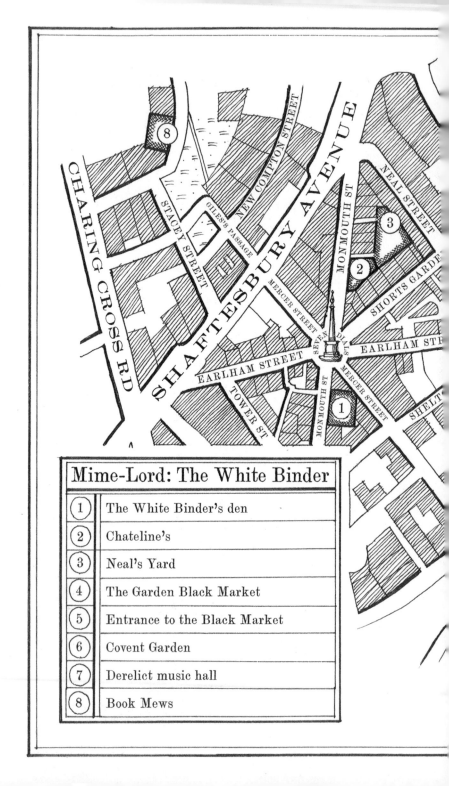

## Mime-Lord: The White Binder

| | |
|---|---|
| ① | The White Binder's den |
| ② | Chateline's |
| ③ | Neal's Yard |
| ④ | The Garden Black Market |
| ⑤ | Entrance to the Black Market |
| ⑥ | Covent Garden |
| ⑦ | Derelict music hall |
| ⑧ | Book Mews |

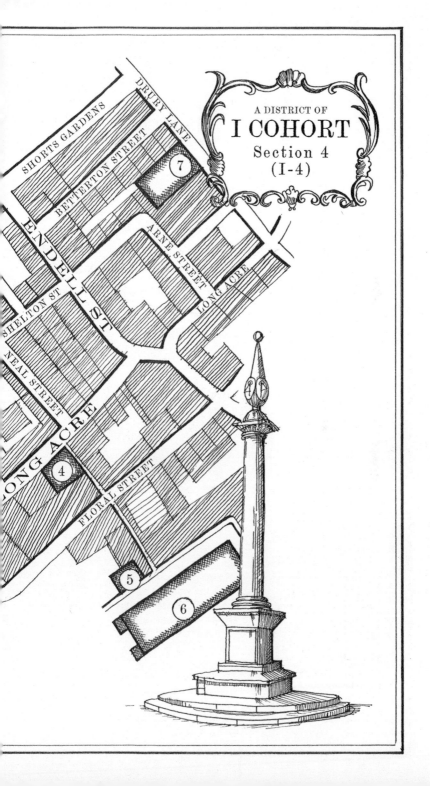

A DISTRICT OF
I COHORT
Section 4
(I-4)

SHORTS GARDENS

DRURY LANE

BETTERTON STREET

ARNE STREET

LONG ACRE

LINDELL ST

SHELTON ST

NEAL STREET

LONG ACRE

FLORAL STREET

7

4

5

6

# A Note to the Reader

At the back of this book you will find a record of the members of the Unnatural Assembly, composed of the clairvoyant mime-lords and mime-queens who operate in each section of Scion London, as well as additional maps of key sections. You will also find a chart of the Seven Orders of Clairvoyance and a glossary of terms unique to Scion and the slang of the clairvoyant underworld.

# PART I

## The Rogue Dial

*For are we not vastly superior to them, we Unnaturals? For though we pick the Bones of Society, though we crawl in Gutters and beg for our Keep, we are living Conduits to the World Beyond. We are Proof of an auxiliary Existence. We are Catalysts of the ultimate Energy, the eternal Æther. We harness Death itself. We unhorse the Reaper.*

—An Obscure Writer, *On the Merits of Unnaturalness*

1

# Alight

It's rare that a story begins at the beginning. In the grand scheme of things, I really turned up at the beginning of the end of this one. After all, the story of the Rephaim and Scion started almost two hundred years before I was born—and human lives, to Rephaim, are as fleeting as a single heartbeat.

Some revolutions change the world in a day. Others take decades or centuries or more, and others still never come to fruition. Mine began with a moment and a choice. Mine began with the blooming of a flower in a secret city on the border between worlds.

You'll have to wait and see how it ends.

Welcome back to Scion.

\*\*\*\*

## September 2, 2059

Each of the train's ten cars was upholstered in the style of a small parlor. Rich red carpets, polished rosewood tables, the anchor—Scion's symbol—stitched in gold on every seat. Classical music drifted from a hidden speaker.

At the end of our car, Jaxon Hall, mime-lord of I-4 and leader of my gang of London voyants, sat with his hands folded atop his cane, staring straight ahead without blinking.

Across the aisle, my best friend Nick Nygård gripped a metal hoop that hung from the ceiling. After six months away from him, seeing his gentle face was like looking at a memory. His hand was strung with swollen veins, and his gaze was fastened to the nearest window, watching the safety lights that flashed past every now and then. Three other members of the gang were slumped across the seats: Danica sporting a head wound, Nadine with bloody hands, and her brother, Zeke, grasping his injured shoulder. The last of us, Eliza, had stayed behind in London.

I sat apart from them, watching the tunnel disappear behind us. There was a fresh scorch on my forearm where Danica had disabled the Scion microchip under my skin.

I could still hear the last command Warden gave me: *Run, little dreamer.* But where would Warden run? The closed door of the station had been surrounded by armed Vigiles. For a giant he could move like a shadow, but even a shadow couldn't have slipped past that door. Nashira Sargas, his erstwhile fiancée and leader of the Rephaim, would spare no effort to hunt him down.

Somewhere in the darkness was the golden cord, linking Warden's spirit to mine. I let the æther wash over me but felt no answer from the other side.

Scion couldn't be unaware of the uprising. Something would have got out before the fires destroyed the communication systems. A message, a warning—even a word would have been enough to alert them to a crisis in their colony. They'd be waiting for us with flux and guns, waiting to send us back to our prison.

They could try.

"We need to do a headcount." I stood. "How long until we reach London?"

"Twenty minutes, I think," Nick said.

"Do I want to know where the tunnel ends?"

He gave me a grim smile. "The Archon. There's a station right underneath it. S-Whitehall, it's called."

My stomach dropped a notch. "Don't tell me you were planning an escape through the Archon."

"No. We're going to stop the train early and find another way out," he said. "There must be other stations in this network. Dani says there might even be a way back into the Underground proper, through the service tunnels."

"Those service tunnels could be crawling with Underguards," I said, turning to Danica. "Are you sure about this?"

"They won't be guarded. They're for engineers," she said. "But I don't know about these older tunnels. I doubt anyone at SciORE has ever been in them."

SciORE was Scion's robotics and engineering division. If anyone would know about the tunnels, it would be someone from there. "There must be another way out," I pressed. Even if we did get back into the main Underground network, we'd be arrested at the barriers. "Can we divert the train? Or is there a way up to street level?"

"No manual override. And they're not stupid enough to have access to street level from this line." Danica lifted the rag from her head wound and inspected the blood that soaked it. There seemed to be more blood than rag. "The train's programmed to go straight back to S-Whitehall. We're setting off the fire alarm and leaving through the first station we find."

The idea of taking a large group of people through a decaying, lightless tunnel system didn't seem sensible. They were all weak, hungry, and exhausted; we needed to move fast. "There must be a station under the Tower," I said. "They wouldn't use the same station to transport voyants and Scion staff."

"That's a long way to walk for a hunch," Nadine cut in. "The Tower's miles away from the Archon."

"They keep voyants in the Tower. It makes sense to have a station underneath it."

"If we assume there's a station at the Tower, we need to time the alarm carefully," Nick said. "Any ideas, Dani?"

"What?"

"How can we identify where we are?"

"Like I said, I don't know this tunnel system."

"Take a wild guess."

She took a little longer than usual to answer. Her eyes were ringed with bruises. "They . . . might have put markers on the lines so the workers didn't get disoriented. You find them in Scion tunnels. Plaques stating the distance to the nearest station."

"But we'd need to get off the train to see those."

"Exactly. And we've only got one shot at stopping it."

"Sort it out," I said. "I'll find something to set off the alarm."

I left them to debate and walked toward the next car. Jaxon turned his face away. I stopped in front of him.

"Jaxon, do you have a lighter?"

"No," he said.

"Fine."

The train's sections were separated by sliding doors. They couldn't be sealed shut; nor was the glass bulletproof. If we were caught in this thing, there would be no getting away.

A crowd of faces looked up at me. The surviving voyants, all huddled together. I'd hoped Julian might have boarded when I wasn't looking, but there was no sign of my co-conspirator. My heart clenched with grief. Even if he and his unit of performers survived the rest of the night, Nashira would have them all trimmed at the neck by sunrise.

"Where are we going, Paige?" It was Lotte, one of the performers. Still wearing her costume from the Bicentenary, the historic event we'd just ruined with our escape. "London?"

"Yes," I said. "Look, we're going to have to stop the train early and walk to the first exit we find. It's heading for the Archon."

There was an intake of breath, and wild looks were exchanged. "That doesn't sound safe," Felix said.

"It's our only chance. Was anyone awake when they put us on the train to Sheol I?"

"I was," an augur said.

"So there's an exit at the Tower?"

"Definitely. They took us straight from the cells to the station. But we're not going through there, are we?"

"Unless we find another station, yes."

While they murmured among themselves, I counted them. Not including myself and the gang, there were twenty-two survivors.

How would these people survive in the real world after years of being treated like animals? Some of them would barely remember the citadel, and their gangs would have forgotten them. I pushed the thought away and knelt beside Michael, who was sitting a few seats apart from the others. Lovely, sweet-tempered Michael, the only other human that Warden had taken under his wing.

"Michael?" I touched his shoulder. His cheeks were blotched and damp. "Michael, listen. I know this is scary, but I couldn't just leave you at Magdalen."

He nodded. He wasn't quite mute, but he used words carefully.

"You don't have to go back to your parents, I promise. I'll try and find you a place to live." I looked away. "If we make it."

Michael wiped his face with his sleeve.

"Do you have Warden's lighter?" I said, using a soft voice. He dug a hand into his gray jacket and pulled out a familiar rectangular lighter. I took it. "Thank you."

Also sitting alone was Ivy, the palmist. She was a testament to Rephaite cruelty, with her shaved head and hollow cheeks. Her keeper, Thuban Sargas, had treated her like a punching bag. Something about her twisting fingers and trembling jaw told me that she shouldn't be left on her own for long. I sat down opposite her, taking in the bruises that bloomed beneath her skin.

"Ivy?"

Her nod was barely visible. A dirty yellow tunic hung from her shoulders.

"You know we can't take you to a hospital," I said, "but I want to know you're going somewhere safe. Do you have a gang that can look after you?"

"No gang." Her voice was a wasted husk. "I was . . . a gutterling in Camden. But I can't go back there."

"Why?"

She shook her head. Camden was the district in II-4 with the largest community of voyants, a busy market town that clustered around a stretch of the Grand Canal.

I placed the lighter on the gleaming table and clasped my hands. Old moons of dirt sat under my fingernails.

"Is there no one at all you can trust there?" I said quietly. More than anything I wanted to offer her somewhere to stay, but Jaxon wouldn't put up with strangers invading his den, especially as I wasn't intending to go back there with him. None of these voyants would last long on the street.

Her fingers pressed into her arm, stroking and grasping. After a long pause, she said, "There's one person. Agatha. She works at a boutique in the market."

"What's it called?"

"Just Agatha's Boutique." Blood seeped from her bottom lip. "She hasn't seen me in a while, but she'll take care of me."

"Okay." I stood. "I'll send one of the others with you."

Her sunken eyes were set on the window, far away. The knowledge that her keeper might still be alive made my stomach roil.

The door slid open, and the other five came in. I picked up the lighter and walked across the carpet to meet them. "That's the White Binder," someone whispered. "From I-4." Jaxon stood at the back, grasping his bladed cane. His silence was unnerving, but I had no time for games.

"How does Paige know him?" Another, frightened whisper. "You don't think she's—?"

"We're ready, Dreamer," Nick said.

That name would confirm their suspicions. I focused on the æther as best I could. Dreamscapes teemed within my radius, like a seething hive of bees. We were right underneath London.

"Here." I tossed Nick the lighter. "Do the honors."

He held it up to the panel and flipped the lid open. Within a few seconds, the fire alarm glowed red.

"*Emergency*," said the voice of Scarlett Burnish. "*Fire detected in rear car. Sealing doors.*" The doors to the last car snapped shut, and there was a low-pitched drone as the train glided to a halt. "*Please move toward the front of the train and remain seated. A life-preservation team has been dispatched. Do not alight from the train. Do not attempt to open any doors or windows. Please operate the slide mechanism if extra ventilation is required.*"

"You won't trick it for long," Danica stated. "Once it sees there's no smoke, the train will go again."

The end of the train was home to a small platform with a guard rail. I hitched my legs over it. "Pass a flashlight," I said to Zeke. When he did, I aimed the beam at the tracks. "There's room to walk next to them. Any way to turn the tracks off, Fury?" The switch to her syndicate name came naturally. It was part of how we'd survived for so long in Scion.

"No," Danica said. "And there's a fairly high probability that we might suffocate down here."

"Great, thanks."

Keeping a wary eye on the third rail, I let go of the platform and dropped on to the ballast. Zeke started to help the survivors down.

We set off in single file, giving the rails and sleepers a wide berth. My filthy white boots crunched through the trackbed. The tunnel was vast and cold, and it seemed to stretch on forever, dark in the long intervals between the security beacons. We had five flashlights between us, one with a flagging battery. My breath echoed in my ears. Gooseflesh raced up the backs of my arms. I kept my palm pressed to the wall and concentrated on putting my feet in the right places.

After ten minutes the rails trembled and we threw ourselves against the wall. The empty train we'd taken from our prison came hurtling past in a blur of metal and lights, heading for the Archon.

By the time we reached a junction signal, where a single green lamp shone, my legs were shaking with exhaustion.

"Fury," I called, "know anything about these?"

"Says the track ahead is clear and the train was programmed to take the second right turn," Danica said.

The left turn was blocked. "Should we take the first one?"

"We haven't got much of a choice."

The tunnel widened around the corner. We broke into a run. Nick carried Ivy, who was so weak I marveled that she'd reached the train at all.

The second passageway was illuminated with white lights. A filthy plaque had been drilled on to a sleeper, reading WESTMIN-STER, 2500M. The first tunnel yawned before us, utterly black, with a plaque reading TOWER, 800M. I held a finger to my lips. If there was a squad waiting on the Westminster platform, they would have received an unoccupied train by now. They might even be in the tunnels.

A slim brown rat darted through the ranks. Michael recoiled, but Nadine shone the flashlight after it. "Wonder what they're living on."

We found out, of course. As we walked, the rats multiplied, and the sounds of chattering and teeth clicked through the tunnel. Zeke's hand shook when the flashlight beam found the corpse, rats still feeding on the last of its flesh. It was clad in the sorry rags of a harlie, and the ribcage had clearly been crushed by a train more than once.

"The hand's on the third rail," Nick said. "Poor bastard must have come without a flashlight."

One voyant shook her head. "How did he get so far on his own?"

Someone let out a quiet sob. He'd so nearly made it home, this harlie who'd escaped his prison.

At last the flashlights fell upon a platform. I stepped across the rails and pulled myself on to it, my muscles throbbing as I lifted the flashlight to eye level. The beam cut through the crushing darkness, revealing white stone walls, a hygienic strip-sprayer, and a storage unit full of folding stretchers: a mirror image of the receiving station on the other end. The stench of hydrogen peroxide was eyewatering. Did they think they'd catch the plague off us, these people? Did they bleach their hands once they'd dumped us on the train, scared clairvoyance might rub off on them? I could almost see myself pinned to a stretcher, racked with phantasmagoria, manhandled by doctors in white coats.

There was no sign of a guard. We swung our flashlights into every corner. A giant sign was bolted to the wall: a red diamond chopped in two by a blue bar, with the name of the station written across it in tall white lettering.

TOWER OF LONDON

I didn't need a map to know that Tower of London wasn't a registered Underground station.

Beneath the sign was a small tablet. I leaned closer, blowing

11

dust from the embossed letters. THE PENTAD LINE, it read. A map showed the locations of five secret stations under the citadel. Tiny lines of text told me that the stations had been built during the construction of the Metropolitan Railway, the old name for the London Underground.

Nick came to stand beside me. "How did we let this happen?" he murmured.

"They keep some of us in the Tower for years before they're sent down here."

He gave my shoulder a gentle squeeze. "Do you remember being brought here?"

"No. I was fluxed."

A gust of tiny spots crossed my vision. I raised my fingers to my temple. The amaranth Warden had given me had healed most of the damage to my dreamscape, but a faint sense of malaise hung around my head, and from time to time my vision faltered.

"We need to get moving," I said, watching the others climb on to the platform.

There were two exits: a large elevator, big enough to accommodate several stretchers at a time, and a heavy metal door marked FIRE EXIT. Nick opened it.

"Looks like we're taking the stairs," he said. "Anyone know the layout of the Tower complex?"

The only landmark I knew was White Tower, the keep and heart of the prison complex, run by an elite security force called the Guard Extraordinary. In the syndicate we called them Ravens: cruel, black-clad Vigiles with a limitless number of torture methods.

"I do." Nell raised her hand. "Some of it."

"What's your name?" Nick said.

"It's 9. I mean, Nell." She resembled my friend Liss enough to have fooled the Overseer with a mask and costume—curling black hair, the same sylphlike build—but her face was made of harder lines. Her skin had a deep olive tone, and where Liss's eyes had been small and very dark, Nell's were a limpid aqua.

Nick's voice softened. "Tell us what you know."

"It was ten years ago. They might have changed it."

"Anything's better than nothing."

"They didn't use flux on a few of us," she said. "I was pretending to be unconscious. If those stairs come up near the elevator doors, I think we're going to be standing right behind the Traitors' Gate, but it'll be locked."

"I can deal with locks." Nadine held up a leather pouch of picks. "And Ravens, if they want a fight."

"Don't get cocky. We're not fighting." Nick looked up at the low ceiling. "How many of us are there, Paige?"

"Twenty-eight," I said.

"Let's move in small groups. We can go up first with Nell. Binder, Diamond, can you keep an eye on—?"

"I hope very much," Jaxon said, "that you are not presuming to give me orders, Red Vision."

In the blur of getting off the train and finding the platform, I'd scarcely noticed him. He was standing in the shadows, his hand on his cane, straight and bright as a newly lit candle.

After a moment, Nick flexed his jaw. "I was asking for your help," he said.

"I will stay here until you clear a path." Jaxon sniffed. "You can dirty *your* hands plucking feathers off the Ravens."

I took Nick by the arm. "Of course we can," he muttered, not quite loudly enough for Jaxon to hear.

"I'll watch them," Zeke said. He hadn't spoken for the whole train journey. One of his hands was clamped over his shoulder, the other wrapped into a white-knuckled fist.

Nick swallowed and beckoned to Nell. "Lead the way."

Leaving the prisoners, the three of us followed Nell up a flight of steep, winding steps. She was quick as a bird; I found myself struggling to keep up. Every muscle in my legs was burning. Our footfalls were too loud, echoing above and below us. Behind me, Nick's boot caught on a step. Nadine grabbed his elbow.

At the top, Nell slowed down and cracked open another door. The distant howl of civil defense sirens came rushing into the passageway. If they knew we were missing, it was only a matter of time until they worked out where we were.

"All clear," Nell whispered.

I took my hunting knife from my backpack. Using guns would draw out every Raven in the keep. Behind me, Nick took out a small gray handset and punched a few keys.

"Come on, Eliza," he muttered. "*Jävla telefon . . .*"

I glanced at him. "Send her an image."

"I have. We need to know how long she'll be."

As Nell had predicted, the entrance to the stairwell was opposite the deactivated elevator. To the right was a wall of enormous bricks, sealed with mortar, and to the left, built under a sweeping stone archway, was Traitors' Gate: a solemn black construction with a latticed lunette, used as an entrance during the monarch days. We were low down here, too low to be seen from the guard towers. A flight of stone steps stretched beyond the gate, lichen-splotched, with a narrow ramp for stretchers.

The moon illuminated what little I could see of the White Tower. A high wall stood between the keep and the gate—something we could hide behind. A powerful searchlight beamed from a turret. The sirens roared a single, unbroken note. In Scion, that signaled a major security breach.

"That's where the guards live." Nell pointed to the keep. "They keep the voyants in the Bloody Tower."

"Where will the steps take us?" I said.

"The innermost keep. We have to hurry."

As she spoke, a unit of Ravens came marching up the path, directly opposite the gate. We flattened ourselves against the walls. A bead of sweat trembled at Nick's temple. If they saw that the gate was secure, they might not check it.

Luck was on our side. The Ravens moved on. Once they were out of sight, I pushed myself from the wall with trembling arms. Nell slid to the ground, swearing under her breath.

Above our hiding spot, several more sirens joined their voices to the warning. I tried opening the gate, to no avail. The chains were held together with a padlock. Seeing it, Nadine knocked me out of the way and took a tiny flathead screwdriver from her belt. She slid it into the lower half of the keyhole, then pulled out a silver pick.

"This could take a while." It was getting hard to hear over the noise. "The pins feel rusty."

"We don't have a while."

"Just get the others." Nadine didn't take her eyes off the padlock. "We should stay together."

As she spoke, Nick held the phone to his ear and whispered, "Muse?" He spoke to Eliza in a low voice. "She'll be here as soon as she can," he said to me. "She's sending Spring-heel'd Jack's footpads to help us."

"How long?"

"Ten minutes. The footpads should be here sooner."

Ten minutes was too long.

The searchlight moved overhead, searching the innermost keep. Nell drew away from it, her eyes narrowed against the glare. She pushed herself into the corner and folded her arms, breathing through her nose.

I paced between the walls, checking every brick. If the Ravens were circling the complex, it wouldn't be long before they came back. We had to open the gate, get the prisoners out of the way, and return the padlock to its place before then. I dug my fingers into the groove between the elevator doors, trying to pry them apart, but they wouldn't open an inch.

A few feet away, Nadine took out another pick. She was working at an awkward angle, given that the padlock was on the other side of the gate, but her hands were steady. Zeke emerged from the stairwell with a flock of nervous prisoners at his back. I motioned for him to stay where he was, shaking my head.

At the gate, Nadine sprang the padlock. We helped her pull the heavy chains from the bars, careful not to let the links make too much noise, and together we pushed open the Traitors' Gate. It scraped against the gravel, its hinges groaning with disuse, but the sirens drowned out the noise. Nell ran up the steps and beckoned us.

"They'll have blocked all the exits," she said when I was close. "That padlock was the only weak point in this place. We'll have to climb over the south wall."

Climbing. My forte. "Vision, get the others," I said. "Be ready to run."

I crept up the steps, keeping low, my revolver gripped in both hands. Another set of steps led up to one of the towers on either side of the archway. A quick jump would take us between two battlements in the adjacent wall, which was much lower than I'd expected. Clearly Scion didn't expect voyants to get this far in the rare event that they escaped the Bloody Tower. I signaled to Nick to bring the others, then headed up the second set of steps, light-footed, keeping to the shadows. When I reached the gap between the battlements, my chest tightened.

There it was.

London.

Beyond the wall was a steep bank leading to the Thames. To the left was Tower Bridge. If we went right, we'd be able to circle around the complex unseen and reach the main road. Nick took a pouch from his pocket and rubbed chalk between his palms.

"I'll go first," he murmured. "You help the others down. Eliza will be waiting on that road."

I looked up at the bridge, scanning for snipers. There were none to be seen, but I sensed three dreamscapes.

Nick squeezed between the battlements and gripped one in each hand, turning to face the wall. His feet sought purchase against the stone, dislodging small fragments. "Careful," I said, though I didn't need to say it. Nick was better at climbing than he was at walking. He shot me a quick smile before lowering himself and dropping the final few feet, falling straight into a crouch.

It made me uneasy that the wall now stood between us.

I held out my hands for the first prisoner. Michael was there with Nell, both supporting Ivy. I took her by the elbows, guiding her to the battlements.

"Up here, Ivy." I shucked Nick's coat and buttoned it around her, leaving me in what was left of my white dress. "Give me your hands."

With Michael's help, I got Ivy over the wall. Nick took her narrow hips, carrying her on to the grass. "Michael, get the injured people up here, quickly," I said, my tone harder than I'd intended. He went to help Felix, who was limping.

One by one, they went over the wall: Ella, Lotte, then a shaken crystalist, then an augur with a broken wrist. Each one stayed close to where they landed, guarded by Nick and his pistol. As I held out a hand to Michael, he was swept aside by Jaxon. He climbed on to the battlements with ease, tossing his cane over first, then leaned down to whisper in my ear.

"You have one more chance, O my lovely. Come back to Dials, and I will forget what you said in Sheol I."

I stared straight ahead. "Thank you, Jaxon."

He leaped down from the battlements, so elegant he almost seemed to glide. I looked back at Michael. Blood was flowing from his cut face, down his neck, soaking his shirt.

"Go on." I grasped his wrists. "Just don't look down."

Michael managed to swing a leg over the wall. His fingers dug into my arms.

A gasp tore from Nell's throat. A long bloodstain was blossoming through the leg of her trousers, coating her fingers. She looked up at me, her eyes wide with fear. A current coursed through my body.

"Get down!" I shouted over the sirens. "Get down, *now!*"

There was no time for anyone to obey. A torrent of bullets tore through the line of prisoners on the steps.

Bodies falling, twisting and jerking. A piercing scream. Michael's wrists slipped through my fingers. I threw myself down behind the balustrade and covered my head with my arms.

Containment would be paramount: kill on sight, don't ask questions.

Nick was roaring my name from below, telling me to move, to jump, but I was paralyzed by fear. My perception narrowed until all I was aware of was my heart and my shallow breathing, and the muffled beat of the guns. Then hands were grasping me, lifting me over the wall, and I was falling.

The soles of my boots slammed against earth, jarring my legs to the hip, and I was pitched forward a few more feet. With a dull *whump* and a grunt of pain, another human shape landed beside me. Nell, her teeth clenched tight. She dragged herself along the ground, then to her feet, and limped as fast as she could. I crawled in the same direction until Nick pulled my arm around his neck. I twisted away from him.

"We have to get them—"

"Paige, come *on!*"

Nadine had made it over the wall, but the other two were still climbing the battlements. A fresh barrage of gunfire from White Tower had the survivors running in all directions. Danica and Zeke jumped, two silhouettes in the glaring moonlight.

I sensed the sniper above us. A fleeing amaurotic girl went down, her skull blown open like soft fruit. Michael almost tripped over her. The sniper set her sight on him.

Every nerve in my body burst into red flame. I wrenched my arm from Nick's grip. With the single drop of strength I still had left, I threw out my spirit and seared right through the sniper's dreamscape, sending her spirit into the æther and her body over the balustrade. As her empty corpse hit the grass, Michael vaulted over the wall to the riverbank. I screamed his name over the sirens, but he was gone.

My feet moved faster than my thoughts. The cracks in my dreamscape were widening, like freshly opened wounds.

We were close to the road now, getting closer, almost there. There were the streetlamps. The guns boomed from the keep. Then the roar of a car engine, and the blue-tinged glare of headlights. Leather under my hands. Engine. Gunfire. A single high-pitched note. Round the corner, over the bridge. And then we were gone into the citadel, like dust into shadow, leaving the sirens to howl in our wake.

# 2

# Long Story

She appeared at 6 A.M. She always did.

My hand snatched a revolver from the table. The theme for ScionEye was playing. A sweeping, theatrical composition, based on the twelve chimes of Big Ben.

I waited.

There she was. Scarlett Burnish, Grand Raconteur of London, white lace frothing from the top of her black dress. She always looked the same, of course—like some hellish automaton—but on occasion, when some poor denizen had been "killed" or "assaulted" by an unnatural, she could exude manufactured distress. Today, however, she was smiling.

*"Good morning, and welcome to another day in Scion London. Good news as the Guild of Vigilance announces an expansion of its Sunlight division, with at least fifty more officers due to be sworn in this Monday. The Chief of Vigilance has stated that the New Year will bring new challenges to the citadel, and that in these perilous times, it remains critical for the denizens of London to pull together and—"*

I switched it off.

There was no breaking news. *Nothing*, I thought, over and over. No faces. No hangings.

The gun clattered back on to the table. I'd been lying on a couch all night, flinching upright at the softest sound. My muscles were stiff and painful; it took some time to maneuver into a standing position. Every time the ache began to ebb, a fresh wave would come, surging from a jolted bruise or strain. I should be heading for bed, as was my custom at dawn, but I had to get up, just for a minute. A glint of natural light would do me good.

Once I'd stretched my legs, I switched on the music player in the corner. Billie Holiday's "Guilty" drifted out. Nick had dropped off a few forbidden records from the den on his way to work, along with the small amount of money he could spare and a pile of books I hadn't touched. I'd found myself missing Warden's gramophone. You could get used to being lullabied by the lovelorn crooners of the free world.

It had been three days since the escape. My new home was a dingy doss-house in I-4, tucked away in a warren of Soho backstreets. Most voyant establishments were ramshackle dumps, hardly fit to live in, but the landlord—a cleidomancer, whom I suspected had opened a doss-house just so he could finger keys for a living—had kept this one free of rodents, if not the creeping damp. He didn't know who I was, only that I had to be kept out of sight, as I'd been beaten badly by a Vigile and he might still be out looking for me.

Until we sorted things with Jaxon, I'd have to keep moving between rented rooms, one every week or so. It was already costing a fortune—I was managing, so far, with money Nick had given me—but it was the only way to know for sure that Scion couldn't track me.

With the blinds down, not a single ray of light entered the room. I opened them, just a little. Golden sunshine struck my raw eyes. A pair of amaurotics hurried past on the narrow street below. On the corner, a soothsayer was on the lookout for voyant clients who might fancy a quick reading. If he was desperate, he might risk approaching an amaurotic. Sometimes they got curious; sometimes they were spies. Scion had long since had agents provocateurs on its streets, tempting voyants to give themselves away.

I closed the blinds again. The room turned black. For six months I'd been nocturnal, my sleeping pattern matched to my Rephaite keeper's; that wouldn't change in a hurry. I sank on to the couch, reached for the glass of water on the table and gulped it down with two blue Nightcaps.

My dreamscape was still fragile. During our confrontation on the stage—when she'd tried to kill me in front of an audience of Scion emissaries—Nashira's fallen angels had left hairline fissures there, allowing memory to drip into my sleep. The chapel, where Seb had met his end. The chamber in Magdalen. The filthy, twisting slum of the Rookery and Duckett's psychomanteum, where my face grew monstrous and misshapen and my jaw snapped off, brittle as old ceramic.

Then Liss, her lips sewn shut with golden thread. Dragged outside to be fed to the Emim, the monsters that had haunted the woods around the colony. Seven bloody cards spun in her wake. I reached for them, straining to see the final card—my future, my conclusion—but as soon as I touched it, it screamed in a tongue of fire. I jerked awake at dusk, drenched from scalp to toe in sweat. My cheeks were damp and burning hot, and my lips tasted of salt.

Those cards would haunt me for a long time. Liss had predicted my future in six stages: Five of Cups, King of Wands inverted, the Devil, the Lovers, Death inverted, Eight of Swords. But she'd never reached the end of the reading.

I groped my way to the bathroom and washed down another couple of the painkillers Nick had left for me. I suspected the large gray one was some kind of sedative. Something to ease the tremors, the churning stomach, the need to grip my gun and not let go.

There was a light knock at the door. Slowly, I picked up my gun, checked it for ammo and held it behind my back. With my free hand, I cracked the door open.

The landlord stood in the corridor, fully dressed, with an antique iron key on a chain around his neck. He never took it off.

"Morning, miss," he said.

I managed a smile. "Don't you ever sleep, Lem?"

"Not often. The guests are up at all hours. There's a séance upstairs," he added, looking weary. "Making a right racket with the table. You're looking much better today, if I may say so."

"Thank you. Did my friend call?"

"He'll be here at nine tonight. Do give me a ring if you need anything."

"Thanks. Have a good day."

"And you, miss."

For a doss-house landlord, he was oddly helpful. I closed the door and locked it.

At once, the gun slipped from my hand. I sank to the floor and buried my face against my knees.

After a few minutes I went back into the tiny, airless bathroom, peeled off my nightshirt, and inspected my injuries in the mirror. Most visible were the deep gash above my eye, closed with stitches, and the shallow wound that curved across my cheek. Everything was worn thin, whittled down. My fingernails were flimsy, my skin was sallow, and my ribs and hipbones bulged. The landlord had given me a wary look when he'd brought my first tray of food, eyeing my lacerated hands and black eye. He hadn't recognized me as the Pale Dreamer, mollisher of his section, protégée of the White Binder.

As I stepped into the cubicle and turned the dial, darkness crept into my vision. Hot water poured over my shoulders, softening my muscles.

A door slammed.

My hand swiped a hidden blade from the soap dish. My body pitched itself from the cubicle, straight against the opposite wall. I concealed myself behind the door, buzzing with adrenaline, holding the blade to my heart.

It took a few minutes for my heart to slow down. I peeled myself from the wet tiles, slick with sweat and water. *Nothing, it's nothing.* Just the séance table upstairs.

Shaking, I leaned on the sink. My hair hung in damp coils around my face, brittle and dull.

I looked my reflection in the eye. My body had been treated as property in the colony, dragged and grabbed and beaten by Rephaim and red-jackets. I turned my back to the mirror and ran my fingers over the little threads of scar tissue on my shoulder. XX-59-40. That brand would be there for as long as I lived.

But I'd survived. I pulled my shirt over the brand again. I had survived, and the Sargas would know it.

****

When I opened the door to Nick for the first time in two days, he gathered me into a gentle embrace, minding my slices and bruises. I'd seen him in so many memories, summoned by Warden's numen, but they couldn't come close to the real Nick Nygård.

"Hey, *sötnos*."

"Hi."

We smiled at each other. Small, dour smiles.

Neither of us spoke. Nick spread our meal on the table while I opened the doors to the small balcony. The wind blew in the smell of Scion's autumn—gasoline and smoke from buskers' pit fires—but the scent from the boxes was so divine I hardly noticed. It was a feast: tiny hot pies packed with chicken and ham, freshly baked bread, golden fries scattered with salt and pepper. Nick pushed a small nutrient capsule across the table.

"Go on. Not too fast."

The pies were glazed with melted butter and poured out a thick, rich sauce when opened. Dutifully, I placed the capsule on my tongue.

"How's your arm?" Nick took it in his hands and peered at the circular burn. "Does it hurt?"

"Not anymore." And any pain was worth getting rid of that microchip.

"Keep an eye on it. I know Dani's good, but she's not a doctor." He felt my forehead. "Any headaches?"

"No more than usual." I tore a slice of bread into small pieces. "Still nothing on ScionEye."

"They're keeping quiet. Very quiet."

We were quiet, too. The sacks under his eyes betrayed the sleepless nights. The wondering. The endless waiting. I clasped my hands around my coffee cup and looked out at the citadel, that rising shatterbelt of metal, glass, and lights that led up to an endless depth of space. Michael was out there somewhere, probably huddled under a bridge or in a doorway. If he scraped together some money he could sleep in a penny hangover, but the Vigiles checked those places every night, looking to fill their arrest quotas before they returned to their stations.

"I got this for you." Nick pushed a handset across the table, identical to the one he'd used at the Tower. "Burner phone. Keep switching the identity modules and Scion won't be able to trace you."

"Where did you get this?" Scion had never manufactured these phones; it had to have been imported.

"A friend at the Old Spitalfields market. Ideally you would throw the whole phone away, but the traders charge a lot of money for the handsets." He handed me a small box. "They're not much good for receiving calls as you'll have a different number each time, but you can make them. It's just for emergencies."

"Right." I pocketed the phone. "How was work?"

"Good. I think." He palmed the stubble on his jaw, a nervous habit. "If anyone saw me get on that train—"

"They didn't."

"I was in a Scion uniform."

"Nick, Scion's a big organization. The chances of anyone linking the respectable Dr. Nicklas Nygård to the penal colony are minuscule." I crowned the bread with butter. "It'd look a hell of a lot more suspicious if you didn't go back."

"I know. And I didn't train in their universities for all those years so I could give up." When he saw my face, he forced a smile. "What are you thinking about?"

"We lost a lot of people at the Tower." Suddenly I had no appetite. "I told them I'd get them all home."

"Stop it, Paige. I'm telling you, you'll destroy yourself if you think like that. Scion did this, not you."

I didn't answer. Nick knelt beside my chair. "Sweetheart, look at me. Look at me." I raised my head, met his tired eyes, but the sight of them only deepened the ache. "If it's anyone's fault it's that Rephaite's, isn't it? He put you on the train. He let you go." When I didn't answer, he wrapped an arm around me. "We'll find the other prisoners, I promise."

We stayed like that for some time. He was right, of course he was right.

But perhaps there was someone to blame. Someone behind the veil of Scion.

Had Warden known the train would end up at Westminster, in the belly of the beast? Had he betrayed me at the eleventh hour? He was a Rephaite, after all—a monster, not a man—but I had to trust that he'd done what he could.

Once we'd eaten, Nick cleared away the leftovers. Another knock at the door had me scrambling for my gun, but Nick held up a hand.

"It's okay." He opened the door. "I called a friend."

When Eliza Renton came in, her ringlets lank with rainwater, she didn't pause to say hello. She rushed straight to the couch with a look that said she was going to sock me in the face, but she ended up yanking me into her arms.

"Paige, you idiot." Her voice was thick with anger. "You bloody idiot. Why did you take the Underground that day? You knew there were Underguards—you knew about the checks—"

"I took a chance. I was stupid."

"Why didn't you just wait for Nick to drive you home? We thought Hector had bumped you off or—or Scion had—"

"They did." I patted her back. "But I'm fine."

Gently but firmly, Nick detached her from my neck. "Careful. She's got bruises on bruises." He steered her to the opposite couch. "I thought more than one of us should hear this, Paige. We need as many allies as we can get."

"You *have* allies," Eliza snapped. "Jax is worried sick about you, Paige."

"He didn't seem too worried when he was throttling me," I said.

This was news to her. She looked between us, an exasperated frown clinching her features.

I drew the curtains. Soon we were sitting on the couches in the gloom, clasping glass cups of saloop from Nick's flask. It was a creamy infusion of orchid tubers and hot milk, sprinkled with cinnamon, popular in coffeehouses. The taste of it was a comfort after months of biting hunger.

On the TV screen, one of Burnish's little raconteurs was on air.

"*Vigile numbers are expected to double in I Cohort over the next few weeks, with the installment of a second prototype Senshield scanner, the only technology known to detect unnaturalness, expected before December. Denizens should expect an increase in the number of spot checks on the Underground, the bus network, and in Scion-authorized taxis. The Underguard division asks that denizens cooperate with the demands of their staff at this time. If you have nothing to hide, you have nothing to fear! Now, moving on to this week's weather."*

"More Vigiles," Nick said. "What are they doing?"

"Trying to find the fugitives," I said. "I don't understand why they haven't said anything."

"That might not be the reason. It's Novembertide in two months," Eliza pointed out. "They always boost security for that. And this year they're inviting the Grand Inquisitor of Paris."

"Aloys Mynatt was at the Bicentenary—Inquisitor Ménard's assistant. If he's dead, I doubt Ménard will be in a party mood."

"They wouldn't cancel it."

"Trust me—if Nashira says 'cancel it,' they'll cancel it."

"Who's Nashira?"

Such a guileless question. No easy answer. Who *was* Nashira? A nightmare. A monster. A murderer.

"Senshield will change everything," I said, watching the screen. "Has the Unnatural Assembly done anything about it yet?"

The Unnatural Assembly, made up of the thirty-six mime-lords and mime-queens of the citadel, each of whom was supposed to oversee all syndicate activity in their assigned section. They were all relatively autonomous, but the Underlord, Haymarket Hector, was responsible for convening their meetings.

"There was some talk in July," Nick said. "Grub Street sent out messages saying they were aware of the situation, but there's been nothing since then."

"Hector has no idea what to do," I realized. "Nobody does."

"That prototype Senshield isn't the worst one we'll see. It can only detect the first three orders, according to the grapevine."

The reminder made Eliza look away. She was a medium. Third order. Nick took her hand.

"You'll be fine. Dani's working on a jamming device," he told me. "Something that will interfere with Senshield. It's complex work, but she's smart."

Eliza nodded, but her brow was creased. "She thinks it might be ready by February."

That wasn't soon enough, and we all knew it.

"How did you get to the colony?" I said to Nick. "There must have been incredible security."

"Jax had almost given up by August," Nick admitted. "By that point we were sure you weren't in London. We had no ransom notes from the other gangs, no evidence that you'd been killed, and there was no sign of you at your father's apartment. It wasn't until the Trafalgar Square incident that we had any leads, when you said they'd taken you to Oxford."

"You were Jaxon's only focus after that," Eliza said, with a pointed look. "He was obsessed with getting you back."

It only half surprised me. To Jaxon, losing his prized dreamwalker would have been infuriating, even humiliating—but I still wouldn't have expected him to risk everything to retrieve me from Scion's clutches. That was the kind of sacrifice you made for people, not property.

"At work I tried to find out more about Oxford, but the data was all encrypted," Nick continued. "It was a few weeks before I was able to get into the head supervisor's office and use her computer. That took me to a kind of dark Scionet, a part of the network that can't be accessed by the public. There weren't many specifics, just that the city of Oxford was a Type A restricted sector, which we knew, and that there was a train station beneath the Archon, which was new to us. There was also a list of names that went back for what looked like hundreds of years. Missing people. Yours was there, close to the bottom of the list."

"Dani took it from there," Eliza said. "She found the access tunnel. Only a unit of specially chosen engineers was allowed in, but she worked out when it would be opened. The train was due for repairs on the thirty-first of August. Jax said that was when we'd go. I stayed to keep an eye on things here."

"It's not like Jax to get his hands dirty," I said.

"He cares about you, Paige. He'd do anything to keep us safe. You most of all."

It wasn't true. Eliza had always thought the world of Jaxon Hall—after all, he'd given us a world—but I'd seen too much from him that said otherwise. He was *capable* of kindness, but he wasn't kind. He could *act* like he cared, but it would always be an act. It had taken me years to wake up and see it.

"That night, after the repairs had been done," Nick said, "Dani got into the tunnel with a card she'd stolen from one of the unit members. She let us in."

"Didn't anyone recognize you?"

"They didn't see us. By the time they put the emissaries on the train, we'd already locked ourselves into a maintenance compartment at the back. The Vigiles had no way to access it, so we were safe for that part of the journey. Then, of course, we had to get off the train."

"With sighted Vigiles escorting the emissaries? How the hell did you manage that?"

"We waited until the emissaries had been taken through the door. A guard on the other side locked it, which left us stranded, but we found an old utility tunnel behind a grate. That took us up on to the street. We got into the Guildhall through a back door."

A utility tunnel. If Warden had known about that, he would have been able to leave safely, too. I released a breath. "You're all off the cot."

"We had to get you back, Paige," Eliza said. "Jax was willing to try anything."

30

"Jax is not stupid. Putting a ragtag group of gangsters on a Scion train without a clue what to expect at the other end *is* borderline stupid."

"Well, maybe he got bored of sitting in the office."

"We got you back. That's what matters." Nick leaned forward. "Your turn."

I looked down at my saloop. "It's a long story."

"Start with the night you were taken," Eliza said.

"That's not where it starts. It starts in 1859."

They looked at each other.

It took a long time. I explained how, in 1859, two races called the Rephaim and the Emim had arrived from the Netherworld—the halfway point between life and death—after the breaking of the ethereal threshold, when the number of drifting spirits had grown too high and thinned the veils between the worlds.

"Okay," Eliza said, looking as if she might burst out laughing, "but what *are* the Rephaim?"

"I still don't know. They look like us," I said, "but their skin looks like metal, and they're tall. Their eyes are yellowish, but when they feed, they reflect the color of the aura they've just fed on."

"And the Emim?"

Words failed me at that. "I've never seen one when it wasn't dark, but . . ." I blew out a breath. "In the colony they called them Buzzers, or *rotten giants*. Spirits won't go near them. They feed on human flesh."

I hadn't thought it possible for Nick to be any paler, but he managed.

I told them about the pact between the Rephaim and the government—protection from the Emim in exchange for voyant slaves—that had led to the establishment of Scion. About the penal colony of Sheol I, built in the ruins of Oxford to act as a beacon of spiritual activity, drawing the Emim away from citadels like London.

I told them how I'd got on an evening train and been subjected to a spot check. How I'd attacked two Underguards, been pursued from my father's apartment, been hit with flux by the Overseer. How I'd woken up in the detainment facility.

I told them how I was given to Arcturus Mesarthim, otherwise known as the Warden—Nashira's betrothed—to be trained as a soldier. I explained the system of the penal colony, giving them descriptions of each class. The elite red-jackets, who courted the favor of the Rephaim in exchange for their services as soldiers; the performers, cast into the slum, used as a source of aura; the amaurotic hands, held behind bars when they weren't being worked to death. I told them how the Rephaim would beat and feed on humans, evicting them if they didn't pass their tests.

The drinks turned cold.

I told them how Seb's death had pushed me up to the next jacket. How I'd trained on the meadow with Warden. I told them about the deer and the Buzzer in the woods, and about Julian, and about Liss. About our attempt to detain Antoinette Carter in Trafalgar Square, which had resulted in Nick shooting me.

My throat was starting to ache from talking, but I told the story to the end. Everything but the truth about my relationship with Warden. With every new revelation about the Rephaim, waves of disgust and horror washed over their faces. They wouldn't understand if I told them how close I'd become to my keeper. I didn't tell them about the salvia memories, or his music in the chapel, or the time he'd allowed me to enter his dreamscape. From my abridged description, he was a reticent creature with whom I'd rarely spoken, who'd occasionally fed me and finally let me go. Of course, Nick spied the hole in my evidence.

"I don't understand," he said. "When you were brought to Trafalgar Square, he could have left you, but he took you back to Sheol. Now you're saying he *helped* you?"

"So I would help him. He tried to overthrow the Sargas in 2039. Nashira tortured him."

"And then decided to *marry* him?"

"I don't know if that was a consequence. They could've been betrothed since before they came here."

Eliza pulled a face. "That's some engagement." She was on her side now, her bare feet propped up on the cushions. "Anyway, isn't treason reasonable grounds for ending the contract?"

"I think it was part of the punishment. She knew how much he hated her. It was more torture for him to stay as her consort, despised by other Rephaim."

"Why wouldn't she have just killed him? Why did she keep any of them alive?"

"Death might not be a punishment for them," Nick said. "They're not mortal. Not like humans."

"Maybe we humans have more important things to think about." I fixed my gaze on the TV. "Warden doesn't matter any more."

*Liar.*

I heard his voice as clearly as if he were in the room with me, a memory so lucid I felt it. It sent tremors working down my arms, right the way to my fingertips.

"Do you think their deal is still on?" Nick asked. "We broke out of the colony—that means their secret is in danger."

"It must be." I nodded to the news. "I don't think that security is to do with Novembertide. They need to wipe out everyone who knows."

"And then what?" Eliza said.

"Another Bone Season. To replace all the humans they just lost."

"But they'll have to put them somewhere else," Nick said. "They can't carry on using the first colony, not now its location has been exposed."

"They're planning to build Sheol II in France, but I don't think they've even started to convert it yet," I said. "Finding us will be their first objective."

There was a short silence. "So the Warden wants to help humans," Eliza said. "Where did he go?"

"To hunt Nashira."

"We have no real proof that he's on our side, Paige." Nick tucked his data pad away. "I don't trust anyone. The Rephaim are enemies until categorically proven otherwise. Including the Warden."

Something twisted inside me, like a nail in my gut, as Nick stood and looked out at the citadel.

I couldn't tell him about the kiss. He'd think I was insane. I trusted Warden, but it was true that I didn't really understand his intentions; who he was, *what* he was.

Eliza leaned across the table. "You will come back to Dials, won't you?"

"I quit," I said.

"Jax will take you back. Dials is the safest place for you, and he's a good mime-lord. He's never made you sleep with him. There are far worse people to work for."

"So I owe him for not turning me into his nightwalker? For not being Hector? You didn't see him. You didn't get this from him." I yanked up the sleeve of my blouse, showing her the ridged white scar on my right arm. "He's off the cot."

"He didn't know who you were when he did that."

"He knew he was beating the stuffing out of a dreamwalker. I'm the only dreamwalker we know."

"This isn't helping." Nick massaged the corner of his eye. "Eliza, you tell Jax that Paige and I will be back to Dials soon. In the meantime, we need to come up with some kind of action plan."

Eliza frowned. "What do you mean, 'action plan?'"

"Well, something has to be done about the Rephaim. We can't just let them carry on with the Bone Seasons." "I don't know about that." Eliza pulled on her coat. "Look, we rescued Paige. We should all just . . . try to focus on getting back to work. Jax says we've lost a lot of income since you went missing," she said to me. "We really need you back at the Garden."

"You want to send me back to the black market?" I couldn't help but stare at her. "Scion is a puppet government. They're keeping voyants in a death camp."

"We're just lowlifes, Paige. If we keep our heads down then we'll never be sent there."

"We're not just lowlifes. We're the Seven Seals, one of the most notorious gangs in the central cohort. And we wouldn't have to keep our heads down at all if not for Scion. We wouldn't *be* criminals. Or lowlifes, for that matter. We have to bring the syndicate together, fast, before they introduce Senshield."

"And do what?"

"Fight."

"Scion?" She shook her head. "Paige, come on. The Unnatural Assembly would never agree to it."

"I'll ask for an audience and explain the situation."

"And you think they'll believe you?"

"Well, you believe me, don't you?" When her expression didn't change, I stood. "Don't you?"

"I didn't see it," she said weakly. "Look, I'm sure they do have some kind of prison facility in that area, but—but you were fluxed, and it just sounds—"

"Eliza, stop it. I was there, too," Nick said.

"I have not had a six-month flux flash," I hissed. "I saw innocent people die trying to get out of that hellhole. And it's going to happen again. Sheol II, Sheol III, Sheol IV. I will *not* pretend it wasn't real."

For a long time, nobody spoke.

"I'll tell Jax you'll both be back soon," Eliza said finally, wrapping her scarf around her neck. "I hope I'll be telling him the truth. There are already rumors that you've left his service."

"And what if I have?" I said softly.

"Just think about it, Paige. You won't last long without a gang, and you know it."

She closed the door behind her. I waited until her footsteps had receded before I let loose.

"She's lost her mind. What the hell does she think is going to happen when they put Senshield on the streets?"

"She's afraid, Paige." Nick heaved a sigh. "Eliza's never known anything but the syndicate. She was dumped on the street and raised in some miserable cellar in Soho. She'd be nightwalking if Jaxon hadn't given her a chance."

I faltered. That was unexpected. "I thought she worked at the penny gaff?"

"She did. She got that job to pay her rent, but ended up spending all her wages on aster and flash houses. When she got in touch with Jaxon, he recognized her talent. He gave her expensive paints, a safe place to sleep, muses beyond her wildest imagination. I remember the day she turned up at the den," he said. "She was so overwhelmed she broke down in tears. Keeping the Seals together is more important to her than anything."

"If she was captured tomorrow, Jax would replace her within a day and you know it. He doesn't care about us. Just our gifts." I stopped for a moment, rubbing the tender spot above my eye. "Look, I know this is big. Bigger than any of us. But if we bend, they'll win."

Nick just looked at me.

"The Rephaim know the syndicate is a threat," I continued. "It's a monster they created, a monster they can't control. But under Hector's leadership, it's nothing but a den of thieves. We have hundreds of voyants in the syndicate. It's organized. It's powerful. If we could use it against the Rephaim, instead of playing tarocchi and killing each other, we might be able to get rid of them. I *have* to talk to the Unnatural Assembly."

"How? Hector hasn't called a meeting in—" He paused. "Hector has never called a meeting."

"Anyone can ask for one."

"Can they?"

"I have learned some things as a mollisher." I took a writing set from the nightstand. "Any member of the syndicate is entitled to send a summons to the Underlord so he can call the Assembly." I wrote it out, added my section at the end, then popped it into an envelope and handed it to Nick. "Could you deliver this to the Spiritus Club, please?"

He took it. "This is a summons? To the Assembly?"

"Hector's dead drop will be full—he never empties it. The Club will send a courier to deliver it in person."

"Jaxon will be furious if he finds out."

"I quit, remember?"

"You might not get far without a mime-lord. Eliza's right. You need a gang, or the syndicate will shut you out."

"I have to try."

He tucked the envelope into his pocket, but he looked uncertain. "This isn't something that will happen overnight. They won't believe a word of what you have to say, and Hector won't particularly care. Even if they did, you're up against decades of tradition and corruption. Centuries. You know what happens when people upset the apple cart."

"The apples fall out." I put my hands on the windowsill. "We can't wait. The Rephaim need to feed, and they don't have many voyants left in their city. Sooner or later they're going to come for us. I don't know how we can fight them—I don't even know *if* we can fight them—but I can't lie down and let Scion decide how my life will look. I can't do it, Nick."

Silence.

"No," he said. "I can't, either."

# 3

# Then There Were Five

The next day was the same. And the next. Sleeping when the sun shone, waking at night.

There was no word from the Unnatural Assembly in response to my summons. I'd give it a week before I sent another. The Spiritus Club's couriers were fast, but Hector might not look at the note for days.

I could do nothing but wait. Without knowing what was happening in the Archon, I couldn't make much of a plan. For now, the board belonged to Nashira.

On the fifth day, I assessed my injuries. The bruising on my back had faded to a spill of sallow brown, and most of the small cuts had healed. After checking the news—still nothing of interest—I sat on the couch and bolted down the breakfast the landlord brought me.

Nick had collected a few more supplies for me from Seven Dials, including $PVS^2$, the oxygen mask that kept me alive when I used my gift for long periods of time. I lay down on the bed and clamped it over my mouth and nose. I hadn't looked into my dreamscape for days, but if I was to even attempt to fight, both my body and my gift had to be fully functional. Now that it had matured, my spirit would be my best weapon. I switched on the mask and withdrew into my mind.

It hurt to immerse myself. When I finally broke through, wilting poppies brushed my cheeks. I opened my dream-eyes. I was standing at the edge of my sunlit zone, my feet pillowed by petals, and the sky beat red and hot above me. An arid wind whipped at my hair.

Great patches of the field had been uprooted. That was the fabric of my mind, torn and scarred, as if it had been ploughed by some infernal engine.

I knelt beside a dying poppy and scooped its seeds into my palm. At the touch of my hand, each one grew a tiny stalk and flowered—but they weren't quite poppies now. A deeper red. A smaller bloom. The smell of fire.

Blood of Adonis. The only thing that could do harm to the Rephaim. They broke across my dreamscape like a red wave.

A hundred thousand poppy anemones.

\*\*\*\*

I didn't try dreamwalking. A mental storm of that magnitude would take time to dissipate. It would be a few more days before I could enter the æther.

I thought about my options. There was a good chance that Hector wouldn't listen to the summons. If he didn't, I'd have to strike out on my own.

There were two serious problems: money and respect. Or, more specifically, my lack of them.

If I left Jaxon's service, I'd need a lot of money to survive. I had some cash sewn into my pillow at the den. Maybe Nick and I could start our own gang. If we pooled our savings—his money from Scion, mine from Jaxon—we might have enough to buy a small den in one of the outlying cohorts, if nothing else. Then we could start looking for allies.

I walked over to the balcony, my arms folded. There was the second problem. The only thing money couldn't buy was respect. I wasn't a mime-queen. Without Jaxon, I wasn't even a mollisher.

There were rules. If Nick and I were to form our own gang in another section, we'd have to seek permission from the mime-lord or mime-queen there. The Underlord would have to give his blessing, which he almost never did. If we did it anyway, we'd have our throats cut, as would anyone we'd been foolish or selfish enough to employ.

If I returned to the Seven Seals on the other hand, Jaxon would welcome me back with an open wallet and a dance for joy. If I refused to work for him, I'd not only lose every drop of respect I'd ever had, but I'd also become a pariah in the syndicate, shunned by other voyants. And if Frank Weaver put a bounty on my head, those voyants would be falling over themselves to sell me out to the Archon.

Jaxon hadn't explicitly said that he wouldn't help me work against the Rephaim, but I'd seen things in him that I couldn't unsee. Maybe it had taken him beating me senseless in Trafalgar Square or throttling me on the meadow before I'd got the message that Jaxon Hall was a dangerous man, and he wasn't above hurting his own.

Yet he might be my only hope of having a voice in the syndicate. Maybe my best chance was to move back to Seven Dials and keep my head down, as I always had. Because if there was one thing more dangerous than having Jaxon Hall as a boss, it was having him as an enemy.

Frustrated, I turned away from the window. I couldn't stay in here forever. Now that I was healed, I should go to Seven Dials and face him.

No. Not yet. First I should go to Camden, where Ivy had said she would go. I wanted to make sure she'd made it.

My bag of clothes hung on the back of the door. I took it into the bathroom, where I stood in front of the mirror and set about disguising myself. I belted on a black woolen coat, turned the collar up to cover my neck, and tugged a peaked hat over my hair. If I ducked my head, my dark lips were hidden by the bloodred cravat draped around my neck.

Warden's gift to me—a sublimed pendant, able to deflect malicious spirits—was hanging from the bedpost. I pulled the chain around my neck and held the wings between my fingers. The metalwork was like filigree, complex and delicate. An item like this would be valuable on the streets, where some of London's most notorious murderers still wandered in their spirit forms.

Once I had loved throwing myself into the labyrinth of London, loved living on its corruption. Once I wouldn't have thought twice about going outside, even with the NVD roaming the streets. I'd kept a handle on my double life, as many voyants did. It was easy enough to slip past Scion's security unnoticed: avoid streets with cameras, keep a safe distance from sighted guards, don't stop walking. Head down, eyes open, as Nick had always taught me. But I knew now that I lived in a façade, and that puppet masters dwelled in the shadows.

I almost lost my nerve. But then I looked at the couch where I'd lain crippled with terror every morning and night, waiting for Scion to break down the door, and I knew that if I didn't go out now, I'd never go out again. I pushed up the window and swung my legs on to the fire escape.

Cold wind clawed at my face. For a minute, I just stayed there, paralyzed with dread.

Freedom. This was what it looked like.

The first tremor hit me. I gripped the windowsill, pulling my legs back. The room was safe. I shouldn't leave it.

But the streets were my life. I'd fought tooth and nail to get back to this, shed blood for it. With clammy hands, I turned and took hold of the ladder, taking each step as though it were my last.

As soon as my boots touched asphalt, I looked over my shoulder, reaching for the æther. A couple of mediums stood beside a phone booth, talking in low voices, one wearing dark glasses. Neither of them looked at me.

Camden was a good forty minutes' walk. My fingers worked under my cap, tucking every strand of blonde away.

People brushed past, talking and laughing. I thought about all the times I'd walked through London. Had I ever stopped to look at someone's face? Unlikely. Why should anybody look at me?

I headed out to the main road, where engines roared and headlights blazed. The buck cabs were all in use, and no unlicensed rickshaws stopped for me. White cabs, white velotaxis, white pedicabs with patent black seats. White triple-decker buses with curving black windows. Buildings loomed above me, all neon glow and banners bearing anchors, and skyscrapers that seemed to touch the stars. Everything was too bright, too loud, too fast. I was used to streets with no electric lights, devoid of noise pollution. This world seemed mad in comparison. My sordid, sacred SciLo, my prison and my home.

Piccadilly Circus soon came into my line of sight. Hard to miss, with those gargantuan screens stacked high on the buildings, showing off an electronic spectrum of advertising and information and propaganda. The hot spots were held by Brekkabox and Floxy, the commercial bigwigs, while smaller screens showed off the latest data pad programs: Eye Spy, Busk Trust, KillKlock—all for helping denizens spot, avoid, or entertain themselves at the expense of unnaturals. One wide monitor scrolled through a series of security alerts from Scion: BEWARE OF CIVIL INATTENTION. NIGHT VIGILES ARE NOW ON DUTY IN THE CAPITAL. ALERT THE GUILD OF VIGILANCE IF YOU SUSPECT UNNATURAL BEHAVIOR. PLEASE STAND BY FOR

PUBLIC SAFETY ANNOUNCEMENTS. The clamor was incredible: snatches of music, engines, sirens, talking and shouting, voices from the screens and the throaty rattle of the rickshaw rank. Glym jacks stood under lamp posts, holding their green lanterns, offering protection from lurking unnaturals. I headed toward the rickshaws.

An amaurotic woman stood in front of me, a cream coat folded over her arm. A Burnish-style dress, ruched red velvet, was molded to her figure. She had a phone pinned between her shoulder and her ear.

". . . be *stupid*, it's just a phase! No, I'm just off to the $O_2$ bar. Might be able to catch that hanging."

She climbed into a rickshaw, laughing. I waited by the railing, my fist clenched around the metal.

The next rickshaw to arrive was mine. They were electric-assist pedicabs with a lightweight, closed cab behind the driver, able to take one or two passengers. I clambered in.

"Camden Market, please," I said, using my best English accent. If they were looking for me, they'd be looking for a brogue.

The rickshaw cut through I Cohort, heading north to II-4. I kept well back in the seat. This was risky, but there was something exhilarating about the ride. My blood rushed in my veins. Here I was, riding through the very heart of SciLo, bold as brass, and no one seemed to notice. Fifteen minutes later, I was stepping off the rick and groping in my pocket for the fare.

Camden Town, the nexus of II-4, was its own small world, where amaurotics and voyants jostled in an oasis of color and dance music. Hawkers came every few days on the canal, bringing merchandise and food from other citadels. Costermongers sold numa and aster, hidden inside fruit. It was a hotbed of illegal activity, as safe a place as any for a fugitive. The clairvoyant night Vigiles had never exposed this market; a lot of them relied on its trade, and a hell of a lot more still spent time here when they were off-duty. It was home to the only underground cinema in the citadel, the Fleapit, one of its many risqué attractions.

I set off toward the lock, past tattoo parlors, oxygen bars, and racks of cheap cravats and watches. Soon I happened upon Camden Hippodrome: luxury dress shop by day, discothèque by night. A man with a lemon-yellow ponytail stood outside. I knew he was a sensor before I got close: the voyants here often colored their hair or nails to match their auras, though you'd only get the link if you were sighted. I stopped in front of him.

"Are you busy?"

He glanced at me. "Depends. You a local?"

"No. I'm the Pale Dreamer," I said. "Mollisher of I-4."

With that, he turned his head away. "Busy."

Eyebrows raised, I stood my ground. His face was carefully blank. Most voyants would have jumped to attention at the sound of the word *mollisher*. I gave him a hard push with my spirit, making him yelp.

"What the fuck are you playing at?"

"I'm busy, too, sensor." I grabbed him by the collar, keeping my spirit close enough to his dreamscape to make him feel nervous. "And I don't have time for games."

"I'm not playing any. You're not a moll anymore," he spat. "Word is that you and Binder have had a disagreement, Pale Dreamer."

"Is it, now?" I tried to sound unmoved. "Well, you must have heard that wrong, sensor. The White Binder and I don't disagree. Now, do you *really* want to risk a slating, or do you want to help me?"

His eyes narrowed a little, assessing me. They were shielded by yellow contact lenses.

"Get on with it, then," he said.

"I'm looking for Agatha's Boutique."

He jerked his collar from my grip. "It's in the Stables Market, past the lock. Ask for a blood diamond and she'll help you out." He folded his copiously tattooed forearms. Skeletons were the theme, wrapping his muscles in painted bone. "Anything else?"

"Not right now." I let go of his collar. "Thanks for your help."

He grunted. I resisted giving him another push as I walked past, heading for the lock.

Doing that had been risky. If he'd been a Rag Doll, he wouldn't have let me push him around. They were the dominant gang here, one of the few to have invented their own distinctive "uniform": pinstriped blazers and bracelets made of rat bones, as well as the colored hair. Their mime-lord's name was whispered throughout II-4, but only a handful of people had ever laid lamps on the elusive Rag and Bone Man.

Jaxon must have put word out on the street that I was no longer his mollisher. He was already destabilizing my position in the syndicate, trying to force me back to him. I should have known he wouldn't wait long.

I smelled Camden Lock as soon as I got close. Narrowboats floated on the scummy green water, their sides coated with algae and old paint, each manned by a costermonger. "Buy, buy," they shouted. "Strings for your boots, two quid for ten!" "Hot pies, toss or buy!" "Five bob for an apple and white!" "Chestnuts baked fresh, a note for a score!"

My ears pricked at that one. The boat was a deep red, trimmed with plum and swirls of gold. It must have been beautiful once, but now the paint was peeling and faded, the stern disfigured by anti-Scion graffiti. Chestnuts roasted away on a stove, scored with X-shaped cuts through which the innards peeped.

When I approached, the costermonger smiled down at me with crooked teeth. The glow of the stove scorched in her eyes beneath the brim of her bowler hat.

"A score for you, little ma'am?"

"Please." I handed her some money. "I'm trying to find Agatha's Boutique. I was told it was near here. Any idea?"

"Right round the corner. There's a hawker selling saloop that way. You'll hear her when you're close." She filled a paper cone with chestnuts and smothered them with butter and coarse salt. "Here you are."

I picked at my chestnuts as I traversed the market, letting myself soak up the atmosphere of humans going about their business. There had been none of this vigorous energy in Sheol I, where voices had been whispers and movements had been quiet. Night was the most dangerous time for voyants, when the NVD were on the prowl, but it was also the time when our gifts were at their strongest, when the urge to be active smoldered inside us—and, like the moths we were, we just had to emerge.

The boutique's windows glistened with fake gemstones. Outside was a girl selling saloop, a petite botanomancer with orchids in her sky-blue hair. I sidled past her.

A bell tinkled above the door. The owner—a bony, elderly woman, wrapped in a white lace shawl—didn't look up when I came in. To match her aura, she'd gone fluorescent green in the extreme: green hair in a razor cut, green nails, green mascara, and green lipstick. A speaking medium.

"What can I do for you, love?"

To an amaurotic she would have sounded like a chain-smoker, but I knew that rasp was from a throat ill-treated by spirits. I closed the door.

"A blood diamond, please."

She studied me. I tried to imagine what I'd look like if I colored myself to match my red aura.

"You must be the Pale Dreamer. Come on down," she croaked. "They're expecting you."

The woman led me to a rickety staircase, hidden behind a rotating curio cabinet. She had a persistent, carving cough, like a chunk of raw meat was stuck in her windpipe. It wouldn't be long before she became mute. Some speaking mediums cut their tongues out just to stop the spirits using them.

"Call me Agatha," she said. "This here is the bolthole of II-4. Haven't used it in years, of course. Camden voyants scatter all over the place when there's a scare."

I followed her into a cellar, which was lit by a single lamp. The walls were crammed with penny dreadfuls and dusty ornaments. Two mattresses vied for the remaining space, covered by patchwork quilts. Ivy was asleep on a pile of cushions, skin and bones in a button-down shirt.

"Don't wake her." Agatha crouched down and stroked her head. "She needs her rest, poor lamb."

Three more voyants shared the second mattress, all with the Sheol look: dead eyes, hollow bellies, faint auras. At least they had clean clothes. Nell was in the middle.

"So you got away from the Tower," she said. "We should get a badge for surviving that."

In the penal colony I'd hardly spoken to Nell. "How's your leg?"

"Just a scratch. I expected more from the Guard Extraordinary. More like the Guard Mediocre, really." She still winced when she touched it. "You know these two troublemakers, don't you?"

One of her companions was the julker boy I'd once helped in Sheol I. He was brown-eyed and dark-skinned, wearing baggy dungarees over his shirt, and his head was tucked under Nell's arm. The fourth survivor was Felix, nervous-looking and a little too thin for his height, with a shock of black hair and a smattering of freckles. He'd been instrumental in delivering messages during the rebellion.

"Sorry. I don't think I ever asked your name," I said to the julker boy.

"It's all right," he said in a light, sweet voice. "It's Joseph, but you can call me Jos."

"Okay." I looked into the corners of the cellar, my heart filling my throat. "Did anyone else escape?"

"I don't think so."

"We got a buck cab from Whitechapel," Felix said. "We had two others with us, but they're both—"

"Dead." Agatha held a cloth to her mouth and hacked from her throat. When she took it away, it was flecked with blood. "The girl wouldn't hold down food. The boy jumped into the canal. I'm sorry, love."

A cool prickling started along the backs of my legs. "The boy," I repeated. "He wasn't mute, was he?"

"Michael got away," Jos said. "He ran down to the river, I think. Nobody's seen him."

I shouldn't have felt relieved—at the end of the day, another voyant boy had died—but the thought of Michael hurting himself was physically painful. Felix scratched the side of his neck. "So you haven't found anyone else?"

"Not yet," I said. "I'm not sure where to look."

"Where are you based?"

"I'm in a doss-house. It's best you don't know where. Are you safe here?"

"They're safe," Agatha said, patting Ivy's arm. "Don't you worry, Pale Dreamer. I shan't let them out of my sight."

Felix gave her a tentative smile. "We'll be fine for now. Camden seems safe. Besides," he said, "anything's better than . . . where we were before."

I crouched beside Ivy, who didn't stir. "I was her kidsman," Agatha said. She took off her lace shawl and draped it around Ivy's shoulders. "Thought she'd given me the slip. I had all the little horrors out searching for her, but we got nothing. Knew they must have nibbled her."

Now I was on edge. Kidsmen picked up gutterlings and trained them to steal and beg, often giving them cruel injuries to attract sympathy. "I'm sure you missed her terribly," I said.

If she picked up on my tone, she didn't acknowledge it. "Aye," she said. "I did. She's been like a daughter to me, this one." She stood and rubbed the small of her back. "I'll leave you to your business. I've got my own to run."

The door clunked shut behind her. Coughing echoed through the stairwell. Felix gave Ivy a gentle shake.

"Ivy. Paige is here."

It took Ivy a while to come to. Jos helped her into a sitting position, propping her up with cushions. Her hand came to rest on her ribs. When her dark eyes finally focused on me, she smiled, giving me a glimpse of a missing tooth at the front of her mouth. "Not dead yet."

Jos looked worried. "Agatha said you shouldn't get up."

"I'm fine. She's always been a worrywart," Ivy said. "You know, we should really send Thuban an invitation to my deathbed. I'm sure he'd love to see the fruits of his labor."

Nobody smiled. The sight of her bruises shook me to the core. "So," I said, "Agatha's your kidsman?"

"I trust her. She's not like other kidsmen—she took me in when I was starving." She pulled the lace shawl more tightly around her shoulders. "She'll hide us from the Rag and Bone Man. She's never liked him."

"Why do you need to hide from him?" I took a seat on the mattress. "Isn't he your mime-lord?"

"He's violent."

"Aren't most mime-lords?"

"Trust me, you don't want to get on the wrong side of this one. He won't want a bunch of fugitives causing trouble in his section. No one knows his face, but Agatha's met him once or twice. She's been in charge of the bolthole for years, since before I worked for her."

"Who's his mollisher?" Nell asked.

"I'm not sure." Ivy lifted a hand to her shorn head, looking away. "They're secretive here."

I'd have to ask Jaxon more about this guy. If I ever spoke to Jaxon again. "Why come back here at all, then?"

"Nowhere else to go," Nell said, pulling a face. "We've got no money for a doss-house and no friends who could afford to put us up."

"Look, Paige," Felix cut in, "we ought to work out what to do, and do it soon. Scion's going to be on the hunt for us, given what we know."

"I've called a meeting of the Unnatural Assembly. We need to spread the word about the Rephaim," I said. Ivy's head jerked around. "Let every voyant in London know what Scion has been doing to us."

"You're mad," Ivy said, staring at me. There was a tremor in her voice. "You think *Hector* would do anything about it? You think he would care?"

"It's worth a try," I said.

"We have our brands," Felix pointed out. "We have our stories. We have all the voyants who are still missing."

"They could be in the Tower. Or dead. Even if we did tell everyone, there's no guarantee it would change anything," Nell said. "Ivy's right. Hector won't believe a word. Friend of mine tried to report a murder to his henchmen once, and they beat him senseless for his trouble."

"We need a Rephaite to prove the story," Jos piped up. "The Warden will help us, won't he, Paige?"

"I don't know." I paused. "I don't know if he's alive."

"And we shouldn't work with Rephs." Ivy looked away. "We all know what they're like."

"But he helped Liss," Jos said, frowning. "I saw it. He got her out of spirit shock."

"Give him a medal, then," Nell said, "but I'm not working with him, either. They can all rot in hell."

"What about the amaurotics?" Felix said. "Can we work with them?"

Nell snorted. "Sorry, remind me why the rotties would give a rat's ear what happens to us?"

"You could show some optimism."

"Yeah, the weekly executions make me *really* optimistic. Anyway, London rotties outnumber us ten to one, if not more," she added. "Even if we got a tiny number of them on our side, the rest would overpower us. So there goes that brilliant plan."

You could tell they'd been stuck in a small room for a while.

"The amaurotics could end up helping us. Scion have always taught their denizens to hate clairvoyance," I said. "Imagine how the average denizen would react if they found out Scion was *controlled* by voyants. The Rephs are more clairvoyant than we are, and they've had us wrapped around their finger for two centuries. But we need to focus on voyants first, not rotties or Rephaim." I went to stand by the window, watching the narrowboats pass with their wares. "What would your mime-lords say if you asked them for help?"

"Let's see. Mine would beat me," Nell mused, "then . . . hm, probably throw me out to beg with cuts on my arms, seeing as he'd think I was such a good liar."

"Who's your mime-lord?"

"Bully-Rook. III-1."

"Right." The Bully-Rook was as much of a brute as his name suggested. "Felix?"

"I wasn't a syndie," he admitted.

"I wasn't, either," Ivy said. "Just a gutterling."

I sighed. "Jos?"

"I was a gutterling, too, in II-3. My kidsman wouldn't help us." He hugged his knees. "Will we have to stay here, Paige?"

"For now," I said. "Will Agatha ask you to work?"

"Of course she will. She's already got twenty gutterlings to feed," Ivy said. "We can't just sponge off her."

"I understand, but you've all been through a lot. Nell, you've been away for ten years. You need time to adjust."

"I'm just grateful she's putting us up." Nell leaned back against the wall. "Getting back to work will do me good. I'd almost forgotten what it was like to be *paid* for doing a job," she added. "What about your mime-lord, anyway? You're with the White Binder, aren't you?"

"I'm going to talk to him about it." I looked at Ivy, who was pushing at a callus on her knuckle. "Does Agatha know about the colony?" She shook her head. "What did you tell her, then?"

"That we broke out of the Tower." Ivy kept shaking her head. "I just . . . couldn't face explaining it. I want to forget it all."

"Keep it that way. The truth is our best weapon. I want it to be heard for the first time at the Unnatural Assembly, or they'll think it's just a rumor that's gone out of control."

"Paige, *don't* tell the Assembly." Her eyes widened. "You didn't say anything about fighting back or going public. You said you'd get us *home*. That's it. We have to stay hidden. You could put the rest of us in—"

"I don't want to stay hidden." Jos's voice was small, but firm. "I want to make it right."

Agatha chose that moment to return, carrying a tray of food. "Time to leave, love," she said to me. "Ivy needs her rest."

"If you say so." I glanced back at her four charges. "Stay safe."

"Wait a second." Felix scrawled a phone number on a scrap of paper. "Just in case you need us. It's for one of the hawkers, but she'll take a message if you call her."

I tucked the paper into my pocket. On my way up the rotting

stairs, I cursed Agatha. What kind of idiot was she that she'd let two voyants die on her watch? She seemed kind enough, and this burden had been dropped on her unexpectedly, but Ivy would follow them to the æther if she wasn't careful. Still, to see four survivors safe and clean and fed, with a place to sleep and other voyants to protect them, was more than I could have hoped to gain from this excursion.

A light rain was falling when I left Agatha's Boutique. I wandered through the covered market, where naphtha lights burned down on a wealth of hot street food. Shiny buttered peas, steaming in paper ramekins; masses of mashed potato, some fluffy white, some tinged with pea-green or rose; sausages spitting in a cast-iron pan. When I passed a tray of drinking chocolate, I couldn't resist. It was silky sweet, and it tasted like conquest. Everything I ate and drank was another way to spite Nashira.

It soon sat oddly on my stomach. Liss would have given an arm for a sip of this drink.

A shoulder knocked against mine, sending the rest of the cup flying.

"Hook it."

The voice was gruff and male. I almost said something back, but the sight of their stripes and bone bracelets stopped me. Rag Dolls. This was their turf, not mine.

With a few hours until sunrise, I left the night market and headed south, keeping an eye out for any passing rides. It didn't take long to arrive at the border of I Cohort. When I reached an alley, I leaned against a wall to check my watch. It was an abandoned busker hideout, dirty and silent, full of burned-out rubbish bins from fires made near the doorways. In retrospect, it was a bad place to stop.

My sixth sense was slow. I didn't feel them coming until they were right on top of me.

"Well, look who it is. My old friend, the Pale Dreamer."

My stomach plummeted into my boots. I knew that oily voice, all right. That was Haymarket Hector.

# 4

## Grub Street

The Underlord of the Scion Citadel of London was not a pleasant sight at any distance. Still, now his face was only inches from mine, I was reminded why darkness suited him so well. A scabrous nose, broken rods of teeth, and eyes threaded with blood vessels were all arranged in a grin. Beneath his bowler hat, his hair was limp with grease. His horde—the Underbodies—clustered around me, forming a tight semicircle.

The Undertaker, the binder of I-1, brought up the rear, recognizable by his top hat. His right arm had been hewn with so many names, it was little more than a sleeve of scar tissue. Beside him was the Underhand, Hector's enormous bodyguard.

"The little Dialer is a long way from home," Hector said softly.

"I'm in I-4. I *am* home."

"What sweet sentiment." He passed his lantern to the Underhand. "We missed you, Dreamer. How lovely it is to see you again."

"I'd love to say the same for you."

"Your time away from London hasn't changed you. Binder didn't tell us where you'd gone."

"You're not my mime-lord. I don't report to you."

"But your mime-lord does." A thin smile. "I understand you two have had a quarrel."

I didn't answer that. "What are you doing in I-4?"

"We got a few bones to pick with your boss." Magtooth grinned at me, showing a left incisor inked with a tiny tarot image. He was a dab hand at tarocchi, Magtooth. The most gifted cartomancer I'd ever played. "One of his lackeys has summoned a meeting of the Unnatural Assembly."

"It's our right to summon meetings."

"Only when I feel like it." Hector pressed his thumb to my throat. "As it happens, I'm not in the mood for any tedious gatherings. Imagine if I were to answer *all* the summons I get in my dead drop, Pale Dreamer. I'd never be doing anything but listening to the woes of my more pious mime-lords and mime-queens."

"Their woes might be important," I said coolly. "Isn't it your job to answer summons?"

"No. It's my underlings' job to deal with the herd. It's *my* job to keep you all in line. The petty problems of this syndicate are important only if I deem them to be important."

"Do you think Scion is important? Do you think it's important that they're about to crush us with Senshield?"

"Ah." Hector placed a finger on my lips. "I think we've found our suspect. It was *you*, wasn't it, Pale Dreamer? You called the meeting, didn't you?"

The words were met with raucous laughter. My spirit felt as if it were swelling, overflowing.

"You think you can summon *us*?" Magtooth sneered at me. "What are we, her fucking lapdogs?"

"Yes, Magtooth, it seems she does. How presumptuous of her." Leaning close, Hector whispered in my ear: "The White Binder will feel my displeasure for allowing you to be so bold as to *summon* me, Pale Dreamer."

"Don't act like a king, Hector." I didn't move. "You know what London does to kings."

As soon as I said it, the æther gave an ominous tremor. The night air blew down my spine as a poltergeist seeped from the walls. "This is the London Monster," Hector said. "Another old friend. Do you know him? He walked these streets in the late eighteenth century. Had a particular penchant for splitting the skin of young ladies."

That blot in the æther was enough to bring bile to my throat and chills to my legs. Then I remembered the pendant, and courage sparked inside me. "I've seen worse," I said. "That thing's a cheap Ripper knock-off."

Hector's speaking medium, Roundhead, let out a ghastly snarl. "Blast your eyes, you damned bitch," he barked. The poltergeist was talking with Roundhead's tongue.

The Undertaker crooked a long finger. Reluctantly, the poltergeist retreated. Roundhead choked out a handful of ugly curses before falling silent.

"Any other party tricks?" I said.

"I'll show you one."

The promise came from Hector's mollisher, Cutmouth. Several inches taller than her mime-lord, she wore knives around her hips and her long red hair in a French braid. Eyes of a deceptively soft brown stared into mine. Her mouth was tugged into a permanent snarl, the result of an S-shaped scar that slashed through both her lips.

"I know a trick or two, Pale Dreamer." The blade of a long knife caught the lantern as she held the tip to the corner of my mouth. "I think they'll make you smile."

I held still. Cutmouth could only be one or two years older than me, but she was already as cruel as Hector.

"A mollisher should have scars." Her thumb traced the faint line on my cheek. "Where'd you get this? Break a nail, did you? Slap on too much greasepaint? You're a sham. A nothing. You and your Seven Seals make me want to spit."

And she did. The others burst out laughing, save the Undertaker, who never laughed.

"Now that's out of the way"—I wiped my face with my cuff—"maybe you could tell me what you want, Cutmouth."

"I want to know where you've been for the last six months. The last person in London to see you was Hector."

"I've been away."

"Yes, you dumb mort, we know you've been *away*. Where?"

"Nowhere near your turf, if that's your issue."

Cutmouth thumped me in the ribs, hard enough to knock every breath from my body. Pain exploded from my old injuries, doubling me over like a snapped twig. "Don't try and toy with me. You're the toy here." While I clutched my ribcage, she aimed a kick at my knee, bringing me to the ground, then pulled my hair free of my hat and twisted it around her hand. "Look at you. You're no mollisher."

"She's a charlatan," one of the flimps said. "Thought she was supposed to be a dreamwalker?"

"Well said, Mr. Slipfinger. She doesn't seem to do much, does she? Bit of a chair-warmer, I say." Cutmouth pressed the blade against my throat. "What are you *for*, Dreamer? What does Binder do with you? We're honor-bound to get rid of charlatans, so you'd better open that trap of yours and talk. I'll ask you again: where have you been?"

"Away," I repeated. She gave me such a smack across the face, my head cracked against the wall.

"Talk, I said. Would you like to be a stiff as well as a fucking brogue?"

I bit back a foul retort. Even voyants parroted Scion's hatred of the Irish. Hector stood by, looking at the golden pocket watch he always carried. There was no way I'd win this fight, not with the other injuries I was hiding. I didn't want Hector to know how much my spirit had changed. As far as he knew, I was still just a mind radar, good for nothing but counting dreamscapes.

"Oh, she won't talk. Give us your wallet, Dreamer," Slipfinger said to me. "We'll buy something more fun."

"And that pretty necklace." His companion, a thickset woman, grabbed my hair. "What metal's that?"

My dirty fingers groped for the pendant. "It's just plastic," I said. "From Portobello."

"Liar. Give it."

The metal tingled against my palm. It was sublimed against poltergeists, but I doubted it would protect me from London gangsters.

"We'll let her keep her trinket," Hector said after a moment. "Although I must say that a necklace would look *dazzling* on you, Miss Slabnose." While the others snickered, the Underlord extended a hand. "Your wallet."

"I don't have one."

"Don't lie, Dreamer, or I may have to ask Bloatface to search you."

My gaze flicked to the man in question. Thick-fingered, with a hairless, doughy head and two greedy black eyes, Bloatface the maggot was the one who did all Hector's really dirty work. The one who did the killing and dumped the bodies, if the situation called for it. I dug into my pocket and threw my last few coins at Slipfinger's boots.

"Consider that payment," Hector said, "for your life. Cutmouth, put the knife away."

Cutmouth stared at him. "She hasn't talked yet," she bit out. "You just want to let her go?"

"She's no use to us mutilated. The White Binder won't want to play with a damaged doll."

"The bitch can tell us where she's been. You said we would—"

With a clap of one hand, Hector struck her. One of his rings caught her cheek, drawing blood. "You," he whispered, "are not my master."

Hair had come loose from her braid, falling over one side of her face. She caught my eye, then looked away, clenching her fist. "Forgiveness," she said.

"Granted."

The other gangsters all looked at one another, but Magtooth was the only one smiling. All of them had small scars on their faces. With a last look at me, Hector placed his hands on his mollisher's waist and guided her away. I couldn't see her face any longer, but her back was tense.

"Boss," Magtooth called. "Forgetting something?"

"Oh, yes." Hector waved his hand. "A hit for the cards, Dreamer. If you bother me again, your light will be put out."

The Underhand parted the others. Before I could duck, his fist smashed into the side of my face, then straight into my stomach. And again. Sparks flew from the center of my vision. The ground lurched up to meet my palms. If he'd been a smaller man, I would have at least tried to land a punch, but if I pissed him off he might just kill me—and I'd fought too hard to live to let that happen. He gave me a few kicks for good measure.

"Mort."

He spat on me and went loping like a dog after his mime-lord. Laughter echoed through the mews.

Pain leaped from the roots of my teeth. I wheezed and coughed. *Gutless bastard.* Magtooth had been itching for a fight since he'd lost our last tarocchi match, although setting the Underhand on me hardly counted as a fight. It seemed so down-right *stupid* now, so stupid to shed blood over a game—but that was all Hector's people really did. They had made a game board of the syndicate.

I pushed myself on to my hands and knees. Now I really was a gutterling. I took out the burner phone from my jacket and dialed. It rang twice before a courier picked up.

"I-4."

"The White Binder," I said.

"Yes, ma'am."

Three minutes passed before Jaxon's voice came down the line: "Is that you again, Didion? Look, you wretched jackanapes, I have neither the time nor the money to waste on capturing yet another one of your escaped—"

"It's me."

There was a long, unbroken silence. My voice usually sent him into fits of prolixity.

"Look, Hector just cornered me. He says he's coming to talk to you. He's got the Underbodies with him."

"What do they want?" he said curtly.

"I summoned a meeting of the Unnatural Assembly," I said, just as curtly. "They didn't like it."

"You wretched *fool*, Dreamer. You should have known better than to think Hector would convene a meeting. He hasn't called a single one in all the years he's been Underlord." I heard him moving around. "You say they're coming here? To Seven Dials?"

"I think so."

"Then I suppose I will have to deal with them." Pause. "Are you hurt?"

I wiped blood from my lips. "They knocked me about a bit."

"Where are you? Shall I send a cab?"

"I'm fine."

"I would like you back at Seven Dials. I've already been forced to inform the nearest sections that you've considered leaving my service."

"I'm aware of that."

"Then come back, darling. We'll talk this over."

"No, Binder." The words came out before I'd even thought about them. "I'm not ready. I don't know if I'll ever be ready."

This time the silence was much, much longer.

"I see," he said. "Well, I await your *readiness*. In the meantime, perhaps I shall begin my search for a replacement mollisher. Bell's commitment is encouraging. After all, not all of us have time to lounge in lavish doss-houses while our mime-lords dust away our problems."

The dialing tone pierced my ear. I yanked the module from the phone and dropped it down a drain.

So Jaxon was considering Nadine, the Silent Bell, as his new mollisher. I shoved the empty phone into my pocket and headed for the end of the mews, my cheek throbbing. Nick was staying on Grub Street, where pamphlets were produced. I should go to him. Talk to him. It was better than spending another night alone, waiting for the red-jackets to drag me from my bed. I hailed a rickshaw and asked for I-5.

****

There would be no meeting of the Unnatural Assembly. It had been optimistic to hope that Hector would listen, but a tiny part of me had thought he might at least be curious enough to hear me out.

I'd have to get word out some other way. I couldn't go shouting about the Rephaim on the street. People would think I'd lost my mind. And I couldn't fight them alone, not when they had the military might of Scion behind them. The sheer size of the enemy was frightening. If I didn't have the syndicate, I had nothing.

Rain was pouring by the time the rickshaw dropped me off at the entrance to the street. I promised the driver I'd come back with coin, wrapped my cravat over my face and walked beneath the archway.

Since the 1980s, Grub Street had been home to the *haute bohème* of the voyant underworld. It was more of a district than a single street, a seam of sedition in the heart of I-5. Its architecture was an eccentric mix of eighteenth-century Georgian, mock-Tudor, and modern, all crooked foundations, cobblestones, and leaning walls, interspersed with neon and steel and a single, modest transmission screen. Shops sold all the supplies a wordsmith could desire: thick paper, moonbows of inkwells, old collectors' tomes—the kind that opened, like doors to other worlds—and bejeweled fountain pens.

There were at least five or six coffeehouses and a solitary cook-shop, already open for business. The smell of coffee drifted from most windows. You could tell it was home to most of the biblio-mancers and psychographers in the citadel, who dwelled in mildewed garrets with only their muses, coffee, and books for company. Victorian parlor music floated from the open door of an antiques shop.

Short alleys twisted off on all sides of the main street, each lead-ing to a small, enclosed court. It was into one of these that I walked, heading for the single doss-house it housed. A sign hung over the door, with letters spelling out BELL INN. When I sensed Nick's dream-scape, I gave it a nudge.

After a few moments, a worried face appeared at the garret window. I waited by the streetlight until he came through the door of the doss-house.

"What are you doing here? What happened?"

"Hector," I said, by way of an explanation.

A shadow crossed his brow. "You're lucky to be alive." He kissed the top of my head. "Quickly. Inside."

"I need to pay for the rick."

"I'll do it. Go on."

I stepped into the hall and shook the rain off my coat. When Nick returned, he led me past the firelit parlor, where a large man was hunched over a book, smoking a pipe. He was perhaps sixty, of sallow complexion. A neat, dark beard, shot with gray, grew out from below his large nose.

"Evening, Alfred," Nick said.

The man started so violently that the chair let out a gunshot crack. "Oh—Vision, my good friend." His accent was distinctly upper class, oddly so, like he should have been born in the monarch days.

"You don't look too good, old man."

"Yes, well." He sank back into his seat. "Minty's out looking for me, you see. Rather on edge."

"You thought I was Minty? I'm flattered." Nick took his key from the doorkeeper. "You work too hard. Why don't you get out of Grub Street for a few days, take a break?"

"Oh, no fear. Your mime-lord would throw a fit, for one thing. He likes me to be available at all hours in case of literary emergencies. Not that he's in my good books—still owes me a blasted manuscript." With a gnarled finger, the man forced his pince-nez to the end of his nose. When he spotted me, his eyebrows sprang up. "And who is this fair maiden you're sneaking into the garret?"

"This is Paige, Alfred. Jaxon's mollisher."

Alfred looked at me over the tops of his lenses. "My word. The Pale Dreamer. How do you do?"

"Alfred is a psycho-scout," Nick said to me. "The only one in London. He discovered Jaxon's writing."

"I hasten to add that the 'psycho' is short for 'psychographer.' Most of my clients are writing mediums, you see." Alfred kissed my grimy hand. "I've heard a great deal about you from your mime-lord, but he never deigned to introduce you."

"He doesn't deign to do much," I said.

"Ah, but he's the mastermind! He need not lift a finger." Alfred released my hand. "If I may say so, dear heart, you look as if you've been in the wars."

"Hector."

"Ah. Yes. Our Underlord is not the most peaceful of men. Why we voyants fight each other so passionately, yet do nothing to fight the Inquisitor, I shall never know."

I studied the drooping face. If this man had discovered Jaxon's writing, he was at least partly responsible for the publication of *On the Merits of Unnaturalness*, the pamphlet that had turned voyant against voyant and caused the terrible fault lines that still divided our community.

"It is strange," I said.

Alfred glanced up at me. His downturned eyes were gunmetal blue, and beneath them hung two swollen pouches of skin.

"So, Nick. Tell an old man the latest Scion scandals." He folded his hands on his stomach. "What sort of devious new experiments are they performing? Are they chopping up voyants yet?"

"Nothing that juicy, I'm afraid. Most of the doctors are testing the new Senshield prototype for SciORE."

"Yes, I imagine they are. How is your Danica faring around that?"

I was certain Danica hadn't met this man in person; she wasn't exactly a social butterfly. Jaxon must have told him about us, real names included. "She's sixth-order," Nick said. "It can't detect her yet."

"Yet," Alfred said.

I wondered whether Danica would have gone back to work immediately after the escape, and felt lower than dirt when I realized I had no idea. She only worked part-time for SciORE, but I was willing to bet that she'd reported for her shift after the rescue.

"The new Senshield won't be ready by Novembertide, in any case," Nick said. "Not for citadel-wide use."

"They have them in the Archon already, my friend. They'll want them in the Grand Stadium. Mark my words, they'll have a lavish welcome ceremony for *Inquisiteur* when he arrives."

"I look forward to all fifty celebratory hangings." Nick steered me towards the staircase. "Sorry, Alfred—I should get Paige some pain-killers. Good luck avoiding Minty."

"Hmph, not to worry. 'Fortune, seeing that she could not make fools wise, has made them lucky.'"

"Shakespeare?"

"Montaigne." With a click of his tongue, the scout returned his attention to his book. "Farewell, halfwit."

It was gloomy in the inn. We creaked up the stairs to the attic floor, where the carpet was worn thin and the walls were the dull brown of an old bruise.

"Alfred and Jaxon go back a very long way." Nick unlocked the door. "He's remarkable—probably the most talented bibliomancer in the citadel. Fifty-seven years old and works eighteen hours a day. He claims he can read anything and just *sense* if it's going to sell."

"Has he ever been wrong?"

"Not to my knowledge. That's why he's the only psycho-scout. He put all the others out of work."

"What does he do for Jax?"

"Pitches his pamphlets to the Spiritus Club, for one thing. He made a small fortune from *On the Merits*."

I didn't comment.

Nick switched on the light. The room was fairly nondescript, furnished with nothing more than a mirror, a cracked sink, and a bed with threadbare blankets. It didn't look as if it had been dusted in a century. A few essential items from his apartment were dotted around the room.

"Do you rent this?" I said.

"I do. It's not exactly Farrance's, but sometimes I just need to be around other voyants, not including Jax. Call it a holiday home." He steamed a flannel with hot water and passed it to me. "Tell me what happened with Hector."

"He said he was going to see Jaxon."

"Why?"

"The summons." I dabbed my lips. "He was going to find out who'd sent it. He realized it was me and got the Underhand to do this."

He grimaced. "I wish I could say I was surprised. No meeting, then?"

"No."

"Were they still going to see Jaxon?"

"I called him to warn him. He wanted me to come to Dials. I said no."

"He wasn't angry about the summons?"

"Not as angry as I expected." When I took the flannel from my face, it was smeared with blood and grime. "He's threatening to make Nadine his mollisher, though."

"He's been grooming her for it, *sötnos*." When I frowned, he sighed. "Nadine was pushing to be mollisher as soon as you went missing. They've been having private meetings, and he's let her do a lot of your work—collecting rent, Juditheon auctions, that sort of thing. It'll stop if you go back, but Nadine won't be happy about it."

"Why did he choose Nadine? I would have thought it'd be Zeke or Dani, as they're furies."

He raised his hands. "Far be it from me to guess at the workings of Jaxon Hall's mind. Anyway, he won't make her mollisher unless you tell him outright that his dreamwalker will never work for him again. Do you really want to quit?"

"No. Yes. I don't know." I chucked myself on to the bed. "I can't forget what he said. That he'd make my life hell if I ever left his service."

"And he will. You'll be shut out of everything if you quit. You need money. Scion watches all its employees' bank accounts," he warned. "I can't keep withdrawing cash for your rent, or they'll start asking questions. Say what you like about Jax, but he pays good money."

"Yes, he pays me to bully Didion and sell fake paintings at the black market. He pays Nadine to play her violin. He pays Zeke to be his lab rat. And what the hell is the point?"

"He's a mime-lord. It's his job. It's your job."

"Because of Hector." I stared at the ceiling. "If he was gone, someone else could take over the syndicate and unite us."

"No. Both the mime-lord and the mollisher supreme need to be gone before a scrimmage can be called. If Hector died, Cutmouth would become Underqueen," he said, "and she's no better. Hector's only in his forties, and he certainly isn't starving. He won't be heading to the æther for a while."

"Unless someone gets rid of him."

His head turned. "Even the most violent mobsters would condemn a coup," he said, his voice low.

"Only because Hector supports their violence."

"Are you suggesting that someone should organize a coup?"

"Do you have any better ideas?"

"They'd have to oust Cutmouth as well. Even if it did happen, the Unnatural Assembly still wouldn't put up a fight against Scion," he said gently. "Most of them got those positions through murder or blackmail, not bravery. Hector's only part of the problem." He poured some saloop from a flask. "Here. You look freezing."

I took it. He sat down on the bed opposite me and sipped from his own cup, looking down at the court.

"I've been having visions since we got back," he said. "It's probably nothing, but some of them . . ."

"What did you see?"

"A waterboard," he said, as if he were still seeing it, "in a room with white walls and a blue tiled floor. I've had visions like that before, but this one feels more specific. There's a wooden clock on the wall behind the board, with leaves and flowers carved around the face. When midnight strikes, a tiny metal bird springs out and sings an old song from my childhood."

My pulse tripped. An oracle's gift mostly involved *sending* images, but sometimes they'd receive unsolicited messages from the æther, too. To Nick, they were an endless source of fear and fascination "Have you seen a clock like that before?"

"Yes. It's called a cuckoo clock," he said. "My mother had one."

Nick hardly ever spoke about his family. I shifted a little closer to him. "Do you think it was meant for you, or about someone else?"

"The song felt personal." Every time he looked at me, the shadows on his face seemed deeper. "I've had visions since I was six years old, and I still don't really understand them. Even if the waterboard isn't meant for me, they'll find out what I am sooner or later. We like to think we're brave, but in the end, we're only human. People break bones trying to get off the waterboard."

"Nick, stop it. They can't torture you."

"They can do what they like." His eyelids lowered. "In all the years I've worked for Scion, I've saved thirty-four voyants from the gallows and two from Nitekind. It's kept me sane. It's what I live for. We need someone in there, or there's nobody to fight for them."

I'd always admired Nick for what he did. Jaxon hated the fact that his oracle worked for Scion—he wanted him to be utterly committed to the gang—but it had been part of his contract that he kept the day job, and he was happy enough to share his earnings when he could.

"But you, *sötnos*—you can still leave," Nick continued. "We can't get you over the Atlantic, but there are ways to reach the Continent."

"It's just as dangerous there as it is here. What would I do? Join a freak show?"

"I'm serious, Paige. You're streetwise and your French is good. At least you wouldn't be here in the heartland. Or you could go back to Ireland. There's only so far they'll go to find you before they give up."

"Ireland." I let out a dull laugh. "Yes, Inquisitors have always had great respect for Irish soil."

"Not Ireland, then. But somewhere."

"Wherever I go, they'll follow."

"Scion?"

"No. The Rephaim." Nashira wouldn't give me up that easily. "Only five people definitely survived the escape. I'm the only one of those five people who has sway enough to make a difference."

"So we stay."

"Yes. We stay and change the world."

His face lifted in a tired smile, but it looked like hard work. I couldn't blame him. The prospect of going up against Scion wasn't exactly heartening.

"I need to get to the cookshop," he said. "Do you want some breakfast?"

"Surprise me."

"All right. Just keep the curtains closed."

He shrugged on his coat and headed outside. I pulled the heavy curtain past the window.

The revolution in Sheol I had beaten the odds. With the right reasons, at the right moment, even the most beaten and broken of people could rise up and reclaim themselves.

The mime-lords and mime-queens of London were not broken. Scion's indoctrination and cruelty had given them the opportunity to rise. They were comfortable in their underworld, with a sprawling network of couriers, pickpockets and footpads to do their dirty work. Somehow, they had to be convinced that overthrowing Scion would give them better lives—but while Haymarket Hector lived, his people would stay lazy and corrupt.

I leaned over the sink and rinsed saliva out of my hair. Nick said Hector wasn't worth killing, but when I looked at the rising bruise on my cheek, I had to wonder. He was a symptom of the diseases in the syndicate: the greed, the violence and, worst of all, the apathy.

Murder wasn't exactly a capital crime to people who were certain of an afterlife. Hector got rid of plenty of syndies, and no matter how brutally he did it, no one batted an eyelid. But killing the leader of the syndicate . . . That would be a very different matter. You could kill a busker or a fellow gang member, but you couldn't go against your own mime-lord, or your Underlord. It was an unwritten rule. The syndicate's high treason.

Maybe—just maybe—I could talk to Cutmouth. Away from Hector, she might be different. But that was about as likely as Hector voluntarily handing the crown to someone competent.

Keeping a cold compress against my cheek, I sat back on the bed. It seemed I had no choice but to take up the mantle of mollisher of I-4 again. To turn the syndicate against Scion, I had to be close to the Unnatural Assembly, close enough to command respect and be privy to its workings—but unless Warden returned, I had no proof of the Rephaim's existence. I'd have to spread the word without a shred of evidence. I pulled on the golden cord again.

*You needed me to start this,* I thought. *I need you to help me end it.*

No answer. Just the same, grave silence.

# 5

# Weaver

Nick left for work a few hours later. The room at Bell Inn was free for me to use, and it was about time I left the I-4 doss-house. I rested there for a few hours, but it felt bare without Nick. In the evening, I set off to find something to eat. Music drifted from a record shop and doors were left ajar for séances. I passed a voyant beggar, wrapped head-to-toe in filthy blankets. It was always the augurs and soothsayers who found themselves on the streets as winter approached, fighting for their lives.

Were Liss's parents still alive? Were they out there in the cold, offering card readings, or had they returned to the Highlands when their daughter went missing? Either way, they would never know what had happened to her. They would never have the chance to face her killer, Gomeisa Sargas. He might be in the Archon now, coordinating a response to the rebellion.

*That is how we see your world, Paige Mahoney*, he'd told me. *A box of moths, just waiting to be burned.*

It was strange to be back in I-5, the financial center of Scion, where I'd lived since I was nine. Long before Jaxon Hall had come into my life, I'd spent my free time ambling through the green spaces that slithered between the skyscrapers, trying not to notice as my gift struggled to emerge. My father had rarely stopped me. So long as I had a phone, he'd been content to let me wander.

When I reached the end of the street, a coffeehouse lurched up on my left, hardly visible in the thick fog. I stopped dead. The sign above the door read BOBBIN'S COFFEE.

My father was a man of habit. He always liked to have a coffee after his shift at work, and he almost always went to Bobbin's. I'd been there with him once or twice myself when I was in my early teens.

It was worth a try. I could never approach him publicly again, but I had to know that he was alive. And after everything I'd seen, everything I'd learned about the world, I wanted to see a face from before. The face of the father I'd always loved, but never understood.

As always, Bobbin's was crowded, the air dense with the smell of coffee. Glances came in my direction—sighted glances, assessing my red aura—but nobody seemed to recognize me. The voyants of Grub Street had always considered themselves to be a cut above syndicate politics. A thin, bruised girl was no immediate threat, even if she *was* some sort of jumper. I still chose a seat in the darkest corner possible, hidden by a screen, feeling as if I'd been stripped. I shouldn't be outside. I should be behind curtains and locked doors.

When I was certain that no one had identified me, I bought some cheap soup with the handful of money Nick had left me, careful to use an English accent and keep my eyes down. The soup was made with barley and garden peas, poured into a hollowed loaf of bread. I ate it at my table, savoring each mouthful.

Nobody in this coffeehouse had a data pad, but most people were reading: Victorian tomes, chapbooks, penny dreadfuls. I cast a glance at the nearest patron, a bibliomancer. Behind his newspaper, he was thumbing through a well-worn copy of Didion Waite's first anonymous poetry chapbook, *Love at First Sight; or, the Seer's Delight*. At least, Didion liked to think he was anonymous. We all knew who'd written the dreary collection of epics as he named every muse after his late wife. Jaxon was waiting on tenterhooks for the day he tried to write erotica.

The thought made me smile until a bell clanged above the door, diverting my attention from the book. Whoever had just come in had a familiar dreamscape.

An umbrella was hooked over his arm. He transferred it to the stand by the counter and stamped his boots on the doormat. Then he was walking past my table, waiting in line for a coffee.

In the last six months, my father's hair had flecked itself with gray, and two faint lines cupped his mouth. He seemed older, but he didn't have a torture victim's scars. Relief came crashing into me. The voyant waitron asked for his order.

"Black coffee," he said, his accent less noticeable than usual. "And a water. Thank you."

It took all my willpower to stay quiet.

My father sat at a table by the window. I hid behind the screen, watching him through a swirling pattern of glass panes in the wood. Now I could see the other side of him, I noticed a purple welt on his neck, so small you'd think it was a shaving cut. My hand strayed to the matching flux scar on my lower back, gained on the night I'd been arrested.

Another clang, and an amaurotic woman came into the coffee-house. She caught sight of my father and went to join him, swinging her coat from her shoulders as she went. Small and plump, she had brown skin, light eyes, and black hair in a loose braid. She sat down opposite my father and leaned across the table, her hands clasped in front of her. Ten delicate silver rings shone on her fingers.

A frown creased my brow as I watched them. When the woman shook her head, my father seemed to lose control of himself. He dropped his forehead into his hand, and his shoulders slumped and shook. His friend placed both her hands over his free one, which was balled into a fist.

Fighting down a sudden thickness in my throat, I concentrated on finishing my soup. The jukebox played "The Java Jive" when someone dropped a coin in it. I watched him take the woman's arm and walk into the darkness.

"Penny for your thoughts, dear heart?"

The voice startled me. I found myself looking at the sinking face of Alfred the psycho-scout.

"Alfred," I said, surprised.

"Yes, that tragic fool. I hear he's far too old to approach beautiful ladies in coffeehouses, but he never learns." Alfred examined me. "You look far too glum for a Saturday evening. In my many years of experience, that means you haven't had quite enough coffee."

"I've haven't even had one."

"Oh, dear me. You are clearly not of the *literati*."

"Evening, Alfred." The waitron raised a hand, as did some of the patrons. "Haven't seen you in a while."

"Hello, hello." Alfred raised his hat, smiling. "Yes, I'm afraid the powers that be have been nipping at my heels. Had to pretend I had a real job, the muses forbid."

A round of good-natured laughter went up before the voyants went back to their drinks. Alfred placed a hand on the chair opposite mine. "May I?"

"Of course."

"You're very kind. It can be absolutely unbearable to be surrounded by writers every day. Ghastly lot. Now, what can I get you? *Café au lait? Miel? Bombón?* Vienna? Or perhaps a dirty chai? I do enjoy a spot of dirty chai."

"Just a saloop."

"Oh, dear." He placed his hat on the table. "Well, if you insist. Waitron! Bring forth the beans of enlightenment!"

It was easy to see why he and Jaxon got on so well. They were both completely off the cot. The waitron almost ran to fetch the beans of enlightenment, leaving me to face the music. I cleared my throat.

"I hear you work at the Spiritus Club."

"Well, I work in the building, yes, but they don't employ me. I show them pieces of paper, and occasionally they buy them."

"Fairly seditious pieces of paper, I hear."

He chuckled at that. "Yes, sedition is my field of expertise. Your mime-lord is a fellow connoisseur. His Seven Orders system remains the one true masterpiece of the voyant world."

Debatable. "How did you find him?"

"Well, it was really the other way around. He sent me a draft for *On the Merits of Unnaturalness* when he was about your age. A prodigy if ever I saw one. Possessive, too. Still goes into paroxysms whenever I take on a new client in the I-4 area," he said, shaking his head. "He's a talented man—fiercely imaginative. I wonder why he gets himself so worked up about these things." He paused as the waitron delivered his tray. "Thank you, good sir." The coffee was poured, thick as mud. "I knew there were risks in publishing such a pamphlet, of course, but I've always been a gambler."

"You withdrew it," I said. "After the gang wars."

"A symbolic gesture. Too late by then, of course. *On the Merits* had already been pirated by every halfwit with a printer from here to Harrow, affecting voyants' mindsets as it went. Literature is our most powerful tool, one Scion has never fully mastered. All they've been able to do is sterilize what they put out," he said. "But we, the creative, must be very careful with seditious writing. Change a word or two, even a single letter, and you change the entire story. It's a risky business."

I stirred rosewater into my saloop. "So you wouldn't publish anything like that again."

"Oh, mercy, don't tempt me. I've been a pauper since the withdrawal. The pamphlet is still alive and well, while the poor scout lives in squalor in his rented garret." He took off his spectacles, rubbed his eyes. "Still, I do take a fair cut from every other pamphlet and chapbook that finds its way to the shelves, apart from Mr. Waite's 'romances,' which are—and I think you'll agree—no loss to me, or indeed, to literature."

"They're not exactly subversive material," I agreed.

"No, indeed. No voyant literature is, really, apart from Jaxon's. It's only subversive in that it's in a forbidden genre." He nodded to a woman at the window. Her chin was tucked against her collar, her face tilted toward her lap. "Isn't it wonderful, how words and paper can embroil us so? We are witnessing a miracle, dear heart."

I looked at the penny dreadful she was hiding under the table; at the way the bibliomancer's eyes were welded to the printed words, ignoring everything outside them. She wasn't just paying attention. She was learning. Believing what would seem insane if you heard it on the street.

The transmission screen above the counter turned white. Every head in the coffeehouse came up. The waitron reached up and turned down the lamps, so the only source of light was from the screen. Two lines of black text had appeared.

REGULARLY SCHEDULED PROGRAMMING HAS BEEN SUSPENDED
PLEASE STAND BY FOR LIVE INQUISITORIAL BROADCAST

"Oh, dear," Alfred murmured.

An instrumental rendition of the anthem began to play. "Anchored to Thee, O Scion," the hymn I'd been forced to sing every morning at school. As soon as it ended, the anchor disappeared—and then Frank Weaver took its place.

The face of the puppet. There it was, staring down at us. The coffeehouse fell silent. The Grand Inquisitor was rarely seen outside the Archon.

It was hard to tell how old he was. At least fifty, probably older. His face was an oblong, framed by greased sideburns. Hair the color of iron lay flat across the top of his head. Scarlett Burnish was poised and expressive; her lips could soften even the most dreadful tidings. Weaver was her polar opposite. His stiff white collar was fastened under his chin.

"*Denizens of the citadel, this is your Inquisitor.*" A cacophony of guttural voices boomed from every speaker in the citadel. "*It is with grave news that I waken you to another day in the Scion Citadel of London, the stronghold of the natural order. I have just received word from the Grand Commander that at least eight unnatural fugitives are at large in the citadel.*" He lifted a square of black silk and dabbed the spittle from his chin. "*Due to circumstances beyond the Archon's control, these criminals escaped the Tower of London last night and vanished before the Guard Extraordinary was able to apprehend them. Those responsible have been relieved of their public duties.*"

It was thought that Weaver was a being of flesh, but no emotion touched his features. I found myself staring at him, fascinated and repelled by this ventriloquist's dummy. He was lying about the time of the escape. They must have needed a few days to coordinate their response. "*These unnaturals have committed some of the most heinous crimes I have seen in all my years in the Archon. They must not be allowed to remain at large, lest they commit such crimes again. I call upon you, the denizens of London, to ensure that these fugitives are detained. If you suspect a neighbor, or*" *even yourself of unnaturalness, you should report immediately to a Vigile outpost. Clemency will be shown."*

Sensation drained away. The urge to run screamed through my blood, beating at my frozen muscles.

*"Only five of these criminals have been named at present. We will update the denizens of London once the others have been identified. For the foreseeable future, the Scion Citadel of London will be placed under emergency red-zone security measures while we hunt these fugitives. Please pay close attention to the following photographs. My thanks to you, and to that which keeps the natural order. We will purge this plague together, as we always have. There is no safer place than Scion."*

And he was gone.

The slideshow of the fugitives was silent, except for a mechanical voice stating each name and the crimes committed. The first face was Felix Samuel Coombs. The second, Eleanor Nahid. The third, Michael Wren. The fourth, "Ivy"—no surname—with her old haircut, dyed brilliantly blue. That photo was against a grey background rather than the white of Scion's official database of denizens.

And the fifth—the most wanted, the face of public enemy number one—was mine.

Alfred didn't even pause for breath. He didn't wait to read my crimes, or to check my face against the woman on the screen. He swept up both our coats, took me by the arm and led me toward the door. Everyone in the coffeehouse was talking by the time the door swung shut.

"There are voyants in this district that would sell you to the Archon in a heartbeat." Alfred hurried me along, hardly moving his lips as he spoke. "Buskers and beggars and the like. Your imprisonment could buy them life. Jaxon will know where to hide you," he said, more to himself than to me, "but reaching I-4 may present a challenge."

"I don't want to—"

I was about to say *go to the Dials*, but I stopped myself. What choice did I have? Scion would catch me within hours if I didn't have a mime-lord's protection. Jaxon was the only option.

"I can try the rooftops," I said instead.

"No, no. I should never forgive myself if you were caught."

This had Nashira's gloved fingers all over it. Forcing myself to quash the volcano of anger, I buttoned my jacket to the chin and buckled it loosely to hide my waist. Alfred held out an arm. With little choice but to trust him, I let him drape half of his coat around me.

"Keep your head down. There are no cameras in Grub Street, but they will see you at once outside it."

Alfred put up his umbrella and walked briskly, but with no outward sign of a hurry. Every step took us farther from the transmission screen and closer to I-4.

"Who's that you got, Alfred?"

It was the augur who had been sleeping outside the coffeehouse. "Oh, er—just a pretty trinket, old girl." He pulled me deeper into his coat. "I'm afraid I'm in rather a hurry—but you'll pop in for a cup of tea in the morning, won't you?"

Without waiting for a reply, he kept on walking. I could hardly keep up with his strides.

We slipped under the archway, out of Grub Street and on to the streets of I-5. The night air was frigid. Yet all around us, London was stirring. Denizens spilled out of apartment buildings and oxygen bars in their hundreds to gather around the transmission towers. I didn't need to feel their auras to tell which ones were voyant—there was terror in their eyes. They buffeted past us as they hurried toward the Lauderdale Tower, where the I-5 screen played the emergency broadcast on repeat. Frank Weaver's face cast lights across the sky.

They were pouring from the bars, shouting from the windows. "Weaver! Weaver!" Their roars were blood and thunder. "WEAVER. WEAVER."

Too many dreamscapes. Each and every one of these people was pressed flush to my senses: their emotions, their *frenzy*, the bright flames of auras as they passed. Voyant. Amaurotic. Voyant. A supernova of invisible colors. When a gap emerged in the tide of human bodies, Alfred pulled me off the street and into the doorway of a jerryshop, where I fought to regain control of my sixth sense. He reached into his pocket, took out a handkerchief, and mopped at his brow.

Away from the crowd, a strange calm came over me. Little by little, I tuned out the æther. All I had to do was focus on my own body: my shallow breaths, my beating heart.

We waited until a large part of the throng had walked past before moving again. Alfred grasped my arm and strode back on to the street.

"I'll take you to the intersection. You can continue to Seven Dials from there."

"You shouldn't."

"Oh, you think I should leave you here in I-5? And expose myself to Jaxon's fury?" He clicked his tongue. "As if I would ever abandon his mollisher to such a fate."

We kept to the backstreets as much as we could, away from the crowds and the transmission screens. As we drew closer, we picked up our pace. There was only so much time until the Archon stopped repeating the broadcast. Without the magnetic influence of the screens, the denizens would be all over the citadel, hunting for traitors. I'd heard of vigilante action during red zones.

By the time we reached the intersection between I-4 and I-5, Alfred was puffing like a locomotive. I was so focused on the border that I didn't sense an aura until it was too late, and a Vigile stepped out in front of me.

Knuckles smashed into my stomach, sending me sprawling against the wall. When I got a good look at my assailant, hot fear surged through me. The Vigile pulled out her machine gun and pointed it at my head.

"Unnatural. Up. Get up!" Making no sudden movements, I rose back to my feet. "Freeze," the Vigile barked at Alfred, who hadn't moved. "Hands up!"

"I *am* sorry, Vigile, but I think there may have been a mistake," Alfred said. He was red in the face, but his smile was perfectly congenial. "We were just on our way to see Inquisitor Weaver's—"

"Put up your hands."

"All right, all right." Alfred raised his hands. "Aside from having no sense of direction, may I ask what we've done amiss?"

The Vigile ignored him. Beneath her visor, her eyes were darting over us. Sighted eyes. I held still.

"Jumper," she whispered.

There was no greed in her expression. She wasn't like the Underguards on the train, thrilled with their catch, already picturing the wealth they'd get for a red aura.

"On your knees," she barked. "On your *knees*, unnatural!" I did as she ordered. "Both of you," she said. With difficulty, Alfred lowered himself to the pavement. "Now, put your hands behind your heads." We both obeyed. The Vigile took a step back, but the red sight of the gun still hovered at the center of my forehead. I made myself look down the barrel. A finger on a trigger was all that stood between us and the æther.

"That won't hide you." The Vigile pulled off my hat, exposing my white-blonde hair. "You're going straight to Inquisitor Weaver. Don't think I won't send you, murderer."

I didn't dare answer. She may have known the Underguards I'd killed. Maybe she'd been on the scene when they found the second man, driven insane, salivating garbled pleas for death. Satisfied with my silence, the Vigile reached for her transceiver. I looked at Alfred. To my shock, he *winked*, like he got detained in the street every day.

"Perhaps," he said, reaching into his pocket, "I can tempt you with this. You're a cyathomancer, aren't you?"

He held up a small gold cup, about the size of a fist, and raised his eyebrows. "This is 521," the Vigile said into her transceiver, ignoring him. "Request immediate backup in I-5, subsection 12, Saffron Street east. Suspect 1 is in custody. I repeat, Paige Mahoney is in custody."

"You're unnatural, too, soothsayer," I said. "You need a numen. Talking into that radio won't change a thing."

The gun jerked back up. "Shut your mouth. Before I put a bullet in it."

"How long do you have before they exterminate you? Noose or NiteKind, do you think?"

*"This is 515. Detain suspect until our arrival."*

"Mind your tongue or I'll break your legs. We know you can run." The Vigile reached for the handcuffs at her belt. "Hold out your hands, or I'll break those, too."

Alfred swallowed. The Vigile grabbed my wrists with one hand.

"Bribes won't help you," she said to Alfred. "If I bring this one to Weaver, I'll be free to buy whatever I like."

My vision shook. Red didn't just come running, but *gushing* from the Vigile's nose. As she raised a hand to stanch it, dropping the handcuffs, I pushed my spirit into her body.

The dreamscape I found was a room full of filing cabinets, lit by stark white lights. This was a clean, precise person. She fitted every thought and memory into a sterile box. It was easy for her to separate what she did at work from her own identity as a clairvoyant. There was color in here, but not a great deal; it had been diluted, washed away by her hatred of herself. In the darkness were her fears, taking the form of specters in her hadal zone: the amorphous figures of other clairvoyants, cruel unnaturals in the shadows.

I was glad, then, when I took her over.

At once I could feel the difference in my body. My new heart took up a staccato rhythm. When I looked up, I saw my own corpse. Paige Mahoney was crumpled on the ground, deathly pale, and Alfred was shaking her with both hands.

"Speak to me," he was saying. "Not yet, dear heart. Not yet."

I stared, transfixed. That was *me*.

And I was . . .

My fist clenched around the transceiver. It was like lifting a dumb-bell, but I raised it to my mouth. "This is 521." My voice came out as a slur. "Suspect has escaped. Heading towards I-6."

I could hardly hear the response. The silver cord was drawing my consciousness away from my host. Her eyes were failing to see, rejecting the foreign body behind them. I was a parasite, a leech on her dreamscape.

And then I was expelled. I opened my eyes and almost head-butted Alfred as I sat up, trembling and sweating. My throat was closed. He slapped me on the back, and I took a gasping breath.

"Good gracious, Paige—are you all right?"

"Fine," I heaved.

And I was. My head was aching, like a hand had gripped the front part of my skull, but it was a tolerable pain.

The Vigile lay unconscious, blood leaking from her ears, nose, eyes, and mouth. I pulled her pistol from its holster and pointed it.

"Don't shoot her," Alfred said. "The poor woman is voyant, at the end of the day. Traitor or otherwise."

"I won't." My temples throbbed. The sight of that bleeding face was ghastly. "Alfred, you can't tell anyone about this. Not even Jaxon."

"Of course. I understand."

He didn't.

I kicked the transceiver from the Vigile's limp hand and brought my boot down on it. After a moment, I crouched down and pressed two fingers to her neck. A huff of relief escaped me when I felt a pulse ticking above her red collar.

"Dials isn't far," I said. "I'm going on alone."

"If you can make denizens bleed at your command, far be it from me to stand in your way." Alfred forced a smile, but he was visibly shaken. "Keep to the fog, dear heart, and move swiftly."

He left the Vigile and dashed away, his umbrella shielding his face. I went in the opposite direction.

I kept to the backstreets, looking for an opportunity to climb. I joined a large crowd heading down the Grandway and broke away at the first right turn, into the smaller roads behind Holborn station. The freezing wind made my bruises ache, but I only allowed myself to stop when I reached the concrete playground of Stukeley Street, where Nick had trained me to fight and climb when I was seventeen. There were huge bins and rails and low walls in abundance, and all the buildings were derelict. My bare palms burned as I dragged a bin across the road and climbed on to it to reach a drainpipe. At the top, I hooked my fingers into the gutter and pulled myself on to a flat roof. The muscles in my shoulders screamed. They were screwed up tight, lacking their old flexibility.

By the time I reached my territory, I was drenched in sweat and hurting all over. I saw the sundial pillar first, rising red-hot from the fog. When I reached the right building, I pounded on the door.

"Jaxon!"

There were no lights in the windows. If they weren't here, there was nowhere else to go. I was sure I could feel a dreamscape.

I looked over my shoulder. No voyants were on my radar. Seven Dials was abandoned—even the oxygen bar across the street was empty of patrons—but Frank Weaver was still talking in Piccadilly Circus, where the enormous I-4 transmission screen was located.

Was Jaxon doing this to spite me? I was still his mollisher. Still his dreamwalker. He couldn't just leave me out here to die.

Could he?

Panic set in. The cold was in my face, in my hands, in my head. I was dizzy with it. Then the door opened, and light came pouring out.

# 6

# Seven Dials

As I crossed the threshold of the den, my knees almost gave way. A strong pair of hands got me up the first flight of stairs and into a wing chair. My nose was streaming, my ears ached and a vicious burn clawed at my cheeks. It was only when sensation returned to my lips that I looked up to see who had rescued me.

"You're blue," Danica said.

I managed a laugh, though it sounded more like a cough.

"It's really not funny. You're probably hypothermic."

"Sorry," I said.

"Don't know why you're apologizing. You're the one who's probably hypothermic."

"Right." I unbuckled my boots with clumsy fingers. "Thanks for letting me in."

Save a single lamp on a filing cabinet, the den was completely dark—every curtain drawn, every light put out—but it was wonderfully warm. Someone must have fixed the boiler at last. "Where are the others?" I said. I was getting déjà vu.

"Out searching for you. Nadine saw the broadcast when she was walking back from the Juditheon."

"Jaxon went, too?"

"Yup."

Maybe he cared more than I thought he did. Jaxon rarely did search work ("I'm a mime-*lord*, O my lovely, not a mime-peasant"), but suddenly he was leaping to my rescue. Danica took a seat on the footstool and pulled a familiar machine toward the wing chair.

"Here." She unhooked the oxygen mask from the tank. "Take a few breaths. Your aura's all over the place."

I lifted the mask to my face and inhaled. *Fear is your real trigger*, Warden had told me. Warden, who had known more than anyone about dreamwalking.

"How's your head?" I said.

"Concussed." As she turned her head to the light, I could make out the long cut above her eye, held together with a series of thin stitches.

"Are you all right now?"

"As 'all right' as you can be with mild traumatic brain injury. Nick stitched it up."

"Have you been back to work since we got back?"

"Oh, yeah. They would have been suspicious if I didn't go. I did a job the next day."

"While concussed?"

"Didn't say I did a *good* job."

I took another breath from the oxygen mask. A botched job by Danica Panić was probably still a lot better than what most engineers could manage on top form.

"Going to turn off the light downstairs. Jax said we had to be in lockdown mode." She got up. "Don't turn anything on."

As soon as she was gone, the æther flickered at eye level,

disturbing my vision. Pieter Claesz, Eliza's favorite art muse, was beaming deep reproach at me.

"Hi, Pieter," I said.

He floated into the corner to sulk. If there was one thing Pieter hated, it was people leaving for months at a time without a word of explanation.

Danica puffed her way back up to the landing. "I'll be in the garret," she said. "You can finish my coffee."

Warmth was finally reaching my core. I took in the familiar surroundings as I sipped the tepid coffee. In the mirror, I caught sight of a greyish stain around my lips. My fingertips had the same discoloration.

The smell of the den fell like dust around me: tobacco, paint, lignin, rosin, cutting oil. I'd spent most of my first year working at one of these tables, doing research into the history and spirits of London, studying *On the Merits of Unnaturalness*, sorting out old newspaper clippings from the black market, making and updating lists of the voyants registered in I-4.

My heart caught at the sound of keys in the lock. Boots thundered on the stairs, and the door was flung open. Nadine Arnett stopped dead when she saw me. Since I'd last seen her, she'd cropped her dead-straight hair so it just covered her ears.

"Wow," she said. "I just *ran* all over I-4 looking for you, and here you are, drinking coffee." She dumped her coat on the back of an armchair. "Where have you been, Mahoney?"

"I was on Grub Street."

"Well, you could have sent us a memo. Why haven't you been here since we got back?"

I was saved from answering when the door slammed again, and Zeke came charging up the stairs.

"There's no sign of her," he said, out of breath. "If you call Eliza we can head over to—"

"We're not going anywhere."

"What?"

She pointed. When he saw me, Zeke came straight to my side and wrapped me in a tight hug. The gesture took me by surprise, but I returned it. He and I had never been close. "Paige, we were so worried. Did you come here by yourself? Where have you been?"

"I was with Nick." I looked first at him, then at Nadine. "Thank you, both of you. For coming to get me."

"Didn't have much of a choice." Nadine unzipped her boots. One of her shoulders was hooded by a thick scab, encircled by livid skin. "Jax hasn't stopped going on about you since we got back from Oxford. 'Where's my mollisher? Why can't someone find her? Nadine, you do it. You find her. Do it now.' You're damn lucky he pays me, or I might be irritated."

"Stop it," Zeke murmured. "You were just as worried as the rest of us."

She kicked off her boots without comment. I glanced at the doorway behind them. "Did you split up to search?"

"Yeah," Zeke said. "Did Jaxon say to lock up, Dee?"

"Yes, but don't. We're not leaving them outside." Nadine looked between the curtains. "You two get some sleep. I'll keep an eye out."

"I'll do it," I said.

"You look like you're about to keel over. Just take forty."

I didn't move from the chair. The warmth of the den had made me drowsy, but I had to stay alert. I might still have to run tonight.

Zeke opened the doors of his box-bed (so Jaxon called it, though it looked remarkably like a cupboard) and sat on the quilt to pull off his shoes. "Is Nick at work?"

"He might be back at Grub Street by now," I said.

"I tried calling him earlier." He paused. "Do you think they suspect him?"

"Not unless he's said something to make them suspicious."

There was silence after that. He lay on the quilt and closed one of the doors, gazing at the photographs and posters he'd glued to the top of the box. They were mostly of free-world musicians, with a single shot of him and Nadine in a nondescript bar, wearing bright clothes and smiles. None of the rest of his family, or any friends from back home. Nadine stood at the window, her pistol tucked against her side.

I turned on the small TV in the corner. Jaxon hated us watching it, but even he liked to keep an eye on what Scion was saying. The screen was split down the middle, with Burnish on one side, in the studio, and a little raconteur on the other. This one was standing outside the front gate of the Tower, her red coat whipped and battered by the wind.

"... *Guard Extraordinary say the prisoners were able to escape by using Felix Coombs's unnatural influence on their newest guard member, who had no idea what to expect from the detainees.*"

"*Of course,*" Burnish said. "*What a horrifying experience that must have been. We're going to leave you now and talk about the most notorious of these individuals: Paige Eva Mahoney, an Irish immigrant from the southern farming province, situated within the Inquisitorial region of the Pale.*" The area was highlighted on a map. "*Mahoney is charged with murder, high treason, sedition, and evasion of arrest. First, we'll speak to renowned Scion parapsychologist Dr. Muriel Roy, who specializes in the study of unnaturalness in the brain. Dr. Roy, do you suspect that it was Paige Mahoney that coordinated this escape? She lived with her father, Dr. Mahoney, for nearly two decades without him having any idea of her condition. That's some real deception, isn't it?*"

"*It is, Scarlett—and as Dr. Mahoney's long-time supervisor, I can only emphasize that Paige's unnaturalness was just as much of an awful shock to him as it was to us . . .*"

They showed a short video of my father leaving the Golden Lane complex, shielding his face with his data pad. My fingers dug into the arm of the chair. When she talked about him, Burnish used his birth name, making puzzled faces as she sounded out the syllables: Cóilín Ó Mathúna. He'd had his name anglicized to Colin Mahoney on our arrival in England, as well as changing my middle name from Aoife to Eva, but apparently Burnish didn't care for petty legalities. By exposing that name, she labeled my father as *alien*, as Other. Heat stroked my eyes.

All my life my father had been distant. The night I'd gone missing had been the first time in months that he'd shown me affection, when he'd offered to make me breakfast and called me by my childhood nickname. He'd been shaking in the coffeehouse, grasping the hands of the woman who'd been sitting with him. But to avoid the accusation of harboring an unnatural—a crime that could lead him to the block—he would have to publicly disown me. To deny that he'd ever seen the part of me that had defined my existence since I was a child.

Did he hate me for what I was, or Scion for bringing us here?

****

The bed was divided from the rest of the room with a translucent curtain. On the left of the pillow was a large window with wooden shutters, which looked down on the beautiful courtyard behind the den. Beyond the curtain, a Lanterna Magica, a white noise machine, and a portable, leather-bound record player stood in a large cabinet: all atmospheric tools, designed to put me in a fit state for dreamwalking. Opposite the door was a bookshelf, cluttered with stolen bits of memorabilia and cases of dreamwalker fuel: painkillers, Nightcaps, adrenaline.

I stirred from sleep with my sixth sense trembling. My old room, with its crimson walls and the ceiling painted with a thousand stars. Jaxon Hall was sitting on the armchair, watching me through the veil.

"Well, well." His face was half in shadow. "The sun rises red, and a dreamer returns."

He wore his silk brocade lounging robe. When I didn't reply, a smile pulled at one corner of his mouth.

"I always rather liked this room," he said. "Quiet. Close. A fit place for my mollisher. I understand Alfred brought you back."

"Some of the way."

"Sagacious man. He knows where you belong."

"I don't know about that."

We studied each other. In four years of knowing him, I'd never really sat down and looked at Jaxon. White Binder. King of Wands. The man who had made me his sole heir, giving me unparalleled respect from people three or four times my age. The man who had taken me into his home and sheltered me from the eye of Scion.

"We are overdue a little *tête-à-tête*." Jaxon crossed one leg over the other. "We have our differences, I know, my Paige. I sometimes forget that you are nearly twenty years of age, drunk on the sweet ambrosia of independence. When I was twenty, my only friend in this world was Alfred. I had no mime-lord, no mentors, no friends of whom to speak. An unusual situation, given that I started life under the watchful gaze of a kidsman."

I pulled the curtain from between us. "You were an urchin?"

"Oh, yes. Surprising, isn't it? My parents were hanged when I was only four. Probably blockheads, or they wouldn't have let themselves get captured. They left me alone in the citadel, penniless. I couldn't always afford fine clothes and famous spirits, my mollisher.

"My kidsman made me steal from amaurotics. She worked with two others, and together they controlled a flock of eighteen sorry gutterlings. Any money I earned was taken from me, and in return, I was tossed the occasional scrap of food. I had always dreamed of going to the University, of being a man of letters—some great, scholarly clairvoyant—but all the trio did was laugh. They told me, dear Paige, that I had never been to school, and while I could pry watches and data pads from amaurotics, I never would. School would cost money, and besides, I was unnatural. I was worthless. But when I turned twelve, I felt an *itch*. An itch beneath my skin, impossible to reach."

His fingers strayed to his arm, as if he could still feel it. There was a reason he'd always worn long sleeves. I'd seen the scars before, long white marks that ran from the creases of his elbows to his wrists.

"I scratched the itch until my arms bled and my fingernails broke. I would scratch my own face, my legs, my chest. My kidsman threw me out to beg—she thought my wounds would attract public sympathy, you see—and indeed, I never made as much coin as I did when I was itching."

"That's sick," I said.

"That's London, darling." His fingers tapped his knee. "By the time I was a young man of fourteen, nothing had changed, except that I carried out more dangerous crimes for mouthfuls of bread and sips of water. I grew ill with fever; I burned for independence, for *vengeance*—and for the æther. Though I was sighted and had an aura, the true nature of my gift had never revealed itself to me. At least if I understood my clairvoyance, I would think, I could make my own money and keep it. I could read people's palms or show them cards, like the buskers in Covent Garden. Even they laughed at me."

He told the tale with a smile; I wasn't laughing.

"One day, it all became too much. Like a doll dropped to the ground, I broke. It was winter, and I was so very, very cold. I found myself sobbing on the ground in I-6, half-mad and ripping at my arms. Not a single soul helped me: no amaurotics, no voyants." He said all this in a sing-song tone, as if he were telling a bedtime story. "I was close to shouting out my clairvoyance to the world, to *begging* the SVD to take me to the Tower, or Bedleem, or some other hell on earth—until a woman knelt beside me and whispered in my ear,

'Carve a name, sweet child, a long-dead name.' And with those words, she disappeared."

"Who was she?"

"Someone to whom I owe a great debt, O my lovely." His pale eyes were in the past. "I knew no long-dead names—only the names of those I *wanted* dead, which were plentiful—but I had nothing else to do but die. In light of that, I walked four miles to Nunhead Cemetery. I couldn't read the names on the graves, but I could copy the shapes of the letters.

"I was too frightened to carve. Instead, I chose a grave, cut my finger and wrote the name in blood along my arm. As soon as the last letter was finished, I felt the spirit stir at my side. I spent a long, delirious night in that cemetery, sprawled among the headstones, and all night long I felt the spirits dancing from their graves. And when I woke, the itch was gone."

A muddled image drifted through my thoughts: a little girl in a poppy field, her hand outstretched, and the blinding pain of the poltergeist's touch. I'd been younger than Jaxon when my gift had first emerged, but until I'd met him, I'd had no idea what I was.

"I cut the spirit's name into my skin, and he taught me how to read and write. When he had served that purpose, I released him and sold him for a modest sum, enough to get me a month's worth of hot meals," Jaxon recalled. "I returned to the kidsmen for a short while—long enough to practice my art—and then, at last, I left."

"Didn't they come after you?"

"Later," he said, "I went after them."

I could only imagine the sorts of deaths he must have given those three kidsmen. *Fiercely imaginative*, Alfred had called him.

"After that, I began my research on clairvoyance. And I found out what I was," he said. "A binder."

Abruptly, Jaxon got to his feet and walked to the forbidden

Waterhouse painting that hung on the wall. It depicted two half-brothers, Sleep and Death, lying on a bed together with their eyes closed.

"I told you this because I want you to know that I understand. I understand what it is to be fearful of your own body's power. To be a vessel of the æther," he said. "To never trust yourself. And I empathize with that burning desire for independence. But I am not a kidsman. I am a mime-lord, and I consider myself a generous one. You are allowed a little coin for your own uses. You are given a bed. All I ask is that you obey my orders, as any mime-lord asks of his or her employees."

I knew it could be worse—that I was lucky. Eliza had told me as much. Jaxon turned to look at me again.

"I lost my temper in Oxford. I suppose you did, too. That you don't *really* wish to leave Seven Dials."

"I wanted to help other voyants. Surely you can understand that—you of all people, Jax?"

"Of course you wanted to help them, sweet, selfless soul that you are. And I, perhaps, was too concerned about protecting you to think of those other voyants. It was beastly of me to threaten you, and I fully deserve your displeasure." He touched the backs of his fingers to my cheek. "You know I would never surrender you to those awful barbarians in Jacob's Island. No splanchomancer will ever lay a finger on my dreamwalker, I promise you."

"Did you try to find me?" I said. "When I went missing."

He looked wounded. "Of *course* I did. Do you think me so heartless, darling? When you didn't arrive on that Monday I had every trusted clairvoyant in I-4 out looking for you. I even involved Maria's and Didion's nitwits in the search. I had to keep the information out of Hector's oily clutches, of course, so the operation was conducted *sub rosa*. But I did not give up, I assure you. I would sooner return to the streets in rags than let Scion take my dreamwalker." With a sniff, he turned to the two reservoir glasses on my nightstand. "Here. The green fairy heals all."

"You never take this out."

"Only on extraordinary occasions."

Absinthe. His long fingers dealt lithely with the accoutrements: the slotted spoon, the sugar cubes, and water. The liquid turned opalescent. Few Scion denizens had the constitution for alcohol, but my injuries were deep enough for me to risk the headache. I took the glass.

"You were meeting with Antoinette Carter," I said. "That day in London, when Nick shot me. Why?"

"I came across some old recordings of her performances while I was at the Garden that month. I was interested in studying her gift and managed to contact her via Grub Street, who publish her writing here." He took a delicate sip from his glass. "Alas, thanks to the Rephaim's interference, she slipped between my fingers."

"They'll be interfering a lot more if we don't fight them, Jax," I said. "We can't let them carry on with the Bone Seasons."

"Darling, your lamp-eyed friends can be dealt with later. Let them play with their puppets."

It was all I could do not to raise my voice. "We *have* to warn the syndicate. They're installing Senshield in two months. If we don't pull together—"

"Paige, Paige. Your enthusiasm is to be commended, but let me remind you that we are not freedom fighters. We are the Seven Seals. Our duty is to I-4 and to London. As members of the syndicate, we must protect our assigned section. That is our sole purpose."

"Everything we know will be meaningless if the Rephs come here. We're living in their lie."

"A lie that sustains the syndicate. That gave birth to it. You cannot, and will not, change its character."

"You did. Your pamphlet did."

"That was quite a different matter." He placed a hand over mine. It was a soft hand; mine was callused, hard from climbing and handling weapons. "There is a reason I forbade you all to take long-term partners. I require your complete commitment to I-4. And while you think of the Rephaim, you are not thinking of I-4. In these restless days, I simply can't afford to have a mollisher whose mind is not entirely focused on her tasks. Do you understand that?"

I didn't understand at all. I wanted to grab him by the lounging robe and shake him.

"No," I said. "I don't."

"You will, my mollisher. Time heals all things."

"I'm not going to stop, Jaxon."

"If you want to keep your place in the syndicate, you will." He stood. "There is one thing that you gained during your time away from Seven Dials. You realized your potential for leadership."

I kept my face still. "Leadership?"

"Don't play the fool. You organized an entire rebellion in that rotting cage they put you in."

"Not alone."

"Ah, modesty. It's a vice. True, you might have struggled without your friends. But on that meadow, you were a queen. You even made a speech! And words, my walker—well, words are everything. Words give wings even to those who have been stamped upon, broken beyond all hope of repair."

I wished I had words now.

"Do you know how old I am, Paige?"

The question took me by surprise. "Thirty-five?"

"Forty-eight," he said. I couldn't help but stare. "As a member of the fifth order of clairvoyance, my life expectancy is rather low. And when I join joyfully with the æther, you will come into possession of I-4. You will be a young, capable, and intelligent mime-queen, part of the highest order, with many loyal clairvoyants at your beck and call. You will have the citadel at your feet."

I tried to imagine it: the Pale Dreamer, mime-queen of I-4. Owning this building. Knowing that every voyant in the section would follow me. Having a voice far louder than a mollisher's.

Jaxon held out his hand. "A truce," he said. "Forgive my poor judgment, and I will give you everything."

I was a fugitive now. A wanted fugitive. Without the gang, and with the fear of the White Binder's retribution, I'd be fair game for every busker and beggar who'd ever thought about selling information to Scion. Everyone else would pretend I wasn't there. Jaxon was my only link to the syndicate, and the syndicate was the only organized force of voyants that could possibly stand against Scion. I had no intention of being silent, but for now, I'd have to play along. I took his hand, and he shook it.

"You've made the right decision."

"I hope so," I said.

His grip grew tight. "Two years. Until then, you remain my mollisher."

My heart squeezed, but I forced myself to nod. His stiff little smile returned.

"Now, we ought to discuss this wretched fugitive situation with the others." He placed a gentle hand on my back and guided me out to the landing. "There are certain precautions we must take if we're to continue living as spiders in Weaver's web. Danica!" He rapped on the ceiling with the end of his cane. "Danica, drop those mechanisms and send for my darlings. We are having a *huddle*, and we are having one forthwith."

Without waiting for a reply, Jaxon led me into his office. His *boudoir*, as he called it. Chenille curtains fell past the windows, blocking out all natural light. A chaise longue idled on splayed legs. Behind it was the tall cabinet where the absinthiana was usually locked, and a bookshelf full of Grub Street titles, not including Didion's. The room smelled of tobacco smoke and rose oil. An antique lampshade threw tiny fragments of color across the floor, as if we were walking across shattered jewels: amethyst and sapphire, emerald and tiger's eye, orange garnet, fire opal and ruby. Jaxon sat in his bergère and lit a cigar.

He wanted me to forget. The Rephaim were dangerous and they were out there, lying in wait, and I seemed to be the only one who gave a damn about it.

Danica came trudging into the room, looking sour. The other three followed half a minute later, all looking different degrees of exhausted. When Eliza saw me, she grinned. "Knew you'd come back."

"Can't keep away," I said.

"The spirits led her to us, my medium. Just as I said they would." Jaxon waved them all in, trailing smoke. "Sit, my lovelies. We have important matters to discuss."

I still couldn't believe he was forty-eight. There was scarcely a line on his face, and his black hair showed no hint of gray.

"First of all, payment. Nadine, for you." With a flourish, he handed her an envelope. "You did well in Covent Garden this week. There's also a small cut from the last spirit we sold."

"Thanks."

"For you, Ezekiel. You've done your tasks superbly, as usual." Zeke caught his packet with a grin. "As for you, Danica, I'm withholding your pay until you show me some progress."

"Fine," she said, looking bored.

"And, finally, Eliza. My dearest." He held out the thickest envelope, and she took it. "We received an excellent sum of money for your last painting. Here, as always, is your fair cut."

"Thank you, Jax." She tucked it into the pocket of her skirt. "I'll put it to good use."

I tried not to look at the envelope in Zeke's hands, full of precious notes. If I'd gone back to Jaxon sooner, I could have had a week's salary under my belt.

"Now, to business. As there is a wanted fugitive living under my roof, I thought we ought to run through emergency protocol for I-4, and for leaving the den during red days." Jaxon tapped away his cigar ash. "First and foremost, you are to continue avoiding the London Underground. If you need to travel to another section, I will personally arrange for an I-4 buck cab to take you there."

"Can we walk?" Eliza sat up straighter, looking startled. "Short distances, at least?"

"If you must. Always, *always* use your aliases within the syndicate, and any other name outside it. Avoid streets with cameras—you know where they are, but look out for wireless additions. Cover as much of your lovely faces as you can when leaving the den, and leave the den only when absolutely necessary."

"So we don't have to go to Didion's bullshit auctions anymore?" Nadine said, looking pleased.

"Auctions are perfectly safe, as is the black market." Jaxon patted the back of her hand. "I abhor the very air he has the nerve to keep inhaling, darling, but his particular brand of bullshit is lucrative. Besides, now our wonderful Paige is back, she will be taking over the bidding. Along with her other duties as mollisher."

Nadine's jaw flexed. "Right," she said. "Good."

I raised an eyebrow. With a quick, measuring glance between us, Jaxon settled back in his chair.

"Now, to business. For the next two weeks, the hunt will be at its most intense. After that, we will be able to lower our defenses a little."

"Jaxon," I interrupted, "the Rephaim know about us and where we live. They know about *you*. Shouldn't we have an escape plan?"

There was a ring of china as Eliza knocked her cup against the table. "They know where we live?"

Jaxon raised his eyes to the ceiling. It was clear that he didn't want the Rephaim mentioned within earshot of the others, but I didn't care. I might have agreed to work for him again, but he couldn't just brush them under the carpet. "They had voyants doing séances," I continued, "and they were getting flashes of the sundial pillar. It's only a matter of time before they find out where it is."

"Oh, come now. There are plenty of pillars in the citadel, not to mention a vast number of sundials." Jaxon stood. "Let them hunt. This citadel will crumble into dust before we permanently abandon our den. I will not desert this territory based on strangers' séances."

"They wanted you as well as Antoinette. And they won't wait long to try again."

"I have higher concerns than the vagaries of monsters." He snatched up his cane. "But to soothe your young minds, I shall show you something."

He led us down the staircase to the ground floor of the den. There wasn't much to see in the hallway; just a dusty, wall-sized mirror, Zeke's bike, and a locked back door, which led out to the courtyard. Jaxon indicated the narrow space under the stairs.

"Do you see those floorboards?" He gave them a smart rap with his cane. "Beneath those floorboards is the bolthole of Seven Dials."

Eliza frowned. "We have a bolthole? An escape route?"

"We do."

"We've all lived here for years, and you never thought to show us?" Nadine said.

"Of course not, my lovely. Where was the need? You and Zeke are presumed dead as doornails, and nobody particularly cared about the rest of us. Until now," he added, looking at me. "Besides, it wasn't always there. I had it built after an unexpected raid on I-4. Eliza and Paige will remember it." That was when we'd had to flee to Nick's apartment. "This is primarily a hiding place. If the NVD were to come here looking for Paige, she could simply tuck herself into the bolthole for a few hours. If the situation were to escalate, she could push a panel at the back, which would lead to a tunnel that runs from here to Soho Square."

He removed the blade from his cane and used it to pull up one of the floorboards. The space beneath the panel was about six feet deep and nine feet wide.

"That looks like somewhere you'd be buried alive." Eliza looked dubious.

"Note that keyword, my medium. Alive. The antonym of *dead*." Jaxon pushed the board back down. "Bear it in mind. For now, remember my rules, and we will all be perfectly safe." He snapped his fingers. "Get back to work, now. Paige, you come with me."

I followed him. Nadine gave me an angry look as I passed, but she was gone before I could ask why.

"Don't frighten the others, darling." Jaxon closed the office door behind me. "They don't need to hear about the Rephaim."

"Apart from Eliza, they were all in Sheol I," I said, trying to sound calm. "They saw it for themselves."

"I don't want them preoccupied. With a red zone in place, this is a perilous time for us all." He swept paperwork from his desk. "Now, back to business. We've been losing a great deal of money in I-4. Nadine has done a halfway decent job as a temporary mollisher, but she isn't *you*, and you were terribly good at making coins appear in my coffers. With you at the Juditheon, I can send Nadine back to Covent Garden with her violin."

I sat. "She might not like that."

"Well, she did it before, didn't she? Did I not employ her for the specific purpose of busking?"

"Yes, Jaxon," I said, as patiently as I could, "but she might not appreciate having her income cut. Were you paying her my wages?"

"You didn't need them, did you?" he said, looking for all the world like I'd asked him if grass was green. "She's a whisperer, Paige.

Music is her equivalent of a numen." He whipped a scroll of paper from a drawer, sealed with what looked like a miniature bow tie. "Here it is. An invitation to the next Juditheon auction." He tossed it to me. "I'm sure Didion will be *delighted* to see you."

I tucked it into my back pocket. "I thought you wanted us all to stay inside?"

"As I just said, Paige, we are losing income. Unless you wish to stay in here and watch our money roll away like water off a crystal ball, you will have to work."

"You're not losing your touch, are you?"

"Silly girl. Never blame your mime-lord for the failures of his dogsbodies. There are a number of reasons for the loss," he said, sitting on the edge of his writing table. "Several of our most lucrative buskers have been detained—not being cautious enough, clearly, wretched fools—no offense to you, of course, dolly. Two key establishments have failed to pay their rent. On top of that, the whole section has been slacking off since you were taken. I need that surveillance camera of a spirit, darling." He unlocked a cabinet and sifted through a line of bottles. "Oh, and one more thing: we can't have you walking around looking like that."

"Like what?"

"Like *you*, my lovely. That hair of yours is far too easy to spot." He held out a glass bottle and a small container. "There. You have the tools," he said. "Make yourself invisible."

# 7

## Under the Rose

"Do I hear one hundred?"

A single white candle burned in an alcove, the only light in the underground crypt. Wax dripped as the flame swayed in a draft, watched by a stone cherub with stumps where its wings had been. My boots were propped up on a velvet footrest, my arm slung over the back of the upholstered chair. A few moments passed before a paddle was raised.

"One hundred to IV-3." Didion Waite cupped a hand around his ear. "Do I hear two hundred?"

Silence.

"Can I tempt you with one hundred and fifty, my mollishers and mobsters? Your mime-lords and mime-queens will be thrilled with this one, truly. Ask the sergeant for his secrets, and you might just bag yourself a Ripper lady. And if you bag yourself a Ripper lady, who knows? You might just bag yourself a Ripper." Another paddle went up. "A believer! One hundred and fifty from VI-5. You've come a long way to claim this prize, sir. Anyone for two hundred, ladies and gentlemen? Ah, two hundred? No, *three* hundred! Thank you, III-2."

Auction by candle was always tedious; the damn thing never seemed to burn down. I picked at a loose thread on my blouse. When Didion called for four hundred, I raised my paddle.

"Four hundred to—" Didion twirled his gavel. "I-4. Yes. Four hundred to the Pale Dreamer. Or perhaps we should call you *Paige Eva Mahoney?*"

A few people gave me curious glances. My back stiffened.

Had he just . . . ?

"Will we be auctioning you off next, madam," he continued, plainly enjoying himself, "given your current status with Scion?"

Murmurs blew from ear to ear. My skin prickled.

Didion Waite had just unmasked me.

Although the Pale Dreamer was well known, her face and real name were not. Some syndicate members had abandoned their legal identities, giving themselves wholly to the underworld, but the other half still held on to respectable jobs in Scion, forcing them to hide behind masks and aliases. I'd always been one of those who led a double life. Given my father's position, and my desire to stay in touch with him, Jaxon had always made me wear a red cravat over my lips and nose when I carried out my duties as his mollisher. I recovered quickly enough to call out, "Only if you'll bid on me, Didion."

Laughter rose from the front rows, making him bristle.

"Well, I shall have to pass on that option, being utterly committed to the memory of my Judith. You look like your mime-lord's doppelgänger, madam," he said, his face florid. "Is the White Binder so in love with his own reflection that he's painted it on to his mollisher?"

My hair had been dyed black and cut so it was level with my chin, baring the length of my neck. The contact lenses were hazel rather than Jaxon's pale blue, but Didion wouldn't have noticed that.

"Oh, no. I'm sure Binder knows that one of him is quite enough for you, Didion," I said, cocking my head. "You've already lost one pamphlet war against him, after all."

Nobody bothered to suppress their snickering. Spring-heel'd Jack let out such a hoot of mirth that the Pearl Queen started in her seat, and Didion turned from pink to puce. "Order," he snapped, then muttered: "And I am working on a new pamphlet, madam, thank you very much—one that will wipe that rag *On the Merits* from the pages of history, you mark my words . . ."

Jimmy O'Goblin, who was sitting next to me, shook with laughter as he drank from his hip flask. A tap on my shoulder made me turn my head. A courier whispered in my ear, "You're really the girl Scion's after?"

I crossed my arms. "No idea what he's talking about."

"Do I hear five hundred?" Didion asked, with dignity.

I forced myself to pay attention, trying to ignore the looks and whispers. It was rare for a syndicate member to be publicly unmasked. Didion had seen my face once, about a year ago. He must have loved giving me away like that, but his spite had made me twice as vulnerable.

The spirit up for grabs was one Edward Badham, a police sergeant of the famous H Division. They'd been the law enforcers of the monarch days, specifically those assigned to the Whitechapel area. It was only after Queen Victoria had died and her son had been ousted as an unnatural that V Division, the blueprint for Scion's clairvoyant police force, had been founded by Lord Salisbury. Any spirit with a connection to H Division could provide an excellent Ripper lead. I could see Spring-heel'd Jack, Jenny Greenteeth, and Ognena Maria at the front, throwing their paddles up at every opportunity. On the other side of the room was the Highwayman, the hard-faced mol-lisher of II-6. I'd never heard of him missing a Ripper-related auction.

As the candle burned, the price of Sergeant Badham's essence climbed. Soon there were only six of us bidding. Jaxon was probably the richest mime-lord in the citadel, but in Juditheon auctions, the candle kept things fair. I watched for the tell-tale burst of light before it died. When it happened, I raised my paddle—and a split second later, so did someone else.

"Five thousand."

Heads turned. It was the Monk, mollisher of I-2. As always, his face was shadowed by a black hood.

"Five thousand! A clear winner," Didion proclaimed. Presumably that would keep him in powdered wigs and ill-fitting trousers for a while longer. "The candle is extinguished, and the spirit of Sergeant Edward Badham belongs to the Abbess of I-2. Commiserations to everyone else!"

Groans and curses filled the crypt, along with bitter mutterings of those from poorer sections. I pursed my lips. Waste of time. Still, at least I'd been able to leave the den for a few hours.

The enormous Highwayman stood, knocking his chair to the floor. Silence fell at once.

"Enough of this charade, Waite." His voice boomed. "That spirit is the property of II-6. Where did you get it?"

"This spirit came into my keeping *legally*, sir, like all my spirits do." Didion bristled. "If you really believe that all the spirits of II-6 want to stay there, why do I keep finding them in my territory, sir?"

"Because you're a macer and a crook."

"Can you prove these allegations, sir?"

"One day," was the dark reply, "I will find the Ripper, and you will prove it with your life."

"I hope that is not a threat against my person, sir, verily I do." The auctioneer was all of a quiver. "I shall not endure that sort of talk in my wife's very own auction house, sir. Judith would never have allowed such wanton verbal abuse, sir."

"Where's your wife's spirit?" a medium shouted. "Shall we auction her off, too?"

Didion purpled like a bruise. You knew things were getting serious when Didion Waite ran out of *sirs*.

"Enough." One of the mime-queens stood. Her short, bright auburn hair was slicked in a pompadour style, and she spoke with a light Bulgarian accent. "The candle is to blame, Highwayman, not the one who lit it. Look to your own streets for your bloody Ripper."

With a snarl of anger, he stormed from the crypt. Spring-heel'd Jack ran off as well, laughing to himself in that insane way of his, and Jenny Greenteeth growled as she left. As I picked up my jacket and satchel, Didion rushed towards the Monk, but he was already halfway up the steps.

"I'll take it," a young woman said. Her red hair was worn in a braided bun, with a fan-shaped comb to hold it in place.

Didion handed her a binding bond. "Of course, of course." He kissed her hand, which bore a long gold ring. "Tell the Abbess to send her binder when she pleases."

The girl gave him a gracious smile and pocketed the bond. "I'll see to it that you have your money within a few days, Mr. Waite."

The Abbess was certainly flush with cash these days. Most of the central gang leaders were wealthy, but I wasn't convinced that many of them had five grand to throw at a spirit.

"Pale Dreamer?"

A mime-queen had stopped in the aisle in front of me, the one with auburn hair. I touched three fingers to my forehead, as was expected around members of the Unnatural Assembly. "Ognena Maria."

"You look different. I was about to say I hadn't laid lamps on you in a while, but your face has been all over London."

"Broke out of the Tower." I pulled the strap of my bag on to my shoulder. "I didn't know you were a Ripper hunter."

"I'm not. I just desperately need more spirits, and the Juditheon seemed like the best place to get them."

"You could have chosen one that *wasn't* from H Division."

"I know, but I like a challenge. Not that I'm rich enough to win."
She held out an arm. "Heading up?"

There was nothing more to do down here. I knew I should be
hightailing it outside—Jaxon was waiting on the street—but what
she'd said was curious. "You must have plenty of spirits," I said as
we walked up the steps. The brooches on her jacket clinked. "Why
this one?"

"We had quite a few of them leave I-5 recently. They seem to be
repelled by one street in particular. I can't see anything wrong with
it, unless someone's botched a séance in one of the houses." A line
creased her forehead. "It worries me more than I'll admit to my
voyants. I don't suppose you've had the same in I-4?"

"Binder would have said."

"Oh, Binder's so far off the cot he's in the grave. I really don't
know how you work for him." She worried at her nail ring. "I don't
suppose he'd be interested in renting a pitch in Old Spitalfields?"

"I can ask him."

"Thank you, sweet. He's better off than I'll ever be." Maria
pushed open the trapdoor.

"Should I tell him about your problem?"

"He won't care, but you can try."

The panel took us up into the shell of what had once been a
church. Shafts of pale sunlight sliced in through the broken roof
of Bow Bells, one of the few churches in London that hadn't been
gutted and repurposed as Vigile stations. It had been disfigured in
the early twentieth century, of course, like all things associated
with the afterlife and the monarchy—the wings struck off the
cherubim, the altars destroyed by republican vandals—but its bells
still hung in the tower. The whole place reminded me of Sheol I.
A vestige of an older world.

I pushed the cover of the crypt back into place. Another woman
was standing near the altar, talking to the Monk and the courier. She

was tall and slim, dressed in a tailored suit, and a top hat was pinned over thick furls of chestnut hair.

The Abbess herself had turned up to meet her mollisher. Mime-queen of I-2, founder of the largest night parlor in London.

"Maria!" She clapped her hands. Her voice put me in mind of a match being struck. "It is you, isn't it, Maria?"

"Congratulations, Abbess," Maria said stiffly. "What a dazzling prize."

"You're very kind. I don't have as fine a collection of spirits as some, but I do occasionally like to bid. Tell me, how are you coping with the red zone?"

"Well enough. You know the Pale Dreamer, don't you?"

The Abbess studied me through a birdcage veil. I could just make out her light brown skin, long nose, and a red feather of a smile. "Of course I do. The White Binder's prodigy. What joy." She took my chin in her lace-clad hand. "Oh, but you'd make a lovely nightwalker."

"She's a little busy being Weaver's quarry." Maria sniffed. "I'd love to stay and chat, but I've a market to manage."

"I want a word." The Abbess released me. "Either we talk now, Maria, or we talk tonight."

"I only leave my voyants once each red day."

"Tomorrow, then. I'll send one of my couriers to arrange it."

With a terse nod, Maria walked on. I followed.

"Bloody madam." She flung open the doors. "Glad someone's got time for chin music."

"What do you think she wants?"

"Probably more nightwalkers. I told her, none of my voyants are interested. Doesn't stop her asking." Maria turned up the collar of her coat against the wind. "You keep safe, sweet. There's always a place for you in I-5, you know, if you ever fancied moonlighting."

"I'll keep it in mind."

She walked briskly in the direction of Bank station. I'd been approached with offers of work before, as had Eliza—poachers often trekked between the sections, trying to bribe skilled voyants into moonlighting for a different boss—but I'd turned them down every time. Jaxon paid enough, and it was risky to work a second job. Most mime-lords would consider it a betrayal worthy of banishment, if not a death sentence.

But Maria had looked genuinely concerned about the loss of spirits, about the possible threat to her voyants' welfare. She might make a useful ally, if only I could get the word out. And if I didn't scrape some money together, moonlighting might be my only choice.

A buck cab was waiting for me on the corner. "Binder said you're to go to the Garden," the driver said.

"Really?"

"Really. Hurry up, will you?" She wiped at her neck with a handkerchief. "Risky enough taking a fugitive in my cab without her dragging her feet."

I climbed in. Eliza must have finished a painting.

SciLo was still in the red, with security higher than Old Paul's spire. Underguards at station barriers round the clock, military vehicles patrolling the central cohort during the day, Vigiles armed with double the weapons. As the cab passed a transmission screen, my face flashed up for the thousandth time. To a stranger, this face would look hostile: unsmiling, too proud for pity, with chill gray eyes and the pallor of a corpse. It was not the face of an innocent. She was unnaturalness incarnate, this woman on the screen. Her eyes held death and ice. Just as Warden had said.

*Warden.* While I was in the citadel, hiding from my own reflection, my Rephaite collaborator was a fugitive as well. I pictured him in the Netherworld, harvesting amaranth, using its essence to soothe his scars. Looking over his shoulder for the Sargas. I didn't know what the Netherworld looked like, but I imagined it as a dark, glorious realm, teeming with half-living things. And Warden with his black-handled blade, tracking the blood-sovereign as she fled her kingdom, like Edward VII before her. Warden in the heat of the hunt. The image shook me to the core, saturating my blood with adrenaline.

"*If I never return,*" he'd said, "*it will mean that everything is all right. That I have ended her.*" Well, he hadn't returned, and it was clear that nothing was all right. Something was happening behind the masquerade of Scion, and if Nashira had killed my only real Reph ally, I might never find out what it was.

He had risked—and lost—everything to help me escape my prison. In return, I'd gone crawling back to my petty treasons with my tail between my legs, failed to convince Jaxon to fight, and cursed Hector's name where he couldn't hear me.

When I got out of the cab, I slammed the door a little too hard. Zeke was waiting for me under the stone archways. He'd scrubbed up nicely, as he always did on selling days: silk brocade waistcoat, neatly parted hair, thick-rimmed glasses that looked fifty years old.

"How are you, Paige?"

"Chipper. Nice glasses." I checked my cravat. "What's the story?"

"Eliza's finished three paintings. Jax wants them all sold by the end of the night. Plus all the junk." He fell into step beside me. "We could use your help with selling. I'm terrible."

"You'd be better if you didn't think you were terrible. You said he wants us to sell *everything*? Does he need a new antique cane, or something?"

"He did say we were low on money."

"I'll believe that when he stops buying cigars and absinthe."

"He hardly stopped drinking while you were away. Absinthe every night, Nadine said."

Behind the eccentric lenses, his eyes were bloodshot. He looked as if he'd been at the absinthe himself.

"Zeke," I said, "did Jaxon really look for me?"

"Oh, yeah. He didn't stop searching until July. Then he seemed to give up, and he took Nadine as a temporary mollisher. When Nick got word about you in August, after we saw you in Trafalgar Square, he was . . . well, a little mad with joy. That was when he started the search again." He adjusted his glasses. "Has he said he'll do anything about the Rephaim?"

"Nope," I said.

"Are *you* going to do something?"

"He's told me not to," I said, trying not to sound bitter. "He requires our complete commitment to I-4."

He shook his head. "That's insane. We have to do something."

"If you have any suggestions, I'm all ears."

"I don't," he admitted. "I don't know where we'd start. I was talking about it with Nick the other day, and I thought we could do some kind of national broadcast, but we'd have to get into the Archon to do that. And even if we could, how do you tell people what you know they won't believe?"

I hadn't realized Zeke was that ambitious. Much as I liked the idea, ScionEye's security was far too tight for us to even consider broadcasting a transmission from the inside. "We can't run before we can walk, Zeke," I said gently. "If we're going to do something, we have to work from the bottom. Let the syndicate know, then the rest of the citadel."

"Yeah, I know. It was wishful thinking." Zeke cleared his throat. "By the way, did Nick tell you—?"

"Tell me what?"

"Nothing. Forget it. Did you get the spirit?" he asked quickly.

"The Abbess snagged it. But what were you going to—?"

"It doesn't matter. I don't think Jax really cares about H Division. He almost admitted he was doing it to spite Didion."

"What else is new?" Didion and Jaxon had been at war for years, jabbing at each other with pamphlets and, occasionally, physical violence. Didion despised Jaxon for being "the most discourteous sir I ever did meet"; Jaxon hated Didion for being a "useless, curly-haired fribble," and for having terrible teeth. It was hard to argue with either assessment.

We walked together along the colonnade until we reached a lantern. Instead of the muted blue of the average Scion streetlamp, its panes were made of a deeper, cobalt glass, tinged with green, hard to see unless your eye was attuned to it. It hung above the door to a second-hand clothes shop. Zeke gave a subtle signal to the shopkeeper, a voyant, who nodded.

A winding staircase took us into the basement of the shop. There were no customers down here; just racks of second-hand clothes and three mirrors. Zeke looked over his shoulder, then pulled one of them open like a door. We sidled through the gap and into the long tunnel.

The black market was situated between Covent Garden and Long Acre. An underground cavern of about fifteen thousand square feet, it had been the hub of illegal trading for decades. Most hawkers earned their flatches on the fringes of the amaurotic markets, but this one was entirely voyant, and entirely secret. The NVD had never surrendered its location to Scion, probably because so many of them still bought their numa from its stalls. Their employers gave them food and shelter, but no means to touch the æther. It was a wretched life they led, fighting their own natures.

The cavern was poorly ventilated, thick with the heat of hundreds of bodies. Stalls sold thousands of numa, every kind imaginable. Mirrors: hand-held, full-length, framed. Crystal balls too heavy to lift. Smoked-glass shew stones, small enough to fit inside a palm. Séance tables. Burning incense. Teacups and cast-iron kettles. Keys for locks that might never exist. Small blunted blades. Boxes of needles. Blacklisted books. Tarot decks of all designs. Then there were the augurs' stands, where flowers and herbs were sold in abundance. Past that were bottles of medicine for mediums—muscle relaxants, adrenaline, lithium—and fine instruments for whisperers, and pens for psychographers, and smelling salts to block out the foul odors that sniffers would pick up on.

Zeke stopped by a booth selling masks and put one on. A cheap one caught my eye, plastic with a coat of silver paint, just big enough to cover the top half of my face. I dug into my pocket and paid with a little of the money Jaxon had given me for the auction.

The flagship booth of I-4 specialized in funerary art, winding sheets and other morbid luxuries for the affluent clairvoyant. No cheap numa on our stall. All our goods were laid out on crushed velvet, arranged around glass vases of roses. Behind the table, Eliza was a vision in a deep-green velvet dress. Her golden hair fell in polished ringlets down her back, and her arms were wound in delicate black lace. She was talking with an augur in a trader's attire. When she saw us, she said something to him, and he left.

"Who was that?" I said.

"Art collector."

"Great. Now go behind the curtain."

"All right, all right." She brushed a spec of dust from the largest painting. "Zeke, can you pick up some more roses?"

"Okay. You want a coffee?"

"And some water. And some adrenaline." Eliza wiped her brow with her sleeve. "We'll be here all night if we don't get these sold."

"You need to be out of sight." I took her elbow and led her to the back of the stall, where a curtain concealed our coats and bags. With a sigh, she sat down and took out some work Jaxon had given her. She liked to be there so we could consult her, but if anyone saw an art medium near our paintings, they'd put two and two together at once. Zeke put his head around the curtain.

"Where's Jax?"

"He said he had business somewhere else," Eliza said. "As per usual. Just get the roses, will you?"

With a slight frown, Zeke went on his way. Eliza was usually in a foul mood after a possession, riddled with tics and spasms. I unloaded a few human skulls from a box. "Do you want a break?"

"I need to be here."

"You look shattered."

"Yes, Paige, I've been up since Monday." Her eyelid gave a hard twitch. "Jax sent me here as soon as I finished with Philippe."

"We'll sell them. Don't worry. Where's Nadine?"

"Hawking."

I couldn't blame her for being short with me. By rights she ought to be asleep in a dark room after a trance, waiting for the tremblings to subside. I helped her with the wares, piling up skulls, hourglasses, pocket watches, specimen frames. Most of them were made by skilled soothsayers in Jaxon's employ, then sold for five times what he paid for them.

A dispute soon broke out on the opposite stall, where a pair of palmists were offering readings. The querent was an acultomancer, and he seemed to be slightly unhappy with what his palm had told him.

"I want *all* of my money back! Charlatan!"

"Your palms are your enemies, friend, not me. If you want your own version of the truth," the palmist said, his eyes hard as flint, "perhaps you should try knitting it."

"You what, you dirty augur?"

There was a crunch as he was hit right on the nose. The nearest voyants stamped and jeered. Palmists were good with their fists. The acultomancer fell into the table, then lunged forward with a roar. Blood flashed across the carpet. The second palmist smashed a duo of spirits into his assailant's face, only to be hit in the throat with a sharpened awl. Her scream was drowned by choking, and by the crowd's cheering.

"Anyone else?" the acultomancer roared.

A lone whisperer raised her voice. "You think you're a big man, don't you, needle boy? Compensating for your tiny pinprick?" Laughter rose everywhere.

"Say that again, hisser"—he flicked another awl into his hand—"and this might just put a pinprick in your heart."

He shoved a table over as he left. Eliza shook her head and went back behind the curtain. *How could I ever hope to unite this rabble? How could anyone?*

The mess was cleared away. Business as usual. I'd sold three watches and a finger-sized hourglass by the time Zeke came back, his vintage glasses clouded by the heat. I took him behind the curtains to Eliza. "Did you hear about the fight with the palmists?" he said.

"We saw it."

"There was another one near the coffee stand. The Crowbars and the Threadbare Company again."

"Idiots." Eliza gulped down half her coffee. "Did you find any adrenaline?"

"They're out," he said. "Sorry."

She was swaying on her feet. "Take a break." I took the paper-work from her hand.

"I'll come back. Just keep selling."

"Half an hour." Zeke grasped her shoulders and moved her away from the stall. "No arguing, okay?"

"Fine, fine, but you two have to get your facts straight," she said, exasperated. "Philippe was Brabançon-born, but he was *from* the Duchy of Brabant. Brabançon is not a place. And Rachel used *liquor balsamicum* when she helped her father. Do not say 'balsamic vinegar' again, Paige, or I swear on the æther I will break a vase over your head."

She picked up her knitted bag and was gone. Zeke and I looked at each other. "Skellet bell?" he said.

"Go for it."

I searched through the box. It was a heavy, hand-held bell, once used for medieval funeral processions. As I unwrapped it, Nadine slammed a creel of wares down on the table. I stared at the full basket.

"You didn't sell *anything*?"

"Unsurprisingly," she said, "nobody wants table junk."

"They're not going to want it if you call it 'table junk.'" I picked up one of the skulls, checking it for breaks, but there was nothing aesthetically wrong with it. "You have to make them tempting."

"Tempting? 'Oh, hello, madam—would you like to buy the skull of some plague-addled fourteenth-century churl for the price of a year's rent?' Yeah, that's sex appeal."

I couldn't bring myself to argue with her; instead, I handed her the bell. With pursed lips, she walked out in front of the stall and rang a single note, startling a sensor. The sound made at least fifty people look up.

"Ladies, gentlemen, do you remember your mortality?" She held out a rose to the sensor, who laughed nervously. "It's so easy to forget, isn't it, when you live alongside death? But even voyants die."

"Sometimes," Zeke said, "you need a gentle reminder. *He aquí*, the lost masterpieces of Europe!" He swept a hand towards the paintings. "Pieter Claesz, Rachel Ruysch, Philippe de Champaigne!"

"Roll up, roll up for the sale of the month!" Nadine rang the bell. "Don't forget death—it won't forget you!"

Soon we'd attracted a large crowd. Nadine described the species of butterflies in the frames, lavished praise on the largest painting, and demonstrated the speed of the sand in the hourglasses. Zeke spent the time charming people with stories of his years in Oaxaca. They clung to him like flies to honey, desperate for tales of a country beyond Scion's influence. The free-world was a paradise in their eyes, a place where voyants could find peace. A few noticed Nadine's accent, too, but she changed the subject if they asked. Zeke handed out the flowers while she did the talking and I took the cash, keeping my head down.

Most of the listeners bought a trinket or two. I counted coins in silence. It was as if Sheol I had never happened.

*Yellow-jacket*, I thought to myself.

\*\*\*\*

Eliza didn't return for two hours. When she did, she looked gray.

"Anything?"

"Everything." I nodded to the empty table, exhausted. "Pieter's painting went to I-3, and I've got two traders interested in the Ruysch."

"Great."

She took a rose from a vase and fastened it to her hair. The ringlets were falling out. "Did you get any sleep?" I said, hoisting yet another crate on to the table.

"Where do you think I've been?"

I watched her. She slid back into her chair and stared blankly at her work.

The fake Ruysch sold to a group of Welsh botanomancers. At quarter to five, I was ready to go. The NVD came on duty at five during the autumn and winter, and Jaxon had insisted that I didn't spend more than a few hours at the market.

"I'm off," I said to Nadine. "Are you all right to carry on?"

"If you can get Eliza back down here."

I'd thought she was right behind me, but she was nowhere to be seen. "I'll try."

"If you don't find her, keep an ear out for the phone booth. I might need to call you." Nadine scraped a hand through her hair. "I hate this."

My head ached from hours of noise and concentration. Near the exit, I spotted a stall selling metallic numa: needles, small blades, bowls for cottabomancy. The metallurgist looked up when I approached.

"Hello," he said, frowning. "You're no soothsayer."

"Just a passing trader." I unclipped the chain from around my neck, trying to ignore the twinge of unease. "How much would you give for this?"

"Give it 'ere." I placed Warden's pendant in his palm. He squeezed a jeweler's loupe against his eye and held it up to the light. "What's this made of, love?"

"Silver, I think."

"Weird charge coming off it, in't there? Like a numen. Never heard of a necklace being a numen, though."

"It repels poltergeists," I said.

He almost dropped the loupe. "You what?"

"Well, so I was told. I haven't tested it." A sigh escaped him, somewhere between relief and dismay. "But say it *did* repel 'geists— how much would you give me for it?"

"Hard to say. If it's silver, then a thousand, give or take."

My face fell. "Only a thousand?"

"I'd give you a few hundred for your average chunk of silver. A thousand seems reasonable for a chunk of silver that gets rid of 'geists."

"Spirits like the Ripper," I pointed out. "That must be worth a lot more than a grand."

"All due respect, miss, I don't know what macer's tricks have been used on this. The metal ain't silver, and it ain't gold. I'd need to take it away and give it a closer look. If the metal's proper and it works, and I can understand exactly *why* it works, I could give you a fair bit more." He handed the necklace back to me. "Depends if you want to part with it for a bit."

It was true that Warden had given me the necklace, but I had a feeling he wouldn't have wanted me to sell it. *"Keep it,"* he'd said. Not *"it's yours."* Not *"do what you like with it."* This wasn't something I should throw at a stranger.

"I'll think about it," I said.

"As you like."

The next customer was getting fidgety. I pulled back the curtain and made my way back up the tunnel.

"I thought you might be here, Dreamer."

I spun to face Cutmouth with a blade in my hand. Her elbow rested on a crate of supplies. She wore a wide-brimmed hat and as much of a smile as her lips would allow.

"How's the face?" she said.

"Still better than yours, I think."

"Oh, I rather like my scar." Her thumb pulled along its length, lip to chin. "You must be pretty busy keeping out of Scion's way. I'm getting a bit sick of seeing your face on every screen."

Her face was lined with cruelty, but I tried to see what she was beneath that smokescreen. A young woman, alone in the world, who'd found a harbor in the arms of the Underlord. Perhaps she'd been like me once, safe with a family. Perhaps she'd sought freedom in the syndicate.

After a moment, during which we stared each other out, I tucked the blade back into my belt. "Cutmouth," I said, "drop the act for a minute."

She cocked her head. "Act?"

"The mollisher act." I kept eye contact. "Does Hector really not care about anything Scion is doing? Does he think he'll survive it all just because he's the Underlord? He's voyant. A soothsayer, at that. Senshield will—"

"Are you *frightened* of Frank Weaver, Dreamer?"

"You're in denial," I said. "And if you stay with Hector, you'll be dead within the year."

"Hector," she snapped, "will be Underlord for the rest of his life. And when he dies, I'll be there to take over." Just for a moment, the scarred face looked naked and vulnerable. "You should know the feeling. What else do we mollishers do it for, Dreamer, if not the love of a mime-lord?"

"I do it for myself," I said.

Her mouth twisted. "Well, it's not getting you far. You're still a useless bit of Binder's furniture." She took something from her back pocket and wrapped her fist around it, concealing it from view. "But you might be good for something. Tell me where Ivy Jacob is hiding."

I tensed. "Ivy?"

"Yes, *Ivy*. The girl whose face is on the same screens as yours every day," she spat, circling me. "Where is she?"

"How should I know?" I said. If the Underlord's mollisher was looking for Ivy in particular, she had to be in deep shit. "You think all of Scion's most wanted know each other personally?"

The briefest flicker of uncertainty crossed her face, but it didn't last. She glanced at the doorway to the market, then set an empty gaze on me. "If you won't tell me," she said, "I'll still find out."

I saw the knife a second too late. Her hands were stronger than mine. One clapped over my lips and shoved me into the wall, cutting off my shout before it could be heard. The blade flashed across the inside of my elbow, and the lip of a vial pressed against my skin.

Blood was her numen. If she was any good, she could use a bit of mine to find out certain things about me: my past, my future. As soon as the pain registered, my spirit whipped out. Cutmouth reeled away from me with a scream of agony. I got a glimpse of the inside of her mind: an empty shipyard, light at the center, dark at the edges, rotten boats floating on greenish water. In the second she was disoriented, I knocked the vial from her hand and wrenched her arm behind her back until I felt the joint in her shoulder strain.

"Trying to spy on me, haematomancer?" Blood was weeping

from my cut. I gritted my teeth, keeping her in the hold. "Tell Hector to keep his nose out of other people's business. I'll break your arm next time."

"Fuck you."

Cutmouth slammed her head into my nose, knocking me back a step, and took off at a dead run. The vial was in pieces on the floor, along with a spatter of my blood. I took a cloth from my pocket and picked up the mess.

Why the hell was she so concerned about Ivy in particular? Was Hector after her? She'd said she wasn't a syndie . . .

Keeping a hand clamped over my cut arm, I made my way back through the shop. Once I was out on the street, I kicked a bollard, flushed with anger. I had the stamina to sell hourglasses and paintings, but I couldn't think of how to rouse the syndicate. I'd have to go behind Jaxon's back—that much was clear—but how to gain support? How to get the message out?

Nadine and Zeke wouldn't last long at the market without Eliza. I glanced into some of our local haunts—Neal's Yard, Slingsby Place, Shaftesbury Avenue—but she was nowhere to be seen. It took a minute to reach the den, where her painting room was empty. That was strange. She must have gone back to the market. I locked the front door, showered and changed into my nightshirt. Once I'd dabbed some fibrin gel onto my arm, I sat on my bed and took out my knife.

Ever since Jaxon had employed me, I'd kept my savings hidden in my room. I unpicked a few stitches and extracted a roll of money. Then, carefully, I counted it.

There wasn't enough.

I scraped my fingers through my hair. With this cash, if I was very lucky, I could buy a tiny room in VI Cohort and use it as a den. Nothing more. Jaxon had always paid well, but not well enough for any of us to be financially independent of him. He made quite sure of that. We'd always have to spend a good half of our wages on little things for the section, things that picked at our income: couriers, spirits, supplies for the den. Any money we made ourselves was handed to Jaxon to be redistributed.

There was no other choice but to stay here. I wouldn't last more than a few weeks on this.

Several of the muses had drifted from the painting room upstairs. They were hovering at my door in a pointed manner. "We sold yours, Pieter," I called. "And yours, Rachel."

The æther quivered.

"Don't worry, Phil, it'll sell. You're a luxury."

I could sense his doubt. Philippe was prone to melancholia. The trio lingered, drawn to my aura like flies to a lamp, but I shooed them back to the painting room. They were always restless when Eliza was away.

Outside, the night was drawing in. I carried out the checks—lights off, curtains drawn, windows locked—then returned to bed and slotted my bare legs under the covers.

As usual, Danica was silent upstairs. The only sound was Jaxon's record player sighing out Fauré's "Elegy." I listened to it, remembering the gramophone at Magdalen. I thought of how Warden had often sat in silence in his chair, gazing at the flames, alone with his wine and whatever thoughts had lived in that desolate dreamscape. I remembered the gentle precision of his touch as he'd tended to my injured cheek, the same hands on the organ, his fingers tracing my lips, framing my face in the gloom of the Guildhall.

I opened my eyes and fixed a hard gaze on the ceiling.

This had to stop.

I reached up to one of the shelves and switched on the Lanterna Magica. There was already a slide inside, left there since the day I was taken. I angled the mirror toward the ceiling, directing a beam of light through the painted glass, and a scarlet field of poppies appeared. This was the slide Jaxon had always used when I was dreamwalking. It was so detailed you could almost believe it was real, and that the ceiling opened out into my dreamscape. As if the axis of the earth had tilted, tipping me into my own mind.

But my dreamscape was different now. This was the dreamscape of before. A relic of another time.

I flicked through a box of slides until I found one that Jaxon had shown me when I was about seventeen, when I'd first confessed my interest in Scion's history. An old photographic slide, hand-painted. Fine black text read THE DESTRUCTION OF OXFORD BY FIRE, SEPTEMBER 1859. As I focused the lens, a familiar skyline materialized.

Black smoke choked its streets. Fire whipped at its towers. Hellfire. I looked up at it for what seemed like hours, and drifted off to sleep with Sheol I on fire above me.

# 8

## On the Devil's Acre

"Paige."

Not again. It couldn't be time for the night-bell yet. I shifted on to my back, uncomfortably hot.

"Warden?"

A chuckle answered, and when I opened my eyes, it was Jaxon looking down at me. "No, my sleeping walker, you're not in that dreadful slum any longer." A strange smell hung on his breath, eclipsed by the scents of white mecks and tobacco. "What time did you return here, darling?"

It took a few moments to remember where and when I was. The den, yes. London.

"When you said." My voice lolled behind my thoughts. "About five."

"Was Eliza here?"

"No." I rubbed my eyes. "What time is it?"

"Almost eight o'clock. A courier informed me that there is still no sign of her at the market." He straightened. "You sleep, my lovely. I shall wake you if the situation escalates."

The door closed, and he was gone. I dropped my head back into the pillow.

The next time I woke, the room was pitch-black and someone was shouting. Two people. I reached for the lamp and crouched on the mattress, ready to spring out of bed and sprint to the bolthole.

". . . *selfish*, we wouldn't have—"

That was Nadine. I held still, listening, but her voice wasn't raised in panic. She sounded angry.

I followed the raised voices to the floor below, where I found Zeke and Nadine, still in their market finery, and a trembling Eliza. Her hair was a mess of wet tangles, her eyes puffy.

"What's going on?" I said.

"Ask *her*," Nadine snarled. A bruise was swelling on her left cheek. "Ask her, go on!"

Eliza wouldn't meet my eye. Even Zeke was looking at her with something like exasperation. His lower lip looked like a split grape.

"Hector came to the market with the Underbodies, all steaming drunk. He started asking us questions about the paintings. We argued with four different traders, all convinced we were selling fakes." With a wince, he reached for his side. "Long story short, to please the traders, Hector confiscated the Champaigne so they could have it examined. They took all the rest of our wares, too. We tried to stop them, but—"

"It was nine to two," I said, but my heart was sinking. "You couldn't have stopped them."

This was a delicate situation. Philippe was going to hit rock bottom when he found out his painting had been stolen, but that was the least of our problems if any local traders twigged that we sold forgeries. We'd always been careful to sell them to smugglers, who couldn't give two hoots that they were fake, or to traveling dealers who were unlikely to come back. If we were discovered, Jaxon would flip his lid.

"I'm sorry." Eliza looked close to collapsing. "I'm sorry, both of you. I just . . . had to sleep."

"Then you should have called us so we could get out of there. But no, you left us standing there waiting for you. And let us get beaten up for you. And then you come waltzing in here at half past nine, expecting us to let you go to sleep?"

"Wait." I turned to Eliza. "Where were you until half nine?"

"I fell asleep outside," she murmured.

That wasn't like her at all. "Where? I checked all our locals."

"Goodwin's Court. I was disoriented."

"You're a liar." Nadine pointed at her brother. "You know what? I don't care where you were or what you were doing. But on top of the damn painting being taken, Zeke has a cracked rib. How are we going to get that fixed?"

Now the spotlight was on me. As I was Jaxon's mollisher, his authority rested in me when he was away. It was my job to dole out punishment if the situation called for it.

"Eliza," I said, trying to sound reasonable, "you slept during your first break. That was for two hours. I know you need more than that after a long trance, but you should have gone back and packed up the stall if you were that tired, so Zeke and Nadine could get you back to the den. Better to deal with an angry Jax than lose potential clients."

There were some twenty-three-year-olds who wouldn't take a lick of criticism from someone four years their junior, but she'd always respected my position. "I'm sorry, Paige."

There was such defeat and exhaustion in her expression, I couldn't bring myself to lecture her for any longer. "It's done, then. We're moving on." When Nadine's jaw dropped, I folded my arms. "Look, she fell asleep. What do you want me to do—put her on the waterboard?"

"I want you to do *something*. You're supposed to be the mollisher. We got the shit beaten out of us and she just gets away with it?"

"Hector reefed you because he's a pitiful excuse for an Underlord and he deserves to be killed by the same people he claims to lead. Eliza shouldn't have been at the market in the first place. And don't you think her painting being stolen is enough? You know how much time she spent on it."

"Yeah, must be exhausting to go into a trance while poor Philippe does all the work."

"Just as hard to play the violin and get money thrown at you for doing what a *rottie* could do." Eliza squared up to her, her aura blazing. "What exactly do you contribute to this section, Nadine? What would happen if Jaxon threw *you* out tomorrow?"

"At least I do my own work, puppet princess."

"I make Jax the most money out of any of us!"

"Pieter makes Jax money. Rachel makes Jax money. Philippe makes Jax—"

Eliza's cheeks were red with anger. "You're only here because of Zeke! Jax didn't even want to hire you!"

"Enough," I snapped. Eliza was heaving out sobs, one hand clenched in her hair, and Nadine had been shocked into silence.

"Yes. That *is* enough."

The deep voice silenced us. Jaxon had appeared in the doorway, his face bloodless. Even the whites of his eyes seemed paler.

"Explain," he said, "what is happening."

I stepped in front of Eliza. "I've sorted it."

"Sorted what, precisely?"

"Eliza slacked off, all our goods have been stolen, and Zeke's got a cracked rib," Nadine exploded. "How exactly have you 'sorted it,' Mahoney?"

"You should have applied for the NVD, Nadine," I said coldly. "You might like that line of work. We'll get Nick to check on Zeke, but I'm not going to punish anyone for being tired."

"I will make that decision, Paige. Thank you." Jaxon held up a hand. "Eliza, explain yourself."

"Jax," Eliza started, "I'm so sorry. I just—"

"You 'just' what?" His voice was sleek as a ribbon.

"I was—I was tired. I fell asleep."

"And you didn't manage to find your way back to the Garden. Am I correct?"

Her head tipped down, but she whispered, "Yes."

"She passed out on the street, Jax," I said. "She shouldn't have been selling at all."

For a long time, Jaxon said nothing. Then he stepped toward her, wearing an odd smile.

"Jax," I warned, but he didn't even glance at me.

"Dear, sweet Eliza, my Martyred Muse." He took her chin in one hand, hard enough to make her flinch. "On this particular matter, I'm afraid I must agree with Nadine." His grip on her chin tightened. "I have no idea what sort of knot you have looped yourself into when it comes to your sleeping pattern, but I will not have any indolence in this den. And martyr you may be, at least by name, but I will not have you weeping like one. If you are finding it particularly difficult to control yourself, leave. You may have to leave either way. If we are unable to sell your art on the black market, my lovely, then you are about as useful to me as a mirror to a summoner."

From the look on her face, he couldn't have hurt her more if he'd stabbed her in the heart. The silence was terrible. In all my years of knowing Jaxon, I had never once heard him threaten anyone with expulsion.

"Jax." Her lips trembled.

"No." The end of his cane whipped toward the door. "Go to the garret. Reflect on your fragile position in this group. And hope, Eliza, that we can resolve this dilemma. If you decide you would like to keep your job, inform me before sunrise, and I will consider it."

"Of *course* I want my job." She looked half-dead with fear. "Jaxon, please, please . . . don't do this—"

"Try not to snivel, Eliza. You are a medium of I-4, not some importunate beggar."

To her credit, Eliza didn't cry. Jaxon watched her go upstairs with not so much as a drop of discernible emotion.

I shook my head. "That was cruel, Jax."

He might have been a well-dressed piece of wood for all the response I got.

"Nadine," he said, "you are excused."

Nadine didn't argue. She didn't quite looked ashamed of herself, but she didn't look triumphant, either. The door slammed behind her.

"Zeke."

"Yes?"

"Your box. Go to it."

"Was that true, Jaxon? That you only gave my sister a job because of me?"

"Do you see many buskers living in my home, Ezekiel? What use do you suppose I had for a violinist with a panic disorder?" He pinched the bridge of his nose, his teeth clenched. "You're giving me a headache. Get out of my sight, you wretched boy."

For a while, Zeke just stood there. He opened his mouth, but I shook my head at him. Jaxon was in no mood for debate. Defeated, Zeke took off his broken glasses, picked up a book from the writing table and shut himself away. There was nothing we could do for his cracked rib.

"Come upstairs with me, Paige." Still grasping his cane, Jaxon went to the staircase. "I have something to tell you."

I followed him back to the second floor, hot around the eyes. In the space of five minutes the whole gang had fallen apart. He directed me to an armchair in his office, but I stayed on my feet.

"Why did you do that?"

"Do what, my lovely?"

"You know they depend on you. On us." There was something about his inquisitive look that made me want to box his ears. "Eliza was exhausted. You know Philippe had her for fifty-six hours, don't you?"

"Oh, she's fine. I've heard of mediums going for up to two weeks without sleep. It causes no lasting damage." He waved a hand. "I shan't fire her, in any case. We can always relocate the stall to Old Spitalfields if we butter up Ognena Maria. But Eliza has had the morbs of late, sobbing to herself in the garret. It's *very* trying."

"Maybe you should ask her why she's been down. There might be something wrong."

"Matters of the heart are quite beyond me. Hearts are frivolous things, good for nothing but pickling." He steepled his fingers. "The stolen painting may prove problematic if Hector finds himself an art specialist, who will see at once that the paint is fresh. I want it returned to I-4, or failing that, thrown into the Thames."

"What makes you think he'll hand it over?"

"I'm not asking him to hand it over without incentive, darling. A carrot must be offered to the ass." He reached into the desk drawer. "I want you to take said carrot to the Devil's Acre on my behalf."

I looked closer.

In a leather-bound case was a solitary knife, about eight inches long, cradled in a bed of crimson velvet. When I reached a finger toward it, Jaxon grabbed my wrist. "Careful. This kind of numen is treacherous. If your fingers so much as kiss it, it will send a nasty shock wave into your dreamscape. And, quite possibly, affect your sanity."

"Whose is it?"

"Oh, some dead person. When numa are left without a voyant for a long time, they do not respond well to being handled. Only someone of the same order as the dead owner has a chance of touching it without injury." He snapped the case shut and handed it to me. "I have no use for it, but Hector is a macharomancer. He should be thrilled with a blade for his collection. An *expensive* blade, I should add."

It didn't look too special to me, but far be it from me to question Hector's taste. "Should I be going that close to the Archon?" I said. "At night?"

"Therein lies the quandary. If I send anyone less than my mollisher, it will wound Hector's pride. If I send anyone to accompany you, he will accuse me of trying to dragoon him into handing over a valuable piece of mime-art."

"I met Cutmouth on the way out of the market. She tried to take blood from me," I said.

"That meddlesome fool must still want to know where you've been. He was demanding to know when he came to Seven Dials. The stench of him still lingers on the curtains."

"They could take the blood from me if I go there."

"Cutmouth," he said, "is a vile augur. Her particular 'art' is clumsy and savage. Even if she could somehow read images of the penal colony from your blood, she wouldn't be able to make a smidgen of sense of them." He drummed his fingers on the desk. "Still, I can't have my mollisher being bled. I will have a courier take you to the I-1 border. A glym jack will accompany you to the Devil's Acre and ensure that you emerge in one piece. Make sure Hector knows he's there. He'll be waiting for you on the steps of the Thorney."

There was no getting out of this. "I'll get changed," I said.

"That's my girl."

In my room, I took out steel-capped boots, cargo trousers, and leather half-gloves. I had to be ready for Hector this time. More likely than not, one of the Underbodies would give me a hefty thump for being in I-1, even if I was there for a reason.

I stole upstairs and took a stolen NVD stab vest from the back of the kitchen door. On the other side of the landing, the door to the painting room was closed.

"Eliza?"

There was no reply, but I could feel her dreamscape. I opened the door, and the smell of linseed floated out. Tubes of oil paint littered the floor, spilling colors on to the dust sheet. Eliza was sitting on her fold-down bed, her knees drawn up to her chin. The muses hung like clouds above her.

"He won't fire me, will he?"

She sounded like a lost child. "Of course not," I said gently.

"He looked so angry." Her fingers framed her temples. "I deserve to go. I messed up."

"You were shattered." I stepped into the room. "I'm going to talk to Hector now. I'll get the painting back."

"He won't give it to you."

"He will if he wants to keep his spirit in his sunlit zone."

She managed a sad smile. "Just don't do anything stupid." Tears seeped to her chin, and she wiped them with her sleeve. "I still have to talk to Jax."

"He knows you want your job. Get some sleep." I turned to leave, then stopped. "Eliza?"

"Mm?"

"If you need to talk, you know where I am."

She nodded. I switched off the lamp and closed the door.

Once I was dressed and disguised, with the stab vest zipped over my blouse and covered by a black jacket, I slung the strap of my bag across my chest and tucked the numen inside it. Even in the box it gave me an unpleasant chill. The sooner it was with Hector, the better.

\*\*\*\*

The Devil's Acre, time-honored home of the Underlord, was almost within spitting distance of the Westminster Archon. The Underlord considered himself to be the other leader of the citadel, with every right to settle in I-1. It was the last place in the world a fugitive should be heading.

The buck cab drove along Embankment, where I disembarked. A spasm of fear almost welded me to the spot, but I made myself walk toward the Archon. I was well disguised, but I had to do this quickly.

When I reached the Archon, I stood beneath it, close to where the river heaved against the walls. That clock had the largest dials in the citadel. Its opal-glass face shone volcanic scarlet.

Nashira could be in there. I wanted more than anything to look, to know what they were doing, but there was no safe place to dream-walk here.

Close by was a vast, decaying abbey, where the kings and queens of old had been crowned. Locals called it the Thorney. As promised, a glym jack was waiting. He was all muscle, hooded, with a green lantern in one hand. Their purpose in the citadel was to escort amaurotics to their destinations at night, ensuring protection from unnaturals and their crimes, but Jaxon had one or two on his side.

"Pale Dreamer." He inclined his head. "Binder says I'm to escort you to the Devil's Acre and wait outside."

"Fine by me." We walked down the steps. "What's your name?"

"Grover."

"You're not one of Binder's."

"I'm from I-2. Surprised the Binder let you out at all, if I may say so." He walked beside me, close enough for him to look like a bodyguard. "Your face was on my newspaper this morning."

"It's up there, too." I nodded to a transmission screen, where the fugitives' faces were being shown again. "But I've got a job to do."

"That makes two of us. Stay close and keep your head down. I'm charged with keeping you alive tonight."

I wondered how much Jaxon was paying him. What price he placed on the life of a dreamwalker.

Before Scion, the high lords of Westminster had planned to eradicate the disease-ridden rookeries of London and replace them with modern, sanitary dwellings. Urban renewal had been put on a backburner when unnaturalness arrived, of course. Most other problems had. Although some attempts at clearance had been made after the Ripper killings, particularly in Whitechapel, there were still four slums in the citadel, mostly populated by buskers and beggars. The Devil's Acre was the smallest by far, confined to three streets that ran between a few decrepit lodgings.

The area around the Archon was heavily guarded. At one point a troop of Vigiles came far too close, but the glym jack pushed me into an alley before they could spot my aura. "Hurry," he said, and we broke into a jog.

When we reached the perimeter of the Devil's Acre, I approached the entrance. A sheet of corrugated metal served as a door on Old Pye Street, barred from the other side. I knocked, hard.

"Doorman!"

Nothing. I gave the door a kick.

"Doorman, it's the Pale Dreamer. I have an urgent proposal for Hector. Open up, you lazy bastard."

The doorman didn't answer—not so much as a snore—but there was no way I was going back to I-4 without the painting. Eliza wouldn't get a wink of sleep until it was found.

"Wait here," I said to the glym jack. "I'll find a way in."

"As you will."

These walls were no friend to a climber. Coils of razor wire would tear my hands to shreds, and the corrugated metal was streaked with oily anti-intruder paint. I made a few rounds of the acre, searching for gaps, but everything was sealed. Clearly Hector was a tad more intelligent than he was hygienic. I was almost ready to admit defeat when the sole of my boot hit something hollow. A manhole cover.

Crouching, I heaved the metal lid to one side. Instead of the small access chamber I'd expected, a tunnel curved under the wall, dimly lit by a portable lantern.

Hector's bolthole. Strange that he hadn't put a padlock on it.

The tunnel was padded with soiled cushions and foam so caked in dirt it looked like stone. I lowered myself in and replaced the bolthole's lid. At the end of the passage I found a grate. Dim light sifted through it. I focused on my sixth sense, letting everything else drain away. There were no dreamscapes or spirits at all. Odd. Hector was always boasting about his enormous collection of spirits, from wisps to ghosts to poltergeists. Hector and the gang must have left again, unless they'd decided to wreak havoc in another section before returning home. Still, they should have a guard watching the bolthole, and there was no reason for all those spirits to have left.

This was my chance. I could sneak in, grab the painting and sneak out again. Job done. My heart raced. If I was caught trespassing in the Devil's Acre, I was worse than dead.

I surfaced from the tunnel in a shack, where the air was close and smelled of petrichor. Keeping low, I cracked open a door. Beyond it was a tiny collection of low-lying houses, cobbled together with brick and metal. I'd expected more from the Underlord's lair.

Each and every building was empty. When I came to the largest, which looked as if it might once have been a grand town-house two centuries ago, I knew it was where Hector lived. The walls were lined with blades of all kinds. Some of them were definitely imported, bought in secret from the black market; they were too fine to be street weapons.

Across the hallway, another set of double doors was ajar. A smell skimmed my nose, stale and unpleasant. I took the hunting knife from my bag and hid it behind my jacket. Warm light flickered across the carpet, but there was no sound.

I pushed open the doors. And I saw the drawing room, and I saw what was inside it.

Hector and his gang were here, all right.

They were all over the floor.

# 9

# The Bloody King

Hector lay on his back in the middle of the drawing room, legs splayed wide, with his left arm resting across his abdomen. Dark blood was spilling from his neck, and no wonder: his head was nowhere to be seen. I could only identify him from his eternally dirty clothes and the golden pocket watch.

A row of red candles had been lit along the mantelpiece. Their dim light made the lake of blood look like crude oil.

Eight bodies lay on the floor. The Underhand was at his master's side, as always. Head still attached, glaze-eyed and open-mouthed. The others were in pairs, like couples in bed. All lying in the same direction, with their heads facing the windows of the west-facing wall.

The insides of my ears tingled. I looked back through the doors and reached for the æther, but there was no one else in the building.

And there was Eliza's beautiful painting, propped against the wall. Arterial spray dripped down the canvas.

The sour stench of urine reached my nostrils. And the *blood*. So much blood.

*Run.* The word drifted through my thoughts. But no, the painting. I had to get the painting. And I had to take note of what was here; they'd clear it all away when word got out that Hector was dead.

First, the corpses. From the spray, they must have been killed here, not moved. I'd seen bodies before, some in the late stages of decay, but these identical positions were grotesquely theatrical. Streaks of blood led up to each body. They must have been dragged around the room like dummies before being posed. I pictured faceless hands propping up legs, lifting arms and tilting heads to the desired angle. Each face was resting on the left cheek. Each right arm lay on the floor, parallel to the torso. All the furniture—armchairs, a séance table, and a coat rack—had been pushed against the walls to make room for them all.

I crouched down by the nearest body, my breath shaking. Bile crept into my throat. This corpse had been Magtooth. It seemed impossible that he'd been taunting me a few days ago, his lips sneering and his eyes alight with malice. His cheeks had been hacked with a knife, most of his nose was missing, and small, V-shaped cuts split his eyelids.

The killer would have known that Hector was never by himself. There must have been more than one person here to take down the whole gang. I checked the corpses again. Hector, the Underhand, Slabnose, Slipfinger, Bloatface, Magtooth, Roundhead. At the bottom right corner of the arrangement, next to Magtooth, was the Undertaker, his mouth still set in a line. Death had hardly changed his expression. That explained why all the spirits had fled. Once a binder's heart stopped beating, his boundlings were free to go.

There was one person missing. Cutmouth. Either she'd escaped, or she'd never been here.

As well as arranging the bodies, the killer had left a calling card. Each body had the right palm turned toward the ceiling, and in each was a red silk handkerchief. A few of the gangs had calling cards—the Threadbare Company left a handful of needles, the Crowbars a black feather—but I'd never seen this one.

Cautiously, I rested the backs of my fingers against Magtooth's bloody cheek. Still warm. His watch was stuck at quarter past three. The clock on the mantelpiece told me it was now almost half past the same hour.

A chill bolted down my spine. I had to leave. Get the painting and run.

The spirits of the Underbodies would need the threnody, the essential words of release from the physical world. If I denied them that basic mercy, they would almost certainly develop into poltergeists, but I didn't know most of their names. I stood over the decapitated body and touched three fingers to my forehead as a sign of respect.

"Hector Grinslathe, be gone into the æther. All is settled. All debts are paid. You need not dwell among the living now."

There was no response from the æther. I turned to Magtooth, unsettled.

"Ronald Cranwell, be gone into the æther. All is settled. All debts are paid. You need not dwell among the living now."

Nothing. I focused, straining my perception until my temples ached. I'd thought they might be hiding, but they didn't emerge.

New spirits almost always lingered close to their empty bodies. I stepped back, into a pool of blood.

The æther, which had been still, began to vibrate. Like water touched by a tuning fork. I ran between the two rows of corpses, heading for the painting, but the quake soon caught up with me. The candles blew out, the ceiling cracked, and a poltergeist exploded through it.

The breacher's impact threw me against the floorboards. I realized my mistake at once: the pendant was in my pocket, not around my neck. Then the agony came, and so did a gut-wrenching scream. Spasms rocked my insides. Hallucinations seared past my eyes: a woman's cry, a torn and bloody dress, a spike concealed by artificial flowers. I gasped for air, clawing the floor until my nails ripped, but the thing was writhing like a snake inside me, digging its claws into my dreamscape, and every breath I took seemed to freeze inside my lungs.

Somehow, my fingers got to my pocket, gripped the pendant, and slammed it against my heart. The spirit thrashed in my dreamscape. I thrashed, too, my neck straining—but I kept it pressed to my skin, like salt to a wound, burning out the infection, until the poltergeist was expelled from my mind. It sent out a burst of tremors before it took off through the window. Glass burst from the frame. I lay on the floorboards, covered in the Underbodies' blood.

After what felt like hours, I drew in a breath. My right arm, which I'd thrown out to protect myself, was already beginning to stiffen. I dragged myself onto my hands and knees. Shards of glass fell from my hair. I opened my eyes slowly, blinking tiny crystals from my lashes.

With gritted teeth, I took hold of the painting and concealed it inside my coat before snatching up my bag. That poltergeist must have been waiting to spring on the first person that happened upon its old master's corpse, purely for its own entertainment.

Leaving the bodies, I made my way back through the bolthole. When I emerged, Grover took my good hand and pulled me up.

"Done?"

"He's dead," I said. "Hector, he's—"

I could hardly speak. Grover dropped my hand and looked at his own. It was wet with blood.

"You killed him," he said, stunned.

"No. He was dead."

"You've got blood all over you." He stepped away. "I'll have nothing to do with this. Binder can keep his coin." He took his lantern from the wall and broke into a run.

"Wait," I shouted after him. "It's not what it looks like!"

But Grover was gone. Dread sank into my veins.

He would tell someone. Probably the Abbess. I thought about sending my spirit after him, knocking him dead so he'd take what he'd seen to the æther—but I couldn't just kill innocent bystanders. And it wouldn't change the fact that I was covered in blood, all alone, and miles from Seven Dials.

There was no way I could walk back to I-4 like this, and I doubted any rickshaws would take me. Calling Jaxon wasn't an option; I didn't have my burner. But there was a lake about five minutes from here, in Birdcage Park. It would be dangerous to go there—it was close to Frank Weaver's estate in Victoria—but unless I found a water fountain, I didn't have much choice.

I ran, cradling my arm to my chest. The slum was swallowed up behind me. I dumped the painting in a waste container on the corner of Caxton Street. It was too heavy to carry any farther.

Birdcage Park was one of the few remaining green spaces in SciLo. Fifty-seven acres of grass, trees, and winding flower beds. Now, in late September, fallen leaves scattered the paths. When I reached the lake, I waded in up to my waist and washed the blood from my face and hair. I couldn't feel a thing above the elbow, while my forearm was in so much pain I wanted to hack off everything below the shoulder. A silent scream wrenched at my throat; I had to press a fist to my mouth to hold it in. Hot tears filled my eyes.

There was a pay phone near the edge of the lake. I dragged myself inside, took a coin from my pocket. My fingers stumbled on the code for the I-4 booth.

No answer. There was no courier standing by.

Somewhere in the fog, instinct returned. I lurched back to my feet. My ears were sizzling. Was there a fire? It didn't matter. I had to hide, to carry the pain somewhere where I wouldn't be seen. The trees by the lake cast deep enough shadows. I stumbled into the undergrowth and curled up in a bank of fallen leaves.

Time slowed. And slowed. And slowed. All I could register was my shallow breathing, the sound of fire, and the pain that pounded through my arm. I couldn't move the joints in my fingers. A Vigile was bound to do a patrol of the lake before dawn, but I couldn't get up. Nothing worked. Pitiless laughter filled my ears, and I blacked out.

****

Pain welled behind my eyes. I opened them a little. The smells of rose oil and tobacco told me where I was.

Someone had propped me against the cushions on Jaxon's couch, switched my bloody clothes for a nightshirt, and covered me to the chest with a chenille throw. I made to turn over, but every limb was stiff and I couldn't stop shivering. Even my jaw was locked. When I tried to lift my head, my neck muscles contracted painfully.

The night's events came flooding back. Anxiety trembled in my stomach. Trying to use only my eyes, I looked down at my arm. The wound was covered with what looked like green slime.

A creak on the landing announced Jaxon's arrival. He had a cigar wedged between his back teeth on one side of his mouth. Behind him were the others, minus Danica and Nick. "Paige?" Eliza crouched beside me and placed a hand on my forehead. "Jax, she's so cold."

"She will be." Jaxon blew out a cloud of bluish smoke. "I must admit, I did expect some minor injuries to contend with—but not to find you unconscious in Birdcage Park, my walker."

"You found me?" My jaw ached with each word.

"Well, I collected you. Dr. Nygård sent me an image of your location. It seems the æther finally sent him something useful."

"Where is he?"

"At that dratted Scion job of his. Into a buck cab I leaped, only to find my own mollisher in a heap of leaves, covered in blood." He knelt beside me, sweeping Eliza aside, and dipped a cloth in a bowl of water. "Let's have a look at this injury."

He washed away the poultice. The sight of the wound made me sick to my stomach. It was a collection of slices in a rough "M" shape, surrounded by splaying, blackened veins, with a glistening inkwell where the two middle lines met. Jaxon studied it. His colobomata swelled, heightening his spirit sight.

"This is the London Monster's work." He touched a finger to the mark. "A very distinctive phantom blade."

Sweat poured off my forehead, and the stiff tendons in my neck strained with the effort of not making a noise. His touch was like liquid nitrogen on the wound; I half-expected it to steam. Eliza risked a closer look. "There's a *blade* in there?"

"Ah, this is a much more sinister weapon. I trust you are all familiar with the concept of a phantom limb?" Nobody answered. "It's the sensation of something existing where it does not. It often happens to amputees. They might feel an itch in a severed arm, or pain in a pulled tooth. A phantom blade is a purely spiritual phenomenon, but similar in theory—poltergeists can inflict their own phantom sensations, usually something they specialized in when they were alive. It's a particularly nasty breed of *apport*, the sort of ethereal energy commanded by breachers, which allows them to affect the physical world. A strangler might leave phantom hands around a victim's neck, for example. It is, in essence, a supernumerary phantom limb."

"Just so I understand," Zeke said, touching a hand to my good shoulder, "she has an invisible knife in her arm. Right?"

"Correct." Jaxon tossed the cloth back into the bowl. "Did Hector set the creature on you?"

"No," I said. "He's dead."

The word hung in the air. "What?" Nadine looked between us. "Haymarket Hector?"

146

"Dead," Jaxon repeated. "Hector Grinslathe. Hector of the Haymarket. Underlord of the Scion Citadel of London. That particular Hector?"

"Yes," I said.

"Deceased." His words were slow, as if each syllable was gold and he was weighing it. "Departed. Shuffled off this mortal coil. Silver cord forever severed. Lifeless. No longer. Is that correct, Paige?"

"Yes."

"Did you touch the blade? Did anyone touch the blade?" His nostrils flared. "What about his spirit?"

"No. And not there."

"Pity. I would have loved to bind that miserable curl of slime." A cruel chuckle escaped him. "How did he meet his end, then? Drink himself senseless and fall into the fireplace, did he?"

"No," I said. "He was beheaded."

Eliza raised a hand to her mouth. "Paige," she said, her voice weak with dismay, "please don't tell me you killed the Underlord."

"No." I stared at her. "They were dead when I arrived. All of them."

"The whole *gang* is dead?"

"Not Cutmouth. But the others."

"That would explain the generous amount of blood on your coat." Jaxon traced his jaw with his thumb. "Did you use your spirit?"

"Jax, are you listening to me? They were already dead."

"Convenient." Nadine was lounging in the doorway. "What was that you were saying earlier, about Hector deserving to be killed by his own people?"

"Don't be ridiculous. I wouldn't have *actually*—"

"Whose blood was it, then?"

"It's theirs," I bit out, "but the poltergeist—"

"I do hope you are not the responsible party, Paige," Jaxon said. "To murder the Underlord is a capital offense."

"I didn't kill him." My voice was quiet. "I would never kill anyone like that. Not even Hector."

Silence. Jaxon brushed an invisible mark from his shirt. "Of course." He took a long drag from his cigar, his eyes oddly vacant. "This dilemma must be rectified. Did you destroy the painting?"

"I dumped it in Caxton Street."

"Did anyone see you leave?"

"No one but Grover. I checked the æther."

"Ah, yes. The glym jack. Zeke, Eliza: go to the Devil's Acre and make sure there is no trace of Paige's presence. Hide your faces. If you're caught, say you were supposed to give Hector a message. Then take the painting from Caxton Street and destroy it. Nadine: I want you to spend the rest of tonight in Soho and monitor the gossip. No doubt that wretched glym jack is already chaunting from the rooftops that the Underlord is dead, but we can discredit any mention of Paige. Our witness is an amaurotic. We can find some way to sully his reliability. "

The three of them made for the door.

"Wait." Jaxon raised a hand. "I hope this is glaringly obvious to you all, but if any of you ever lets slip that we knew of Hector's death before its official announcement, we will all be under suspicion. We will be dragged before the Unnatural Assembly. People will come forward from the market and tell them all about the painting debacle. You will find that loose tongues oft lead to loose necks." He looked at all of us. "Do not boast of it. Do not joke of it, speak of it, whisper of it. Swear it on the æther, O my darlings."

It wasn't a request. Each of us said "I swear" in turn. When he was satisfied, Jaxon stood.

"Go, you three. Hurry back."

They others left, all giving me different looks. Zeke was worried; Eliza, concerned; and Nadine, mistrustful.

When the door closed downstairs, Jaxon came to sit beside the

chaise longue. He stroked a hand over my damp hair. "I understand," he said, "if you felt you couldn't tell the truth in front of
them. But tell me, now. Did you kill him?"

"No," I said.

"But you wanted to kill him."

"There's a difference between wanting to kill someone and killing
someone, Jax."

"So it would seem. You're certain Cutmouth wasn't there?"

"Not that I could see."

"Fortunate for her. Not so fortunate for us, if she makes her
claim to the crown." His eyes were jewel-bright, and two spots of
color glowed on his cheekbones. "I have a way to deal with this.
Cutmouth's absence is conspicuous. All it would need is a whispered
rumor that she did the deed, and the sheer weight of suspicion will
force her to flee for her own safety. And you, darling, will be out of
the firing line."

I shifted onto my elbow. "Do you think she really could have
done it?"

"No. She was devoted to him, the poor fool." He looked thought-
ful. "Were they all beheaded?"

"The Underbodies weren't. They looked like they'd been ripped.
And all of them were holding a red handkerchief."

"Intriguing." The corner of his mouth quirked. "There's a
message in the murder, Paige. And I don't think it's simply a refer-
ence to Hector running around like a headless chicken for the last
eight years."

"Mockery," I ventured. "He was getting too big for his boots.
Acting like a king."

"Quite. A very Bloody King." He sat back and tapped his knee.
"Hector needed to die, no question of that. We have been quivering
in his shadow for almost a decade, watching him turn the syndicate
to a vague association of lazy rogues and low criminals, but no

more. Oh, I remember when Jed Bickford was Underlord, when I was still a gutterling. You would get more morals from a rock than from Jed Bickford, but he wasn't idle."

"What happened to him?"

"They found him in the Thames with a knife in his back. His mollisher was dead by dawn the next day."

Nice. "Do you think Hector killed them?"

"Unlikely, though he naturally favored blades. He wasn't clever enough to kill the Underlord without anyone noticing. But he was clever enough to win the ensuing scrimmage. And now"—his smile widened—"well, if Cutmouth does flee, someone must be clever enough to win the next one."

Only then did it sink in.

A new Underlord. We were getting a new Underlord.

"This could be our chance," I said. "If someone else takes Hector's place, we could change things, Jax."

"Perhaps. Perhaps we could." In the ensuing silence, Jaxon leaned over to his cabinet and procured a slim crutch. "The wound may weaken you, and your muscles will be stiff for a few hours." He pressed the crutch into my hands. "You won't be running for a while, my injured lamb."

A mollisher knew when she was dismissed. I left with my head high. As I opened the door to my room, I stopped dead.

Jaxon Hall was laughing his head off.

# PART II

## The Rephaite Revelation

*For the Merits of Unnaturalness are many, and ought to be known throughout our Underworld, from the Devil's Acre and the Chapel to the brave Stronghold of I Cohort.*

—An Obscure Writer, *On the Merits of Unnaturalness*

# Interlude

## Ode to London Under the Anchor

The Cheapside steeple was pale against the sky, and all across the citadel the homeless were scattering dirt on their pit fires. Night Vigiles were returning to their barracks after twelve long hours of hunting and harrowing. Those that hadn't filled their arrest quotas would be beaten black and blue by their commandants. Still they seemed no closer to finding Paige Mahoney.

At the Lychgate, three corpses swayed in the breeze. An urchin stole the laces from their shoes, watched by crows with bloody beaks.

On the banks of the Thames, the mudlarks crept from their sewers and dug their fingers into the dirt. Prayed for a glint of metal in the silt.

A handful of buskers checked their watches and set off for the Underground, hoping for change from heavy-eyed commuters. They were trading cash for coffee, plucking the *Daily Descendant* from a vendor and looking at the faces on the cover without seeing them. Deep in the financial district, with their own silk nooses pinned to their shirts, they would count out the coins that would pay for the cycle.

And the homeless were still homeless, and the corpses still danced. Puppets on a hangman's string.

On the night of
November the first, 2059,
the Spiritus Club shall exhibit

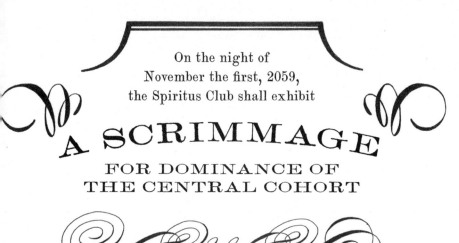

# A SCRIMMAGE

## FOR DOMINANCE OF
## THE CENTRAL COHORT

N.B.—Venue to be confirmed closer to the Date.
All Participants shall be matched in close Combat
within the confines of the Rose Ring.

A memorial bell will be rung for our erstwhile
Underlord at dawn on the first of October.

Let the signs of the æther guide your way.

*Minty Wolfson.*

Secretary of the Spiritus Club, Mistress of Ceremonies

*On behalf of the Abbess,*
*Mime-Queen of I-2,*
*Interim Underqueen of the*
*Scion Citadel of London*

# 10

# Ding Dong Bell

In the darkness before dawn, the voyants of I Cohort waited for the sign. Bow Bells would ring for one reason, and one only. To acknowledge the death of the Underlord.

A single chime rang out. Traditionally, one brave voyant would steal into the church at dawn and ring the bells for as long as possible before the Vigiles arrived. One of the Abbess's people had been chosen to do the deed.

Eleven chimes later, sirens keened from the Guild of Vigilance. Other voyants had climbed up buildings and trees to watch the courier's climb, but they soon began to leave.

Three of us had camped out on the roof of the old tower on Wood Street, part of yet another former church. Once we'd climbed it, the night had been spent waiting for the dawn, watching the stars, laughing at old memories of Jaxon.

It was rare for me to spend such a long time with Zeke, and I found that I was glad he'd come with us. Sometimes it was easy to forget that we were all friends, despite the bizarre circumstances. It hadn't been so easy to forget that today I would face the Unnatural Assembly.

The courier's silhouette darted away across the rooftops of Cheapside. Nick, who'd been watching Bow Bells in silence, sat down and poured three flutes of sparkling rose mecks. "Here's to Haymarket Hector, friends," he said in a grave tone, raising one towards the church. "The worst Underlord the citadel has ever seen. May his reign be swiftly forgotten by history."

With a long yawn, Zeke sat down and helped himself to a flute. I stayed where I was.

Two days after the killings, a letter had appeared in our dead drop, along with a sprig of hyacinth. The mistress of ceremonies had called for anyone with knowledge of the murder to come forward and give evidence. After four days, another notice had been sent out, giving Cutmouth three further days to present herself to the Unnatural Assembly and clear her name before she could claim the crown. Finally, a third letter had appeared to announce the date of the scrimmage.

Haymarket Hector had been buried by I-2 footpads beneath the ruins of St. Dunstan-in-the-East. Overgrown and beautiful, with a canopy of leaves, it was where all syndicate leaders were interred.

The first sunrise of October bathed us in a golden haze, burning away the mist and dew. The Vigiles, finding nothing at the church, retreated back to their headquarters.

Jaxon and I had received a formal summons to the Assembly, the first time such a summons had been sent in many years. Neither of us knew what it was about, but they'd most likely ask me about my involvement in Hector's death. If they found me guilty, I would end up in the Thames.

The wind whipped my hair as I looked out at the citadel, as it worked its dark enchantment on my state of mind. To the south was the bleak needle spire of Old Paul's, the highest building in all of Scion London and the seat of the Inquisitorial courts, where voyants were occasionally given televised sham trials before they were sentenced to death. The sight of it gave me a chill.

"There's something beautiful about it, isn't there?" Nick murmured. "The very first time I saw London, I wanted to be part of it. All those layers of history and death and grandeur. It makes you feel as if you could be anything, do anything."

"That's why I wanted to stay with Jax." I watched the lights fade from the buildings as the sun rose. "To be part of it."

There was another major building nearby. The Bank of Scion England stood on Threadneedle Street, the heart and soul of the financial district. A vast hologram of the anchor rotated above it. That was the bank that sustained this citadel, funded the capital punishment of voyants, and pumped money to Scion's network of citadels and outposts. No doubt it was also responsible for ensuring that the Rephaim were kept in extraordinary opulence.

And this was what I was trying to fight. The empire and its riches against one woman and her pillowcase of pennies.

"Were there any voyant organizations in Mexico, Zeke?" I asked.

"Not many. I heard some of them call themselves healers or witches, but most people don't know what they are." He toyed with his shoelace. "There weren't that many voyants at all in the city where I lived."

A sharp pang of nostalgia. It had been a long time since I'd been a free-worlder. Since I'd lived in a world where clairvoyance wasn't even acknowledged, let alone treason. "Sometimes I wonder which is worse," Nick mused. "Not knowing at all, or being defined by it."

"Not knowing," I said, with certainty. "I'd rather know what I am."

"I'm not so sure." Zeke rested his chin on his knees. "If I hadn't known—if word of Scion hadn't reached us . . ."

He turned his head away. Nick glanced at me, shook his head. Something had happened to Zeke that had made him lose his original gift and become unreadable. Jaxon and Nadine both knew, but the rest of us were in the dark.

"Paige," Zeke said, "there's something you should know."

"What?" I said. He was looking at Nick, whose jaw was clenched. "What's the matter?"

"We've heard rumors," Nick said. "We dropped into a bar in Soho the other night. There were voyants there taking bets on who might have killed Hector."

The glym jack must have talked. "Who were the candidates?" I said, trying to sound calm.

Zeke clasped his elegant hands. "Cutmouth and the Highwayman were both mentioned."

"But you were the favorite." Nick didn't look happy. "The clear favorite."

A flicker of trepidation started inside me.

As the sun rose higher, we packed up our camp. To get down, we had to make a leap between the tower and the nearest building. When he landed, Nick fell straight into a roll: a quick, lithe turn of limbs, from the balls of his feet to his shoulder and straight into a run. I was next. The jump was easy enough, but as soon as my boots hit the concrete, the muscles in my right arm went rigid. I landed hard on the top of my spine and ended up sprawled on my back, my hand clapped over the nape of my neck. Nick came straight back for me, his face white.

"Paige, are you all right?"

"I'm fine." I said it through clenched teeth.

"Don't move." He touched the small of my back. "Can you feel your legs?"

"Yeah, they feel great." I took his hands, and he eased me to my feet. "I'm just a bit rusty."

Above us, Zeke was still grasping the parapet, white-knuckled. "Any chance of some help?" he shouted.

Nick stood with his arms folded, a laugh in his eyes. "You're not scared of a little ninety-foot drop, are you?"

A muttered curse was the only answer he got.

Zeke blew out a long breath, took a few steps back and broke into a run. When he jumped, he sailed over the tower's parapet, down toward the lower rooftop. Not quite far enough. His arms hooked over the edge of the building, but his legs swung down toward the street, kicking at nothing. Panic widened his eyes. I started toward him, my heart in my throat.

Nick got there first. With a strength born of two decades of training, he grasped him under the arms and lifted him away from a long fall. Zeke clamped a hand over his chest, laughing between gasps for air.

"I don't think I'm cut out for this," he said.

"You're fine." Nick grasped his shoulder. Their foreheads were close together, almost brushing. "Paige and I have been doing this for years. Give it time."

"I don't think I'll be doing this again in a hurry." He grinned at me. "No offense, but I think you're both insane."

"We prefer 'intrepid,'" Nick said solemnly.

"No," I said. We looked up at the three Barbican towers, where my face was still on the screens, close enough for my father to see over his breakfast. "I think 'insane' works."

And it was. It was insane that we'd once spent every day clambering up buildings and hanging by our fingertips from ledges, inches from death. Knowing how to run and climb had almost saved me from the red-jackets, that fateful day in March. If that flux dart hadn't caught me, I might have escaped without ever setting foot in the penal colony.

We set off for I-4 as quickly as possible. The Vigiles would be on high alert after that breach. Zeke was nervous about jumping again, but Nick was just as patient with him as he'd been with me at the beginning. When we reached the den, I headed up to my room to get ready, dread coursing its way through my body. As I opened the door, Nick caught my arm.

"Jax will protect you. Good luck," he said, and left me alone.

Tiny prickles ran down the backs of my thighs. Taking slow breaths, I tidied my hair into ringlets with a curling iron, then buttoned myself into a long-sleeved silk blouse and high-waisted trousers. When I was done, I pushed up one sleeve to look at the poltergeist's mark. I took in a deep breath at the sight of it. The gnarled black "M" was about five inches wide and wept a clear fluid that reeked of metal.

A knock came at the door, and in walked Jaxon Hall with his favorite rosewood cane. He wore a black coat and a wide-brimmed hat over his best waistcoat and trousers.

"Are you ready, darling?"

I stood. "I think so."

"Dr. Nygård said you took a tumble on the rooftops." Leather-clad fingers stroked my cheek. "Devious, vicious creatures, poltergeists. They whittle at the will to live. Fortunately, we can now bind him."

My heart jumped. "You found his name?"

"Eliza did. Naturally there are conflicting reports of the London Monster's identity, but this fellow was imprisoned for the crimes. A vendor of artificial flowers named Rhynwick Williams." Jaxon sat down on my bed and patted the duvet beside him. I lowered myself on to it. "Hold out your arm, darling."

I did. With his eyes fixed hungrily on the scar, Jaxon removed a small knife from the end of his cane. A boline, with a rounded bone handle and a silver blade, used by binders and haematomancers for bloodletting. He pushed up his left sleeve, revealing the underside of his forearm. It was marked with faint white lines, each spelling out a full name.

"Now," he said, "let me explain. The Monster was unable to

occupy your dreamscape, but it has forged its own passageway into it. This tiny crack in your armor allows the Monster to cause you pain whenever it so desires. You are very lucky, darling, that the creature's touch failed to destroy your mind . . . perhaps something to do with your childhood encounter with a poltergeist."

It was the pendant that had shielded me, but let him think what he wanted. "So how do we close the passageway?"

"With skill. Once the creature is bound, it will pose no further threat."

The tip of Jaxon's blade touched the Monster's mark, wetting the blade with that strange fluid. Then he turned it on to his own skin, drawing a thread of blood from his inner arm.

"Allow me to educate you in the noble art of binding." The letter "R" bled from his arm. "Observe the bloodletting. The source of my gift. You see, while the spirit's name is written in my flesh, I have the power to control it. It belongs to me. It is my subject. If I intend to keep a spirit temporarily, I have only to carve the name in a shallow hand. Only until the wound heals is the spirit in my possession." Blood dripped down his pale fingers. "But if I wish to keep a spirit, I must scar myself with its name."

"Nice calligraphy," I said.

The name was beautifully written, with painful-looking flourishes. "One can't carve one's skin with any old lettering, darling." Jaxon continued slicing. "Names are important, you see—more important than you can possibly imagine."

"What if someone never gets given a name?" I said. "Or if more than one person has the same name?"

"That is why you should never identify with one name. Anonymity is your best protection from a binder. Now, watch."

He carved the last letter.

A shock wave went through my dreamscape, resonating through every bone in my body, as the London Monster came rushing back across the citadel. My head felt as though it was about to implode. I hunched over myself, gasping, as an unseen force pulled at the fabric of my mind, knitting the tiny opening together. As the spirit hurtled through the window, Jaxon flexed his fist, pushing blood down to his fingertips.

"Stop, Rhynwick Williams."

The spirit stopped dead. Ice spread across the mirror on the wall.

"Come to me, now." Jaxon held out a hand. "Leave the lady be. Your reign of terror is over."

The tension rose from my dreamscape as the spirit obeyed. I slumped against the wall, breathing in sharp bursts, drenched in sweat. Bound, mute, and obedient, the London Monster gravitated toward Jaxon.

"There. Mine. Until I sell him to the Juditheon for an obscene amount of money, of course." His eyes flicked down to the monster's mark, which had turned a muted gray. "The scar, I'm afraid, will always remain."

I pushed myself up on trembling arms. "Is there no way to get rid of it?"

"Not that I know of, darling. Perhaps if we had an exorcist to send the creature to the last light, but alas, we do not. Daphnomancers say that essence of the bay laurel can allay the pain. Probably augurs' drivel, but I shall ask one of my couriers to pick up a bottle of its oil from the Garden." With a smile, he handed me my long black coat. "Let me do the talking today. The Abbess won't condemn you with-out evidence."

"She was Hector's friend."

"Oh, she knows very well that Hector was an insufferable buffoon. She will have to acknowledge her glym jack's report, but she won't linger on the subject." He held open the door for me. "You're going to be fine, my lovely. Just don't show them that scar."

****

One of Jaxon's trusted buck cabbies was waiting outside the den. The meeting would be held at a derelict bathhouse in Hackney, and all members of the Unnatural Assembly were expected to attend. "Not that many of them will show up," Jaxon said. "The central mime-lords and mime-queens will, but those from outlying sections are unlikely to bother. Lazy, impertinent rogues."

While Jaxon soliloquized on how much he despised them all (and how very fortunate it was that Didion Waite hadn't wheedled his way on to the Unnatural Assembly), I sat in silence and nodded from time to time. The Abbess had seemed kind enough at the Juditheon, but it had been clear from her interaction with Ognena Maria that she had a firm hand. What if she asked to see my arm? What if they saw the damning evidence that Hector's poltergeist had felt threatened by me?

The cab pulled over in II-6, and a courier ran to meet us with an umbrella. Rain was thundering from dark, ash-colored clouds, sending water surging through the gutters. Jaxon took my arm and pulled me close to him. As we walked, a few voyants caught sight of our auras and touched their foreheads.

"Who else has arrived?" Jaxon asked the courier.

"There are fourteen Assembly members present, sir, but we expect more within the half-hour."

"What a *delight* it will be to see all my old friends. My mollisher has only had dealings with a few of them."

"They look forward to seeing you, sir."

I doubted it. Most of the Unnatural Assembly were reclusive, preferring to stay holed up in their dens while their employees carried out their wishes. A few had loose friendships, but nothing strong. There was too much bitterness left over from the gang wars.

The public bathhouse of Hackney had been boarded up for well over a century. After glancing over his shoulder, the courier led us down a series of steps and knocked on a heavy black door. A pair of sighted eyes appeared through a slot.

"Password?"

"Nostradamus," the courier whispered.

The door creaked open. Jaxon tightened his arm around me before we walked into the gloom.

Inside, the air was close and musty. Knowing London, there was probably a body in here somewhere. The courier took a lantern from his companion and held it up, guiding us down a narrow passageway and into a vast, gloomy chamber. An arched white ceiling swept above us, painted with neat blue rectangles. Every window and skylight was blocked by heavy boards. Scented white candles had been placed at regular intervals along the edges of the chamber. The walls flickered and the shadows danced. Top notes of sweet blossom stroked my throat, layered like petals over a grave. Despite the candles, the illicit reek of alcohol glanced off my nostrils, mixed in with sweat.

The mime-lords and mime-queens of London had gathered on a tiled floor where a deep pool had once been. The vast majority hid their identities, wearing all sorts of disguises, from simple hoods and scarves to threatening iron masks and stolen Vigile visors. It was illegal to wear decorative masks in public—most syndicate members only wore them at gatherings like this one—but many people did. The fashion had cascaded down from industrial citadels like Manchester, where most denizens wore respirators.

Jaxon had never worn any kind of disguise; he seemed to rely on his silver tongue to get him out of trouble. I still wore my red cravat beneath my eyes out of habit, though thanks to Didion, it wouldn't do much good.

Auras jumped at my senses. Despite years of prejudice against the lower orders, the gang leaders displayed a wide range of gifts.

Most fell somewhere on the middle of the spectrum: mediums, sensors, guardians, with the odd fury or soothsayer in the mix.

Ognena Maria was among those gathered here, talking in a low voice with Jimmy O'Goblin, the clumsy drunkard who ruled II-1. Their mollishers stood on either side of them like bodyguards, both hooded, faces shrouded with colored silk. Then there was the brutal Bully-Rook and his mollisher Jack Hickathrift; the Wretched Sylph, pale and mournful; the elderly Pearl Queen in her finery, the only one to have come alone. I knew most of the others by sight, but had rarely dealt with them.

Ten feet above us in the stalls, the Abbess of I-2, interim Underqueen until the scrimmage, was lounging against the railings in a tailored velvet suit that must have cost her a small fortune. Beneath her hat, her hair fell in sculpted waves down one side of her neck. The Monk and two of her nightwalkers, including the redhead that had been at the Juditheon, were sitting behind her. Her associates were properly called the Nightingales, though they had numerous names on the streets.

"Well, what do you know?" The green-eyed Glass Duchess examined us through a haze of smoke. A smirk crept up one side of her wide mouth. "Assembly, behold! The recluse has emerged from his cave."

"Well met," said her twin and mollisher, the Glass Dell. They were identical except for the wiry brown curls under their bowler hats; the Dell's were long, the Duchess's short. "We haven't seen you in a summer, Binder."

"And how we have missed his presence. Welcome, White Binder," the Abbess called, beckoning us with a warm smile. "And you, Pale Dreamer. Welcome."

Heads turned to look at us: some with curiosity, others with outright loathing. As I looked at the Abbess, I tried to read her aura. Definitely a medium. A physical medium, from the feel of it. Quite a rare gift. She had the sort of dreamscape that called out for spirits to seize control of her.

Jaxon ignored the other mime-lords and mime-queens, but touched his hand to his chest in half a bow. "My dear Abbess, what a great pleasure to see you again. It's been too long."

"So it has. You ought to visit me in the parlor once in a while."

"I have no particular uses for a night parlor," he said, making the Glass Dell choke on her aster, "but perhaps I shall stop by in I-2."

"Binder, you rancid old codger," the Glym Lord boomed, slapping Jaxon on the back so hard he almost dropped his cane. Better known as Glym, he was almost as big as a Rephaite, straining all over with muscle and coarse hair. Matted locks fell down to his waist, restrained by a thick band. "How are you?"

"How's life?" Tom the Rhymer appeared over his other shoulder, clapping down a liver-spotted hand. He was almost the same size as Glym; an old Scottish soothsayer with curtains of blue-rinsed hair beneath his hat. He was the only other jumper in the room. "You know, next time somebody paints a tarot deck, they should stick you on the Hermit card."

I smiled behind my silk. As if he sensed it, Glym gave me a grin that made his eyes glister, his teeth white against dark, leathery skin. Jaxon's eye twitched.

"Leave him be, you pair of monsters. I hope you'll forgive the dismal surroundings, my friends," the Abbess called out to all of us, waving a half-gloved hand toward the ceiling. "I felt it would be inappropriate to meet in the Devil's Acre, given the sad circumstances. Alas, we must convene in places Scion has left to rack and ruin."

It was true. Most of the syndicate's hideouts were derelict places: abandoned buildings, closed stations, sewer chambers from a time long past. We gathered in the under, the hidden, the forgotten.

The minutes ticked on. The Heathen Philosopher arrived in a

cloud of perfume and white powder and greasepaint, trailing a sour-faced mollisher. Two footpads had to keep Didion Waite from entering, and we were treated to his pompous voice piping out arguments for ten minutes ("I may not be a mime-lord, but I am a *valued* member of this community, Madam Underqueen!"). When the doors swung open again, the Wicked Lady came marching in with the Highwayman. She was the brutal mime-queen of this section, presiding over three of the most notorious slums in the citadel: Jacob's Island, Whitechapel, and the Old Nichol, as well as the docklands. A burly Ripper hunter in her thirties, half her mollisher's height, with a klaxon voice and lips purpled by aster. Above us, the Abbess waved her to a seat on her right.

"My dear friend," she said. "Thank you for allowing us to use this space for these proceedings."

"Oh, doesn't bother me." With a snort, the Wicked Lady sat down and crossed her legs, tossing her ash-blonde curls over her shoulder. "Half this bloody section is derelict."

"It has a dark past, as we all know," the Abbess said. She looked at us all, her slender eyebrows lifting. "I asked for all Assembly members from I and II Cohorts to report to this meeting as a matter of urgency. Where is Mary Bourne?"

"She sends her apologies, madam," said a whey-faced courier, curtseying low. "She has a fever. Her mollisher is tending to her."

"We wish her well. And Ark Ruffian?"

"Intoxicated, madam, the wretched bloody scoundrel," Jimmy O'Goblin slurred, waving a finger. "As is his mollisher. We all shared a merry glass last night. In Hector's memory, you understand. I said to him, 'Now, Ark, you know very well that Madam Abbess has called our names in her hour of need, perhaps you oughtn't to drink another,' but I tell you, lady, all he said was—"

"Yes, thank you, Jimmy. I suppose I was optimistic to expect him. Congratulations on arriving so clear-headed." The Abbess's smile faded, and her hands tightened on the railing. "And where, I ask, is the Rag and Bone Man? Does he consider himself too fine for these proceedings?"

A long silence followed her words. "Don't think I've ever seen him," Madam Speaker said.

"He lurks beneath the ground, as always," the Lord Costermonger said. "I hear his mollisher, La Chiffonnière, rules Camden in his name."

"A sloven, as ever. The Rag and Bone Man has always preferred to skulk in his squalid lair, in the company of rats and rot, than answer the call of the syndicate." Something like anger tainted her voice. "No matter. The room will smell a little less foul without his presence. Please, all of you, be seated."

She lowered herself into a chair, as did some of the Unnatural Assembly. I sat beside Jaxon and tried to look calm.

"You will all know by now that Haymarket Hector, my dearest friend, was murdered. It now falls to me to command the syndicate before the scrimmage." A heavy sigh went through her. "As part of my duties as interim Underqueen, to uphold the strength of the Unnatural Assembly, I must investigate the circumstances that led to Hector's death. Pale Dreamer, would you present yourself to the floor?"

I glanced at Jaxon. He gave me the barest nod.

"One of my glym jacks reported that you were present on the night of Hector's death," the Abbess said gently as I walked to the middle of the room. "Is this true?"

My legs turned to columns of ice. "Yes. They were all dead when I arrived in the Devil's Acre. Hector was beheaded. The rest died from cut throats, by the looks of it."

"Disgraceful," the Pearl Queen groused. "In his own parlor, of all places . . . I hope you will hand out the death sentence for this crime, Underqueen. It makes a mockery of our laws."

"I assure you, justice will be dealt in due course." The Abbess turned back to me. "May I ask what you were doing in the Underlord's territory, Pale Dreamer?"

"That's what I'd like to know," the Bully-Rook said, giving me a nasty look.

"I was sent there on my mime-lord's orders."

"Sure you didn't just sneak in and kill him?" the Glass Duchess asked, to murmurs of agreement. "You were seen arguing with Hector's mollisher at the black market, Pale Dreamer."

"I don't deny it," I said coolly.

"My mollisher is trustworthy." Jaxon stood and placed both hands on his cane. "I'm afraid Hector, for all the good work he did for this citadel, was attempting to blackmail me. On the night he was murdered, he stole a valuable painting from I-4's flagship booth at the Garden. I sent my mollisher to negotiate its safe return. Unfortunately, this meant that she was the first to stumble across his corpse. I can vouch absolutely for her good conduct in this matter."

Behind me, Tom the Rhymer chuckled. "You would, though, wouldn't you?"

"May I ask what you're insinuating, Tom?" The veiled courtesy in Jaxon's voice was unsettling. "That I would *lie* to the Assembly?"

"Stop." Above us, the Abbess raised a hand. "I will hear no more of this. We trust in your word, White Binder."

Tom muttered a few choice words, but shut up when Glym gave him a warning look. There were murmurs of assent from most members of the Assembly, though the Pearl Queen didn't take her pale eyes off me for a long while. They wouldn't question me while I had the protection of the interim Underqueen.

When silence had fallen again, the Abbess motioned to the two nightwalkers behind her. "My Nightingales noted that Cutmouth was not present at the scene of the crime. Can you confirm this, Pale Dreamer?"

"There was no sign of her," I said, "and no spirits, either. All of them had left the Acre."

"Even the London Monster, Hector's protector?"

"Yes, Underqueen."

The Glass Duchess shook her head. "Don't know why he kept that thing shackled to his side. Useless."

"Not entirely useless," the Heathen Philosopher drawled, stroking his ample chin. "The London Monster leaves a very distinctive mark, a black 'M' on the skin. If we can find this mark, it will be easy to track down Hector's killer."

My fist clenched behind my back. Above us, the Abbess rested her hands on the railing again. Bluish marks stained the skin under her eyes, making her look gaunt with exhaustion.

"I would ask that all of you order your voyants to keep an eye out for this mark. Maria, my dear," she said, "as you run a market specializing in amaurotic trinkets, I want you to search for the origin of the red handkerchiefs that were found with the body, which would appear to be the only solid lead." Ognena Maria nodded, though she didn't look too pleased with being called *my dear*. "In the meantime, we will begin the process of searching out Cutmouth. Does anyone have any idea where she may have fled?"

Nobody spoke. Before I knew it, I was taking another step forward. This could be my chance.

"Abbess," I said, "I hope you'll forgive the intrusion, but there's something the Unnatural Assembly desperately needs to hear. Something that—"

"—I should have announced at the beginning of this meeting," Jaxon interrupted. "Foolish of me to let it slip my mind. Despite my attempts to keep her off my turf, Cutmouth was a patron of several gambling-houses and night parlors in Soho. Perhaps it would be sensible to begin the search there."

Anger boiled in my gut. He knew very well what I wanted to say.

After a moment, the Abbess said, "Do I have permission for my hirelings to enter I-4 for that purpose, Binder?"

"Of course. We would be delighted to host them."

"You are too kind, my friend. If there are no other points to raise, I shall let you return to your sections in peace. I hope to see you all at the scrimmage." When the Abbess stood, the rest of the Unnatural Assembly followed suit. "Grub Street will organize the ledger of contestants and keep you informed as to the location. Until then, may the æther keep you in these troubled times."

There were a few farewells before they all began to leave. As she passed, the Abbess gave me a soft smile. I glanced three fingers off my forehead and followed Jaxon down the passageway.

"You see?" He took my arm again. "Safe and sound. You have nothing to fear now, O my lovely."

While we waited for another cab, Jaxon lit a cigar and watched the sky. I leaned against a streetlamp. "Jax," I said quietly, "why did you interrupt me?"

"Because you were about to tell them about the Rephaim."

"Of course I was. They need to know."

"Try to use your common sense, Paige. Our focus was to ensure that you weren't strung up for murder, not to tell tall tales." All the warmth in his face had drained away. "Don't try that again, darling, or I may have to show the Abbess this little piece of evidence."

He tapped my arm with one finger.

The threat shocked me into silence. He held up a hand, and a rickshaw braked across the road.

So long as I was with him, I was safe. So long as I was his dutiful Pale Dreamer, my name would be just clear enough for the Unnatural Assembly to quell their suspicions about me. But if I ever struck out on my own, he would expose the dirty secret underneath my sleeve.

Jaxon had never meant to use this meeting to protect me. He'd used it to trap me. To ensure that I would never rise above him.

"Now, back to I-4." With a dashing smile to the driver, he climbed up the folding steps of the rickshaw and took a seat. "The others will meet us in Neal's Yard."

Blackmailing, devious *bastard*. I could hardly get the words out. "To do what?"

"Break our fast," he said, with a private sort of smile. "Every revolution begins with breakfast, darling."

\*\*\*\*

Even a revolutionary breakfast—whatever that might be—had to be eaten in Chateline's. The others met us in our private booth. As always, I sat at Jaxon's right side, where a mollisher belonged. He ordered a spendthrift breakfast: everything on the menu, from salted sprats on scrambled eggs to honeyed corn muffins, glossy sausages, and kedgeree with hard-boiled eggs. The food was delivered on tiered stands and trays covered by silver cloches.

"What's this in aid of, Binder?" The owner poured me a cup of fresh coffee. Chat was a soft-spoken ex-boxer who'd served Jaxon for years until he'd lost a hand to an angry rival. Broken capillaries spread out from his nostrils into his cheeks. "Giving Hector a farewell toast?"

"In a fashion, my friend."

Chat retreated to the bar. Opposite me, Eliza helped herself to a dish, smiling her uncertainty. "In a fashion?"

"You'll see. Or rather, you'll *hear*. When I tell you," Jaxon purred.

"Right. How was the meeting?"

"Oh, quite uneventful. I almost forgot how insufferable they all are. Nonetheless, Paige's reputation is safe, so the meeting served its purpose." *I'll bet it did*, I thought. "Devilled kidney, Danica, my dear?"

He offered her a hot plate. She gave it a surly look before taking it.

"This is the first time we've seen you in days." Zeke slid a plate of muffins toward her. "What are you living on up there?"

Danica was out of her depth outside the den. Wild red hair tumbled from its bun, her freckled cheeks were spattered with oil and fresh soldering burns mottled both her hands. "Oxygen," she said. "Nitrogen. I could go on."

"What are you *working* on, then, brains?" Nadine popped a fried mushroom into her mouth.

"Danica is designing a jamming device," Jaxon intervened. "The same technology that created Senshield, beautifully enrobed in a convenient, hand-held form."

"I took the basic design from Scion," she said. "They're working on a portable version of Senshield."

My fingers tapped the tablecloth. Opposite me, Nick frowned. "Why would they need that?"

"To get rid of the NVD. You don't think they want to use unnatural police for ever, do you?"

Nick looked shocked, and no wonder. If Senshield could be carried by amaurotic Vigiles, they wouldn't need sighted eyes on the streets. The voyants who had turned on their own kind, who had hunted their fellow unnaturals, would no longer serve a purpose in Scion.

"Excellent news for us," Jaxon remarked. "We'll have amaurotics bumbling about with cumbersome bits of equipment instead of sighted clairvoyant soldiers on the streets. Do eat, my lovely," he added to me. "We have much to do over the coming weeks. You'll need your appetite and your wits about you."

I took a bite of bread.

"You look a lot better, Paige." Now they'd made up, Eliza was back to being a true yes-Jaxon. "We've got a ton of rainbow ruses to sort out. I could use a hand tomorrow if you're up for it."

"I wouldn't concern yourself with rainbow ruses for now." Our mime-lord took a delicate sniff of lemon Floxy, as he always did to cleanse his palate. "We have far more important matters to consider,

O my lovely. Matters that, for the first time, may take our thoughts beyond the limits of I-4." He paused, presumably for dramatic effect. "Would you like to hear them?"

Zeke caught my eye and pulled a face. "Yes, Jaxon."

"Good. Gather round, then."

We all leaned closer. Jaxon looked at each of us in turn, his whole aspect aflame with energy.

"As you know, I have been devoted to I-4 for close to twenty years. Together, we have kept it prosperous in the face of Scion's tyranny. You six are my magnum opus. And despite your occasional—well, regular—blunders, I have nothing but the greatest admiration for your skills and dedication." His voice dropped a note. "But we can do no more with I-4 and her people. We are the best of all the dominant gangs in the citadel: the best at trading, the best at combat, the best at *excellence*. For this reason, I have decided to apply for the position of Underlord."

I closed my eyes. No surprise there.

"I knew it." Eliza's face broke into a grin. "Oh, Jax, this is really off the cot, but just *imagine* it. We—we could really be—"

"The governing gang of the Scion Citadel of London." Jaxon took one of her hands, chuckling. "Yes, my faithful medium. Yes, we could." She looked as if she might weep with joy.

"We'd be calling the shots." A smirking Nadine traced the edge of her glass. "We could tell Didion to blow up the Juditheon."

"Or give all its spirits to us." At her side, Eliza was basking in Jaxon's good mood. "We could do *anything*."

"Just the seven of us. The lords of London. It will be exquisite." Jaxon lit a cigar. "Don't you think, Paige?"

Behind that smile was danger. I mustered what I hoped was a convincing grin. The sort of smile a mollisher should give her mime-lord on the receipt of such good news. "Absolutely," I said.

"You have faith that I can win, I trust."

"Of course."

Jaxon had the most money, ego, and ambition out of all the mime-lords in London. Given how ruthless he could be, and how skilled he was in both binding and spirit combat, he had a high chance of winning. A *very* high chance. Nick looked as apprehensive as I felt.

"Good." Jaxon picked up his coffee. "I shall be leaving some homework in your room. Reading material, so you can learn the noble customs of the scrimmage."

Brilliant. While Scion and the Rephaim plotted their next move, I'd be doing my homework. Like a good little mollisher.

"Paige," Jaxon said, almost as an afterthought, "fetch another rack of toast sandwiches, will you, darling?"

It had been years since I'd been the tea girl. Maybe I hadn't shown enough enthusiasm. The gang watched me as I walked over to the bar and waited for Chat to emerge from the kitchen, drumming my fingers on the bar. In the corner, I could just hear two other voyants talking.

". . . argument with I-4." A man's voice. "I heard there was some quarrel with the French girl at the market."

"She's not French," a woman muttered. "That's the Silent Bell, his whisperer. She's a free-worlder, they say. So is the brother."

I tapped the service bell, my nerves looping themselves into tight knots. Chat came out of the kitchen in his apron, his cheeks red from the heat of the ovens. "Yes, love?"

"Some more toast sandwiches, please."

"Coming up."

While I waited, I strained to hear the conversation again. ". . . saw her with Cutmouth, you know. She was wearing a mask, but it was her, I'm sure of it. The Pale Dreamer."

"She's back in London?"

"Aye, and she was there when Hector died," a gruff voice said. "I know the glym jack that went with her to the Acre. Grover. A good man, he is, and honest. He said she was covered in blood."

"She's the girl on the screens. Did you hear?"

"Mm. Shady business, that. Maybe Hector sold her out, and that's why she killed him."

Chat came out with the rack of buttered sandwiches, and I went back to my seat. "They're talking about us," I said to Jaxon, who grew still. "The people behind the screen."

"Are they, now?" He tapped his cigar into a glass ashtray. "And what are they saying?"

"That we killed Hector. Or I did."

"Perhaps," Jaxon sneered, raising his voice so half the bar looked up at us, "they should mind their tongues. I understand the mime-lord of I-4 does not tolerate slander. Least of all from his own people."

There was a brief silence before a trio of soothsayers rose from behind the screen, took their coats from the nearest stand, and left. They kept their faces turned away from our table. Jaxon sat back in his seat, but his gaze followed them as they hurried away into Neal's Yard.

The others went back to their meals. "One of them knew." I glanced at Jaxon. "He knew Grover."

"Perhaps they ought to read the old laws of the syndicate. The First Code states that without sufficient proof, the word of an amaurotic is rotten." He raised his cigar back to his lips. "It's hearsay, O my lovely. Don't fret. You have me to vouch for your good nature. And once I am Underlord, these allegations will disappear."

And with them, any chance of changing the syndicate. That was the bargain he offered: protection in exchange for my compliance. Jaxon Hall had me in a bind, and worse, he knew it.

I tuned out the rest of the conversation. As I sipped my coffee, I sensed two auras nearby. Gooseflesh rose along my abdomen.

Two silhouettes were just outside the window.

The cup fell from my fingers. Two pairs of eyes looked back at me, firefly lights in the gloom of the passage.

*No.*

Not now. Not them.

"Paige?"

Eliza was staring at me. I looked down at the spilled coffee and broken glass, numb. "Apologies, Chat," Jaxon called. "Excitement gives her butterfingers. We would be more than happy to pay double your usual tip." He waved a few notes. "A tremor, I presume, Paige."

"Yes," I managed. "Yes. Sorry."

When I looked back at the window, there was no sign of anyone. Nick gave me a curious look.

It had to be a mistake. A nightmare. My broken dreamscape, blurring memory and reality.

If not, I'd just seen two Rephaim in I-4.

****

Jaxon was planning to order another five courses, but I made an excuse and slipped out of the restaurant. It was only a few seconds' run to the den. Every shadow grew taller; every streetlight flashed like Rephaite eyes. As soon as I was inside, I tore up the stairs and grabbed the backpack from under my bed. I ripped it open with one hand, almost breaking the zip, and crammed a blouse and trousers inside it. Sharp, angry breaths escaped me, verging on sobs.

It hadn't been Warden. Who else would have come for me? Who else could know where I lived? Nashira must have worked out where the sundials led . . . I'd have to go back to the doss-house. Make a plan. Get away. I yanked my coat from the back of the door and pulled it on. When Nick came in, he caught my hands.

"Paige, stop, stop." I struggled, but he held me. "What are you doing? What's wrong?"

"Rephs."

His face stiffened. "Where?"

"Outside Chat's. The alley." I stuffed a spare jacket into my backpack. "I have to go, or they'll target you as well. I have to go to the doss-house and—"

"No. Wait," he urged. "You're safer here, with us. And Jaxon isn't just going to let you leave, not now he's going for Underlord."

"I don't care what Jaxon does!"

"Yes, you do." He spun me to face him. "Just put the bag down, *sötnos*. Please. Are you absolutely sure they were Rephs?"

"I felt their auras. If I stay here, they'll take me to Nashira."

"They could be Warden's allies," he said, though he looked doubtful.

"What was it you said, Nick? 'The Rephaim are enemies until categorically proven otherwise.'" I sifted through my nightstand, pulling out socks and shirts, scarves and glovelettes. "Will you give me a ride, or am I walking?"

"This is the eve of Jaxon's personal revolution. He won't forgive you if you leave, Paige—not this time."

"They'll nip his revolution in the bud if they find us."

Three loud raps came on the door, startling us both, before it almost flew off the hinges. Jaxon seemed to fill the door frame. His cane banged down on the floorboards.

"What is the meaning of this?"

"Jaxon, there were Rephs outside the bar. Two of them." I stood. "I have to go. We all have to go, *now*."

"We are not going anywhere." He used the cane to push the door closed. "Explain. Quietly."

"Where are the others?"

"Still at Chateline's, where they will be staying for the next few hours, blissfully unaware of this conversation."

"Jaxon, *listen* to her. Please," Nick said firmly. "She knows what she saw."

"She may think so, Dr. Nygård, but we all know what recurrent exposure to flux can do."

"What the hell is that supposed to mean, Jax?" I stared him out, livid. I could just about sympathize with Eliza thinking I'd lost my mind, but Jaxon had been there. "You think I'm having flux flashes? Were you having one, too, when you saw the colony for yourself?"

"This isn't a matter of disbelief, O my lovely. This is a matter of decorum. Of dedication. Despite your repeated contact with experimental psychoactive drugs, I do believe your story. As you say, I can hardly deny what I saw with my own eyes," he said, pacing to the window. "I do not, however, see any reason for the people of I-4 to act upon it, nor for the Unnatural Assembly to hear of it. I have already said this to you in as many words. Must I really repeat myself?"

In exchange for his protection, he was asking me to close my eyes to everything I'd learned. "I can't understand you," I said hotly. "They are *here*, in I-4. How can you just ignore it?"

"You don't need to understand my actions, Paige. You need to do as you are told, as we agreed."

"If I'd done as I was told in the colony, I'd still be there now."

There was a long silence. Jaxon turned his head.

"Explain this to me. I find myself puzzled." He stepped toward me, raising a finger. "You've always known that Scion's doctrine is rooted in injustice. You've always known that their inquisition into unnaturalness is reprehensible. But only *now* do you think we should intervene. Were you too afraid to strike when their corruption was only human, my Paige?"

"I've seen what started it. I've seen what indoctrinated them," I said. "And I think we can stop it."

"You think fighting the Rephaim will bring a halt to the

inquisition? Don't labor under the illusion that Frank Weaver and his government will become devoted friends of yours if you destroy their masters."

"Surely we have to *try*, Jax? Who's going to rule I-4 when they come for us?"

"Be careful, Paige." Jaxon's face was losing color again. "You are treading a very fine line."

"Am I? Or am I crossing yours?"

That did it. Jaxon shoved me into the cabinet with one arm, pinning me against the shelves. He was much stronger than he looked. A tall jar of sleeping pills smashed against the floorboards. "Jaxon!" Nick barked, but this was between mime-lord and moll-isher. His right hand gripped my arm, where the poltergeist's mark was burned into my skin.

"Listen to me now, O my lovely. I will *not* have my mollisher raving in the streets like some Bedleem unfortunate. Especially not now that I am considering taking control of this citadel." There was a triangle of lines between his eyebrows. "Do you think the good people of London would support me, Paige, if I were seen to be believing some madman's tale of giants and walking corpses? Why do you think I stopped you from telling the Abbess? Do you think they would take our word for it, darling, or would they laugh and call us fools?"

"Is that it, Jax? All these years later and you're still worried about people laughing at you?"

He smiled an empty smile.

"I consider myself a generous man, but this is your last chance. You can stay with me and reap the benefits of I-4's protection, or you can take your chances out there, where no one will listen. Where they will string you up for Hector's murder. The only reason you are not dead already, O my lovely, is because of *my* good word. My declaration of your innocence. Put one toe out of line, and I will have you dragged before the Unnatural Assembly so you can show them that scar."

"You wouldn't," I said.

"You have no idea what I would do to keep London from war." With a last flex of his fingers, he let go of my arm. "I will have someone paint over the sundials to keep them from being recognized. But know this, Paige: you can be the Underlord's mollisher, or you can be carrion for crows. If you choose the latter, I will let it be known that you are fair game. Just as I did before you returned to the Seals. After all, if you are not the Pale Dreamer . . . who are you?"

He left. I kicked my basket of trinkets from the market, knocking it over, and sat with my head in my good hand. Nick crouched opposite me and grasped my upper arm.

"Paige?"

"It could *strengthen* the syndicate." I took a deep breath. "If we could just convince them . . ."

"Maybe, if you found proof of the Rephs, but the truth would end the syndicate as we know it. You want to turn it into a force for good. Jaxon isn't interested in 'good.' He wants to sit on his throne and gather spirits and be king of the citadel until he dies. That is all he cares about. But an Underlord's mollisher has power, too. You could change things, Paige."

"Jax would always stop me. A mollisher isn't an Underlord—he'd just make me his special errand girl. Only an Underlord could change everything."

"Or an Underqueen," Nick said, with a brief laugh. "We haven't had an Underqueen in a long time."

Slowly, I raised my gaze to his. The smile slid from his lips.

"I couldn't," I murmured. "Could I?"

I watched him. He stood up and braced his hands on the windowsill, and looked down at the courtyard. "Mollishers are never eligible. Their loyalty can't be questioned in a scrimmage."

"Is it against the rules?"

"Probably. If a mollisher goes against their mime-lord, it marks them as a turncoat. It's never happened, not in the whole history of the syndicate. Would you follow a backstabber?"

"I'd rather follow one than walk in front of one."

"Don't be smart. This is serious."

"Fine. Yes, I'd work for a backstabber if she knew the truth about Scion. If she wanted to expose it, to stop the systematic *murder* of clairvoyants—"

"They don't *care* about Scion's corruption. They're all like Jaxon. Even the ones who seem kind. I'm telling you, they'd bleed their own sections dry if it meant they had full pockets. You have no money to pay them all. And you've seen Jaxon, getting us to do the dirty work while he smokes and drinks absinthe. You really think people like him will command an army for you? Put their precious lives at risk for you?"

"I don't know. But maybe I should find out." I sighed. "Say I *was* to apply. Would you be my mollisher?"

His face twitched.

"I would," he said, "because I care about you. But I don't want you to do it, Paige. At best you'll be a traitor Underqueen. At worst you'll lose and wind up getting killed. If you wait two years, Jaxon will give you the section anyway. Is there any wisdom in waiting?"

"In two years it will be too late. We're weeks away from Senshield, and the Rephaim might have taken their next colony. We need to strike *now*. Besides," I said, "Jaxon won't retire in two years. All he's trying to do is keep me quiet. Pat my head with one hand while he chains me with the other."

"Is it worth the risk of losing?"

"People died to get me out of Sheol," I said quietly. "People like us are dying every day. If I hide in the shadows while this continues, I'm spitting at their memories."

"Then you'd better make sure you're prepared for the consequences." Nick stood. "I'll calm him down. You'd better unpack."

He closed the door gently behind him.

It might be the only choice. Painting the sundials wouldn't hold back the Rephaim for long. To transform the London syndicate into an army that could stand against them, I would have to think bigger. Become not just a mollisher, not just a mime-queen, but the Underqueen of the Scion Citadel of London. I had to have a voice too loud to silence.

After a minute, I started to gather up the things I'd scattered across the floor: nineteenth-century newspaper clippings, brooches, antique numa—and a third edition of *On the Merits of Unnaturalness*, confiscated from a busker who had been mocking it in Soho. *By an Obscure Writer*, it read.

*Words give wings even to those who have been stamped upon, broken beyond all hope of repair.*

There were ways to raise my voice. I took out my phone, slotted a new module into the back, and dialed the number Felix had given me.

## 11

# Urban Legend

"A what?"

Nell looked almost impressed by my sudden display of insanity. Her hair had been cut so it fell just past her chin; what was left was ironed straight and dyed at least ten shades of orange. With cinder glasses and glossy black lipstick, she was unrecognizable.

Dawn hadn't yet broken, but the five of us were already huddled on the rooftop terrace of one of Camden's independent oxygen bars. Curving screens divided the tables. The buskers' music from the market below was enough to ward off eavesdroppers.

"You heard me," I said. "A penny dreadful."

On my left, Felix shook his head. His chosen disguise was one of the filtering masks they wore in the north and parts of the East End, which left only his eyes uncovered. "You want to tell a *story* about the Rephaim?" His voice was muffled. "Like it's not real?"

"Exactly. *On the Merits of Unnaturalness* made the syndicate what it is today," I said, keeping my voice low. "It completely revolutionized the way we think about clairvoyance. Just by putting his thoughts on paper, one obscure writer changed everything. Why can't we?"

Felix held his mask away from his mouth. "Okay," he said, "but that was a pamphlet. You're suggesting a penny dreadful. A cut-price horror story for people with too much time on their hands."

"I used to read *Marvelous Songbirds for Sale*. You know, the one about the orthinomancer who's a gutterling and sells talking birds," Jos said, "but my kidsman found my stash and threw them all in a pit fire." He wasn't on Scion's radar yet, but Nell had bundled him up in a scarf and hat anyway.

"Good. That stuff will rot your brain." There were rings under Nell's eyes. "And Grub Street pumps it out at a rate of knots."

"I just don't know if we should make it a horror," Felix continued. "What if people think it's fiction?"

"How do you kill a vampire?" I asked. Felix struck me as the sort of guy who pretended he read Nostradamus in the evenings, but kept a battered copy of *The Mysteries of Jacob's Island* between the pages.

"With garlic and sunlight," he said. Bingo.

"But they don't exist," I said, trying not to smile. "How do you know?"

"Because I read it in—" He flushed. "Fine, fine. I might have read a couple of penny dreadfuls when I was Jos's age, but—"

"I'm thirteen," Jos groused.

"—can't we just write a serious pamphlet? Or something like a handbook?"

"Oh, great. The Rephaim will be shaking in their boots over Felix Coombs and his *handbook*," Nell said, deadpan.

His lips pursed. "I'm serious. Binder could help you, couldn't he, Paige?"

"He doesn't like rivals. And the difference between a pamphlet and a penny dreadful is that pamphlets claim to tell the truth. Penny dreadfuls don't. We can't just shout about the Rephs in the street," I said. "A penny dreadful will turn them into an urban legend."

"What good will that do?" Nell rubbed the skin between her eyebrows. "If we never prove it—"

"We're not trying to prove anything. We're trying to *warn* the syndicate."

Opposite me, Ivy was hunched over an untouched cup of saloop, her breath steaming from below a pair of round, gold-framed sunglasses. The distinguishing feature in her photo—the bright blue hair—had already been shorn away. Bony fingers tapped the table, their knuckles raw with calluses. She hadn't said a word since my arrival, nor looked up from her saloop. She'd been treated like dirt by her Rephaite keeper. Those wounds wouldn't heal easily.

"We should do it," Jos said. "Paige is right. Who's going to listen to us if we say it's real?"

"You're all off the cot. You know that?" When she saw our faces, Nell clicked her tongue. "Fine. I guess I'll have to do most of the writing."

"Why you?" I said.

"I got a job on the silks at the Fleapit. We can use the box office to write." She took a few gulps of cola. "I reckon I can knock a decent story together. Jos can help me smooth it out."

Jos's eyes brightened. "Really?"

"Well, you're the expert." She stifled a yawn. "We'll get working on it tomorrow. Today, I mean."

Some of the tension bled from my neck and shoulders. There was no way I could work on a penny dreadful for days without Jaxon picking up on it. "It might be best to write two copies in case one gets lost. And make sure you include the pollen of the poppy anemone," I said. "That's how they can be destroyed."

"Can you buy it on the black market?"

"Maybe." I had a feeling it wouldn't be there, but black-market traders could get hold of almost anything. "How soon do you think you can get it done?"

"Give us a week. Where should we send it when it's finished?"

"Leave it at the Minister's Cat gambling-house in Soho. I know one of the croupiers there—Babs. She works from five to midnight all week. Make sure you seal it." I sat back. "How's Agatha treating you?"

Jos pulled a face. "I don't like her that much. She wants me to start singing in the market."

"The food she gives us is terrible," Felix added.

"Stop it," Ivy snapped, emerging from her silence so suddenly that Jos flinched. "What's wrong with you? She's hiding us from Rags and feeding us with money from her own pocket. Whatever she's given us, it's all she can afford. And it's a damn sight better than what the Rephaim made us eat. When they let us eat."

There was a brief silence before Jos mumbled an apology. Felix turned pink at the ears.

"Agatha's all right. Staying with her is cheaper than a doss-house." Nell scraped a hand through her hair. A forked scar caught the light, sweeping from the corner of her left eye to her earlobe. It was too pale to be recent. "Hey, who are you betting on in the scrimmage, Paige?"

"Yeah." Felix leaned toward me, rubbing his hands. "Is Binder going for it?"

"Naturally," I said.

"So if he wins, you'll be mollisher supreme." Nell's gaze was piercing. "I think you'd do a decent job as the Underlord's moll, you know. You got us all out of the colony, didn't you?"

"Julian and Liss did a lot to help. And the Warden."

"You got everyone on to the train. You got us all to keep fighting at the end. Besides, you're the only survivor who might be able to get the Unnatural Assembly to do something."

"Like anyone will, after what happened to Hector," Felix said. "Who do you think did it?"

"His mollisher," Nell said. "I always thought she adored him, but if she didn't do it, why wasn't she there?"

"Because she knew she'd be judged for it, no matter how much that lecherous, drunken bastard deserved it." All eyes turned to Ivy, who'd choked out the words as if they were barbs in her throat. "He gave Cutmouth that scar, you know. Got blind drunk one night and did it with one of his knives. She hated his guts."

It was impossible to see her eyes through those lenses, but her fingers bunched into a fist. I exchanged a glance with Nell and said, "How do you know that?"

When she replied, it was hardly loud enough to hear. "Just heard it on the streets. You hear a lot as a gutterling."

Nell looked suspicious now. "Nobody in my district thought Cutmouth hated Hector. People said she was half in love with him, if anything."

"She was not," Ivy bit out, "in love with him."

"You knew her, didn't you?" I said. Ivy looked between us. "I saw her the night Hector died. She asked where you were hiding."

Ivy opened and closed her mouth. "She asked—" Her whole body was trembling as she leaned across the table. "Paige, what did you tell her?"

"I told her I didn't know where you were."

Mixed emotions thrashed their way across her face. Like me, Nell had clearly caught a scent. "How *did* you know her?" she said.

Shoulders hunched, Ivy pulled her knuckles up to her chin. "We grew up in the same community."

"But she got the scar when she was working for Hector, and I've never heard that story about him cutting her," I said, watching her face. "So you stayed friends with her after she became his mollisher, and she confided in you about how much she hated him. That's dangerous information to share with a gutterling."

Something like panic was crashing over Ivy's features now. "You know they're saying it was you who killed him, Paige?" she said, with an edge to her voice. "Agatha told me. The Unnatural Assembly cleared you, but you were at his parlor that night. Why are you so interested in Cutmouth?"

I fell silent and leaned back in my seat, trying not to notice the look of confusion Jos gave me. She had me there. If I could prove Cutmouth guilty, it would clear my name and rid me of the need for Jaxon's "protection"—but I couldn't press Ivy in front of the others, or they'd wonder the same thing.

"I'm tired." She stood, pulling her sleeves over her shaking hands. "I'm going back to the boutique."

Without another word, she walked toward the stairs, her head ducked. As I rose to go after her, Nell caught my arm. "Paige, don't," she murmured. "She's confused. Agatha's been giving her sedatives to help her sleep."

"She's not confused."

I pulled my arm free and swung my legs over the balustrade, on to a wrought-iron stairway that zigzagged down the side of the building, leaving the other three to finish their drinks. Below me, Ivy was making her way out of the bar at top speed, back towards the inner market. I jumped down and jogged after her, into a close pathway that was packed with empty stalls.

"Ivy."

No reply. Her pace quickened.

"Ivy," I said, raising my voice, "I don't particularly care why you know Cutmouth, but I need to know where she might be hiding."

Her shaved head was bowed, her hands shoved into her pockets. When I got within a few feet of her, she turned on her heel and thrust something toward me. A switchblade glinted in the blue light of a streetlamp.

"Just leave it, Paige," she said, with a coldness I'd never heard from her. "It's none of your business."

Her face twitched and her hand trembled, but her eyes were almost black with resolve. Bruises were still fading from her skin. She kept the knife pointed at my heart until I took a step back. "Ivy, I'm not going to hurt her," I said, raising my hands a little. The knife flinched up again. "She could be in danger. Whoever killed Hector will be looking for—"

"You know what, Paige? I don't know if she loved or hated him. I thought I knew her once," she spat, "but I've always had a knack for trusting the wrong people." Her voice was threadbare. "Back off, Pale Dreamer. Run back to your mime-lord."

The knife snapped closed. She cut through a line of hanging rugs and disappeared into the market.

****

It might be nothing. Maybe Cutmouth and Ivy had been friends who'd stayed close enough to share their secrets and that was the end of it. It was clear she had some idea of where Cutmouth was, but she had no reason whatsoever to trust me with the information. She didn't know me from the next person she'd met in the colony. I was just the white-jacket from the meadow whose keeper had been kind to her.

Back near the Underground station, I climbed into a rickshaw and pulled my hood over my eyes, watching the stars sail in and out of the clouds. At least we'd all agreed on the penny dreadful. It was the most secret breed of rebellion I could imagine, putting words on paper. But hadn't Jaxon's pamphlet completely changed the structure of the syndicate? Hadn't it dictated our protocol, our rivalries, the way we looked at one another? Jaxon had been a nobody, a self-educated gutterling, yet his pamphlet had done more than any Underlord, simply because people had read it in droves and found something worth acting on.

Writing didn't carry the same risks as speaking. You couldn't be shouted down or stared at. The page was both a proxy and a shield. The thought was enough to bring a smile to my face for the first time in days, though it faded when I saw the nearest transmission screen.

The rickshaw took me back to I-4. As it rattled into Piccadilly Circus, it swung to the right, jolting me in my seat. The driver glanced over his shoulder. Automatically, I pulled my scarf up to my eyes.

A paddy wagon was parked in the center of the Circus, where a unit of Vigiles had rounded up nine voyants and bound their hands. In front of me, the driver muttered to himself, cursing his job, flexing his fingers on the handlebars. We were hemmed in by the sheer weight of traffic, brought to a standstill by a red light and the curiosity of the passengers. Another rickshaw client was standing up, craning to see the show.

". . . miscreants, seditionists, and the vilest of unnaturals," a Vigile commandant was bellowing through a speaking-trumpet. His pistol was aimed at the heart of a soothsayer, whose head was bowed. Beside him, a medium had broken down in tears of fright. "These nine traitors have confessed to being seduced by Paige Mahoney and her conspirators. If these fugitives are not found, they will spread the plague all over our citadel! They plot to destroy the laws that PROTECT you! Let London BURN before the Bloody King's legacy continues!"

The red light blinked off, and the bus moved on. Another jolt, and the rickshaw was weaving around traffic again.

"Sorry," the driver called, wiping the sweat from his forehead. "Would've taken a different route if I'd realized."

"Have you seen a lot of that?" I asked.

"Too much."

He was amaurotic, but he sounded sad. I didn't speak again. Every move Scion made was controlled by Nashira. Those nine voyants would be dead before the week was out.

The rickshaw dropped me off at the base of the Seven Dials pillar. The vibrant blues and golds on the sundials at the top had been replaced by red, white and black, with silver anchors in the middle of each oval. Chat had painted them during the night, coating their beautiful symbols with Scion's colors. It looked authentic, like something done for Novembertide, but the sight of the enemy's symbol on that pillar hurt my heart. I took out my keys and walked away from it.

When I got back to my room, I found four small Grub Street booklets on my bed. I picked up the nearest and skimmed my fingers over it. *The History of the Great Syndicate of London: Volume I.* This must be what Jaxon had meant by "homework." I sat down in my armchair and opened it.

Originally, the clairvoyant people of London had only ever met in small groups. There had been a few large gangs with voyant members, like the Forty Elephants, but it was a "mirror-reader" named Tom Merritt who had stepped up and taken charge of it all in the early 1960s. Interesting that the first Underlord had been a soothsayer, the lowest of Jaxon's orders. Along with his lover, the "flower-caster" Madge Blevins, he'd divided the citadel into sections, created the black market, and given each clairvoyant a job. The most committed were raised to positions of power, becoming the first mime-lords and mime-queens. In 1964, his work was done. He declared himself Underlord, and Madge his faithful mollisher.

It was strange to see a record that didn't use the Seven Orders classification system. *Mirror-reader* and *flower-caster* had long since been replaced by *catoptromancer* and *anthomancer*. There were other archaisms scattered through the text: *numina* for *numa*, *spirit-reel* for *spool*.

The first scrimmage had been held twelve years later. Good Tom and Madge had both been killed in a freak accident, leaving the syndicate without a leader. The resulting battle for the crown—the first scrimmage—had been won by the first Underqueen, who'd called herself the Golden Baroness. She had ruled for another four years before being brutally murdered by an "axe-diviner."

*Upon the Underqueen's gruesome Demise, it was decreed by the Unnatural Assembly that her Mollisher, the Silver Baron, would inherit the Crown in the style of the deposed Monarchs of England, whose line was interrupted by the arrival of Scion (for are we not, as one Mime-Queen said, the monarchy of those who have been crushed beneath the Anchor?). From that point on, Mollishers would always inherit, except in the rare situation that both Underlord and Mollisher were killed at the same time, or the Mollisher refused or ignored their Claim.*

That might explain Cutmouth's disappearance. It was safe to assume that whoever had killed Hector wanted her dead, too. She'd chosen to go into hiding rather than announce herself to the Unnatural Assembly. When I opened Volume III, published in 2045, I clenched my jaw.

*It is in this period of our History that the great Pamphleteer, known under the pseudonym "An Obscure Writer", stepped forth to reorganize the Syndicate. In 2031, the Seven Orders of Clairvoyance—published in the pamphlet* On the Merits of Unnaturalness—*caused a minor spate of Disagreements (including the historic imprisonment of the Vile Augurs) before its implementation as the official System by which we understand Clairvoyance in the Syndicate. Grub Street is proud to have published this stupendous and ground-breaking Document. As of the present time, Obscure Writer, now formally known as the White Binder, is Mime-Lord of I Cohort, Section 4.*

"A minor spate of Disagreements"? Was that what this historian called all that senseless murder, all those gang wars? Was that what he called the divisions that still riddled us? I turned to the section on syndicate customs.

*The Scrimmage is based on the medieval art of* mêlée. *Mime-Lords, Mime-Queens, and their Mollishers fight in close Combat in a "Rose Ring," an enduring symbol of the Plague of Unnaturalness. Each of the Combatants fights for his- or herself, but a Mollisher may work with his or her Mime-Lord or Mime-Queen at any time during the battle. The last Candidate standing is declared Victor and is presented with the ceremonial Crown. From that moment, the Victor rules the Syndicate, and bears the title of Underlord or Underqueen, depending upon their Preference.*

*When there are only two Combatants left in the Rose Ring, and they are not a Mime-Lord or Mime-Queen and Mollisher duo, they must do battle to the Death in order for a final Victor to be declared. Only by using a specific invocation—"in the name of the* æther, *I, [name or alias], yield"—can a Combatant end the last fight without bloodshed. Once this word is spoken, the other Party is automatically declared Victor. This Rule was introduced by the Golden Baroness, first Underqueen of the Scion Citadel of London (ruled 1976–1980).*

Jaxon rapped on the wall with his cane. I closed the book and laid it on the nightstand.

In the office, I was hit by the waxen smell of flowers. There were cuttings all over his desk, along with a heavy pair of scissors and a length of orange ribbon. On the couch, Nadine picked through the week's earnings. She glanced at me before looking back at the pool of coins in her lap.

"There you are, Paige." Jaxon waved me to a seat. Our argument had already been forgotten. "Where did you go this morning?"

"Just to Chat's for a coffee. I woke up early."

"Don't wander off. You're far too precious to lose, O my lovely." He sniffed, his eyes bloodshot. "Wretched pollen. I'd like my mollisher's opinion, if you'd care to cast your eye over these blooms."

I sat down in the opposite chair. "I didn't have you down as a botanist, Jax."

"Not botany, darling. Custom. Each participant in the scrimmage chooses three flowers to send to Grub Street with their application. They still use the language of flowers as a tribute to the first Underlord's mollisher, who was, legend has it, a talented anthomancer." Each of the flowers had a small label. "Here are the ones I've chosen. Forsythia, to tell them how much I'm looking forward to the fight." That flower was small and yellow. "Ragged-robin, of course, for wit." A second bloom came spinning into my lap, its petals mauve and spidery. "And lastly, monkshood."

"Isn't that poisonous?"

"It is. Symbolically, it can either mean 'chivalry' or 'beware.' Nadine doesn't think I should send that one."

"No," Nadine said, not looking at him. "I don't."

"Oh, come now. It will be fun."

"Why *would* you send it?" I said. The last flower was a shapeless sort of bloom, deep soothsayer's purple in color.

"To be different, darling. Most mime-lords send begonia as a warning, but I rather like monkshood."

"If I was the one receiving it," I said, "I might think you were threatening the organizers."

"Thank you," Nadine sighed.

"Damn you, dullards. There really is not a whit of wit between you." With careful fingers, he tied a length of ribbon around the flowers and held them out to me. "Take these to the dead drop. Nadine and I have something to discuss."

Nadine dropped her chin, and her hand balled into a fist on the arm of the chair. It was tempting to stay and listen in, but my better side told me not to.

Rain spat down from a layer of cloud. I checked the street for Vigiles and ducked out of the doorway, pulling a hood over my hair. Book Mews was a deserted alley just north of Seven Dials, the perfect place for a dead drop. It was only a quick run from the den, but with Scion's increased security, even a short journey could get me killed. When I caught sight of Giles's Passage, I broke into a sprint and vaulted over the fence at the end. As soon as I reached the dead drop in Book Mews, I crammed the envelope and the posy behind a loose brick and shoved it back into place.

Two dreamscapes—armored, Rephaite dreamscapes—converged on me.

In a heartbeat, there was no air in my lungs. It clogged in my throat, almost choking me. Blood siphoned itself from my skin, toward my vitals, leaving a terrible cold in its wake. Even my dreamscape was reacting to it, throwing up barriers, thickening its defenses. *Shit.* They must have been waiting for me to leave the den alone. Now they were blocking my route back to it. If these two were in the thrall of the Sargas, I was already dead.

I wouldn't go back to the penal colony. That was all I knew, all I could think. They could take me in a body bag. I pulled two knives from my jacket before metal touched my neck.

"Put them down." There was nothing warm in that voice. "They will not help you."

"If you're thinking of taking me to Sheol I"—it came out through clenched teeth—"you can cut my throat first, Rephaite."

"Sheol I no longer serves as our penal colony. No doubt the blood-sovereign would find somewhere else to store you, but fortunately for you, I am no friend to her."

The face above me was concealed by one of Scion's exorbitant masks, the sort that reshaped the features with such subtlety it was hard to tell there was a mask at all. When a gloved hand lifted it, a chill of recognition scampered along my spine.

In the penal colony the Rephaim had always been touched by candles or torchlight, or the glow of the late evening. Always radiant, but half in shadow. By daylight, Terebell Sheratan looked almost drained. Deepest brown hair lay on her broad shoulders, and a long, elegant nose swept down from between slightly upturned eyes. Both her lips were spare, making her look disapproving. As with any Rephaite, it was impossible to tell how old or young she was.

If you'd looked closer, you would have seen that her skin was a blend of silver and copper, and her irises were full of fire. *Beautiful* wasn't the right word for her, nor for the male at her side. He was as tall as Warden, lean as a knife, with a hairless head and a complexion like argent satin. His wide-spaced eyes were the dim chartreuse of a Rephaite who had gone without feeding for a while. A long growl quaked from his throat.

"How did you find me?" I said.

Terebell swung her blade back into her belt. "You will be pleased to hear that you were difficult to find. Arcturus told us of your den's location."

Slowly, I put the knives away. "I haven't sensed your dreamscapes since you turned up at the bar."

"We have our ways of staying hidden. Even from dreamwalkers."

My hand strayed to the revolver in my jacket. "Do not make a fool of yourself," Terebell said, seeing it. "Without the red flower, you will find that we are quite immune to bullets."

Both Rephaim were wearing elbow-length, buttoned gloves. They didn't dress like monarchs any longer, but like denizens: long woolen coats, sturdy winter boots, tailored trousers. How they'd found threads that fit them so well, let alone passed through this district without attracting a Vigile, I had no idea.

"Who are you?" I said to the male.

"I, dreamwalker, am Errai Sarin. You may not have seen my kin at all during your time in the old city," he said, looking at the wall. "None of us volunteered as keepers for your Bone Season."

"Why not?" I raised a hand. "I'm here, by the way. Not hiding behind the wall."

Two hot eyes stared down at me. "Our duties," he said, "did not lie in keepership. I had several tenants from the previous season, but I seldom saw them. Myself and ten of my cousins are aligned with the Ranthen."

"That is the true name of the 'scarred ones,'" Terebell said. "I don't believe I ever formally introduced myself, dreamwalker. I am Terebellum, once Warden of the Sheratan, sovereign-elect of the Ranthen."

So she was their leader. I'd always assumed it was Warden. "I didn't realize there were more of you," I said.

"There are other Rephaim with Ranthen sympathies, though not a quarter as many as there are with blind loyalty to the Sargas."

"Alsafi and Pleione," I said, thinking back. "Were they the only others in the colony?"

"There was one more, who was . . . lost to us during our escape from the colony." Her irises dimmed. "Other than that, they were thralls of the Sargas."

Errai scanned the alleyway. "We ought to speak inside, Sovereign."

"We're not in Sheol I any more," I said. "You won't find fancy rooms and chambers in London. Just slums and 'scrapers."

"We do not require tribute. Only secrecy," Terebell said.

"It's private enough here. And with all due respect, I don't want to be in an enclosed space with you until I know what you want."

"Yes, I have observed that you climb out of all such spaces, like a spider. You scuttle. I often wonder why Arcturus chose you as his human underling."

"We didn't have much choice but to scuttle. We'd been starved and beaten for months."

"You do not have that excuse now, fed and watered as you are." She turned her back on me. "We will speak inside. You are beholden to me for shielding you from the Sargas, and I do not forget when I am owed a debt."

There was a short silence, during which I fought down my pride. These two might have news of Warden, and I wanted that more than I could ever admit to them. More than I'd admitted to myself. "Follow me," I said.

It would be a risky walk to Drury Lane. The irises of my companions were dim enough to pass as human, but their height and bearing pulled in curious looks, setting me on edge. I kept my distance and my hood pulled over my eyes. One busker dropped her tin of money when she saw them.

The abandoned music hall was another hideaway for the homeless in the winter. Scion had shut down many such establishments during the reign of Abel Mayfield, conqueror of Ireland, who had often proclaimed that all art propagated dissent. *Give them paint*, he'd raved during one speech, *and they will paint over the anchor. Give them a stage, and they will shout out treason. Give them a pen, and they will rewrite the law.*

I checked the æther, then pulled myself up to an open window. The two Rephaim watched with empty expressions, if they could be called *expressions*. Once I was inside, I opened the stiff door to let them in.

In the hall, all was still. Sepulchral, even. Walnut tables and chairs had been left abandoned, some overturned by squatters and others modestly dressed with dust sheets. The stage curtains sighed with years of dust, but the architecture was still largely intact. An old flyer clung to the threadbare carpet.

*On* Wednesday, 15th May 2047
*Witness* THE MADNESS OF MAYFIELD
*in* "BEYOND THE PALE"!
*A new comedy on recent happenings in Ireland*

My vision clinched to a narrow window. I'd had no idea that Scion denizens had been chuckling away in their music halls while we fought for our freedom from Dublin to Dungarvan. It made me think of my cousin Finn and his fiancée Kay for the first time in months. Their passion, brighter than the low sun on the Liffey. Their rage against the shadow of the anchor. To them, nothing in the world had been more important than keeping Scion out of Ireland.

Twelve years this piece of paper had been here. When I looked up, the evidence of Scion's retribution glinted back at me. Scorches on the stage curtains and carpets. Rusty stains. Chips missing from the paneled walls. Only the stupid had dared make fun of Mad Mayfield, whether amaurotic or voyant.

"This will suffice," Terebell said in a clipped tone. That patina of its history was invisible to her. "A great deal of this citadel is derelict, it seems."

"You look a bit run down yourself, Terebell," I said.

"We did not have a luxury train to take us under No Man's Land. Be grateful that we did not draw any Emite hunters to your door." Terebell held my eye contact without blinking, a disconcerting Rephaite mannerism. "Nashira is determined to reclaim you. She is in the Archon even now, urging the Grand Inquisitor to increase the intensity of the hunt."

"She knows I live in I-4." I took a seat. "Why hasn't she found me yet? The section isn't that big."

"As I said, you were difficult to locate. Nashira's puppets will not want to create further panic by having any more of a Vigile presence on the streets. They may believe that you have left I-4 for your own safety, which would be the most logical course of action for you to have taken."

"So her deal with Scion is still on."

"Of course. Weaver will not question Rephaite rule while he fears the Emim." She looked me over, like she was waiting for something fantastic to jump out at her. "You wish to destroy Nashira. So do we."

"Why can't you destroy her by yourselves?"

"There are a mere two hundred of us with Ranthen sympathies, and only a few on this side of the veil," Errai snapped. "Against the thousands of supporters the Sargas has amassed, that is a feeble number."

"*Thousands?*" I stared at them. There had only been about thirty Rephaim in the penal colony. "Please tell me you're joking."

"Jokes are the declarations of fools."

"She will gather humans, too." Terebell looked faintly revolted. "You are all so full of self-loathing, so enslaved to your guilt . . . I have no doubt the Sargas doctrine will appeal to certain humans."

The mere thought of thousands of Rephs brought tremors to my back.

"Only the Ranthen stand against the might of the Sargas," Errai said curtly. "And we want you to find the Warden of the Mesarthim for us."

I raised my head. "He's alive?"

"So we hope." Terebell's face was taut. "We failed to destroy Nashira and Gomeisa in the colony. The two of them barred themselves inside the Residence of the Suzerain, along with every loyal red-jacket that had not been killed, to wait out the destruction. Once it was clear that we would never reach them in that stronghold, Arcturus made for London to warn you of her hunt. He is an upholder of our dying movement," she said. "He must be found."

"What makes you think I have the faintest idea where he is? I haven't seen him since—"

"The Bicentenary, yes. But you do know where he is." She leaned down to meet my eyes. "You are fortunate that the Sargas have not yet heard of your golden cord with Arcturus. Breathe a word of it to any Rephaite but the two of us, dreamwalker, and I will cut out your tongue."

Warden had said that the cord had been formed when we'd saved each other's lives, three times each. "May I ask why?"

"You do not seem to understand our culture." Errai dealt me a withering look. "Any intimacy between Rephaim and humans is forbidden."

"The cord," Terebell said, "is undesirable, and a complication. Without it, however, it will take a long time for Errai and me to track him down. Perhaps too long. But you can, Paige Mahoney. You know where he is."

"He didn't teach me much about the cord," I said.

"You do not need to be taught. You are not dull-witted, and you know at least a little of how the æther works."

I pushed my hands into my pockets. "When did you last hear from him?"

"When he arrived in London, on the fifth of September. It was agreed that he would perform a séance as soon as he found you, but we never received word."

My mouth turned dry. "Are you *sure* Nashira hasn't got him?"

"She would have made it very clear if she had captured the flesh-traitor. More likely he has fallen prey to opportunistic humans."

"That doesn't seem like him," I said.

"No. It does not." There was a softness in her voice that caught me off-guard. "We may be known to you as slavers, but there is greed among humans, too. I will not see him sold like livestock to fill a callous trader's pockets." She straightened. "If you wish to see his loyalty, check the backpack you took from the colony."

"My backpack? Why?"

Terebell didn't dignify the question with an answer.

To agree would be madness. I was being hunted, I hadn't felt so much as a quiver from the golden cord, and London was too big to search alone. But there were so many questions that had gone un-answered; so much I still had to ask him. To tell him.

"Fine," I said quietly.

Errai said nothing, but I glimpsed doubt in the way he looked at Terebell. She reached into her coat and handed me two large silk pouches.

"The white contains salt; the red, pollen of the poppy anemone," she said. "Use the red pouch sparingly."

"Thank you." I tucked them both into my inside pocket. "How do I contact you?"

Terebell peeled open the door, letting watered-down sunlight into the hall. "When you find Arcturus, he will send word through a séance. In the meantime, dreamwalker, see to it that you stay hidden. If there is one thing we Rephaim excel in, it is biding our time. Nashira has plenty. She will not stop hunting you until your face is fixed in plaster in her halls."

The death masks lined up in her residence. I could never forget those sleeping faces, taken from the victims of her reign. As Terebell replaced her mask and turned to leave, Errai caught her arm.

"We must feed."

"Don't even think about it," I said.

They looked at each other and left without another word. By the time I reached the street, they were nowhere to be seen.

\*\*\*\*

Trying to find one man in the Scion Citadel of London would be no mean feat, even if he was a Rephaite. It was a sprawling snarl of streets and jostling bodies, radiating out for miles in all directions, and there was almost as much of it underground as there was above. If Warden *had* been taken by opportunist traffickers—which was possible, if he'd been dressed well and traveling alone—then they might well already be plotting to nab themselves a few more Rephaim. They would see at once that he wasn't human, that he might be worth a lot of money.

Then again, Warden wasn't exactly an easy target. He was nearly seven feet tall and muscled to match; he would have been difficult to catch and restrain. His captors must have gone prepared, which meant they'd been watching him. Someone out there knew about the Rephaim.

That night, I sat high on the rooftops of Seven Dials, watching the sun set. This was the most beautiful time of the day, when the light shone through the gaps between the buildings and turned the skyscrapers to blades of gold.

Jaxon and the others were all in the den, having spent the night feasting on real wine and smoked cheese to celebrate his application, but I couldn't bring myself to join them. It would be too obvious that my mind was elsewhere. I'd dislocated my spirit, searching within my radius for any hint of Warden's dreamscape, but he was nowhere to be found.

In the distance, I could just see a transmission screen. It cycled through the list of fugitives three times before switching back to the Scion anchor. I pulled my knees up to my chin.

I might just see him again. Arcturus Mesarthim, the mystery I'd never solved.

Nick's head appeared as he climbed on to the roof. "Paige?" he called out.

"Here."

A smile lit his face when he saw me. "Party food for you." He tossed me a package, wrapped in a cloth napkin, and sat down beside me. "He notices when you're not there, you know."

I did know. All too well. "Nick, I need you to cover for me tonight." I turned the package over in my hands. "Just for a few hours."

"Now?" He made a sound that was something between a sigh and a groan. "Paige, you're a fugitive. The most wanted person in this citadel. You can't keep going out at night."

Scion had taken many things, but they wouldn't take the night from me. "It needs to be now," was all I said.

"At least let me know where you're going."

"I'm not sure yet. Just keep an ear out for the phone booth."

Nick reclined against the chimney. My stomach was alive with nerves, but I unfolded the serviette and picked at the crystalized ginger inside.

In the distance, Big Ben began to chime out five o'clock. The SVD would be returning to their barracks for their twelve hours' rest by now. All across the citadel, their sighted, clairvoyant counterparts would be taking up their posts. Determination settled over me. It was dark enough to begin the search.

"Paige," Nick said, "I've been meaning to tell you, but with all that's happened . . . it never seemed to be the right time." The contours of his face grew deeper. "I told Zeke. When Warden took you away. I was distraught, and he was with me for a long time, and—" He coughed. "Well, it just came out."

His right hand was shaking. I covered it with mine.

"And?"

The corners of his mouth turned up, just a little. "He said he felt the same."

Behind my ribs, there was the briefest falter in my heartbeat. Nick watched me with a deep groove between his eyebrows. I leaned across the space between us and kissed his cold cheek.

"You deserve it," I said softly. "More than anyone, Nick Nygård."

A wide smile answered mine. He wrapped both arms around me and held me close, and a rich laugh rang through his whole body. The sound glowed like an ember in my chest.

"I'm happy, *sötnos*," he said. "For the first time in years, I feel like it could be all right. Everything." He rested his chin on the top of my head. "That's delusional, isn't it?"

"Definitely. But if you're both delusional together, you'll be fine."

His heart was beating fast against my ear, as if he'd run for years to reach this state of mind. "We can't tell Jaxon," he said, very quietly. "You'll keep it secret, won't you?"

"You know I will." Jaxon had always forbidden us from having *relationships*—said with a suitable measure of disgust—lasting more than a night. He'd blow a gasket at the thought of a relationship within his own gang. Given how unpredictable he'd been of late, he might even turf them both out.

We stole back through the garret window and stepped over Eliza's scattered paint palettes. The outline of a horse had been sketched out on the canvas. "Jax got her a new muse," Nick said. "George Frederick Watts, the Victorian painter."

"There's something wrong. She's not herself."

"I asked her about it, and she said she had a friend who was ill."

"'The Seven Seals do not have friends. Only those who would break us, and those who can't,'" I said, quoting Jaxon.

"Exactly. I think she's seeing someone."

"Maybe." Eliza was often approached by other voyants, usually from gangs that didn't have Jaxon's stringent rules on commitment. "But who? She never has any time to herself."

"Good point."

Nick and I parted ways on the second-floor landing. As he headed down the stairs, I noticed that the way he held himself had changed. His shoulders were relaxed, his face free of tension. He almost had a spring in his step.

Had I given the impression that I wanted him to be alone? He must have felt so guilty all this time, thinking I'd be hurt, that I might still love him in some deep vault of my heart. I knew what he was like, for ever trying to lift people's happiness on to his shoulders. There was no need for it this time. I would always adore him, but what we had was more than enough.

The others were still talking and laughing on the other side of the door, but I'd never felt less like joining them. It hurt that Nick had to hide this one source of comfort from Jaxon. Danica wouldn't be there, either, but she generally got away with it. I, on the other hand, was expected to be at Jaxon's side whenever he desired my presence. To soothe his wounds, to boost his ego, to follow his orders to the letter.

Frankly, I had better things to do.

I crouched beside the bed, where my backpack was hidden behind my trunk of market trinkets. All my possessions were still tucked into the side pocket. I searched until my fingers closed around two tiny vials, each smaller than my little finger. A scroll dangled from the red ribbon that bound them together. I unraveled it to find a note, written in a familiar hand.

*Until next time, Paige Mahoney.*

One of the vials was brimful with a lambent, yellow-green liquid. Ectoplasm, the blood of Rephaim.

When the other vial caught the light, kindling its coy glow, I knew exactly what it was. Relief welled up inside me, so pure and strong I laughed out loud. I sank on to the carpet, bared my arm, and tipped the precious vial of amaranth on to the poltergeist's mark.

Warmth flowered underneath the stone-cold skin. The twisted wound cracked open, like old paint. As I circled my finger over it, it washed away, leaving my skin smooth as buttermilk.

And just like that, Jaxon could no longer blacken my name before the Unnatural Assembly.

But Warden needed this vial. Wherever he was, he would suffer for his sacrifice.

*Until next time, Paige Mahoney.*

Next time would be now.

# 12

## Fool's Errand

London—beautiful, immortal London—has never been a "city" in the simplest sense of the word. It was, and is, a living, breathing thing, a stone leviathan that harbors secrets underneath its scales. It guards them covetously, hiding them deep within its body; only the mad or the worthy can find them. It was into these ageless places that I might yet have to venture to find Warden.

He had been looking for me; it made sense that he should have been abducted from my district. They couldn't have taken him far. Even if they had knocked him out, he was a conspicuous load to carry.

While Jaxon and the others drank themselves senseless next door, I lay on my bed and set the oxygen mask over my mouth. With my eyes closed, I reached as far as I could out of my body without leaving it. The dislocation wasn't smooth; more like trying to tear a thick, coarse piece of fabric. I'd let myself get rusty. When I finally felt the æther, it was singing with dreamscapes and spirits, as it always was in the inner citadel.

Toward the end of my time with him my sixth sense had been perfectly tuned to Warden's presence, to the point that I had some sense of his emotions. Now there was nothing.

They'd taken him too far. I sat up and pulled off the mask, frustrated. My limit was one mile. Beyond that, I couldn't sense a thing.

It would take a long time to cover the whole citadel alone, and I'd have to be alert for Vigiles. I owed Terebell a debt, but paying it could cost me my life. And Warden's, if I failed to find him. His captors—if there *were* captors—might even have taken him out of London. Smuggled him across the channel, perhaps, or just killed him and sold him to a black-market taxidermist. I'd heard of stranger things.

Out of options, I threw on my cravat and hat. As I got to the windowsill, I looked again at the ectoplasm.

Warden wasn't the type to spell out his intentions, but he wouldn't have planted such a thing in my backpack without purpose. I pushed the stopper from the second vial and knocked it back. It shocked my teeth like a mouthful of iced water, leaving an aftertaste of metal.

At once, everything sharpened. The vial slipped from my fingers and bounced off the carpet. It had the opposite effect to alcohol on my sixth sense, jolting it into hyperactivity. I felt the motions of the spirits upstairs like finger-strokes; felt the dreamscapes and the auras of the others like bright lights through the wall, screaming their emotions at me. I was a conductor, flowing with energy. I caught the wall, sick and breathless, my head whirling.

On an impulse, I submerged my sight into my dreamscape. As a dream-form, I cut my way through the overgrown poppy anemones, searching for any clue, any difference. Dusk had fallen in my mind. The flowers tangled around my knees, brilliantly red beneath the night sky. Each petal was edged with chartreuse light, as if my mind was bioluminescent. A breach between the clouds let in a single ray of light from the æther, illuminating my sunlit zone.

And there it was. Golden light was streaming from the center of my mind and blazing a path into the æther, well beyond the range of my spirit.

His blood had made him visible.

When I jerked out of my dreamscape, my hands were sweating and trembling. I threw the backpack over my shoulders and flung open the window, leaving it ajar, before I climbed the back of the den and broke into a run across the rooftops.

It was as easy as reading an internal compass. Instinctual, as though this were a path I'd walked before. I had a feeling that if I were sighted, I'd be able to see the cord with my naked eyes, like an arrow pointing me to him. Across streets, between buildings, over rooftops and under fences. I followed the call, avoiding the Vigiles, ducking into alleys and scrambling over walls. By the time I reached the edge of I-4 and climbed into a rickshaw, I knew he was close. Less than a mile. And when the rickshaw crossed into II-4, I could almost see the beacon in the æther, beckoning me to a familiar district.

Warden was in Camden.

**\*\*\*\***

The market was as hectic as ever when I arrived. It was easy to blend in with the crowd. I still walked with my head down and one hand on the pistol in my pocket. The Rag Dolls would tolerate a rival mollisher's presence if they caught wind of it, but they wouldn't let me run around unchecked. I had to get this done before the ectoplasm left my system.

As I dashed down Camden High Street, I spied Jos, wearing a peaked cap over his cornrows, perched like a curious bird on a statue of Lord Palmerston. A whisperer stood beside him, playing a slow tune on her piccolo while Jos sang in a delicate voice. A large crowd watched in reverent silence. Polyglots sang best in their own, true language—Glossolalia, the Rephaite tongue—but they could make the most grisly street ballad sound beautiful.

> *Five ravens feasted on a winter's day,*
> *On the White Keep's highest tower, so they say,*
> *When the coffin carried the queen.*

> *Not one raven chose to leave the fray*
> *While the queen turned cold down Frogmore-way,*
> *And the widow wore snow-white on the day*
> *That London was in mourning.*

> *Five ravens feasted on a summer's day*
> *On the White Keep's highest tower, so they say,*
> *When the king fled from his throne.*

> *Every raven turned and flew away*
> *While the blood turned cold down Whitechapel-way,*
> *"He was stained," they claimed, "by the Ripper's blade*
> *He is our king no more."*

At the end of the song, the crowd clapped and tossed coins at them both. Jos caught them in his hat, and the girl took a bow as the audience dispersed. The pair of them scrambled for the remaining coins and shoved them into their pockets. The girl ran off. When he spotted me, Jos waved me over.

"Hello, you," I said, and he smiled. "Who was that?"

"Just someone I busk with." He jumped down from the statue. "What are you doing here?"

"I'm looking for someone." I pushed my icy hands into my pockets. "Where are the others?"

"Ivy's at the bolthole. I think Felix is out working, too. Nell said she'd meet me to get dinner—she gets wages for doing the silks now," he added, "but she didn't show up."

"Why does Nell need to buy you dinner? Is Agatha not feeding you?"

"She gives us rice milk and bloaters." Jos looked sick at the thought. "I give the bloaters to her cat. I know it's better than what the Rephs gave us, like Ivy said, but I'm sure she could afford something else. She has a huge slice of pie and a whole spice cake every night."

Bloaters were awful. Nasty little fish from the canal, all guts and eyeballs. He was right: Agatha must be able to feed them something better than that, given all the coin they gave her.

Jos walked with me through the market, tipping his hat to the odd gutterling. I tried the golden cord again, but it was trembling now, difficult to pin down. All I knew was that Warden was close.

"Where are you going to look for this person?" Jos asked.

"I don't know yet." I scanned the nearest buildings. "How's Agatha treating you, aside from the food?"

"She's kind to Ivy, but she's quite strict with the rest of us. If we don't bring back fifty pounds a night, we don't have supper. Most of the soothsayers are too scared to busk now, thinking they might be arrested."

If only I had more money, I could get them all out of there. "How's the writing going?"

"We're nearly finished. Nell is brilliant," he said. "She could be a psychographer."

"What's the story about?"

"It's . . . well, it's sort of our story. About a Bone Season and all the humans escaping and the Rephaim coming to hunt them, but a few of them helping us, too." His dark eyes peeked up at me. "We made Liss the main character. As a tribute. Do you think that's okay?"

A tight knot pushed into my throat. Liss, the unsung hero of the slum, who had got me through those first few weeks. Liss, who had suffered every wrong with dignity. Liss, whose life had been cut short before she could break free.

"Yes," I said. "I think it's okay."

Jos looked better for the reassurance. As we walked, I cast my eye toward the beggars of this district, huddled in doorways with their threadbare blankets and half-empty tins.

Jaxon must have been like that once. Perhaps he'd spent his nights in Camden, lingering around the costermongers, hoping for a bite of hot food or a coin to buy a drink. I could almost see him: a thin, pale boy with hair he cut himself, angry and bitter, loathing himself and what circumstance had done to him. A boy who begged for books and pens as often as he did for coin. A boy with arms torn to ribbons by fingernails, plotting his escape from poverty.

But he'd made a name for himself in the end, unlike the beggars died on his streets. Any empathy he'd had for them—if ever—was gone.

In the Stables Market, I spent a few pounds on a cup of saloop, a hot penny pie, and a wedge of spice cake for Jos. He ate voraciously as we walked, hardly speaking. I thought of what Jaxon would say if he knew I was spending my wages on spice cakes for fugitive street singers ("What an abysmal waste of good coin, O my lovely"), then decided I didn't care.

I grasped the cord again. It was pointing to an enormous building that loomed over the market. A derelict, by the looks of it, though the red brick was in good condition.

"You said you were looking for someone," Jos said quietly. "Is it one of the other survivors?"

"In a manner of speaking." I nodded to the building. "What's that place for?"

"It's called the Interchange. Nobody's been allowed in there since I've been in II-4."

"Why?"

"I'm not sure, but Agatha's gutterlings think it's the Rag Dolls' den. There's a door to get into it, but they always have a guard. Nobody goes in the Interchange except them. You won't try and break in there, will you?" Jos said, looking worried. "Nobody's allowed. The Rag and Bone Man's orders."

"Have you ever seen this famous Rag and Bone Man?"

"No. The Rag Dolls tell the district what to do."

"How?"

"They call all the kidsmen and the séance-masters to a meeting and get them to spread the word. They send the dates with their gutterlings. My friend Rin said she had to take a reply from Agatha to their ringleader once. Chiffon, her name is, short for La Chiffonnière. She's the one who gets the orders from Rags."

"His mollisher," I said, remembering the Unnatural Assembly's meeting. The Lord Costermonger had said that La Chiffonnière ruled this district.

"I think so."

Interesting. *La chiffonnière* sounded French, but it wasn't a word I'd come across at school. "I might have a word with this Chiffon if I see her," I said. "How do I reach the door?"

Jos pointed. "Just go through the market and up the set of steps. There's a big sign. Another lot of steps on your left will take you to the door. The gutterlings dared someone to sneak down to it once. They never saw him again."

"Great." I took a deep breath. "I need to go, Jos. You should try and find Nell."

"I'll come with you," he said. "I can help. Agatha will only send me out to sing again."

"You're still under Scion's radar," I said. "Do you want your face to be all over London?"

"You've stayed out of their way, haven't you? And you need

someone to keep a lookout while you're searching," he said earnestly. "What if the Rag and Bone Man comes?"

My instinct told me to say no, but he had a point. "You have to do exactly as I say. Even if I tell you to leave me behind if there's danger," I said. "If I tell you to go, you run for it and find Nell. Promise me, Jos."

"I promise."

****

The arching sign must once have spelled out a name, but the years had picked the words apart. Instead of CAMDEN INTERCHANGE, it now read CA N I T CHANGE. A graffito of an inverted Scion anchor cut through the middle, and a question mark had been added at the end. Jos and I walked around the side of it until we reached the back.

"You never told me who you were looking for." Jos stepped lightly, hardly making a sound. "It's the Warden, isn't it?" When I nodded, he grinned. "The others won't be happy."

"We need some Rephaim on our side. He helped Liss," I reminded him. "He'll help us, too."

"I think he helped a lot of people. We just didn't see it."

He was right on that. Warden had certainly helped me, bringing me food and refusing to raise a hand to me, at great risk to his position.

The yard was deadly quiet. A few abandoned cars were parked on the cobblestones outside the Interchange: a derelict building, shaped like an upside-down "T," that overlooked a quiet part of the market. The whole place was boarded up; planks had even been hammered over the doors. There was no light whatsoever. Even if I somehow wormed my way inside, the interior might be fitted with alarms to prevent squatters.

"This is it," I said.

"It doesn't look like anyone lives there."

"They might just have the lights turned off." I gave him a nudge toward it. "I need you to climb up as high as you can and keep an eye out. If you see anyone coming, make a noise."

"I can use this." He held up a tiny silver crescent of metal. "Bird warbler. It's loud."

"Good idea. Just be careful."

He ran toward the building and started to climb, using windowsills and protruding bricks to steady himself. I sat by a wall and reached for the golden cord again.

Yes, he was here. I could feel his dreamscape now, an unsteady gleam.

I skirted round the edges of the building until I reached a flight of concrete steps. There were two dreamscapes at the bottom: one animal, one human. I crept down a few steps and peered into the shaft. A woman sat on a crate, smoking with one hand and adjusting a portable radio with the other. An enormous dog slept beside her, curled up in the warmth of a small bin fire. Behind the pair was a black door, daubed with a line of unintelligible red graffiti.

The woman was unreadable. Clever mime-lord. Nothing could affect her mind, not even my spirit. I could try possessing the dog and making a fuss, but the door was padlocked. The guard would only panic and run off with the key.

I retreated back to the yard and looked up at the building again. There were no other entrances. Unless . . . well, if you couldn't go over, you could usually go under.

Close to my feet was a drain. I crouched down, dropped a small stone through the gap and heard it *ping* against a solid floor.

This was no drain. It was a vent. There was open space under the Interchange, right beneath my boots. I'd heard of such passages before, of course—there was a lower world of sewers and passages beneath the streets of London, built during the monarch days—but I'd never heard of a tunnel system in Camden. I dug my fingers into the slats and pulled, but the plate wouldn't budge.

I still had no idea how to use the golden cord to communicate, but I could guess. I thought of an image, like an oracle might create *khrēsmoi*. I pictured the grille, down to the very smallest details: the cast-iron metalwork, the granite sett paving, the seams that ran between metal and stone. And as I held the image in my mind's eye, I felt him again—and this time, it was more than a sting at my senses. The lantern of his dreamscape flared to life, as if he'd woken from a deep sleep. The image I received in return was dark at the edges, like a frame from a silent film. A cell with bars. A chain. A guard with an orange aura.

I was seeing through Warden's eyes. Against all odds, I'd found him.

Jos jumped down from a ledge and ran over. "Nobody's coming. Did you find anything?" he said.

"Something." I straightened, my eyes aching. "What's on the other side of the Interchange?"

"The canal, I think."

"Let's have a look."

We climbed over a set of railings, then a brick wall, and dropped on to a towpath. A bridge curved over the dirty water, right next to the Interchange building. Jos hopped across the roofs of several narrowboats and perched on the other side of the canal.

"Look," he called, pointing. "Look from this side."

I joined him. When I faced the towpath bridge again, I saw what he meant. There was a yawning space underneath it, like the mouth of a cave, where the water disappeared under the building.

"What's that?" I said.

"Dead Dog Hole, the old canal basin." He crouched, squinting at it. "You think that's the entrance?"

"I do." There was a stack of flotsam by the nearest boat. "And I think I've got a way in."

Between us, we got a piece of wood into the water. It looked like part of a crate, large enough for one person to sit on. I'd have to find another way to get Warden out. Jos kept an eye on our surroundings, watching for passers-by as he handed me a plank to serve as a paddle.

"Should I keep watch again?" He clung to the railings with one hand. "What if the Rag and Bone Man comes?"

"I'll handle it." I grasped the sides of the wood. "You keep watch and whistle if you see them."

"Okay."

"Jos." He gave me an expectant look. "Do *not* be seen. Watch from somewhere safe. At the first sign of trouble, you run back to Agatha and pretend I was never here. Got it?"

"Got it."

He watched from the edge as I pushed off on my makeshift raft, into the absolute darkness of Dead Dog Hole.

The silence was broken only by echoing drips. Once I was out of sight of the path and the streetlamps no longer reached me, I switched on my flashlight. Riveted columns ran from the ceiling and vanished into the black water. The walls on either side of me were the red brick of the warehouse, though thick with algae and dirt. They couldn't have taken Warden this way.

Through two archways was what looked like a passage. I tossed my backpack on to the ledge. As I shifted my weight to my feet, ready to leap after it, the wood capsized. My fingers caught the stone, but most of my body plunged into freezing water. A gasp of shock escaped me. I hauled myself into the passage, my arms shaking with the effort. My wet clothes were a second skin. The toes of my boots pushed at the wall, lifting my legs clear of the canal.

I crawled a few feet and grasped two corroded iron bars. There was just enough space between them for my head and body to slip through. I peeled off my soaking jacket and tied the sleeves around my waist. My fingers were already stiffening, and my clothes reeked of whatever slime and dirt was in the water.

Why would the mime-lord of II-4 be holding a Rephaite in his compound? He had to have known what he was doing, or he would never have been able to capture one. As soon as I was through the rusted bars, I sensed the two dreamscapes. One was Warden—I recognized the arc of his mind—but the other was unfamiliar. Human. Voyant. The guard with the orange aura. Whoever had trussed Warden up down here, they didn't want to leave him alone—with good reason. I'd never seen him kill, but if he could fight the Emim, his strength must be immense. I reached into my boot for my hunting knife.

If I was discovered in a rival mime-lord's den, his hirelings would be well within their rights to drag me to the Unnatural Assembly. Or just kill me, so long as they told Jaxon about it.

My boots were soft leather; they hardly made a sound. I walked until I found myself in a man-made tunnel, a remnant of an age of mines and steam and railway wagons. The walls were tangled with chicken wire. Naked, broken bulbs hung in cages from loose wires. I moved into the blackness, avoiding the brooding spirits that drifted past. Just wisps. Nothing dangerous. Jos's dreamscape was somewhere above me. He must have climbed up to the warehouse roof.

It soon became apparent that this place was something like a maze. Perhaps it hadn't been built for that purpose, but with only the occasional glint of light to indicate where you were, it was disorienting. I took note of what was in each vault: barrels of alcohol, mattresses and lanterns, rubble and junk. Decades of accumulated scrap. A den for the Rag Dolls. It must have once have been a basement under the warehouse, but it stretched beyond the Interchange, too.

And manacles. My breath stopped in my throat.

There were *manacles* on the walls.

Jos had said that a gutterling who'd dared to come near this place had never been seen again. I moved slower, listening for footsteps. When I reached one tunnel, I could see people in the market above through circular grates in the ceiling. Their shadows flickered past. I kept close to the walls, though I doubted they could see me.

I dug a bag of climbing chalk from my backpack and drew a tiny line on the wall. As I followed the passages, I marked each one with chalk. One unventilated room was enormous: a great underground vault, at least a hundred feet long, not dissimilar to the Garden's market cavern. The ceiling was low, with vast, sweeping arches. It looked as if it was being refurbished. A spotlight cart stood in the far corner, casting harsh electric light through the arches. Crimson curtains had been hung over the walls, some half-attached to rails, and tables and chairs scattered around the place. I checked the æther and darted across the stone floor, heading for a passage on the other side of the vault.

A thin, filthy cat bounded from under a table and streaked past me with a yowl. I slammed my back against the wall, my heart clobbering my ribs. The animal disappeared into another tunnel.

If a cat had found its way down here, there must be another way out. It was a small comfort in this place. I could imagine them dragging Warden's dead weight through the passages. *Nearly there.* I pictured the room with arches, but got nothing in return.

The fuzzy sound of a radio soon came to my attention, tuned to Scion's only news station. I switched off my flashlight and peered around the corner. An old signal lantern sat on the floor in the next tunnel, illuminating the door of Warden's prison.

The guard was a slim man with artificially orange hair, slouched against the wall, bobbing his head to the radio. A few days' worth of stubble had crawled down his neck, right to the hair on his chest, and a coat of dirty grease lay on his skin. A summoner. I'd have a big fight on my hands if I faced him. Summoners could pull spirits across vast distances if they knew their names.

I fitted myself into an alcove. Like an arrow, my spirit streaked through the wall and into the guard's dreamscape. By the time his defenses came up, I'd already nudged him into his twilight zone. When I snapped back, my temples thumping, I heard a distinct sound of a limp body collapsing on stone.

When I reached the tunnel, I found him on the floor, face down. He was unconscious, but breathing. There was no padlock on the door; just a chain that prevented it from opening more than a few inches. Nobody had expected a break-in. I pulled away the chain and stepped into the cell.

13

# Thief

Handcuffed to a pipe in the light of a dead-flame lamp, his head hanging between his shoulders, Arcturus Mesarthim looked nothing like the keeper I'd shared a tower with for six months. His clothes were plastered with filth and dust, and beads of water seeped from his hair. I dropped my flashlight and fell into a crouch beside him.

"Warden."

He didn't answer.

Fear came snaking around my chest, pushing against anger. Someone—multiple people, by the looks of it—had beaten the shit out of him. His aura was a candle in a draft, flickering and weak.

White breath billowed past my lips. My boots could hardly grip the icy floor around him. With a running nose and trembling hands, I grasped his shoulders and shook him. No breath lifted his chest.

"Warden, wake up. Come on." I tapped his cheek, hard. "*Arcturus.*"

At the sound of his true name, his eyelids parted. A dim, yellowish light bled into his irises.

"Paige Mahoney." It was almost too soft to hear. "Good of you to come to my rescue."

Relief crashed over me. "What did they do to you?" I could hardly get the words out through my chattering teeth. "Does the guard have the key to your chain?"

"Leave the chain." A rattle escaped his throat. "You ought to leave. My captors will return before long."

"I'll be the judge of when I leave."

Outside the door, I rolled the guard on to his back and rummaged through his pockets. With one heavy key I unlocked Warden's manacle, freeing his wrist. I scooped an arm around his shoulders, trying to pull him into a sitting position, but he was a dead weight.

"Warden, you *have* to move. I can't lift you." I pulled the lamp closer. Green-black stains were blooming under his skin in curious patterns, like fern frost. "Tell me where you're hurt."

His gloved fingers twitched. I turned my flashlight downward. A bangle of scarlet poppy anemones hung on his left wrist, the sort of thing I'd often twisted together with daisies as a child. The whole of his arm was peppered with necrotic tissue, shot through the smooth dark gold of his skin.

"They are like irons." His eye-light was fading. When I reached for the first chain, it flared up again. "Don't."

"We don't have time to—"

"I have not fed in days." The last word ended in a growl. "The hunger is taking me."

"It isn't taking you anywhere. I am." I took his face between my hands. "Terebell and Errai sent me to find you."

Some of the light returned to his gaze. "You look different," he said. "The mind-sickness . . . I will not remember you, Paige . . ."

He was delirious. "Warden, what do you need? Salt?"

"That will wait. I have no bites. It is the fever in my mind that must be dealt with first."

"You need aura," I realized.

"Yes." Each breath ground through his throat. "They have tormented me for weeks, letting me take only a little at a time . . . keeping it just out of my reach . . . I confess, I am starving. But I will not take yours."

I smiled grimly. "Good thing there's an alternative, then."

The guard really was having a bad night. I took him by the wrists and hauled him into the cell on his back. Dry groans punctuated each pull on his arms. I shackled him to the pipe and held my knife to his throat. Warden watched in hungry silence.

"Did this one beat you?" I said.

"On multiple occasions."

The guard stirred. Blood slithered from both his nostrils, right down to his chin. "The hell did you do to me?" His breath smelled of stale coffee. "My head . . ."

"You work for the Rag and Bone Man," I said, smiling. "Tell me who he is, or I'll ask my friend to drain you very, *very* slowly of your aura. How would you like to be amaurotic, summoner?"

When he found a knife at his throat and a chain at his wrist, the guard struggled. My knee pinned his free hand. "Better rottie to the core than sleeping with the bloaters," he hissed. "Rags will throw me in with weights on my ankles if I say a word." He took in a deep breath and shouted, "Sarah Whitehead, I summon you to—"

I slapped a hand over his mouth.

"Try that again and we'll skip the draining," I said, leaning close to him. "I'll just shoot you. Understood?"

He nodded once. As soon as I removed my hand, he said, "Bitch."

Warden played his part beautifully. He shifted toward the guard on all fours with the slow precision of a predator, his pale yellow eyes like a wolf's in the gloom. Muscle shifted under his skin. The man yanked at his chain in a panic, kicking at the floor. Even I shivered. Rephaim looked relatively human by daylight, but in the dark, they lost the veneer of humanity.

"Call him off." The closer Warden came, the more the guard pulled at his manacle. "Call him off, brogue!"

"I'm afraid he's not a dog," I said, "but you've treated him like one, haven't you?" My knife dug into his neck. "Tell me who the Rag and Bone Man is. Tell me his name and I might let you live."

"I don't *know* his name!" he shouted. "None of us know his name! Why would he tell us?"

"What was he planning to do with the Rephaite? Who's he working with? Where is he now?" I grasped his throat and angled the knife toward the underside of his chin. "You'd better get talking, summoner. I don't consider myself patient."

He spat at me. Warden's face turned utterly cold. "You'll get nothing out of me," the guard repeated. "Nothing."

I pushed my spirit against his dreamscape, hard. More blood swelled from his nostrils. "Even if I wanted to, I couldn't tell you," he choked. "He's only here once in a blue moon. We take orders from his mollisher." When Warden moved toward him again, he gasped for air. More than air. "You said you'd call him off!"

"I didn't, actually," I said.

There was no violence. Nothing but a look. Warden stared at the guard and breathed in. His chest expanded, and his eyes scalded like signal lights before filling up with vivid orange. The guard slumped against the frozen pipe, his aura thin as tissue paper.

A ripple went right the way through Warden's body. Ectoplasm glowed in the veins beneath his skin, which suddenly appeared translucent. I stayed where I was, keeping a few feet between us. When I lifted the flowers from his arm, a deep growl rumbled up from his chest.

"My captors ventured outside for food," he said. "They will not be long."

"Good. I'd love to meet them."

"They are dangerous."

"So am I. So are you."

His eyes were growing brighter. They flooded me with the stranger memories of my imprisonment. A gramophone's blacklisted music, telling lovers' stories to the gloom. A butterfly held out inside caged fingers. His lips on mine in the Guildhall, hands gliding over my hips, my waist. I tried to focus on removing the next flower chain, but I was too aware of his movements now. Each rise and fall of his chest, each flex of tendon in his neck.

Above us, the pale moon was just visible between the metal slats. When there were no chains left, I took my burner from my backpack and stuck a new module between my teeth while I pried the back cover off. Warden let his head fall back against the wall. I stayed beside him as I called the I-4 phone booth, hoping on hope for a signal. We weren't too far underground.

"I-4," said a courier's voice. The line was bad, but I could just about hear.

"The Red Vision," I said. "Quickly."

"Bear with me."

I didn't have much time to bear with him. Warden's eyes strayed to the summoner again, to the wisp of aura that still clung to him. After a minute, Nick spoke: "Everything okay?"

"I need a lift," I said.

"Where are you?"

"Camden. The warehouse at the top end of Oval Road."

"Ten minutes."

The line went dead. I pulled out the identity module and slid it into my back pocket, then took the signal lantern in one hand and hoisted Warden's heavy arm around my neck. He grasped my shoulder as he stood. The weight of his hand sent tremors down my sides.

"Where is the way out?" he said, his voice low.

"I came in through Dead Dog Hole. The canal basin."

"I was taken through the black door, but the unreadable guard is always there. I presume we will not be leaving through the basin."

"We wouldn't get through," I said.

"Perhaps there is a way to access the warehouse, as this was once its basement." His grip on my shoulder tightened. "You still have the guard's keys, I take it."

"Naturally. Can you walk?"

"I must."

Our progress through the tunnels was slow: Warden was sporting a bad limp, unable to walk on either leg for long. It seemed incredible that a tiny red bloom, as light as a feather, could do so much damage to a Rephaite's anatomy. They were muscular, statuesque creatures, impossible to take down with physical force, yet the key to their downfall could fit in my palm. I handed him the lantern and wrapped my free arm around his waist. His proximity made me cold, then warm. I could feel the labored weight of his breaths against my hair.

The next tunnel curved around a corner. The lantern's light seemed very small, casting a tiny circle around us. I shone the flashlight beam up a vent, but it was a dead end.

"How did the Rag Dolls capture you?"

"With poppy anemone. They must have been watching me for some time, marking my movements. Or perhaps they knew, somehow, that I would go to I-4," he said. We kept going, turning into yet another passage that looked identical to the last. "They came for me during the day, when I was resting. They blindfolded and bound me with the flower, then transported me here in a large vehicle."

My heart rate was climbing. The Rag Dolls shouldn't know a thing about the Rephaim, let alone how to capture them. When I saw a familiar chalk mark, I wilted.

"We're going in circles."

Warden was growing stronger; I could feel it in his hand, its grip. "Do you sense Dr. Nygård?"

"Yes. He's close." I tensed. "There's someone else, too."

"With him?"

"No. They're coming from a different direction." A small group of dreamscapes had detached themselves from the hive of the market. "Three people."

As soon as he said it, a whistling came from above. A bird's call in the middle of the night. Jos. I let go of Warden and took out my revolver. "Are any of the guards full-sighted?"

"No. They are all half-sighted."

Good. It took effort for a half-sighted voyant to keep their sight focused for too long. In the dark, we could elude them.

A door clanged in the distance. Warden grasped my arm and swung me into an alcove, so my back was pressed against his chest. ". . . feed him at some point," someone was saying. A man, gruff and loud, with a shadow of the East End in his accent. Each word echoed through the damp tunnels. "He almost sapped Cloth last time."

"You were holding him too close." A woman. Londoner, like the man, but I couldn't place the district. "They can only feed at a certain distance."

"You sure none of ours have squealed about him?"

A sharp laugh. "Who would they squeal at? The Underlord is dead. Without him, the Unnatural Assembly is a shambles. Not that it was ever more than that."

I kept a tight hold on my revolver. At my side, Warden leaned heavily against the wall. His eyes were already cooling back to chartreuse.

A shout of alarm rang from the cell, so close to our hiding place that I started. "What the hell is this?" the man roared. "Where's the creature?" Rattling chains. "*Where is it?* You think we paid you to lose our leverage?"

My mouth was dry as dust. "Chiffon," the guard groaned, "some . . .
brogue bitch came in and took him away. Her aura was . . . red."

The woman must be La Chiffonnière, the Rag and Bone Man's
mouthpiece in the district. I wanted to see what the hell she had to
say for herself, but Warden was too weak to leave alone.

"And where's your brogue now?" Footsteps. "What did she look
like?"

"Black hair and a red cravat over her face. She's gone."

"Is she, now?" Chiffon said, her voice strangely flat. "Then
consider yourself unemployed."

A single gunshot echoed through the catacombs. One of the
dreamscapes faded from my perception. "His nose was bleeding,
and we're looking for a brogue with a red aura. Sounds like the Pale
Dreamer's our girl," Chiffon concluded.

*Shit.*

"Rags will have someone killed for this," the man said. "We've
just lost our bargaining chip."

"We weren't the ones guarding him. Besides, I doubt the creature's limped too far. We can still catch him."

"So long as we find him." Footsteps again. "We should keep our
sights up."

Warden took my arm. We kept moving, staying close to the walls.
I flicked my torch beam at them, searching out familiar markers. My
feet were light, but Warden's injuries made him cumbersome. Each
footfall was like a homing beacon, telling the pair where we were
heading, but the clinking jewelry the captors were wearing was just
as useful. Every time we heard metal, we changed direction.

Soon enough we reached the main vault, where I killed the light
and reached for Warden's hand. His fingers slid between mine. As
we passed the spotlight cart, I pulled out the power cord, throwing
us into total darkness again. Warden kept going, his eyes pinpricks
of faint light in the black. I let him lead me. We'd reached another

passage and concealed ourselves behind what felt like a velvet curtain by the time the two strangers reached the vault.

"Now someone's janxed the light."

"Shh. Even dreamwalkers breathe," Chiffon whispered.

I risked a look through the curtains. The two of them walked past with their flashlights, searching behind curtains and under tables.

"Now, where would a giant hide, if he could?" Chiffon passed right by our hiding place, but her senses weren't as keen as mine. "In the biggest room of the house, I'd say."

Warden was still and silent. Beside him, I felt deafeningly human, each breath like a draft.

"There's nowhere to run, Rephaite." The man was close. "All the exits are blocked. If you don't come out, I'll take my sweet time killing your friend. You can keep her in your cell, if you like . . ."

Sweat slithered down my back. I hooked my finger over the gun's trigger. The last thing a murder suspect should be doing was shooting someone, but I might not have a choice. Beside me, Warden touched my arm and nodded toward something that I'd thought was a table. A jukebox was concealed behind the curtain.

The other abductor's heavy footsteps were getting closer. With a quick movement, Warden flicked on the machine, and an old recording fanfared from inside it. My skull rang like a bell as a woman sang out in jubilant, trilling French, accompanied by what sounded like an entire orchestra. Nothing could be heard but the song. We moved to the left, behind the nearest curtain, and edged along the wall. I sensed the two dreamscapes shifting in the other direction.

The vault was a cavern of echoing voices; it was impossible to tell where the music was coming from. "Find it," Chiffon snapped.

There was another tunnel across the vault. We'd have to make a run for it. Treading lightly, I slipped out from behind the curtain. I could just make out the back of the man's head in the flashlight's beam, with short hair that gave way to a bald patch. Warden followed me. We almost reached the tunnel before the spotlight cart blazed back to life, blinding me, and two masked figures whipped around to face us.

"Here she is. The red brogue and her Rephaite," the man said.

The painted masks had mouths that looked as if they had been slashed open, with plastic, sharpened teeth bared in grins. Light glared behind them. Without a moment's hesitation, I flung my spirit straight at the man's dreamscape. He fell back with a scream that raised every hair on my body. As soon as I was back in my own skin, I grabbed Warden by the jacket and ran, blinking lights from my eyes.

Chiffon sent a spool after us. I deflected two drifters and fired a bullet over my shoulder before Warden pulled me to the left, into another tunnel that forced us into single file. I didn't dare stop.

"There's no way out, you know," Chiffon called, laughing. "It's a labyrinth down here!"

Every tunnel looked the same. The abductors' voices boomed in the darkness, sending fear wrenching through my abdomen. Somewhere, a dog was barking, searching for the intruder. And then there was light, right at the end of a long, narrow passageway. I sprinted toward it, Warden limping behind me. On either side of us, crates were piled up to the top of the tunnel. Before I could ask, Warden acted. Even with his strength depleted, he was much stronger than I was. He took hold of a crate and pulled it out from the bottom of a stack. In the narrow tunnel, the noise they made as they crashed down was deafening. Glass shattering, wood breaking apart, manacles and chains rattling against stone. A flood of red wine came pouring from the largest. My boots thumped up a set of steps until I crashed headlong into a set of bars. I picked through the keys, my fingers shaking.

Spools came flying past me, catching the edges of my dreamscape. I crouched down and flung one back, smashing memories into the man's dreamscape. He was bleary-eyed, confused by the shock to his system. A heavy crate crashed down on his legs. This time his scream was cut short.

The right key was made of tarnished steel. As soon as the gate opened, I let Warden through and locked it behind us.

The Interchange building was enormous, derelict and empty. Without stopping for breath, I fired a few bullets into a tall window. When the last one hit, the glass fell from the frame in a cascade of shards. Warden gave me a leg up, and I climbed over the windowsill, swinging my head under a wooden plank. The dog was still barking below, but they'd have to find another way to reach us now.

"Come on." I grasped Warden's elbows. "Just a bit farther. Climb."

His jaw was stiff and his neck strained with the effort, but he got himself through the gap. Even after taking aura, he was so weak. I hooked my arm around him again, and this time he put his weight on me.

A black car with tinted windows was parked on the cobblestones. Nick flashed the headlights. Relief filled me to the brim. He reached over and opened the back door.

"Is anyone following you?"

"Yes. Quickly, go."

"Fine. But—wait, Paige, what are you—?" He stared as I helped the exhausted Warden into the car. "Paige!"

"Just drive." I pitched myself in after Warden and closed the door with a thump. "Drive, Nick!"

A figure came running around from the front of the warehouse, slim and quick, a sawn-off shotgun in both hands. Nick didn't ask questions. His hand yanked at the gearstick, and his foot slammed into the accelerator. The car's engine was twenty years old and janxed to hell, hauled from a pile of scrap at the Garden, but by some miracle, it worked. With a jolt that snapped my teeth together, it roared into reverse. The masked gangster fired, but the range of the shotgun was too short. Nick pulled at the wheel, spinning the car toward the main road.

The gangster lowered the shotgun. Several other people sprinted out from the warehouse, all in those same terrible masks. Together, they converged on a black van.

Sweat stood out on Nick's brow. Our car was a painted rust bucket, used only in emergencies; it was in no state for a chase. He kept his foot down, taking us out of sight of the warehouse and down Oval Road, but he didn't drive straight toward I-4. Instead, he pulled straight around on a crescent.

"We'll double back on them," he said. "Go through the market and down to I-4 through the backstreets."

I looked over my shoulder. The van's red taillights slashed past with a scream of tires, down the road they thought we'd taken. "Watch out for others," I said. "They might have more cars."

"You could have told me you were doing this," Nick gripped the steering wheel with white knuckles. "Who the hell were those people? Rag Dolls?"

"Yes."

Nick swore. Only when he switched on the heating did I realize I was still drenched to the bone and freezing cold. Instinctively, I shifted closer to Warden. Shallow breaths lopped past my ear. As the car continued toward I-4, I pulled the used identity module out of my pocket and flicked it through the window, into the gutter. Nick glanced into the rearview mirror.

"Before you were captured," I said to Warden, "where were you sleeping?"

"An electrical substation on Tower Street." His voice chafed his throat. "We monsters do not sleep on feather beds. Not anymore."

Tower Street was right by the den. If I'd been in Seven Dials when he arrived, I might have sensed his presence before it was too late. His head fell back against the seat, and I felt his consciousness fade. "He can't go to Dials," Nick said to me, looking straight ahead.

"I know."

"Or my apartment."

"He's going to a doss-house. There's nowhere else to go."

****

"That was too close, Paige. Far too close."

In the smallest room in a Soho doss-house, the lights were off and the curtains drawn. We both looked at the bed, where Warden was in a deep sleep. I'd helped him out of his filthy coat, but he'd deposited himself on the bed and withdrawn into his dreamscape before we could do anything more.

"He can't stay here forever."

"Most of the Rephs want him dead, and Scion will be after him." I spoke softly. "We can't throw him out to die."

"He'll have to leave at some point. Neither of us can afford to pay his rent."

With a sigh, I scraped a hand through my limp hair. It was hard to remember a time when I hadn't been regularly caked in dirt and sweat. "Nick," I said, "there's a link between the syndicate and the Rephaim. There has to be, or they wouldn't have known how to capture Warden. I have to find out how much more they know. And get the fugitives out of that district."

He frowned. "You're not going back to II-4, Paige. The whole district will be looking for you."

"Do you think they'll go to the Assembly?"

"No, I don't. They have no evidence that you were there, and I doubt they want to broadcast the fact that they had someone tied up in their den."

I studied his face. "You've been in the syndicate longer than I have. What do you know about this guy?"

"The Rag and Bone Man? Not much. He's been mime-lord of II-4 since I joined the syndicate."

"Have you ever seen him?"

"Not once. Even by the Unnatural Assembly's standards, he's considered fairly reclusive. He and the Abbess have bad blood between them, though nobody knows why." His voice was low. "You're already too caught up in this, Paige. If these people had the guts to capture a Rephaite, they'll have the guts to do the same to you. I know you'll ignore me, but . . . don't do anything stupid."

I offered a tired smile. "As if I ever do."

He clicked his tongue. His finger rubbed a spot just above his left eye in a soothing, circular motion I recognized. Migraines struck him once every few weeks, sometimes accompanied by visions, leaving him bedbound for days at a time. Jaxon always declared that a "headache" was nothing to gripe about, but Nick went to hell and back on those days.

"The thing I'm trying to understand," he said, his face tight, "is how a syndicate mime-lord could know about the Rephaim. Has anyone ever escaped from a Bone Season before?"

My pulse thickened. "Two people. Twenty years ago."

Out of all the prisoners, only two had escaped from the massacre that followed the rebellion. One had been a child; the other, the traitor who had told Nashira about the insurrection. She'd killed every human and tortured every Rephaite involved in it, including her blood-consort.

"Warden might know something," I said. "I need some time with him." When he gave me a look, I raised my eyebrows. "Nick, I was trapped with him for six months. Another day won't kill me."

"He won't wake for a while. Come back to the den for a few hours. Jaxon's been asking about you all day."

"I'm covered in canal. He'll notice."

"I'll keep him busy while you change."

I glanced at Warden. "Give me a moment."

His mouth thinned, but he didn't argue.

As soon as he was gone, I sat on the edge of the bed and lifted my hand to Warden's coarse hair. His body was heavy with sleep, his face turned into the pillow. He didn't make a sound, or move an inch. If anyone discovered him here, in this weakened state, he wouldn't last a minute.

The fact that syndicate members knew about the Rephaim was disturbing. One of the survivors of the first Bone Season rebellion could well have returned to London and concealed himself deep in the catacombs of Camden, where nobody could get to him. I got the sense that I was only scratching the surface of these machinations.

Against my better judgment, I touched the backs of my fingers to Warden's cheek. His face still bore that unusual pattern of bruising, but it was warmer now. He stirred, and his eyelids flickered. My heart pulsed in my fingertips. I remembered when he was wounded the first time, when I'd treated him instead of killing him. Something about this Rephaite had made me want to save him, in that city between life and death. Something that had overridden my natural instinct to destroy him from the inside out.

I hadn't thought of what would happen when he was back in my life, or how he would fit into it. Arcturus Mesarthim belonged to the halls of Magdalen, to red curtains and firelight talks and music from a century ago. To think of him walking the streets of London was almost impossible.

Whatever these people were planning, they didn't have him any longer. I took out a pen and scribbled a note.

*Back later. Don't open the door.*

*Oh, and do me this honor: survive the night. I'm sure you'd rather not be rescued twice.*

*—Paige*

# 14

## Arcturus

When he woke the next afternoon, he did not find himself chained to a pipe in an underground cell. He did not find himself in the custody of the Rag Dolls, starved and beaten at their pleasure. Instead he found himself on a box-spring mattress that wasn't quite long enough for him, with his neck supported by a wilted pillow and a vase of plastic geraniums on the nightstand.

"Well," I said, "this feels familiar."

He looked up at the ceiling: the branching fractures in the plaster, the damp that stained the corners.

"This place does not," he said.

His voice was exactly as I remembered it, dark and slow, rising up from the depths of his chest. A voice that was felt as well as heard.

"You're in I-4, in a doss-house." I struck a match. "Not exactly Magdalen, but it's warmer than the streets."

"Indeed. Certainly warmer than the desolate tunnels of Camden."

As I lit the tall candle on the table, Warden pushed himself on to his elbows and flexed his shoulders. All the bruises had faded in the hours he'd been asleep. "What time is it?" he asked.

"Four in the afternoon. You've been dead to the world."

"I did wake for long enough to read your note. Touché," he said. "May I ask where you went?"

"Seven Dials."

"I see." Pause. "You have returned to Jaxon's service, then."

"I had no choice."

We looked at each other for a long time. So much had happened in the weeks since the escape. We'd never met on neutral ground before.

Over time I'd grown used to his appearance, but now I forced myself to look at him as if for the first time. Irises like flame behind stained glass, pupils of a black that caught no light. The lines of him, hard yet soft: the bow of lips, the cut and curve of jaw. Brown, uncombed hair that brushed the top of his spine and fell over his forehead, oddly human. He hadn't changed at all, except for a slight loss of radiance.

"I take it there's danger," I said.

"Indeed. I planned to be the first to warn you, but it seems the Grand Inquisitor has made the peril clear." His gaze darted over my face. "London suits you."

"Regular meals do wonders." I cleared my throat. "Drink? Wine's in short supply, but there's delicious tap water."

"Water would be welcome. My captors were not as liberal with their supplies as I would have liked."

"I had your clothes laundered. They're in the bathroom."

"Thank you."

I focused on pouring water into glasses as he rose. Considering how prudish the Rephaim had been in the colony, with their gloves and high collars, he seemed quite blasé about nakedness. When he returned, in the plain, black clothes of an amaurotic trader, he sat down on the couch opposite me, keeping the table between us. A re-enactment of Magdalen, minus our colony uniforms. His shirt hung open, exposing the hollow of his throat.

"I confess myself impressed that you found the catacombs," he said. "I did not think it likely that I would be discovered."

"The golden cord helped." I nodded to the candle. "Terebell wants to know where you are. You can do a séance here."

"I would like some time to speak with you first. Once the Ranthen know that you have freed me, it will be difficult for us to be alone together without arousing suspicion."

"'Suspicion,'" I repeated.

"Do not think that the masquerade ends here, Paige. We have merely exchanged one style of dance for another. It is not only the Sargas that fear any prolonged contact between Rephaim and humans."

"They know about the golden cord."

"They know that you started the revolt. Terebell and Errai know about the golden cord. And they know of a Sargas rumor of something more between us." His gaze held mine. "That is all they know."

My heartbeat stumbled.

"I see," I said.

I handed him a glass. Even here, far from the penal colony, this simple exchange felt taboo. "Thank you," Warden said. With a nod, I sat back on the couch and pulled my knee to my chest.

"Are the Sargas looking for you?"

"Oh, I imagine Situla Mesarthim is tracking me as we speak. I am a flesh-traitor. A renegade," he said, indifferent as ever. "All Rephaim have been told of my disloyalty."

"What does being a flesh-traitor entail?"

"It is to be denied access to the Netherworld for all eternity. To be non-Rephaite. A blood-traitor betrays the ruling family, but the flesh-traitor betrays all Rephaim. To earn these punishments, I committed one of the very highest flesh-crimes. I consorted with a human."

With me. "You knew that was the consequence."

"I did."

It was quite a statement, but he delivered it as though he were commenting on the weather.

"Nashira is pressuring the Grand Inquisitor to pour all his resources into finding the fugitives. She already has two survivors of the escape in the interrogation rooms."

"How do you know?"

"Alsafi is one of ours. He is still with Nashira, feeding us information. I do not know the names of the prisoners, but I will endeavor to find out." A shadow crossed his face. "Is Michael safe?"

Michael had been loyal to him long before I had. "We were separated at the Tower," I said. "The Guard Extraordinary killed most of the people who took the train."

His knuckles strained against his gloves. "How many are left?"

"Twelve escaped. Five left that I've seen, including me."

"Five." A hollow chuckle rolled from his throat. "I had better abandon the business of sedition."

"It was never your aim to save voyants. It was mine." I studied him for a long time. I'd forgotten how he looked at me. As if he could see straight into the heart of my dreamscape. "I have so much to ask you."

"We have time," he said.

"I can only spend a few more hours here. Jax will be back from his meeting by midnight. He'll ask questions if I'm gone again."

"Then I will ask one first," Warden cut in. "Why escape Nashira only to give yourself back to Jaxon?"

That got my back up. "I haven't given myself to anyone. I'm staying in his good graces."

"I heard you tell him on the meadow that you had had enough of slavery. This is a man who threatened to kill you if you did not return to his employ. Tell me, why should he not beg for *your* good graces?"

"Because I'm not the mime-lord of I-4. Because I'm the Pale Dreamer, Jaxon Hall's mollisher. Because without Jaxon Hall I am absolutely nothing. And I need status like you need glow." I was biting out each word. "I can't leave Jaxon. That's just the way it is."

"I did not think you had such respect for the status quo."

"Warden, my face is all over this citadel. I needed protection."

"If you have gone to him only out of necessity," he said, "I take it you are thinking of some way to gain your independence."

"I could rob the Bank of Scion England and become the richest woman in London, but I have no good weapons and no soldiers to help me. Revolution isn't quite as easy as treason." When he said nothing, I sat back. "I do have one idea. The Underlord was murdered. If I can win the scrimmage to replace him, I'll be Underqueen."

"The Underlord chose a portentous time to die." He raised his glass to his lips. "I take it you do not know the identity of the murderer."

"Not exactly. The man who captured you might have something to do with it. Did you overhear anything in the catacombs?"

"Nothing of use, but we know Nashira has a vested interest in disbanding the syndicate. How was the Underlord killed?"

"Beheaded in his own parlor. His gang had their throats cut and their faces disfigured, Ripper-style. It wasn't just a hit," I said, with certainty, "or the killer would have taken everything valuable. Hector had a solid gold pocket watch. That was still on the body."

"A statement, then." Warden drummed his fingers on the table-top, a habit of his. "Decapitation is the favored execution style of the Sargas dynasty in the corporeal world. It signifies the removal of the dreamscape. It is quite possible that a Rephaite did it. Or a human in the thrall of the Sargas."

"One human couldn't have taken down eight people," I said.

"But a Rephaite could," he said. I hadn't considered it before. It would have been painfully easy for someone of Warden's size and strength to murder eight drunk voyants. "You seem to know a great deal about the scene of the crime."

"I found the bodies. Jaxon sent me to pacify Hector. He was about to expose a part of our trading network."

Warden clasped his hands. "Have you thought, then, that Jaxon himself might have been involved?"

"He was at Seven Dials the whole time. I'm not saying he wasn't indirectly involved, but I could say that about anyone." I rubbed my temples. "I'm the prime suspect on the streets. And I need to clear my name if I'm ever going to win the voyants' respect."

"I see."

The blaze in his eyes set me on edge. I had to wonder how much he trusted me, after everything. His arms were still in a sorry state, blackened and lustrous from the elbow down.

"What do you need?" I nodded to them. "Blood and salt?" He wasn't having my blood again, but Nick could procure a pack from Scion.

"Salt should suffice. The half-urge remains on the surface."

There was a small cupboard in the corner, filled with odds and ends for tenants to cook their own meals. I emptied what was left of a salt cellar into a glass and handed it to him.

"Thank you." Warden hauled one heavy arm on to his lap.

"Do you have any more amaranth?"

"No. Unless the Ranthen have more, it will have to be harvested from the Netherworld. In any case," he said, "amaranth is no remedy for the half-urge. It heals spiritual injuries."

"Thank you for the vial. It came in handy."

"I thought it might. You seem to attract injuries in the manner that a flower attracts bees."

"Comes with the crime." Without thinking, I touched the scar on my cheek. "The ectoplasm showed me the cord."

"Yes," he said. His attention was focused on his arm now, measuring out saline. "Ectoplasm heightens your sixth sense. Mine in particular allowed you to see the link between us."

"Yes," I said. "The Mysterious Link Between Us."

He glanced up at me. The necrosis in his arms was already melting away. It was almost disturbing how quickly they healed.

"The fugitives have written a kind of instruction manual about how to fight off Rephaim and Emim," I said. "I'm going to try and sell it to Grub Street."

"More Rephaite hunters will begin to appear in the citadel before long, and they will need to feed. I suppose it would be wise for your people to know." He put down the glass. "Tell me, what manner of techniques for Rephaite-slaying are written in this manuscript?"

"Use pollen of the poppy anemone and go for the eyes."

"It is illegal to possess seeds of the poppy anemone in any Scion citadel. The only supply I know of was grown in the greenhouses of Sheol I." He dabbed salt on to his wrist. "It seems they are being illegally cultivated in London, too."

"We'll have to find out where. I brought this for you, by the way." I placed a bottle of brandywine on the nightstand. "From Jaxon Hall's cabinet of prohibited beverages."

"You are too kind." He paused. "I will return to the substation when I am stronger."

"You're not going anywhere near it," I said.

"Where, then?"

I didn't hesitate before I said, "Here."

Warden looked at me, assessing my features. I sometimes wondered if Rephaim had to work hard to gauge the meaning of human expressions. They had so little expression themselves.

A knock on the door brought me back to myself. Warden's gaze flicked to the wall, then to me, before he stood and concealed himself behind the bathroom door. There was no guarantee that we hadn't been followed here. I eased the door open.

"Nick?"

Sweat coated his brow. He was still in his Scion uniform, shaking all over, so pale he looked ill.

"*Jag kunde inte stanna,*" he said faintly. "*Jag kan inte göra det här . . .*"

"What's wrong?" I guided him towards the couch. "What's happened?"

"SciSORS." Shallow breaths passed his lips. "I can't work for them for another day, Paige. I can't."

A gradual stillness came over him. I sat on the arm of the couch, keeping a gentle grip on his shoulder.

"They got one of the Bone Season prisoners. Ella Parsons. They called my entire department to watch when they brought her in."

My skin prickled. "Watch what? Nick, *what?*"

"Watch them test Fluxion 18."

"I thought they were still trying to work out the formula." It was one of the last snippets of information I'd gleaned from my father about the project.

"They must have sped it up to arm the Vigiles for Novembertide." His fingers pressed against his temples. "I've never seen anything like it. She was vomiting blood, clawing at her hair, biting her fingers. The two senior developers started asking her questions. About you. About the colony."

A circle of doctors around the gurney. An operating theatre, the spectators in white coats. The anger I felt wasn't the red, unstable sort, but cold as broken glass.

"Nick," I said, "did Ella recognize you?"

He hung his head. "She reached out to me before she passed out. They asked if I knew her. I said I'd never seen her before. We were sent back to our labs, but I left early." Sweat seeped from his hairline. "They must have guessed. I'll be arrested next time I set foot in that place."

His shoulders were shaking now. I wrapped an arm around him. Scion were stepping up their game.

"Did you know her?" His voice was thick. "Did you, Paige?"

"Not well. She never got past her white tunic. We need to make a plan to get you out of there."

"But all those years—all that work—"

"How much use are you going to be to anyone when you're the one on the waterboard? On the gallows?" My breath caught. "That—that wasn't what your vision was about, was it? With the cuckoo clock?"

"No. I'd have sensed it coming by now." His hand clinched mine. "I have to get a sample of that drug. I have to know what they put in it. Figure out an antidote." He took a breath. "There's more. They're not just going to target public transport when they introduce Senshield. They're going for essential services, too. Doctors' offices, hospitals, homeless shelters, banks. All of them will be equipped with the scanners."

The news turned my stomach and boiled my blood. Using homeless shelters had always been risky for voyants, but the sheer scale of this attack was appalling. Come the New Year, the vast majority of voyants wouldn't be able to access basic medical services. With the banks no longer an option, most would have to give up their double lives. The streets would be overrun with gutterlings. I closed my eyes.

"How do you know this?"

"Oh, they told us." He let out a hollow laugh. "They told us, and you know what we all did, Paige? We gave them a round of applause."

Hatred bubbled in my gut. They had no right to do this. No right to steal away *our* rights.

Nick's head came up when an aura registered on his radar. Standing in the bathroom doorway was Warden. Even weak and tired, he appeared redoubtable. Nick rose to his feet, his face tight, and drew me closer to him.

"I don't think I ever introduced you two," I said.

Nick's grip tightened. "You didn't."

"Right." I cleared my throat. They'd met once before in the colony, but not for long. "Nick, this is Arcturus Mesarthim, or Warden. Warden, this is Nick Nygård."

"Dr. Nygård." Warden inclined his head. "I am sorry not to meet you in a better state. I have heard a great deal about you."

Nick nodded stiffly. His eyes were rimmed with red, but hard. "All good, I hope."

"Very."

There was a pregnant silence. I had a feeling Nick wouldn't be too happy if he learned how much Warden knew about him—how many of my memories he'd stolen. I had shown him the last one of my own free will, the one that had bared Nick's soul as well as my own.

"Give me a minute," I said. "I need my contacts."

Nick nodded, but he didn't take his eyes off Warden. I went into the tiny bathroom and pulled on the light cord, leaving the door ajar so I could eavesdrop. The contact lenses sat in liquid on a shelf above the sink. The silence continued for a while before Nick spoke.

"I'll just come out and say it, Warden. I know you let Paige out of the colony in the end, but that doesn't mean I have to like or trust you. You could have let her go in Trafalgar Square. I had her in my arms and you took her."

At least he cut to the chase. I found myself listening for Warden's response, waiting to see how he would answer the charges.

"Her presence in the old city was necessary," was the quiet reply. "Paige was my only chance of creating turmoil."

"So you were using her?"

"Yes. The human insurgents would not have responded to a

247

Rephaite leader, with good reason. Paige has a fire of rebellion in her gut. I would have been a fool to overlook it."

"Or you could have let her go. For her sake. If you cared about her, you would have."

"Then I would have been forced to use another human for a cat's paw. Would that have been any more ethical?"

Nick huffed out a laugh. "No. But I don't think you people are too good with ethics."

"All ethics come in gray, Dr. Nygård. In your profession, you should know."

"Meaning?"

This wasn't going well, and I wasn't sure I liked being talked about. I went back into the room before Warden could answer, silencing them both.

"Do you want to stay for a while?" I said to Nick.

"No. I should get back to Dials." He glanced at Warden. "How long have you been away from the den?"

"About an hour."

"Come with me, then."

I looked at Warden, and he looked at me. "I don't know," I said.

"We'll make an excuse for you to come back. Just keep Jaxon happy for a while, or he'll give us a curfew." He buttoned up his coat. "I'll wait outside."

I clenched my jaw as he left.

"Go," Warden said, very softly. "I left you often enough in the penal colony, with no words of explanation. Manipulate your mime-lord, Paige, as he has spent his life manipulating others. Use him to your advantage."

"I can't out-Jaxon him. He's the master of manipulation." I stood and swung my jacket on. "Nick's right about the curfew. I'll come back when I can."

"I look forward to it. In the meantime," he said, "I am sure I will find some way to entertain myself."

"You could do that séance."

"Perhaps. Or perhaps I will take a few more hours of peace before the war begins one more."

There was a light in his eyes that I might have thought playful if he hadn't been a Rephaite. I couldn't help but smile as I left him to his own devices.

# 15

# The Minister's Cat

The minute I walked away from the doss-house again, I wanted to go back. I didn't want to leave him there alone. Most of all, I didn't want to scarper back to the den just to keep Jaxon from cutting my pay. My freedom—the freedom I'd fought for, that people had died for—seemed like just as much of a charade in the Seven Seals as in Scion. I was nothing but a dog on Jaxon Hall's leash.

I couldn't keep this up for two more years. I wasn't a good enough actor to keep spinning along in his *danse macabre*. The scrimmage was my only chance to break free of his hold.

We worked our way through Soho. This lattice of backstreets formed the real underbelly of I-4, where the poorest of Jaxon's people eked out a living or died trying. I kept my head down and my eyes peeled for any sign of unfamiliar couriers.

"Paige," Nick said, speaking in a low voice, "I don't trust him."

"I could tell."

"I can't forget that night on the bridge. You pushed him away. You wanted to go home." He caught my arm, and I stopped dead. "Maybe he had his reasons. Maybe he does want to help you overthrow his own kind. But he kept you prisoner for half a year, to use you as his puppet. He threw you into the woods with one of those monsters. He watched them *brand* you—"

"I know. I remember."

"Do you?"

"Yes, Nick."

"But you don't hate him."

Those pale green eyes could slice down every shield I'd ever raised. "I'll never forget those things," I said, "but I want to trust him. If he isn't on their side, he must be on ours."

"What's he going to eat? Aura à gogo? Dreamwalker au gratin? Shall I get him the menu and serve him a busker?"

"Funny."

"It's not funny, Paige. That one in the city gave me my first experience of being fast food."

"He's not going to feed on us. And there's no reason under the sun why he'd tell Scion where we are. They'd kill him just as fast as they'd kill me."

"You do what you like, *sötnos*, but I'm not helping you see him. If anything happened, I'd never forgive myself."

I didn't say anything. He couldn't seem to look at me.

Guilt was written all over him. What they'd done to Ella hadn't been his fault, but I knew that he would always wonder, in the dark hours, if there was anything he could have done to stop her suffering. And whether he helped me or not, he would think the same if I came to any harm in Warden's company.

As I thought of it, Liss Rymore and Seb Pearce rose to the front of my mind for the first time in days, and the agony of their deaths erupted afresh. I'd never had a chance to mourn the fallen of that season. Voyants didn't hold funeral services—it wasn't in our culture to grieve over an empty corpse—but it might have helped. Given me a chance to say *sorry* and *goodbye*.

I schooled my expression so it didn't show. Nick didn't need my grief on top of his.

As we passed the sundial pillar, with its sad, painted faces, a medium in a long coat whistled from behind a phone booth.

"Pale Dreamer."

I stopped. It was one of Jaxon's couriers, someone I recognized. "What is it, Hearts?"

"Got a message for you," he said, stepping towards us. "From somebody called 9. She says the project's finished and it's waiting for you at the location you agreed on."

Nell's number. It must be the penny dreadful. "That's it?"

"That's it."

A mouthful of broken teeth grinned at me. I turned out my empty pockets. With pursed lips, Nick passed him a few coins from his wallet. "When did you get the message?" I said.

"Only ten minutes ago, but the courier who spoke to me said it had taken her two days to deliver the package. The Rag Dolls are checking the pockets of every courier who leaves II-4," he said. "Took some time to smuggle the envelope out of the section without them noticing, apparently."

Hearts doffed his hat and stowed the money in his coat before he slunk into an alley. Nick and I waited until his dreamscape was a good distance away before we continued.

"It's you they're looking for," Nick murmured. "Have you ever heard of couriers being searched?"

"No, but we just smuggled a Reph out of their section. They might be feeling paranoid."

"Exactly. You can't go back."

As soon as we were through the red door of the den, Jaxon summoned us to his office. He was sitting in his bergère with his fingers steepled, wearing his favorite brocade lounging robe and a stiff expression. I stood beside Nick and raised my eyebrows.

"Another stroll, darling?" he said curtly.

"I sent her out to find a busker for me," Nick said. "He owed us money."

"I do not want my dreamwalker leaving the den without my express permission, Dr. Nygård. In future, you will send one of the others." He paused. "Why are you in that ghastly uniform?"

"I came straight from work." He cleared his throat. "Jax, I think my position in Scion has been compromised."

Jaxon turned on his chair. "I am listening."

As Nick explained what had happened, Jaxon picked up a fountain pen and twirled it between the fingers of one hand.

"Much as I despise your moonlighting with Scion, we do need your income, Dr. Nygård," he concluded. "You had better return to your work next week and continue to feign ignorance. It would only incriminate you further if you were to abandon them now."

We couldn't need money that much. Even after what had happened at the black market, I-4 had been running normally. "Jax, he's in danger," I said. "What if they arrest him?"

"They won't, honeybee."

"You're raking in a fortune from the buskers' rent alone. You can't possibly—"

"You may be my heir, Paige, but unless I'm mistaken, I am currently mime-lord here." He didn't deign to look at me. "One glance from a voyant girl is not enough to implicate our oracle in anything."

"So you're happy to risk that oracle's neck for a few more pennies in your coffers?" I said hotly.

He grasped the arm of his chair. "Leave me with my mollisher, if you please, Dr. Nygård. Take a well-deserved break."

Nick hesitated before he left, but only for a moment. He gave my shoulder a gentle squeeze as he passed.

A distorted recording of "The Boy I Love is Up in the Gallery" was warbling from the corner. An empty reservoir glass stood on the desk. I lowered myself into an armchair and crossed my legs, giving him what I hoped was an innocent, expectant sort of look.

"The scrimmage," Jaxon said, in a dangerously soft voice, "is less than a month away. And I have seen no evidence whatsoever that you are attempting to prepare for it."

"I've been practicing."

"Practicing *what*, Paige?"

"My gift. I've . . . tried walking without the mask," I said. It wasn't quite a lie. "I can do it for a few minutes now."

"It's all very well and good to exercise your gift, but your physical health is just as important. They kept you weak and malnourished for a reason, darling: so you couldn't fight back." He placed a small bottle on the desk, full to the brim with greenish liquid. "Worse, you have neglected to treat yourself with the bay laurel I purchased for you."

I drew my arm toward my chest. Something told me not to tell him that the scars had been washed away by amaranth. It would only lead to questions about where I'd procured it.

"It hasn't hurt since you bound the Monster," I said.

"Irrelevant. Until I see some evidence that you are taking care of yourself," Jaxon said, "I will be withholding your wages."

The smile slipped off my lips. "I've done everything you've asked me," I said, trying to keep the bitterness out of my voice. "Everything. Delivered the messages, gone to the auctions—"

"—and through it all, paid not one iota of attention!" He swept the glass off his desk, along with reams of paperwork. "I suggest you manage your time a little better. I shall ask Nick to train you up for the fight."

Absinthe soaked into the carpet. My heart hammered. Jaxon took another glass from the cabinet.

"Off to bed with you, now." He poured the absinthe. "You need your rest, O my lovely."

With a curt nod, I left.

How long had it been since he'd left the den? How long since he'd last seen the streets he wanted so badly to rule?

On the landing, Eliza was gazing blankly at the wall, her mouth ajar. Oil paint sleeved her arms from fingertip to elbow. Her hair hung in greasy coils down her back, reeking of old sweat.

"Eliza?"

"Paige," she slurred, "where have you been?"

"Out." Her eyelids were drooping. I took her by the elbows. "Hey, when was the last time you slept?"

"I'm not sure. Doesn't matter. Do you know when Jaxon's next pay packet is coming in?"

I frowned. "Has he not paid you, either?"

"Said he wanted to see progress. Need to make more progress."

"You've made plenty of progress."

I led her up the stairs by the arm. She was trembling all over. "I have to carry on," she muttered. "I have to, Paige. You don't understand."

"Eliza, I want you to take eight hours off. In that time, I want you to have a meal, take a shower and get some sleep. Can you do that?"

A titter jumped from her lips. I pushed her into the bathroom with a towel and a lounging robe.

Danica, as always, was working on her side of the garret. I knocked on her door and entered when I didn't get an answer.

The corners overflowed with bits and pieces she'd picked out of scrap heaps or bought from mudlarks on the banks of the Thames. Danica was sitting on the end of her daybed, hunched over the heavy oak table that served as her work surface.

"Dani, I need a favor."

"I don't do favors," she said. A circle of dense glass magnified one of her eyes to an absurd size.

"It's nothing too strenuous. Don't worry."

"Not the point. That seat isn't for people," she added as I sat down.

"What are you working on?" I scanned the curled scraps of paper on the floor, all scribbled on in neat Cyrillic script. "The Panić Theory?"

Her hypothesis still required empirical research. Jaxon wanted to include it in his next great pamphlet. The formula was simple: take the order of clairvoyance, multiply by ten, take away from one hundred, and the answer was the average age for a voyant of that order to die. It meant that I would die at thirty, which was a cheerful thought. Then again, cheerful thoughts didn't sell pamphlets.

"Nope." She picked up a spanner. "The hand-held Senshield."

"Why does Jax want you working on that?"

"He doesn't tell me *why*. He tells me *what* and *when*."

I couldn't think why Jaxon would need such a thing. "If you get bored," I said, reaching into my pocket, "do you think you could modify the portable oxygen mask for me? I need it to be a bit smaller."

She turned it over in her callused hands. "That's as small as you'll get it. It needs a decent air chamber."

"How about something I can conceal?"

"Jaxon won't pay me for that. This is the job he gave me."

"It's for the scrimmage. Besides, you haven't bought so much as a sock since last year," I said.

"This may come as a shock to you, but I need the money to pay the mudlarks. They charge me like they're selling gold dust." She dropped the mask on the table. "If I say yes, will you go away?"

"If you also make sure that Eliza eats a full meal before she goes back to work."

"Done."

That was the best I'd get out of her. I passed Eliza as she tottered into her room and collapsed on her bed in a heap. When the muses approached her, I forced them into a spool and knocked them unceremoniously to the other side of the garret.

"She needs to rest. Bother someone else for a while."

Pieter shot off in a huff. The newest muse, George, brooded in the corner while Rachel and Phil hung sadly above the door. Eliza was already sound asleep, her arm hanging off the edge of the bed, face half-buried in the pillow. I pulled a thick blanket over her shoulders.

Jaxon didn't want me to *rest*. If he was interested in giving his voyants rest, Eliza wouldn't be wandering around like an automaton in clothes she'd been wearing for a week.

My mime-lord was waiting in the doorway of his office, watching me. With a slanted smile, he waved me into my room. I slammed the door in his face.

Curled up on my bed, I picked open the pillowcase stiches with the tip of my knife. There was enough money in there to buy one more night for Warden at the doss-house. After that, he was on his own. I turned on to my side and rested my head on one arm, listening to the white noise machine.

After an hour or two, Jaxon's dreamscape dimmed. I lay awake until the den was quiet; until the streetlights bathed the streets with blue and even Danica had succumbed to her exhaustion. The penny dreadful was waiting in Soho. Warden was waiting in the doss-house. Under my pillow, my hand lay on the handle of my knife. I hadn't felt this alone in a long time.

At midnight, my door swung open. I sat up with a pounding heart, the knife still in my hand.

"Shh. It's me." Nick crouched beside my bed. "You're sleeping with a knife?"

"You sleep with a gun." I laid it on the nightstand. "What's the matter?"

"Go." He nodded to the window. "Go back to the doss-house and see Warden. I'll leave Jaxon a note. Tell him we're training."

"I thought you said—?"

"I did, but I'm tired of doing everything by Jaxon's book," he whispered. "I don't like it, Paige, but we need to work out what the Rag Dolls are planning. And I trust that you know what you're doing." He still didn't look happy. "Be careful, *sötnos*. And if you can't be careful—"

"—be quick." I kissed his cheek. "I know. Thank you."

\*\*\*\*

It must have been hard for him to let me go, but it felt good to have Nick back on my side. Even if we both agreed that me seeing Warden was risky, it was better than having no Rephaite help whatsoever.

There was a cold snap in the air. I climbed my way out of the den, bundled up in a jacket and cravat, and took off down Monmouth Street. Jaxon's office window was dark; his dreamscape swam with the muddied tint of alcohol. I spied a unit of Vigiles patrolling on Shaftesbury Avenue and took a different route across the rooftops to Soho.

The district was heaving with denizens, mostly amaurotic, with the odd voyant darting through the throng. The people came here for what little pleasure Scion afforded them: the casinos, the underground theatres, and the 3i's Coffee Bar and its music, played by the few whisperers who'd clawed themselves into amaurotic jobs. This was where Eliza had spent her youth.

When I reached the square, I slipped into one of the more popular voyant establishments in the district: the Minister's Cat, a gambling-house tailored to voyants, with stringent rules on which orders could bet (oracles, soothsayers, and augurs always ineligible, given their prophetic gifts). There was a lottery held here every month, with the winner entitled to a sum of money from Jaxon. It was also the only place in I-4 where members of other gangs were allowed to linger without express permission, as they generated so much money for the section. Most districts had a handful of "neutral" buildings, where turf disputes and grudges were ignored. *Königrufen* and tarocchi were the most popular games. My fingers itched—I loved tarocchi, and winning a few games could get me a pocketful of cash—but I didn't have nearly enough money to enter the tournament.

As always, it was full to bursting with people from all over the citadel. I slid my way between sweating bodies and round tables, leaving looks and whispers in my wake. This particular establishment was a breeding ground for syndicate gossip. Babs was presiding over a game of tarocchi in the corner. I'd have to wait.

Maybe I could find help somewhere else. There were plenty of voyants selling knowledge in here.

*Knowledge is dangerous.*

Dangerous, but useful.

A soothsayer sat in a booth nearby, dark of skin, late twenties. Her hair was a cloud of tiny corkscrews, restrained by a thin band of violet silk. Large eyes looked up at me from below heavy lids. The right was deep brown and the left, green, with a loop of yellow around the pupil and no colobomata. It was the second time in my life that I'd seen a pair of eyes like that.

"Got time for a reading?"

She rubbed the bridge of her broad nose. "If you've got coin for it."

I handed her the meager change in my pocket. "That's all I've got."

It was enough for her to buy another few glasses of mecks. "Well," she said, "I suppose it's better than nothing."

Her deep voice held the remnant of an accent. I sat down in the booth and clasped my hands. She pulled a velveteen curtain along its rail until we couldn't be seen by the gamblers.

"You're an astragalomancer," I said. Her fingernails were painted white, dotted with black. There were flecks of white above her eyes, too. She took two small dice from her sleeve. Knucklebones, flecked with ink.

"Now, here's how this works," she said, holding one up between her thumb and index finger. "Not all 'stragas work the same way I do—most of them do some really complicated shit with answers on paper—but I keep it very simple. You ask five questions and I'll give you five answers. They might be vague, but you'll have to deal with it. Give me your hand."

I did, and she grasped it—then dropped it like it was a frayed wire.

"You're cold," she said, giving me a suspicious look.

At first I didn't realize what she meant—if anything my hands were uncomfortably warm—then I opened my palm and remembered. "Sorry." I spread my fingers, showing her the cuts. "Poltergeist. They're about ten years old."

She shook her head. "It's like shaking hands with a corpse. Give me the other one."

The scars had always been a bit cooler than the rest of me, but I'd never known anyone to react like that to my touch. She took my right hand instead, holding the dice in her free palm.

"Right," she said, relaxing. "Ask your questions."

I didn't miss a beat: "Who killed the Underlord?"

"Dangerous question. Make it better. The æther won't just deliver a name like a vending machine."

I paused, mulling it over. "Did Cutmouth kill the Underlord?"

The dice rolled across the table. A two and a two. The soothsayer lifted her empty hand to her temple.

"Scales," she said, in that strange monotone Liss had used during my reading. "One side of the scale is full of blood, weighing it down. Four figures stand around the scales—two on one side, two on the other."

"Right. Does that answer the question?"

"I said it would be vague. In my experience, the scales usually point toward truth. So you've got two people who are on the right side of the truth and two who aren't," she said. "You should get it. The æther's response to a question is for the querent's understanding only."

If the æther had a personality, I decided, it would be a smug bastard.

"Next question, then," I said. "Did Cutmouth kill the Underlord?"

"You just asked that."

"I'm asking it again."

"Are you testing my abilities, jumper?" She didn't seem insulted; just vaguely amused.

"I might be," I said. "I've seen more than one charlatan in here. How do I know this isn't a rainbow ruse?"

So she did it again. A two and a two. I repeated the question once more and got the same answer. The soothsayer took a few gulps of mecks.

"Please, enough. I get the same damn image every time. And you've only got two more questions."

There were so many I wanted to ask, particularly about Warden, but I had to be careful. "Say I wanted to know about a group of people, but I didn't want to say who they were," I began.

"So long as *you* know who you're talking about, that should work. You're the querent. I'm just the channel."

My fingers tapped the table. "How does . . . the one who lives underground . . . know about the puppet masters?"

It was clumsy, but it had to sound like nonsense to this stranger. From her expression, she'd heard stranger things. The dice rolled across the table and stilled next to my hand, both showing a single dot.

"A hand without living flesh, its fingers pointing to the sky. Red silk surrounds its wrist like a manacle. The hand snatches white feathers from the ground. Two fingers break away, but it keeps snatching."

She shook her head, took another gulp of her drink.

"Meaning?" I said, trying not to sound exasperated.

"No idea what the hand is. Red silk is likely blood, or death. Or neither," she added. No wonder soothsayers had so much trouble making money. "White feathers . . . plucked from a bird, perhaps. They could represent parts of a whole. Or exist as symbols on their own." A vein stood out along the middle of her forehead. "Last question. I'm getting tired."

I was silent for a while, trying to think of something that could point me in the right direction—until I remembered Liss, and that reading she'd done for me.

"Who is the King of Wands?"

She smiled. "You've been to see a cartomancer, haven't you?"

I didn't answer. Talking about Liss would only bring back the pain of her death. The soothsayer flicked the two dice up with her thumb and caught them in the same hand. A two and a five.

"Seven," she said, slamming them down on the table. "That's it."

I raised my eyebrows. "No vision?"

"Sometimes the number's enough. Remember the way they're divided, too," she said. "A two and a five is different from, say, a three and a four. One or the other of the two numbers is usually particularly significant." Her hand jerked out of its own accord, bowling over her glass of white mecks and sending the dice on to the floor. "And that's it. When I start spilling drinks, it's time to stop. I know it seems shady, but there's meaning in the madness."

"I believe you." And I did. No matter how confusing her gift had seemed, I sensed Liss would be right about everything. Even if I didn't understand *everything* yet.

"Don't worry about it too much. Nothing you can do about your future, I'm afraid."

"I don't know about that." I stood. "Thank you."

"If you ever need another reading, you know where to find me."

"No, thanks. But I'll send people I know in your direction."

The soothsayer nodded, nursing her forehead with one hand. I swept the curtain aside and left the booth. My gut was a cradle of snakes.

Babs was back at the bar, freckled and cheerful, pouring the players drinks from a bottle of blood mecks that looked older than she was. Some said the monarchy was still alive and well in Babs: she was a self-declared queen of chin music. She raised a hand when she saw me.

"Pale Dreamer," she exclaimed. "Haven't seen you in a while. How are you?"

"Could be better, Babs." I sat on one of the wooden stools. "I'm told you have a package for me."

"Oh, yes, I have." She rummaged under the counter. "Favor from a beau, is it?"

I shook my head, smiling. "You know the Binder wouldn't allow that."

"Cold as a dead fish on a tomb, that man. You know he's stopped the lottery, don't you?"

"Since when?"

"Back in August. Nobody was happy, but I suppose he was generous to do it in the first place."

Interesting. "You're busy tonight."

"Oh, I know. We've been taking bets on the outcome of the scrimmage. Bless old Hector for dying. We were struggling to get patrons in here for a while," she said. "Gillies used to come, but not so much any more. Scion's got them too scared to sneak out of their barracks after hours."

"Why?"

"Beatings. They're losing patience with this fugitive situation, saying the Gillies must be hiding their own kind." She glanced up at me. "Speaking of fugitives, you've been the talk of the house for a fair few moons. They've been taking bets on you being the one who bumped off Hector."

Of course they had. "And what do you think?"

She snorted. "I've known you for two years, love. I can't imagine you pulling off someone's head. No, I reckon it was Cutmouth. I mean, if it wasn't, why hasn't she come forward to claim the crown?"

"Because she knows she's a suspect."

"She wouldn't care a jot, that girl. She wasn't too bad without Hector pulling her strings. Came in here quite often for a game with one of her girlfriends." With a smile, Babs handed me a thick manila envelope. "Here, love. I haven't laid a lamp on it, sure as I'm a sensor."

"Thank you." I still checked that the seal was intact before I tucked it into my jacket. "I'm a bit short, Babs. I'll pay you when I get my wages."

"Instead of coin, humor me with a game. There's some couriers over there that need a good thrashing."

I looked over my shoulder. "Where?"

"Middle table. They're in most nights."

"Which section do they play for?"

"I-2. They're civil enough, but they win a bit too often, if you know what I mean. Hey, remember when your lot took Magtooth down a peg?" she laughed. "Ah, that was a good night. Seeing him cough up all that money he'd bet on himself . . ."

All of us had been in hysterics that night. It seemed a hollow victory now Magtooth was dead.

A small group of the Abbess's people sat around the table she'd indicated, all involved in a game of tarocchi. They wore the rich, dark velvets and satins favored by her close associates, embellished with lace sleeves and delicate silver jewelry. I recognized the redhead from the Juditheon auction, lounging on the edge of the table, looking over the fan of cards in her hand.

"Maybe next time," I started to say—then stiffened. One of the players had a head of bright blue hair and wore Rag Doll pinstripes on his sleeveless waistcoat. A bracelet of small bones hung around one wrist. On his right upper arm was a small tattoo of a skeleton's hand, ivory-white, outlined in black, its fingers reaching upward to his shoulder.

*A hand without living flesh, its fingers pointing to the sky.* I glanced back at the booth, but the soothsayer was gone.

"That's a Rag Doll," I said quietly.

Babs glanced up. "Hm? Oh, so it is. The Nightingales are always playing friendly games with other sections. They've had a long rivalry with the Wicked Lady's people." She poured me a glass of white mecks. "Though I must say, I'm surprised they'd stoop to playing with a Rag Doll. He must have paid good money to enter their tournament. Binder's still all right with other gangs stopping here, isn't he? I can kick them out if it displeases him."

"No. They're fine." My heart still drummed a little too hard. "Do you know why the Abbess hates their mime-lord so much?"

"This might surprise you, but I've never heard."

It did surprise me. I was wearing my cravat, but I kept my face turned away from the Rag Doll. "What's that symbol on his arm?"

"All the Dolls have it. Looks shit, doesn't it?"

I cracked a smile at that. "I've got to go. Thanks for the drink."

"All right." She reached over the bar to embrace me. "You be careful, Dreamer. The streets aren't very kind these days."

I crossed the room and shut myself into another booth, where I took out the pages of the manuscript and smoothed them out. Two copies. Nell had done well to get them to me so quickly.

They'd called it *The Rephaite Revelation*. The writing was economic, clearly scrawled in a rush by torchlight, but penny dreadfuls weren't supposed to be masterpieces. It described the unholy triangle of Scion, the Rephaim, and the Emim. It went into gory detail about the penal colony and explained the trafficking that had gone on for two hundred years. Most importantly, it told them how to destroy a Rephaite. They'd come up with the idea of coating a blade in anemone nectar, or using a blowpipe to aim its pollen into the eyes.

It was all told through the eyes of 1, a poor card-reader, snatched from the streets and thrown into a nightmare. The sketches didn't show her face, but she had black ringlets, like Liss. I flicked through to the last pages. In the end, this Liss broke free of the colony and rallied London to the defense of voyant-kind. She did what the real Liss hadn't had the chance to do.

She was alive in the pages of the truth. I shoved the envelope back into my jacket and pushed the curtain aside.

The Rag Doll had disappeared from the gambling-house. As I passed the I-2 gamblers, I stopped and rapped on their table. They looked up, startled. The redhead stubbed out her aster and stood.

"Pale Dreamer," she said huskily. Half of her face was concealed by a complex lace mask. "Can we help you?"

I folded my arms. "Binder told you at the meeting that Cutmouth sometimes came in here. Did you follow up on that lead?"

"Oh, yes," one of the men said, not taking his eyes off his cards. "Unfortunately we found nothing of use. A few of these people had seen her in here, but she hasn't come back since."

"Right." Lazy bastards. "Any reason you're playing with Dolls?"

"He challenged us. And insulted our lady. We told him to put his money where his mouth was." One of the other women, an augur, blew lilac smoke at me. "Do you want to challenge us, Pale Dreamer?"

The redhead threw a card at her. "Stop it. This isn't our turf." She touched a hand to my arm. "The Abbess is grateful for your understanding, and for the White Binder's. We hope that this can be resolved."

"Don't we all," I said, and turned away.

Babs was still behind the bar with another croupier, roaring with laughter at something he'd said. I left through the front door, making a bell ring.

I walked faster than usual. Warden's rent was due tomorrow morning; I had to see him now, or the landlord would come knocking on his door.

My heart pounded as I made my way back through Soho, keeping to the quietest backstreets. The back of my neck tingled. At this time of night, the residential areas were eerie and deserted; their voyants were all in the heart of the district, gambling or trading gossip.

I was almost at the doss-house when two dreamscapes closed in on me, and a punch in the face knocked me right off my feet.

# 16

## Flower and Flesh

A bag descended over my head. My arms were wrenched out on either side of me. I arched my back and strained my right hand towards my belt, reaching for my hunting knife with a scream of anger.

Something hard struck the back of my skull, setting off an explosion of colors behind my eyes. A hand clamped over the lower half of my face. I felt myself being dragged along like a ragpicker's cart, the asphalt carving up my knees.

"So terribly sorry to do this, Pale Dreamer"—a rough voice— "but I'm afraid you know too much."

They carried me around a corner. The taste of iron coated the roof of my mouth. Blood was slinking toward the back of my throat, making me gag. Panic stopped my breath. Unless they were planning to kill me here, they had to be taking me to a car. I tried to scream again—some of Jaxon's employees would be nearby, most of whom would help me if they thought there might be a reward in it—but the bag only pressed harder over my lips. Blue lamplight seeped through it.

"Now, Pale Dreamer, here's what we want you to do." A serrated knife bit into the side of my neck. "Tell us where you took the creature, and we shall reconsider cutting your throat."

"What creature?" I spat out.

"The one you stole from the catacombs. Pretty eyes, like jacklights. Shall we jog your memory?"

Another punch, this time in the small of my back, sent me reeling against a wall. My spirit seemed to spring awake; it slashed at the nearest dreamscape. One of the attackers gave a shout, and his knife clattered to the ground near my boots. Blind, I snatched it up and pointed it in the direction of the two dreamscapes, my muscles quivering.

"You won't find him," I said.

"Won't we?"

An augur and a sensor. I tore off the bag. The sensor was exceptionally tall and slim, while the augur was petite. Both of them wore black clothes, with those painted, grinning masks, and carried carving knives.

"It's the Rag and Bone Man who wants me dead, I take it," I said, taking a step away from them.

"Clever of you to have found his sanctuary." The auger pointed a silenced pistol at me. "Far too clever for your own good, Pale Dreamer."

I lunged at her, taking her down at the waist. Her pistol went off somewhere near my right knee. She clawed at me with her free hand while I kept her left wrist pinned to the ground, forcing the gun away from my body.

The second assailant came for me with a knife. I got in a kick to his stomach, winding him. The woman took the opportunity to roll me on to my back and hold down my hands with her knees. The mask tilted to one side as she pressed the pistol to the center of my forehead.

Hot pressure rose behind my eyes, and I felt myself being sucked from my body, bone and spirit tearing far away from one another as I jumped. I pulled against it, but it was an impulse, mechanical. It was kill or be killed. My spirit cut through her mind, throwing her spirit right out of her body. A heartbeat later, the corpse slumped on top of me. The man screamed a name through the slot of his mask. He bunched his fists in my jacket, dragged me out from under the woman, and smashed my back against the wall. I caught his wrist and forced it back, cracking bone, so his knuckles almost kissed his forearm.

A knife stabbed up, aiming for my stomach. I jerked away just in time; the tip of the blade nicked my side. Before he could stab again, I thumped my knee between his thighs. A huff of hot breath came through the mask, past my ear. My fingers let go of his injured wrist and took hold of the knife hand instead. I bit down as hard as I could on his arm, so I felt the bite's weight in the roots of my teeth. He screamed a searing insult in my ear, but kept a rigid hold on me until my teeth punctured skin and my mouth filled with the taste of pennies.

I knew myself too well to use my spirit again. My head was pounding, my vision prickling at the edges. The second his left hand loosened its grip, I delivered a hard kick to the front of his leg and rammed my free fist into his solar plexus. The damaged leg buckled under his weight. My shoulders slid from his grasp, and I was free.

The hitman's knife swung around like a waltzer at a fairground. I picked up the dead woman's revolver and stayed on the balls of my feet, keeping low. The knife whipped past me, almost catching my cheek. His vision would be blurred from that blow to his torso, already hemmed in by the mask's small eyeholes. The instant he turned the wrong way, I bashed the revolver into the spot just behind his ear, then kicked him in the small of his back, so hard it jolted pain into my knee. He lurched into the bins before he hit the ground.

Panting, I let myself fall against the brick wall. Sparks wheeled across my field of vision. I wiped my hands before I crouched down and pulled off both their masks.

The woman's eyes bored into nothing. Both of them wore bone bracelets and pinstripes, like the Rag Dolls. I reached into her coat pocket, and my fingers closed over cool, smooth fabric. Crimson silk pooled in my palm.

A red handkerchief, stained with dark blood.

My fingers curled around it. I knew instinctively that it was Hector's blood on this little slip of silk. They must have been planning to plant it on my corpse, to use my body as evidence that I'd been the killer all along.

The man gave a short groan. Aside from a small scar near his temple and a smattering of stubble along his jaw, he had no distinguishing features whatsoever. I stuffed the handkerchief into my pocket and gave him a hard clap on the cheek.

"What's your name?"

"Not saying." His lids were heavy. "Don't kill me, dreamwalker."

"So you're willing to kill for your boss, but not to die for him. I'd call that the mark of a real coward. Better tell him to send more than two lackeys next time." I held up the handkerchief. "What were you going to do with this? Plant it on me?"

"Just wait until the scrimmage." A laugh rocked through him. "One king falls, another rises."

"You're mad." With a surge of disgust, I shoved him back to the ground. "You're lucky I don't kill you just for being on the White Binder's turf."

"You might as well. Rags will do it if you don't," he said. "But you've got no real power, mollisher. You'll always be someone else's puppet."

There was already one death on my conscience tonight. What mattered was that the penny dreadful was still inside my jacket, safe and sound. I slid off my belt and fastened the hitman's hands to the wrought-iron gate. Using the last of my strength, I bumped the man into his twilight zone and left him to his nightmares by the woman's empty body.

**\*\*\*\***

By the time I reached the doss-house, it was nearly half past midnight. I got myself up the creaking stairs and unlocked the door.

The room was lit by a single candle and the flicker of the transmission screen. Warden was standing by the grimy, rain-strung window, looking out at the citadel. When he saw my swollen lip and bloody head, his eyes flared.

"What happened?"

"He put a hit on me." I snapped the bolts into place, slid the chain along its track. "The Rag and Bone Man."

My heart was still pounding, my vision trembling with lights. I stumbled past him, into the bathroom, and snatched a tin of meager medical supplies from the cabinet.

As I peeled off my trousers and bandaged my shredded knees, I had to wonder what Warden was thinking. No doubt that I was wasting precious time, scrapping in alleys while Scion prepared their empire for war. Only when I opened the door did I realize that my hands were shaking.

Warden didn't ask me if I was all right. The answer was obvious. Instead, he closed the curtains and poured me a glass of brandywine. I sank on to the couch beside him, keeping my distance, and cradled it between my hands.

"I take it you took care of the hitmen," he said.

"They're looking for you."

He took a sip from his own glass. "Rest assured, I have no intention of being caught off my guard a second time."

272

His left hand held the arm of the couch; the right lay on his thigh, the palm upturned. Large, tough hands, scored with scars along the knuckles and an indent at the base of his right thumb.

In the colony he had often watched me as though I were a riddle he couldn't solve. Now his gaze rested on the transmission screen. Scion's most popular comedy was on, the one that revolved around vapid amaurotics and their valiant triumphs over unnaturals. I quirked an eyebrow.

"Were you watching a *sitcom*?"

"I was. I find Scion's methods of indoctrination quite intriguing." He switched to the news, where an earlier broadcast was on its second cycle. "Scion has announced the creation of an elite subdivision of Vigiles called Punishers. Their particular function is to track down known preternatural fugitives so they may be brought to justice."

"Preternatural?"

"A new name for those who commit extreme forms of high treason, it seems. I imagine it was Nashira's suggestion. A means of making your life in London more difficult."

"How creative of her." I drew in a slow breath. "Who are they?"

"Red-jackets."

I stared at him. "What?"

"Alsafi has informed us that, now they have no colony to protect, the red-jackets have been put to work in the citadel. No doubt your friend Carl will be among them."

"He's not my friend. He's Nashira's bootlicker." Even the memory of Carl Dempsey-Brown was irritating. I put down the glass. "I can't pay for you to have more than another night here. Jax is withholding my wages."

"I do not expect you to pay for my bed and board, Paige."

I switched off the news, thickening the darkness, and took a gulp of brandywine. His gaze was almost burning a hole in the wall, as if giving me so much as a glance would cause the roof to collapse. I shifted, pushing my hair behind my ear. My shirt came down to mid-thigh, and I assumed he'd seen me less than fully clothed before—he'd removed a bullet from my hip after Nick had shot me.

Warden spoke first: "I take it your mime-lord has approved of your staying here for another night."

"Do you think I report to him about everything?"

"Do you?"

"No, actually. He has no idea where I am."

We were both fugitives, both separated from our allies, both on the wrong side of Scion. We had more in common than we'd ever had before, but this wasn't the Warden I'd left at the doss-house a few hours ago. Something had changed in the hours I'd been away, but I hadn't got him out of that hovel for him to turn into another monster. There were plenty of those on my doorstep already.

"You have questions," Warden said.

"I'll start by asking you for the truth."

"A grand request. About what, specifically?"

"You," I said. "The Rephaim."

"Truth looks different in every lens. History was made by liars. I could tell you of the great cities of the Netherworld, and the Rephaite way of life—but I sense those are truths for another night."

I tried to smile, just to dispel the tension. "Well, now you've got me curious."

"I could not describe the Netherworld's beauty. No words can." A light rose in his irises, something of the Warden I knew. "If I had my salvia, I would show you. But for now"—he placed his empty glass on the table—"I will tell you of the history of Rephaim and humans. You will need it to understand the Ranthen, and to understand what we fight for."

My head was killing me, but I'd wanted to hear this for a long time. I swung my legs on to the couch. "I'm listening."

"First," he said, "know that the spoken history of the Netherworld has been distorted over the centuries. I can tell you only what I have seen, and what I have heard."

"Noted."

Warden leaned back on the couch, and for the first time in a while, he set his gaze on mine. It was a relaxed posture, human-like. A petty inch of me was tempted to look away, but instead I looked right back.

"The Rephaim are a timeless race," he began. "We have been in the Netherworld for time immemorial. Its true name is She'ol, hence the penal colony's name. We existed only on æther, for nothing grows in the Netherworld. There is no fruit or flesh. Only æther and amaranth, and sarx-creatures, like us."

"Sarx-creatures?"

"Sarx is our immortal flesh." He flexed his fingers. "It does not age, nor can it be extensively harmed by amaurotic weapons."

As he told the story, his voice grew slow and soft. I took another sip of brandywine, turned on to my side and sank into the cushions. Warden glanced at me before he continued.

The Rephaim had always been in the Netherworld. They were not born, like humans, nor had they evolved (to their knowledge); instead, in Warden's words, they *emerged*, fully formed. The Netherworld itself was the cradle of immortal life, the womb in which they were created. There were no Rephaite children. From time to time, more Rephaim would surface, though the waves of creation were sporadic.

Once upon a time, these immortals had seen themselves as the mediators between life and death, between the two planes of Earth and æther. When humans had first appeared in the corporeal world, they elected to keep close watch over them to ensure they did no damage to the fragile balance between worlds. Originally, this watch had taken the form of sending spirit-guides, the psychopomps, to escort the spirits of dead humans into the Netherworld.

But as time went on—and Rephaim, he told me, still had trouble grasping the concept of *time*, a force which had no effect on the Netherworld or its inhabitants—humans had became more and more divided. Full of hatred for one another, they fought and killed over everything imaginable. And when they died, many lingered, refusing to go on to the next stage of death. Eventually, the ethereal threshold had risen to dangerous levels.

At that time, their leaders were the Mothallath family. The star-sovereign, Ettanin Mothallath, had decided that Rephaim should enter the physical world and soothe the ethereal unrest, encouraging the spirits to go into the Netherworld, where they could come to terms with their deaths in peace.

"So that's what the Netherworld is for," I said. "To ease the passage of death. To stop spirits lingering here."

"Yes. We were to prepare them for their journey to the last light. For their true, second death. Our intentions were pure."

"Well, you know what they say about good intentions."

"I have heard," he said.

I was silent as he pressed on with the tale. From time to time, he would pause mid-sentence; his eyes would narrow a little, and his mouth would thin and turn down at the corners. Finally, he would choose a word and press on, still with a faint look of dissatisfaction, as though the English language had failed him in some way.

A proud and respected family of scholars—the Sargas, whose duty had been to study the ethereal threshold—had decided that crossing the veil would be an act of inconceivable desecration. Their belief was that interaction between Rephaim and humans should be avoided, that their immortal flesh would perish on Earth. But the threshold was climbing higher, and the Mothallath rejected their counsel. As the judgment was theirs, they would send one of their own as the first of the "watchers."

The first watcher, the daring Azha Mothallath, had successfully crossed the veils and communed with as many spirits as she could. She had returned safe and sound, and the threshold had lowered. It seemed the Sargas had been wrong. There was no harm in the crossing.

"That must have pissed them off," I said.

"Immensely," he confirmed. "The watchers would go through the veil whenever the threshold pushed too high, wearing armor to protect themselves from corruption. We Mesarthim, who were guardians to the Mothallath, desired to escort them—but we soon discovered that only they could go through."

"Why?"

"That remains a mystery. To protect themselves, the Mothallath made a strict law that they would never reveal themselves to humans. They were always to maintain their distance."

"But someone didn't," I guessed.

"Correct. We do not know exactly what happened, but the Sargas informed us that one of the Mothallath had crossed the veil without permission." His eyes dimmed. "After that, everything disintegrated. That was when clairvoyance entered the human world. That was when the Emim appeared. That was when the veils between the worlds grew thin enough to let all of us through."

I hesitated. "Clairvoyance hasn't always been there, then."

"No. It was only after that event—the Waning of the Veils, as Rephaim call it—that humans began to interact with spirits. You have been here since ancient days, but not quite as long as amaurotics."

I'd always liked to think that we'd been there since humans had existed. In my heart, I'd always known it was a self-indulgent fantasy. Amaurotics *were* the originals, the naturals. I took a long, deep breath and let it go.

War had torn through the Netherworld then, war that turned Rephaite against Rephaite and all factions against the Emim. The creatures had crawled out of the shadows like a plague, rotting the

Netherworld in their wake. The Rephaim stopped being able to exist purely on the æther, which they had once breathed the way humans breathed air. They had starved and perished in their thousands, as the Sargas had predicted. Finally, Procyon, Warden of the Sargas, had declared himself *blood-sovereign* and waged war against the Mothallath and their supporters, blaming them for letting death into their realm. Those who were still loyal to the Mothallath called themselves Ranthen, after the amaranth—the only flower that grew in the Netherworld.

"I'm assuming you were on the Ranthen side," I said.

"I was. I am."

"But?"

"You know the end. The Sargas won. The Mothallath were usurped and destroyed, and the Netherworld could sustain us no longer."

Rephaite faces didn't lend themselves to grief, but there were times when I thought I could see it in Warden. Small things gave the regret away. The dwindling of the light in his eyes. The slight tilt of his head.

An impulse moved my hand toward his. Seeing it, he curled his fingers into a fist and pulled his arm to the left.

Our gazes jarred for the briefest instant. The back of my neck grew hot. I reached for my glass, as if that was what I'd been doing in the first place, and leaned against the opposite arm of the couch.

"Carry on," I said.

Warden watched me. I cradled my forehead in one hand, trying to ignore the warmth that bled into my cheeks.

"To save themselves," he said, "the Ranthen declared loyalty to the Sargas. By that point Procyon was incapable of leadership, and two new members of the Sargas family had risen to take his place. Nashira— one half of this pair—declared that she would take one of the traitors as her blood-consort, to show them that even their leaders would conform to the new order. As ill luck would have it, she chose me."

Warden stood and placed his hands on the dusty windowsill. Rain poured down the panes.

I shouldn't have tried to comfort him. He was a Rephaite, and it was clear that whatever had happened in the Guildhall had been a mistake.

"Nashira was—and still is—the most ambitious of the Rephaim." When he spoke of her, his eyes burned. "As we could no longer connect to the æther, she said we would have to see if we fared any better on the other side of the veil. We waited for the ethereal threshold to reach its highest ever point before a large party made the crossing in 1859. There, we discovered that we could feed on the link certain humans had with the æther. Where we could survive."

I shook my head. "And Palmerston's government just let you in?"

"We could have survived in the shadows, but Nashira was determined that we had to be apex predators, not parasites. We revealed ourselves to Lord Palmerston, telling him that the Emim were demons and we, angels. Almost without question, he surrendered control of the government to Nashira."

The wings struck off the angels in the churches, making way for the new gods. The statue of Nashira in the House. Gomeisa had been right: we'd made it so easy for them to take control.

"Queen Victoria was allowed to maintain an appearance of power, but she had no more sway over England than a pauper. The death of Prince Albert hastened her departure. On the day he was crowned, their son Edward VII was framed for murder and accused of bringing unnaturalness into the world. And the inquisition into clairvoyance—our establishment of control—began." He raised his glass. "The rest, as they say, is history. Or modernity, as the case may be."

We were quiet for some time. Warden emptied his glass, but didn't let go of it. It was strange to think that his world had always existed alongside this one, unseen and unknowable.

"All right," I said. "Now tell me what the Ranthen want. Tell me how you're different from the Sargas."

"First and foremost, we do not wish to colonize the corporeal world. That is the foremost desire of the Sargas."

"But you can't live in the Netherworld."

"The Ranthen believe the Netherworld can be restored, but we do not wish it to be isolated from the human world, as it once was. If the threshold can be lowered to a stable level, we wish to have an advisory presence in the human world," he said. "To prevent the total collapse of the veils."

I sat up straighter. "What happens if they collapse?"

"It has never happened before," he said, "but I feel it will end in a cataclysm, as do many other Rephaim. The Sargas aim to bring it about. The Ranthen aim to stop it."

I watched his face, trying to draw something from it: an emotion, a clue. "Did you agree with Nashira?" I asked. "When you first came here. Did you agree that humans should be subjugated?"

"Yes and no. I believed that you were reckless, destined to destroy both yourselves and the æther with your endless, petty wars. I thought—perhaps naïvely—that you would benefit from our leadership."

My laugh was a tad sour. "Of course. The mindless moths, drawn to the flame of your wisdom."

"I do not think like Gomeisa Sargas." His eyes were cold, but that was nothing new. "Or his relatives. I took no pleasure in the degradation and misery of the penal colony."

"No. You just went along with it." I turned my head away. "Seems like some of the Ranthen should just join the Sargas. I find it hard to believe they want to look after us poor defenseless humans."

"You are right to suspect that motive. Most Rephaim cannot abide living here, as half-things, and many bitterly resent the Sargas for forcing them to stay." He returned to his seat beside me. "To a creature of sarx, Earth can seem . . . unpleasant."

"What do you mean?"

"Everything here is dying. Even your fuels are made of decomposed matter. Humans use death as a means of sustaining life. To most Rephaim, that is an unpleasant thought. They see that as the reason why humans are so bloodthirsty, so violent. Most Ranthen would leave if they had the choice. But the Netherworld is broken, too. Decaying, like the Emim. And so we must stay."

Another chill. I picked up a ripe pear from the fruit bowl. "So to you," I said, "this is rotten."

"We see the rot before it rises."

I tossed it back into the bowl. "That's why you wear gloves. So you don't catch mortality. Why did you want to work with me?" *Or kiss me*, I thought, but couldn't bring myself to say it.

"I do not believe in Sargas lies," he said. "You are alive until your dying day, Paige. Do not let their madness into your mind." Warden didn't break my gaze. He was in there somewhere, behind those hardened features. "The Ranthen believe, unlike the Sargas, that humans stole our lifeline from us inadvertently—but they do not see humans as their equals. Many of them blame human violence and vanity for their own suffering."

"You helped me."

"Do not labor under the illusion that I am a bastion of moral goodness, Paige. That would be a dangerous venture."

Something snapped inside me. "Trust me," I said, "I'm not under any illusions about you. You went through my private memories and took things from me that I'd never told anyone. You also kept me captive for six months so I could start a war for you. And now you're acting like a cold bastard even though I dragged your sorry hide out of a cell."

"I am indeed." He inclined his head. "Knowing that, are you willing to continue our alliance?"

At least he didn't make excuses. "Do you want to explain *why*?"

"I am a Rephaite."

As if I could have forgotten. "Right. You're a Rephaite," I agreed. "You're also Ranthen, but you talk about the Ranthen as if you're not one of them. So what the hell is it that you want, Arcturus Mesarthim?"

"I have many aims. Many desires," he said. "I aim to bring about a settlement between humans and Rephaim. I aim to restore the Netherworld. But above all, I aim to end Nashira Sargas."

"You're taking your sweet time with that."

"I will be frank with you, Paige. We do not know *how* to overthrow the Sargas. They seem to draw their power from a deeper well than ours," he said. I'd expected as much, or they would have dispatched the Sargas years ago. "Our original plan was to extinguish both blood-sovereigns and scatter their supporters, but we are not yet strong enough to do this. Instead of toppling their leaders, we must infiltrate their major source of power: Scion."

"So what do you want from me?"

He leaned back. "We cannot dismantle Scion alone. As you may have noticed, we Rephaim are not particularly generous with our passions," he said. "We cannot inspire insurrection in the hearts of your people. But a human could. Someone with an intimate knowledge of both the syndicate and the Rephaim. Someone with a powerful gift and a taste for revolution." When I said nothing, his voice softened. "I do not ask this of you lightly."

"But I'm the only choice."

"You are not the only choice. But if I could choose anyone on earth, it would still be you, Paige Mahoney."

"You chose me to be your prisoner, too," I said coldly.

"To protect you from having a keeper as cruel and violent as Thuban or Kraz Sargas, yes. I did. And I know it is no excuse for the injustices I did you," he said. "I know that no matter what explanation I offer, you can never truly forgive me for not letting you go when I had the chance."

"I might be able to forgive you. Provided you never give me an order again," I said. "I can't forget."

"As an oneiromancer, I have infinite respect for memory. I would not expect you to forget."

I brushed my hair behind my ear and crossed my arms, prickling with goose bumps. "Let's say I do become your associate," I said. "What will I get in return, apart from your contempt?"

"I have no contempt for you, Paige."

"You could have fooled me. And getting respect is one thing, but I could have all the respect in the world and no money to buy weapons or numa or food."

"If you require money," he said, "that is all the more reason to align yourself with the Ranthen."

I looked up at him. "How much do you have?"

"Enough." His eyes glowed. "Did you think we had planned to go against the Sargas without a penny to our names?"

My heart began to pound. "Where have you kept it all?"

"There is an agent working for the Ranthen within the Westminster Archon, who holds the money in a private bank account. An associate of Alsafi, who deemed it best that their name was known only to him. If you can persuade Terebell that you are capable of handling it, and if you promise her your support, she will be your patron."

I sat back, stunned. All that scraping for coins could be a thing of the past.

"If I become Underqueen," I said, "we *might* be able to rally the London voyants. But I'll be up against every mime-lord and mime-queen in this citadel with half an ego and a head on their shoulders."

"I take it they are all like Jaxon Hall."

"What, bloodthirsty peacocks? Almost uniformly."

"Then you must win. They are feasting on their own corpses,

Paige. If the syndicate is properly governed, I believe it could pose a great threat to the Inquisitor, and to the Sargas. But with a leader like Jaxon Hall, I foresee only blood and revelry—and in the end, destruction."

Liss's last card sprang to my mind. I would never know what image had burned in that little fire, and whether it had pointed to victory or defeat.

"I suppose I should not leave the Ranthen waiting." He rose to his full height. "Do you have another candle?"

"In the drawer."

Silently, he set up the séance table. When it began, he knelt in the light of the candle and murmured in his own language. Gloss had no discernible words, just a long, flowing series of sounds.

Two psychopomps drifted through the walls. I held very still. They were cryptic spirits, rarely seen outside burial grounds. Warden made a soft sound in his throat. They both flew through the candle flame and took off again, leaving the windows and the mirror covered with a light frost.

"Terebell will meet with me at dawn." Warden put out the candle. "I must go alone."

"That's how your séances work?"

"It is. The psychopomps' original duty was to guide spirits to the Netherworld, but now that function is obsolete, they do what they can to assist us on this side. They seldom interact with humans, as you may have noticed."

Jaxon certainly had; he'd been trying to get close to psychopomps for years so he could complete his next pamphlet.

He wasn't leaving. We watched each other for a minute, not speaking. I remembered the rhythm of his heart against my lips. His naked, callused hands sweeping over my body, cradling me close until the kiss was deep and hungry. Looking at him now, a small part of me wondered if I'd imagined it.

With the light switched out, all I could hear was my own quiet heartbeat. He was silent as stone. I thought he'd move to the bed, but he stayed where he was. I turned on to my side and rested my head on a cushion. Just for a few hours, I would sleep outside of Jaxon's grasp.

"Warden."

"Hm?"

"Why did the amaranth bloom?"

"If I knew," was his reply, "I would tell you."

# 17

# Gambler

I hid the red handkerchief in my pillow at the den. I couldn't be caught with such an incriminating object, but something made me want to hold on to it.

With the Rephaim back in the citadel, it was time to put another piece in motion. To let people know what they were up against. The next day, I went back to Grub Street for the first time since I'd fled with Alfred.

Considering its distinguished position as the only voyant publishing house in London, the Spiritus Club, founded in 1908, was a shabby affair. It considered itself to be the stronghold of creativity among voyants, the beating heart of non-violent mime-crime. Tall and narrow, crammed between a poetry lounge and a printing press, it boasted mock-Tudor half-timbering and a buckled beak of roof, with a heavy green door and dirty bow windows.

I checked the æther yet again, making sure I hadn't been followed, before I pressed a finger to the doorbell. Somewhere in the building, a bell clanged. After two more rings and a knock on the door, a woman's voice fluted from a speaker on my right.

"*Go away, please. We've enough poetry collections to paper every house in London.*"

"Minty, it's the Pale Dreamer."

"*Oh, not you. I've had enough trouble with booklice without a fugitive on my doorstep. This had better not be a ploy to get more of my elegies for the White Binder.*"

"He doesn't know I'm here. I'm looking for Alfred," I said. "The psycho-scout."

"*Yes, I know who he is. We are not hiding multiple Alfreds in here, I assure you. Have you been invited?*"

"No." I rattled the handle. "It's freezing out here, Minty. Will you just let me in?"

"*Wait in the foyer. Wipe your feet. Don't touch anything.*"

The door swung open. I stamped my boots on the doormat and waited in the hallway.

It was quaint inside. Flower-patterned wallpaper, sconces, a little rosewood desk on a deep burgundy carpet. The symbol of the Spiritus Club—two fountain pens inside a circle, joined to create the hands of a clock—was carved on to a shield above the mantelpiece. That symbol was printed in the top right corner of every illegal pamphlet and chapbook in the citadel.

"Alfred!" a voice shouted from somewhere above me. "Alfred, get down to the foyer!"

"Yes, yes, Minty, wait a tick . . ."

"Now, Alfred."

I sat on the edge of the desk to wait, keeping a tight grip on my messenger bag.

"Ah, the Pale Dreamer returns to Grub Street!" Alfred thumped his way down the staircase, a smile breaking his lips and teeth apart. When he saw my face, it plummeted. "Oh, dear. What happened?"

The hitman's punch had left a terrific shiner under my right eye. "Just training. For the scrimmage."

He shook his head, squinting at the bruise. "You ought to be more careful, dear heart. But to what do I owe the pleasure?"

"I wondered if you might be free for a few minutes."

"But of course." He extended an arm, which I took, and we walked up to the landing, stepping over gold stair rods with decorative brackets. "I say, you could almost be Jaxon's daughter with that hair. Clever of you to dye it."

Another woman came flying down the stairs, wild-haired and bespectacled, one I didn't recognize. It wasn't Minty Wolfson, in any case. She looked as if she was still in her nightclothes. "Who on *earth* are you?" she demanded, as if I had some nerve to be on earth at all.

"Why, this is the White Binder's esteemed mollisher." Alfred placed his hands on my shoulders. "Currently the most wanted person in London, which makes her very welcome in our midst."

"Bloody troublemaker, from what I've heard. I hope you know where you are, young lady. The Spiritus Club is the finest voyant publishing house in the world."

"It's the only one, isn't it?" I said.

"Ergo, it is the finest. We were built on the glorious foundations of the Scriblerus Club."

"Indeed we were. All great satirists, the Scriblerians. Passionate in their pursuit of dullards." Alfred ushered me through a door. "Be a dear and make us some tea, Ethel. My poor guest is thirsty."

I could have sworn the ruffles of her dress quivered with outrage. "I am not a waitron, Alfred. I do not have time to serve cups of tea to some Dublin doxy. I have work to do—*work*, Alfred. Definition: *exertion* or *effort* directed to produce or *accomplish* something—"

Alfred, sweating, shut the door before she could continue.

"I apologize sincerely for my colleague's conduct. The north will seem peaceful after this lunacy."

I lowered myself into the opposite chair. "You're going north?"

"In a few weeks, yes. I've heard of a very talented psychographer in Manchester." He pushed a tier stand of biscuits toward me. "I must say, I'm very glad to see you made it back to Seven Dials after our last encounter. Close shave, wasn't it? I usually have better luck with bribing them."

"I'm the most wanted person in Scion. A numen was never going to help." I nodded to a monochrome photograph in an elaborate brass frame, propped up on a highboy behind his desk. "Who's that?"

Alfred looked over his shoulder. "Ah, that's my late wife. Floy, she was called. My first, short-lived love." His fingers caressed the frame. The woman inside it was perhaps thirty. Thick, straight hair fell past her shoulders. She looked straight at the viewer with her lips parted a little, as if she'd been speaking when the photograph was taken. "She was a good woman. Distant, perhaps, but kind and talented."

"Was she voyant?"

"Amaurotic, as a matter of fact. An odd match, I know. She died very young, unfortunately. I'm still trying to find her in the æther, to ask her what happened, but she never seems to hear."

"I'm sorry."

"Oh, dear heart, it's hardly your fault." For the first time I noticed the ring on his finger, a thick gold band with no adornments. "Now, how can I help you?"

I opened my bag. "I hope you won't think I'm being presumptuous," I said with a rueful smile, "but I have a proposal for you."

"I confess myself intrigued."

"You said you were looking for something controversial. I have some acquaintances who've written a penny dreadful together, and I was wondering if you might like to have a look at it."

He grinned. "You had me at 'controversial,' dear heart. Let's take a look."

I fanned the pages out across the desk. With a puzzled smile, Alfred reached for his pince-nez and peered at the title.

THE REPHAITE REVELATION

*Being a true and faithful Account of the ghastly Puppet*
*Masters behind Scion, and their Harvest of clairvoyant Peoples*

"My word." He chuckled. "I suppose you did say 'controversial.' Who are these imaginists?"

"There's three of them, but they want to remain anonymous. They're identifying themselves with numbers." I pointed to the bottom of the page. "All part of the story."

"How splendidly meta."

I let him leaf through it for a while. Occasionally he murmured "ah, yes" and "good" and "eccentric." A shiver trailed along my spine. If Jaxon found out I was doing this, he would boot me out of Seven Dials and leave me to my fate. Then again, he wasn't exactly happy with me now.

"Well, Paige, it could use some work, but the idea is quite terrifying." Alfred pressed his index finger against the first page. "You rarely see literature that talks openly about Scion's corruption. It does something to challenge their authority, implying that their minds are weak enough to be controlled by outside forces."

"Exactly," I said.

"Jaxon will be furious if he finds out that I was involved in this, but I always was a gambler." He rubbed his hands together. "Not all writers come through me."

"There is one catch," I said. "The writers need it to be out by next week."

"Next week? Gracious. Why?"

"They have their reasons," I said.

"No doubt, but it isn't just me they have to convince. It's the fastidious Grub Street booksellers, who then have to allocate a certain amount of money to pay the Penny Post. They are the bookshop—a living, mobile bookshop, made up of thirty messengers,"

Alfred explained. "It's how Grub Street has kept itself out of Scion's way for all these years. It would be far too dangerous to sell forbidden stories in one place."

There was a knock on the door before a thin, trembling man tottered in with a tray. His aura almost shouted what he was: psychographer.

"Tea, Alfred," he said.

"Thank you, Scrawl."

Scrawl put the tray down and stumbled back out, muttering to himself. Seeing my expression, Alfred shook his head. "Not to worry. Poor fellow got himself possessed by Madeleine de Scudéry. A prolific novelist, to put it lightly." He chortled into his teacup. "He's been scrawling away for a month."

"Our medium sometimes paints for days without sleeping," I said.

"Oh, yes, the Martyred Muse. Sweet girl. Mediums do get the short end of the stick in this business, don't they? Speaking of which, I must ask—are your friends psychographers? Writing mediums?"

"I'm not sure." I stirred my tea. "Will that affect the Club's decision?"

"I shan't lie to you, dear heart. It may well do. With the exception of Jaxon, they've always believed that unless a story is written by someone whose link to the æther is sustained by writing, it's a story not worth telling. Elitist claptrap, if you ask me, but my opinion only goes so far around here."

"Do you think they'd need proof?"

"Oh, I'm sure they'd let it slide." He twirled his pipe between his fingers. "I hope Minty will see its potential, but this sort of writing could cause Scion to come down on us like so many bricks."

"The Club kept *On the Merits* secret."

"For a while. Scion knows all about it now. It was only a matter of time until a Vigile showed them." He looked down at the pages, stroking his small chin. "There's enough material here for a novella, though that would be much harder to distribute. And a penny dreadful would be read on the spot. May I take these pages for Minty to peruse?"

"Of course."

"Thank you. I shall call you with her verdict in a few hours. How should I contact you?"

"The I-4 phone booth."

"Very good." His damp eyes rested on mine. "Tell me, Paige—truthfully, now. Is there even a slither of truth in here?"

"No. It's all just fiction, Alfred."

He looked at me for some time.

"All right, then. I'll be in touch." Without getting up, Alfred took my hand between his large, warm ones and shook it. "Thank you, Paige. I hope to see you again soon."

"I'll let the writers know you're vouching for them."

"All right, dear heart. But do tell them from me: not a word to the Binder, or we'll all be in for the high jump." He slid the pages into a drawer. "I shall give these to Minty as soon as she's finished writing. Stay safe, won't you?"

"Of course," I said, knowing I wouldn't.

****

The sun burned a deep autumn gold. My next destination was Raconteur Street, where Jaxon had heard of unregistered pickpockets targeting amaurotics ("They're stealing from *our* hapless victims, O my lovely, and I don't like it one bit"). None of the others were available to deal with it. If I wanted my next pay packet, I'd have to do as I was told. I didn't have the Ranthen's patronage just yet.

Alfred called himself a gambler. Maybe I was, too, though I hadn't made a penny from the risks I was taking. If Jaxon found out I'd been seeing Warden—in any capacity—his rage would be incandescent.

There was no sign of the pickpockets, though I could see a few of ours at work. If the offending voyants were here, this would be the perfect opportunity for them to strike. Across the inner citadel, amaurotics were flooding into the vast department stores, buying stacks upon stacks of gifts for Novembertide. It was the most important festival on the Scion calendar, celebrating the formal opening of the Scion Citadel of London at the end of November in 1929. Red glass lanterns were strung between the streets, while tiny white lights, smaller than snowflakes, cascaded from windowsills and snaked in perfect spirals around lampposts. Vast painted banners of previous Grand Inquisitors hung from the largest buildings. The crowds were dotted with students handing out posies of red, white and black flowers.

Would my father celebrate alone this year? I pictured him at the table in the gray light of morning, reading his newspaper, with my face staring back at him from the front page. I'd been a disappointment to him from the moment I'd turned my back on the University, but I was far beyond that now.

"I don't know what you're talking about." A woman's plea reached my ears. "Please, Commandant, I just want to get home."

An enormous, armored black vehicle was parked on the side of the street, marked with SUNLIGHT VIGILANCE DIVISION and the anchor, in the sun. I stepped behind a lamppost and pulled down the peak of my cap, straining to see what had happened. It was rare for the Vigiles to bring out military vehicles, as most of their army was stationed overseas. They'd patrolled the streets of every citadel during the Molly Riots, when Scion had declared martial law and put ScionIDE soldiers in the central cohort.

A young woman had been detained. Her hands were cuffed in front of her, and she had the wary, panicked look of someone who knew they were in trouble.

"You claim to have arrived in 2058," the Vigile commandant was saying. One of his underlings stood by with a data pad. "Can you prove that?"

"Yes, I have my papers," the woman stammered, her Irish accent clear as a bell. She was about my height, though her hair was a darker blonde than mine had ever been, and she wore the crisp red uniform of a paramedic. I could tell from here that she was amaurotic. And a few months pregnant. "I'm from Belfast," she continued when the commandant didn't speak. "I came here to work. There's no work left in the north of Ireland, not now that—"

The Vigile hit her.

The impact radiated through the crowd like a shock wave. He hadn't just slapped her, but punched her in the jaw, hard enough to snap her head around. Sunlight Vigiles never used brutality.

The woman slipped on the ice and fell, twisting at the last moment to spare her rounded stomach. Blood leaked from her mouth, on to her palm. When she saw it, she let out a cry of shock. The commandant walked around her. "No one wants to hear your lies, Miss Mahoney."

My heart lurched.

"You brought your unnaturalness to my shores. If I had it my way," he barked, "we wouldn't employ brogues at all. Especially not dirty, unnatural farm girls."

"I'm from a Scion citadel! Can't you *see* I'm not her? Are you blind?"

"Who's the father?" He pressed his pistol to her stomach, eliciting gasps from the crowd. "Felix Coombs? Julian Amesbury?"

*Julian.*

Instinctively, I looked up at the nearest transmission screen. A new face had been added to the cycle of preternatural fugitives. Deep brown eyes and skin, bald, with a rigid set to his jaw. Julian Amesbury, guilty of high treason, sedition, and arson. If they didn't have him, he must be alive. Surely.

"Who?" The woman shielded the bump with her arms, pushing herself back with her heels. "Please, I don't know who you're talking about . . ."

Murmurs passed through the spectators. I could hear them from here: "Shouldn't do this here," "not for the daytime," "inconsiderate." They wanted unnaturals gone, these people, but not while they were doing their shopping. To them, we were litter being taken to the landfill.

The woman was hauled to her feet by his lackeys. Her cheek was already an enraged red, her eyes brimming with tears. "You're all mad," she choked out. "I'm not Paige Mahoney! Can't you *see* yourselves?"

She was strapped, weeping and thrashing, on to a stretcher in the paddy wagon by a female Vigile. "Move along," the commandant roared, startling the onlookers, who expected courtesy from daytime Vigiles. "Any of you know any brogue immigrants, you can tell them to get ready for questioning. And don't think you can hide them in your homes, or you'll go to the gallows with them."

He climbed into a second paddy wagon. "This is wrong," someone called out. A young, amaurotic man, bright-eyed with outrage. "She isn't Paige Mahoney. You can't just arrest an innocent woman in broad—"

Another Vigile struck him with her baton, right at the front of his skull. He crashed into the pavement, his hands raised to protect himself.

A stunned silence fell over the crowd. When there were no more voices of dissent, the Vigile beckoned to her squad. As the man pushed himself on to his elbows and spat out two teeth, the onlookers surged away from him. His nose was bloody. I could only watch as the paddy wagon and its armored escort drove away, feeling as if the world and all its walls were crashing down on top of me. I had the insane urge to run after them or send my spirit into a Vigile's dreamscape, but what good would that do?

The realization of my powerlessness choked me. Before anyone could notice that the real Paige Mahoney was standing in the vicinity, I raced into the backstreets. Black hair, a cravat and a pair of contacts wouldn't hide me for much longer.

I knew London in a way they didn't. How to wear the shadows like a hood over my eyes. How to pass unseen, even in broad daylight. How to ebb away into the night. Its map was as familiar to me as my own hands. While I had that advantage, they wouldn't find me.

I had to believe it.

When I reached the door of the den, it took three tries to get my key into the lock. In the hallway, Nadine was sitting on the stairs, polishing her violin. She looked up, frowning.

"What's the matter?"

"Gillies." I drew the chain across.

Nadine stood. "The Punishers?" She stared. "I saw them on ScionEye. Are they coming here?"

"No. Not Punishers." I swallowed the thickness in my throat, the acid taste of dread. "Are the others here?"

"No. Zeke's with Nick. I *told* him not to go out today . . ."

She rushed through the door, heading for the phone booth. I ran up the stairs, sick to my stomach.

During the Molly Riots, anyone with an Irish surname, or whom Scion proclaimed to *look* Irish, had been subjected to endless spot checks and interrogations. That poor woman, whose only mistake was to be in the wrong place and from the wrong country, might well be dead by sunrise. And unless I gave myself in, putting everything else in jeopardy, there was nothing I could do to save her.

The snake of guilt tightened its coils. I sat on my bed and squeezed my knees between my arms, drawing myself inward. If Nashira's puppets meant to force me out with brute force, they wouldn't succeed.

A rapping came against the wall. Jaxon Hall demanded an audience. The shadows under my eyes were more like crevices now—he'd know something was wrong at once—but I had to face the beast at some point.

My mime-lord lay on the chaise longue like a statue, eyes half-open, his face warmed by the golden light outside. Empty wine bottles crowded the coffee table, and every ashtray was brimful of ashes. I stood in the doorway, wondering once again how long it had been since he'd last gone outside.

"Afternoon," I said.

"Indeed it is. A chill sort of afternoon. Would that be because the winter is drawing ever closer, and with it, the scrimmage?" He took a swig of absinthe from the bottle. "Did you check for the pickpockets?"

"They weren't there."

"What have you been doing for the other two hours?"

"Collecting money from the night parlors," I said. "I thought we should get it all in before the scrimmage."

"Oh, don't think, darling, it's a dreary habit. But do put the money on my desk."

He didn't take his eyes off me. I reached into my pocket and laid a wad of my own precious notes on his desk. Jaxon picked them up and counted.

"You could do better, but this will get us through the month. Here." With a clumsy flourish, he took about a third of the bundle, popped it into an envelope and handed it back to me. "For your troubles." Bloodshot eyes peered at me. "What the devil happened to your face?"

"Hitmen."

That woke him up. "Whose hitmen?" He stood, almost knocking a glass off the table. "In *my* territory?"

"Rag Dolls," I said. "I dealt with them. They should still be on Silver Place, if you send someone to look."

"When did this happen?"

"Last night."

"On your way back from your training." When I nodded, he snatched a lighter from his desk. "I will have to speak to the Abbess about this." He stuck a cigar between his teeth, lighting it after four attempts. "Do you have any idea why the Rag and Bone Man would target you, Paige?"

"No idea," I lied. Slowly, I sat down on the couch. "Jax, what do you know about him?"

"Next to nothing." His expression was pensive. "Not even what sort of voyant he is, though his name implies osteomancy. In all my years as a mime-lord, I haven't seen him once. He lives a wretched sort of subterranean existence, shunning all human contact, speaking only through his mollishers. I suppose he became a mime-lord during Jed Bickford's reign."

"Wait," I said. "Mollishers?"

"He does keep the Unnatural Assembly posted on his section's changes. He's had three mollishers that I know of. I never heard the first one's name, but the second was called the Jacobite, and the most recent is La Chiffonnière. She became mollisher in February this year."

February. That was around the time I was captured. "What would make him want to change mollishers?"

"Oh, heaven alone knows. Perhaps he or she did something to annoy him." He pulled a glass ashtray across the desk. "Tell me, Paige—have you heard from the local ventriloquists?"

"Who?"

"The Rephaim, darling."

"You're interested?"

"I don't particularly want to know what the Rephaim are doing, and I still have no intention of doing anything about their presence. I merely asked if you had *heard* from them."

I wet my lips. "No. Nothing."

"Good. Then we have no distractions."

"Depends what you mean by 'distractions,'" I said tersely. "The Vigiles are going to interrogate all the Irish settlers this week. They seem to think the brogues are conspiring to hide me."

"The Grand Commander must be *aching* for new ways to waste time. Now, on to more important matters. Come out to the courtyard with me."

Of course. Mass arrests and beatings meant nothing to Jaxon Hall. Did he ever acknowledge Scion, or was it all just background noise to him?

The courtyard at the back of the den was one of my favorite places in all of London: a triangle of tranquility, paved with smooth white stone. Two small trees grew from circles of soil, and Nadine kept the wrought-iron planter-boxes overflowing with flowers. Jaxon sat down on the bench and dropped his extinguished cigar into one of them.

"Do you know the rules of the scrimmage, Paige?"

"I know it's close combat."

"The fight is based on the rather brutal medieval tradition of *mêlée*. You will find yourself engaged in a series of small battles within the so-called 'Rose Ring.'" He closed his eyes, soaking up the sun. "You must be wary of those whose numa can also be wielded as weapons: axinomancers, macharomancers, and aichmomancers in particular. Another point of note is that using amaurotic tactics to end any of your battles—stabbing someone with an ordinary blade, for example—is called a 'rotten ploy.' At one point it was forbidden, but nowadays it's perfectly acceptable, so long as it's carried out with enough flair."

I raised an eyebrow. "Enough *flair*? Is that what the syndicate wants from its Underlord?"

"Would you follow someone with no hint of panache, darling? Besides, the scrimmage would be bland without a little bloodletting, and amaurotic weapons are perfectly adequate for that."

"What about guns?"

"Oh, yes—no firearms permitted. It's considered slightly unfair that a wonderful candidate could make a misstep and be shot dead." He tapped his cane. "We have another, vital advantage, you and I. At any time, we can fight together. Only a mime-lord and mollisher pair may do this."

"Do most participants fight in pairs?"

"All but the independent candidates, who have more to prove. What I suggest, for the purpose of ensuring that both of us survive—"

"Survive?" I frowned. "I thought—"

"Don't be naïve. The rules do state that the aim is to stun, but there are always deaths during a scrimmage. What I suggest," he continued, "is that we both learn a little more about our gifts. That way, we will be able to anticipate and read each other's movements as we fight."

I didn't say anything for a moment. Jaxon had no idea that my gift had matured as much as it had.

"All right." I leaned against the blossom tree. "Well, you know about mine."

"Don't tell me you learned nothing in the colony."

"I was a slave, Jax, not an apprentice."

"Come now. Don't tell me my mollisher didn't try and learn more about her gift." There was a hungry glint in his eye. "Don't tell me you still haven't mastered possession."

Possession was something I fully intended to use at the scrimmage; if I didn't show Jaxon now, he'd only find out later.

For a while there were no hosts to be seen. Finally, a bird flickered overhead, gone in a blink. I made the jump.

It was easy to take control of this body, with its fragile, lilac dreamscape; not so easy when I found myself soaring on the whims of the wind, with nothing to stop me plummeting into the asphalt.

Deep inside me was a trembling—the bird's consciousness—but I focused, quashing its spirit. This wouldn't be like it was with the butterfly. This time I would spread my wings. I squeezed myself into the new bones, as if I were pulling on clothes that were too small, and slammed my wings downward, lifting my light body. Vertigo overwhelmed me.

But the sky was peaceful. Quiet. Not like the violent, bloody citadel. In the sky there was no Scion. The birds refused the anchor's call. Past the encroaching evening, a ribbon of color still lay across the horizon: rosy coral, soft yellow, palest pink. Other birds were flocking around me, twisting and soaring, turning and folding in a unison that seemed impossible. They swirled like rain on their way to roost. There was a pulse between these birds, as if they shared a single dreamscape. As if they had a web of golden cords between them.

My silver cord pulled at my spirit. I turned away from the flock and swept back down to the courtyard. Clumsily, I flapped my way to Jaxon's other shoulder, opened my beak, and chirruped in his ear.

He was still laughing his delight when I snapped back into my own body and took in a gasp of air. The starling teetered on the bench, looking drunk. I'd fallen right into Jaxon's arms.

"Wonderful!"

I extricated myself from Jaxon's grip and dabbed the sweat from my forehead. My heart was palpitating, stiffening my airways.

"You really are extraordinary, O my lovely. I knew I put your gift two orders above mine for a reason, just as I knew you'd turn a bad experience to your advantage. That Rephaite must have taught you a great deal. I owe him a debt. You can even do it without that cumbersome oxygen mask."

"For about thirty seconds." Darkness clouded my vision.

"That's thirty seconds longer than you could do it before. You've made *progress*, Paige, which is more than you made with me. Would it that I could send the rest of the gang to sharpen their skills. Oh, the place sounds like a boot camp for clairvoyants. A whetstone for the spirit. Send them all, I say." He led me back to the bench and sat me down. "The only problem I foresee with possession is the fact that your body is left vulnerable. Perhaps wait until the finale to use it, when there are only one or two opponents left."

A headache was already surging above my eye. He crouched down in front of me, his cheeks brushed with a hint of pink.

"Anything else?"

"No."

"Oh, don't be coy, Paige."

"That's it. Really." I forced a smile. "Your turn."

"My gift is nowhere near as fascinating as yours, O my lovely, but I suppose I did promise."

Jaxon took a seat beside me. "What can you do with the spirits?" I said. I'd always been curious about his gift. "When you say 'control,' what do you mean?"

"My boundlings are free to wander within the confines I set for them. Most of them are simply commanded to stay in I-4 and behave themselves. When I need them, however, I can use them in spirit combat."

"In the same way you'd use other spirits?"

"Not quite. When the average voyant spools the average group of spirits, they simply aim them in the direction of an opponent and hope for the best. The spirits push terrible images into the dreamscape of the enemy, but they're easily driven away by their defenses. But my boundlings carry my strength with them. Unlike the common wisp, which can only produce hallucinations, boundlings can manipulate the fabric of a clairvoyant's dreamscape."

"Can they kill?"

I tried to sound casual. Jaxon looked at the starling with no expression. His lips moved quickly, and the æther shifted as a spirit shot from inside the den. The bird flinched as it approached, then gave a horrible jerk as the spirit cut through its tiny dreamscape, shattering its silver cord.

A moment later, the starling was dead.

"My boundlings can be almost as powerful as you, darling. Some have the power to push weak spirits right out of their dreamscapes." He gave the little corpse a push, and it rolled off the edge of the bench, on to the white stone floor of the courtyard. My stomach turned at the sight of its dead beads of eyes. Bloodless murder. "You see?" he said. "Life, for all its wonders, is rather flimsy in the end."

Flimsy. Like a moth.

Jaxon leaned across the bench and gave me a peck on the cheek. "We will win," he said. "We will triumph, darling. And all will be as it should be."

\*\*\*\*

The citadel was teeming with Vigiles, all out on a voyant-hunting spree, but I had to leave the den before I suffocated. Once Jaxon was locked in his office, I took off down Monmouth Street and slipped down the tunnel that led to Chateline's. Without ordering anything, I took up residence at my favorite table, away from the windows, and dropped my head into my hands.

Jaxon could kill me in the scrimmage. There would always be foul play—I'd expected that—but I'd never thought that murder in the ring would be an acceptable practice.

The transmission screen in the corner showed the great stone arch of the Lychgate, as it often did on weekdays nowadays. NiteKind must be going out of fashion. Perhaps the amaurotic elite didn't want painless punishment for the citadel's unnaturals anymore. I made myself watch as the executioner led two prisoners out on to the lead roof.

The nooses were cast over the heads of the condemned. You could just hear one of them pleading for clemency, his voice amplified so all of London could hear his cowardice. His shift was stained, his face swollen and bruised. His hands were trembling as the masked Grand Executioner cuffed them. The second man stood with his hands behind his back, waiting for the plunge.

Before they could die, the screen flicked to the comedy channel. The patrons cheered.

A silver tray was deposited in front of me. Chat folded his arms, his stump resting in the crook of his elbow.

"That executioner's a piece of work," he muttered. "Cephas Jameson, his name is. Always leaves it as long as possible."

I rubbed my temple. "Did I order something, Chat?"

"No, love, but you look like you need it. That's quite a shiner you've got there." He looked at the screen through his good eye. "I don't know why they show it. Like we don't know what they'll do to us."

"Why don't we do something?" The frustration almost choked me. "This has been going on for *centuries*, Chat. Why don't we just—?"

I gesticulated, like I could grasp the solution.

"Apathy's a killer. The way most people see it, we can survive like this if we stay out of the way." Chat leaned against the table. "You know what they used to call the British Empire? 'The empire on which the sun never set.' That's the very same empire Scion's built on." His mouth puckered for a moment before he said, "If it's us against the sun, who wins?"

I couldn't answer.

Chat returned to the bar, leaving the tray behind. Underneath the cloche I found a bowl of chestnut soup. As I picked up the spoon, I caught sight of my reflection in the tray. My black hair made my face looked pasty. Bags mushroomed out from under my eyes, along with the giant bruise.

The door banged open, and a courier came rushing into the bar. One of Ognena Maria's, wearing the symbol of the Spiritus Club. When he spotted me, he rushed up to my table, panting.

"Are you the Pale Dreamer?"

I nodded. "What's wrong?"

"Message for you, miss. From Grub Street."

He handed me a burner phone. Alfred must have heard back from Minty already. I held it to my ear, cupping my hand around the mouthpiece. "Hello?"

"It's me, dear heart. I thought the poor courier would never find you."

I gripped the phone, my knuckles white. "Did they like it?"

"They loved it!" Alfred sounded jubilant. "Yes, they were all very impressed, even the booksellers. So long as the authors contribute a small amount to the cost of ink and short-notice distribution. We typeset the whole thing today, go to press tomorrow, and distribute as soon as you've paid."

"Oh, Alfred, that's—" I dropped my forehead against the wall, my heart still thumping. "That's wonderful. Thank you."

"I live to serve, dear heart. Now, regarding the delicate matter of money, Minty will need it from the writers before the pamphlet goes out. Tell the courier where she should leave the bill. I shall be far from London by tomorrow, but you must get in touch if you have any questions. The courier will leave you my number."

"Thank you again, Alfred."

"Good luck," he said.

He hung up first. I tossed the courier the phone. "Tell Minty to leave the bill here, at Chateline's."

In exchange, he handed me the slip of paper, which I pocketed. "Understood, miss." He left.

*The delicate matter of money.* Delicate indeed. Even if I committed every waking minute to following Jaxon's orders, I wouldn't make a quarter of what I'd need to cover such an astronomical cost—and it would be astronomical. I had no choice but to impress the Ranthen, to seek the patronage of Terebell Sheratan.

"Chat," I said, "I think I need a drink."

# 18

## The Patron's Puppet

That drink gave me a good night's sleep, but it didn't take away the problem. Until the Ranthen returned, I had no way to pay the Spiritus Club. As predicted, the amount they wanted was more than I made in a year with Jaxon. Minty's rule was clear: no money, no distribution. I tried ringing Felix—maybe the fugitives had enough to help—but the hawker didn't pick up.

I tried the golden cord. Nothing. If Warden didn't come back soon, I'd have to track him down.

In the meantime, I threw myself into my work. The scrimmage was getting closer, and no matter what happened with the pamphlet, I had to be ready for it. Nick and I trained hard in the courtyard, both with weapons and without. Muscle hardened in my arms and legs. My waist and hips reclaimed their shape. I could lift and climb without breaking a sweat. Bit by bit, it was all coming back to me. How to be a mollisher, a fighter, a survivor.

Four days after Alfred's phone call, I knocked on Jaxon's door. No answer. I balanced a tray on my hip and knocked again.

"Jax."

A grunt came from somewhere inside. I went in.

The room was dark and stifling, the curtains blocking any hint of sunlight. Everything smelled of the ends of cigarettes and unwashed skin. Jaxon lay spreadeagled on his back, long fingers clasped around a small green bottle with a cork stopper.

"Fucking hell, Jaxon," was all I could say.

"Go away."

"Jax." I put the tray down and grasped him under the arms, but he was heavier than he looked. "Jaxon, snap out of it, you lazy sot."

His hand came flying up, shoving me into the desk. An ink bottle toppled off the edge and bounced off the carpet, hitting him right on the forehead. A dull groan was his only reaction.

"Fine." I straightened my blouse, irritated. "By all means, stay there."

Curses tangled in his mouth. Out of pity, I shoved a cushion under his head and threw the mantle from the couch over his back.

"Thank you, Nadine." His words weren't quite as crisp as usual, but he stopped just short of slurring.

"It's Paige." I tapped my foot. "Did you speak to the Abbess about the hitmen?"

Even drunk, he managed to sound irritated. "She's looking into it." His arm curled around the cushion. "Goodnight, Paignton."

At least he'd told her. If the Abbess hated the Rag and Bone Man as much as rumor suggested, she'd be happy to investigate. I pulled the mantle over his shoulders and left, closing the door quietly behind me. Jaxon had always liked a drink, but I'd never seen him like this. *Paignton . . .*

Save for Nadine's violin, playing a melancholy tune from the first floor, the den was quiet. We were all trapped indoors by Jaxon's latest curfew. The front door was locked from the inside, and nobody knew where he'd hidden the key. Just to get some air, I went out to the courtyard and lay down on the bench beneath the blossom tree.

London had too much light pollution for most stars to be seen, but a handful pierced through the artificial blue haze. Above the madness of the metropolis, the night sky put me in mind of the æther: a network of orbs, some bright, some dim, pinpricks in the endless folds of darkness that could have been full of knowledge or ignorance. Too much of it to see or comprehend.

The golden cord gave a hard pull.

I sat bolt upright. Warden was waiting behind the gate, in the darkness of the access passage.

"You were away for a while," I said, wary.

"Regrettably. I was with the Ranthen, discussing the state of affairs in the Westminster Archon." He could almost have passed for human tonight, with his eyes that dim. He wore a straight-cut coat, gloves and boots. "Terebell has summoned you."

"Where?"

"She said that you would know the place."

The music hall. Part of me wanted to refuse the demand, but it was a small, bitter part, and I needed Terebell's help.

"Give me a minute," I said.

"I will meet you at the pillar." He withdrew.

I was careful not to make a sound on the stairs. In the bathroom, I set my hat over my hair, chalked my lips and pressed in my hazel contacts. It wasn't enough. Unless I went under the knife, nothing could hide my face forever.

There were two more weeks until the scrimmage. All I had to do was stay alive until then.

When I opened the bathroom door, I found myself facing Nadine Arnett. Her eyelids were puffy, her bare feet raw with blisters.

"Are you all right?" I said. We hadn't spoken in some time. "You look exhausted."

"Oh, I'm just great. I've only been on the street for nine hours. I only had to run from the Vigiles twice." She swung her violin case on to the floor. Deep, purplish grooves ran through her fingertips.

"Going somewhere?"

"Goodge Street. I've got a job to finish."

"Right. Does Jax know?"

"No idea. Are you going to tell him?"

"You know, the only reason he keeps you as mollisher is because you're a dreamwalker. He told me, while you were gone. It's your aura he wants, Paige. That's the asset. Not you."

"All our auras are his assets. Did you think Jax liked our scintillating table conversation?"

"I'm loyal. That's why he chose me when you were gone. It had nothing to do with my aura," she said, and I could tell by her face that she believed it. "You know what he thinks of sensors. He still chose me to be his mollisher."

"I'm trying to work, Nadine." I pushed past her. "I'm not interested in a rivalry."

"Maybe you could do more work if you stepped down," she said, almost biting out the words. "I don't know what you're up to, Mahoney, but I know you're up to something."

Eliza chose that moment to open the kitchen door, letting out the smell of allspice. She looked at us.

"Something wrong?"

"Nothing," I said, and left Nadine to answer her questions. I snatched my coat and cravat from the rack and left through my bedroom window.

Warden was waiting for me near the desecrated sundial pillar. He stood when I approached. The sight of him sent a tremor down my back.

"We must move swiftly," he said. "There are Vigiles nearby."

"It isn't far." I wrapped my cravat over the lower half of my face, checking three times that the knot was tight enough. "We'll attract attention if we walk together."

"I will follow you."

I led him down the east-facing dial street, where cars and rickshaws rumbled past the pavement. I stayed close to the walls and shop fronts, keeping my face turned against my collar. There were no Vigiles that I could see, but every aura set me on edge. There could be Rag Doll spies in the district. A camera peered down from a rooftop, but the peak of my cap shielded me from facial recognition. I waved Warden to the other side of the street, nodding to it. It was madness to be outside with him. This citadel had eyes in every wall.

Once we were both over the main roads, out of the way of the streetlamps, I let myself breathe again. Warden fell into step beside me. He took much larger strides than I did.

"What does Terebell want?"

"To treat with you." He slowed down for me. "The time is ripe for you to request the money you require."

If she said no, it was the end of everything.

We walked without speaking again until we reached the music hall. I slowed down when I sensed a dreamscape nearby.

Standing in the middle of Drury Lane was a single voyant officer, his masked face angled away from us. At first glance he looked like a night Vigile, but the uniform was different. A scarlet shirt with paned sleeves, showing hints of gold lining; a black leather gilet, stitched with the Scion anchor in gold; elbow-length gloves; and tall boots. A more sophisticated take on the old red-jacket's uniform.

"Is that a Punisher?" I whispered.

Warden looked over my head. "Almost certainly."

Whatever this guy was, he was standing between us and our destination. I glanced up at the buildings, scanning for the right window. When I found it, I whistled out a signal, the first few notes of Scion's anthem.

Within seconds, three footpads were climbing from the window of the nearest night parlour. I nodded to the Punisher. They tied scarves over their faces before they ventured towards him. One of them swiped the baton from his belt and threw it to her companion, who leapt over a car and sprinted away. The Punisher watched in silence as they fled, then looked over his shoulder, red visor gleaming. I grabbed Warden's shoulder, pulling him back into the shadows.

For an instant, I was certain the Punisher would come to investigate. His fingers flexed over his radio. Finally, he strode in the direction the footpads had gone.

That wasn't normal Vigile behavior. That silence, the lack of immediate reaction when they'd snatched the baton. He'd be back in a minute.

"Go," I whispered.

Moving quickly, we made our way round to the back of the theatre. I could sense four Rephaite dreamscapes inside, with their distinctive armor. Once we reached the stage door, Warden faced me under the streetlamp and grasped my upper arms. A shock flew down to my fingers, but my back tightened. It was the first time he'd touched me since the catacombs.

"I will not often ask you to conceal the truth," he said, his voice low, "but I ask it of you now."

I didn't speak.

"There is a reason I have been behaving the way I have. What happened between us in the Guildhall is common knowledge among Rephaim. Nashira has spent a great deal of time telling her people that I am a rotmonger and a flesh-traitor." He looked me in the eye. "But you must deny it, repeatedly and emphatically if need be, to the Ranthen."

It was the first time he'd really acknowledged that the Guildhall hadn't been a figment of my imagination. "I thought Terebell and Errai knew," I said quietly. "They know about the cord."

"The cord does not always point toward physical intimacy." His gaze flicked over my face. "I understand if you do not wish to do as I ask. But I ask it for your sake, not mine."

After a moment, I nodded. He released my arms, leaving goose-flesh beneath my shirt. I turned to face the door.

"If she asks," I said, "what should I say happened?"

"Anything but the truth."

Because the truth must be too awful for Rephaim to wrap their heads around.

I kept my distance from Warden as we sidled through the door, parted the dust-laden stage curtains, and descended to the auditorium, where the faded chairs and carpet were lit by several jack-lanterns. Terebell stood in the aisle with three other Rephaim. Warden stopped in the aisle.

"Ranthen-kith," he said, "this is Paige Mahoney. It is to her that you owe my presence tonight."

Terebell ignored this announcement. She went straight to Warden and pressed her forehead to his, murmuring to him in Gloss. They were almost of a height. The sight of it made something wrench behind my ribs.

"Hello, Terebell," I said.

Terebell turned her head, but still didn't speak. Her hand rested on Warden's shoulder. She looked at me the way Jaxon looked at buskers.

"I have brought Paige here to speak with you about her plans," Warden continued. "She has a request for us, as we have one for her."

Errai and Pleione said nothing. Standing between them, Terebell slashed her gaze over me.

"Dreamwalker, this is Lucida Sargas." She motioned to the stranger. "One of the very few with Ranthen sympathies."

My hand flinched toward the pouch in my pocket. "Sargas?"

"Indeed. I have heard a great deal about you, Paige Mahoney."

Lucida had slightly more emotion in her features than the others; she looked almost curious. "From the tales told by my Sargas-kin."

She had Nashira's complexion—somewhere between silver and gold, more on the silver side—and thick hair, but it was loose and cut to her shoulders. An unusual style among Rephaite females in the colony, but all three of them had it here. She looked so much like her relatives, with those hooded eyes.

"What sort of tales?" I said, wary.

"They are calling you the great fleshmonger of London. They say the earth beneath your feet is scorched and rotten." Her gaze slid down to my boots. "It looks decidedly undamaged to me."

Fantastic. "And what do they say about you?" I let go of the pouch. "Do they know you're Ranthen?"

"Oh, yes. I was fool enough to disagree with the violent colonization of Sheol I. Consequently, I was declared a blood-traitor by my dear cousin, Gomeisa. I have lived as a renegade ever since."

"A Ranthen renegade." Terebell paced past her. "I am sure you remember Pleione Sualocin."

"Vividly," I said.

She was the only one sitting, the first Rephaite I'd ever seen. The one who had sapped a voyant's aura on my first night in the colony. Her hair was short now, too, thick curls of black that sat on her shoulders.

"Ah, yes. 40." A low, purring voice that promised danger. "We have much to discuss with you."

"So I've heard." I perched on the back of a seat. Warden remained standing in the aisle. He held himself differently around them, straight-backed and unmoving. "You can drop the 'dreamwalker,' by the way. And the 40, while you're at it. It's Paige."

"Tell me, *dreamwalker*," Terebell said, ignoring me, "have you encountered any Rephaite hunters since we last saw you?"

My jaw flexed. "No," I said, "but they'll come sooner or later."

"Then take care to conceal yourself. Red-jackets are hidden among the Vigiles." Terebell paced past me. "We are at a critical stage in our plans. After several failed attempts to overthrow the Sargas family, we have taken our first step toward bringing about their downfall. But their grip on the corporeal world is strong, and it will only grow stronger as their empire expands. Sheol II's location has been decided."

"Where?"

"We know that it will be in France, but not the precise location," Warden said. "Alsafi will send word when he discovers it."

"Nashira and Gomeisa form the heart of the Sargas doctrine. You will have noticed that Gomeisa was able to ward off four of us in the Guildhall," Terebell continued, with no hint of shame. "That is no natural strength. We had planned to eliminate Nashira quietly, but it seems that opportunity has been snatched." Her gaze drifted towards Warden. "Before we can strike them, it is essential that we dismantle the network they have built in the human world."

"Scion," I said.

"The key purpose of the penal colony was never to fend off the Emim," Warden said, "but to indoctrinate humans. The red-jackets, most of whom were successfully brainwashed, will act as human agents of the Sargas when they reveal their presence to the world."

"You mean the Sargas are going to tell everyone they're here?" I looked between them and found only straight faces. "They're mad. The free-world would declare war on Scion."

"Unlikely. If it came to war, Scion could raise a vast army. It would deter any declaration of war from the countries of the free-world, whose alliances are troubled, at best."

"From our last reports, many of them are closing their eyes to Scion's unsavory practices in order to maintain peace," Terebell said. "President Rosevear, for example, is leaning toward a policy of non-intervention. Scion has also managed to conceal a great deal of their brutality from free-world surveillance."

As a student in a Scion school, I'd dreamed of the free-world coming to their senses. I'd dreamed that, when hard evidence got out of Scion's crimes, the superpowers would raise their banners against my enemy—but it had never been that simple. Free countries were invisible on classroom maps, but through osmosis at the black market and talking to Zeke and Nadine, I'd grasped bits and pieces about how the Americas were governed. Rosevear was a respected leader, but she had her own problems to handle: swollen oceans, toxic waste, financial burdens, countless problems on her own shores. For now, we were on our own.

"We must start with London," Terebell said—a statement, not a suggestion. "If we can destroy the nerve center, the other citadels may begin to crumble. We understand from Arcturus that the Underlord was murdered."

"Yes."

"Evidently," Errai said, "it was a Rephaite assassin. Situla Mesarthim, perhaps. She is fond of decapitation."

"It seems likely," Pleione agreed.

Lucida was still watching me, one eyebrow slightly raised. "And what do you think, dreamwalker?"

Arms folded, I cleared my throat. "It's possible," I said, "but all the evidence is pointing toward a mime-lord called the Rag and Bone Man. The same mime-lord that captured Warden."

"Then there is no clear heir to the crown," Terebell said, and I shook my head.

"We're holding a competition to choose a new leader."

"And do you intend to participate?"

"Yes. I have to win if I'm going to get the word out. I've already had this produced." I took out my spare copy of *The Rephaite Revelation* and handed it to Errai, who looked at my hand as if it were a dead rat. "Once it's distributed, everyone in the citadel will know about you."

"What is this?"

"It's a penny dreadful. A horror story."

Terebell snatched it. Her eyes grew hotter as she read the front page. "I have heard of these. Cheap, sordid entertainment. How dare you belittle our cause with this mockery?"

"I didn't have time to write an epic poem, Terebell. And if I'd tried to tell people without proof—"

Errai actually hissed at me, a sound like water being thrown on a fire. "Do not speak to the sovereign with that tone. You had no right to expose us without permission. You should have waited for us to advise you."

"I didn't realize I needed your advice, Rephaite," I said coolly.

He spat something at Warden in Gloss, and a spirit fled from the hall. With a glance at me, Warden sent a soft tremor across the cord, something that felt a little like a warning.

Lucida took the pages from Terebell. "I do not think this idea so crass," she mused, flipping through the pages. "It will make our movements in the citadel more difficult, but may save arduous explanations when the time comes for us to reveal ourselves."

"The denizens of this citadel fear the onset of unnaturalness," Warden said. "They have no wish to see visions of giants, and if they did, they would certainly not go to the authorities about them."

There was a short silence before Terebell leaned down to my level. I wasn't sure if it was intended to patronize me or not. "If you win this 'scrimmage,'" she said, "then you will have overall command of the London syndicate. We wish to know if you will join your forces with ours."

"I doubt that would work," I said. "Don't you?"

"Explain your meaning."

"You're visibly sickened by my presence. Aside from that, the syndicate's a mess. Getting it organized will take time." I looked her in the eye. "And money."

There was a silence, during which the hall turned cold, as if a sudden draft had blown in.

"I see." Terebell rested her gloved hands on the back of a seat. "Money. The dark obsession of the human race."

Errai turned up his nose. "Material possessions cannot last, yet they fight over them like vultures. Disgusting greed."

"Fruitless greed," Pleione said.

"Okay, stop." I held up a hand, irritated. "If I'd wanted lectures, I would have gone to the University."

"I am sure." Terebell paused. "And what, dreamwalker, if we do not provide you with *money*?"

"Then I won't be able to remodel this syndicate. Even as Underqueen. First, I'll have to give the mime-lords and mime-queens a financial incentive to become my commanders," I said. "Then, if we can start the revolt, I'll need more to keep it going. Buying weapons, feeding voyants, patching them up when Scion fights back—all of it will cost more than I could hope to earn in a lifetime. If you agree to fund me, I can help you. If not, you should ask someone with fuller pockets than mine. There are plenty of rich criminals around."

They all looked at one another. Errai turned around, his muscled back heaving as he growled to himself.

I wouldn't let them recreate the penal colony in London. The syndicate voyants wouldn't be their red-jackets, with me as their Overseer. I had to assert myself as their equal, not their lackey.

"Bear in mind that our reserves are not infinite," Terebell said, studying my face. "At any moment, our agent in Scion could be discovered and the bank account closed. We do not have the resources to fund an extravagant lifestyle for an Underqueen, and at the first sign of careless spending, we will withdraw our support."

"I understand," I said.

"Then you have our word that if you win the scrimmage, we will fund the reorganization of the London syndicate. We will also, where possible, provide natural resources from the Netherworld to contribute to the war effort. It is the place from which both essence of amaranth and Emite blood are harvested."

"What use is Emite blood?"

"It has many properties," Warden said, "the most useful of which is masking the aura. A small dose will corrupt its appearance, so the nature of the gift cannot be determined. Naturally, harvesting the blood is a perilous venture, and tasting it, a deeply unpleasant one."

It sounded priceless. My aura was the one thing that almost always gave me away in London. "When you say 'mask,'" I said, "do you mean from other voyants?"

"Yes."

"And Senshield scanners?"

"Perhaps. We have not yet had the opportunity to test that theory."

"And soon enough, when word reaches the last strongholds of the Netherworld, we will also be able to provide soldiers of our own," Terebell said.

I raised an eyebrow. "Word of what?"

"The amaranth in bloom," Errai said, looking as irritated as Rephaim could look. "It is the Ranthen's call to arms, that which will persuade our old allies to return to us. Why do you think we never acted before now? We were waiting for the true sign. For an opportunity to revive what has faded."

My head was whirring. I tucked my hands into my pockets and took in a long, deep breath.

"We do not have time for you to ponder this proposal," Terebell said. "Answer me now, dreamwalker: will you ally your forces with mine?"

"It's not as simple as 'yes' or 'no.' If I win, I'll do my best to persuade the London voyants that taking down Scion is a good idea, but it won't be easy. They're thieves and con artists with no military training whatsoever. The money should convince them to help us, but I can't guarantee it."

"As you cannot *guarantee* it, we will have to impose our own guarantee." She indicated the nearest two Ranthen. "In order for you to win the scrimmage, you will submit yourself to our training. Errai, Pleione, you will instruct the dreamwalker to ensure she is up to standard."

From the look Errai gave me, you'd have thought she'd asked him to lick the floor. "I will not," he said.

"I will," Pleione said, with a note of menace.

"It would make more sense for me to train with Warden. I'm used to his training style," I said, trying to sound offhand. The thought of these two training me was not a pleasant one.

Tension crept into Terebell's jaw. "Arcturus has other duties. He is no longer your keeper."

"It will save time. We don't have a lot of it."

Her eyes grew hotter. You could almost see her mulling it over, weighing up the pros and cons of leaving the great Arcturus Mesarthim on his own with an upstart human. She turned to Warden and spoke to him in Gloss, her whole body held up as if by a taut rope. He looked at me for a while.

"Paige is right," he said. "It will save valuable time. For the Ranthen's sake, I will do this."

Terebell's features were rigid. "So be it." She reached into her coat and handed me a thick envelope. "Be grateful for this patronage, dreamwalker. And know that if you do not succeed in the ring, I will make you sorry you were ever born."

She spoke to the other three in Gloss, and the four of them left the auditorium without another word. Only Warden remained behind. I tucked the envelope into my coat, out of the reach of pickpockets.

"They're so friendly," I said.

"Hm. And you are a talented diplomat."

"Dreamwalker." Terebell was still on the stage, looking out from behind the curtain. "Before you begin, a word."

My pulse quickened. I glanced at Warden, who said nothing; then I followed her, up the steps and on to the stage. She seized my arm and pulled me behind the curtain, where she slammed me into the wall. My spirit reared up inside me.

"The Sargas have spread a message through the Netherworld. Every chol-bird is singing that Arcturus Mesarthim degrades himself with humans." Terebell forced up my chin. "Is this true, girl?"

"I don't know what you're talking about."

Her grip tightened. "If one more lie falls from your tongue, it will rot to the root. The golden cord may have helped you find him, but its mere existence implies an intimate relationship. I will not allow you to—"

"Rephaim don't consort with humans." I cut her arm away. "Even if I could, I wouldn't touch him."

My tongue, as it happened, did not rot to the root. "Good," Terebell said softly. "I may have agreed to fund your revolution, and I may have saved your hide in the colony. But do not cease to remember your station, Paige Mahoney, or I will see you fall as a crop falls to the scythe."

She let go of my arm. I marched toward the door, more shaken than I dared to show. Fuck her training. Fuck the lot of them.

Outside, it was starting to rain. The Punisher hadn't returned. He was fortunate; at that moment, I probably would have killed him.

With my hands balled into fists in my pockets, I walked away from the music hall, blowing out slow breaths to cool my anger. I'd always known what Rephaim thought of humans, but I never imagined that Warden would care what others thought about him. I had to be impervious, like they were. Let it all run off me, like water.

"Paige."

His voice was close, but I kept walking. "I don't think we should talk," I said, not looking at him.

"May I ask why?"

"I can think of several reasons."

"I have plenty of time to hear them. Eternity, in fact."

"Fine. Here's one: your so-called allies are treating me like filth on their boots, and I don't like it one bit."

"I did not think you could be so easily rattled."

"Let's see how rattled you are when I start talking about what cruel, tyrannical bastards you Rephaim can be."

"By all means," he said. "They would benefit from a lesson in humility."

I stopped beneath a streetlamp and faced him. The rain was already picking up, plastering my hair to my face—and for once he looked as human as I did, standing in the downpour on this London corner. "I don't know what their problem is, or what they know about the Guildhall," I said, "but they need to get over it if we're going to work together. And you need to decide how many of Terebell's orders you'll follow if we go ahead with this alliance."

"What I do is my prerogative, Paige Mahoney. Thanks to you, I am my own master."

"You told me once that freedom was my right." I held his gaze. "Maybe you should do something with it."

A furnace roared to life behind his eyes. It had come out sounding like a challenge.

Was he a gambler, too? And was the gamble worth it, when neither of us could win? I thought of the patronage, of the money and support I needed. I thought of Jaxon, watching the clock, waiting for me to return from my tryst.

"The sovereign-elect orders us to train," he said, "but she did not specify the manner in which I should train you."

"That sounds ominous."

"You will have to trust me." He turned back to the music hall. "Do you?"

# 19

## Ciuleandra

The music hall was empty when we returned, though I still checked for dreamscapes. Warden closed the doors behind us. I sat down on the edge of the stage and brought one knee up to my chest.

"How do you know Lucida isn't a double agent?"

He barred the doors. "Why do you ask that?"

"She's a Sargas," I said.

"Did you agree with your father on everything, Paige? Your cousin?"

"No," I said, "but the Mahoney family aren't tyrants who specialize in brainwashing."

The corner of his mouth gave the briefest twitch. "Lucida broke away from her kin a long time ago. She would not have starved herself for a century without good reason."

"What about the others?" My breathing was slower now, steadier. "What about Terebell?"

"I trust them, but the alliance will not be easy. Terebell has always been a harsh judge of the human race."

"Any particular reason?"

"I have studied many books on human history, and if there is one thing I have learned from them, it is that it is not always possible to find reason in tradition. It is the same for Rephaim."

Truer words had never been spoken.

Warden took a seat beside me, not quite close enough to touch, and clasped his hands. We both looked up at the carved pillars, the high ceiling. Unlike Terebell, he took in the hallmarks of violence that had been wrought on this building. His gaze lingered on the nearest collections of bullet wounds on the walls, the torn and blackened stage curtains.

"I apologize for how I treated you in the doss-house," he said. "I wanted to prepare you for the Ranthen's conduct. Their tolerance for humans waxes and wanes."

"And you thought the best way to prepare me was to act like a—"

"—Rephaite. Most Rephaim are that way, Paige."

I made a noncommittal sound.

In the colony, our relationship had been about fear. My fear of his control. His fear of my betrayal. Now, I realized, it was about trying to understand each other.

But fear and understanding were kindred things. Both involved the loss of the familiar and the terrible danger of knowledge. I didn't know if I understood him yet, but I wanted to. That in itself was a shock.

"I don't want this to be a repeat of the colony," I said softly.

"We will not allow that." Pause. "Ask."

He hadn't even looked at me. "The plan to 'quietly eliminate' Nashira," I said. "That was you."

It was a while before he replied. "Yes. Only when she chose me did I see an opportunity to end her."

"When were you betrothed?"

"Not long before we came to this side of the veil."

"Two centuries," I said. "That's a long time."

"Not by our standards. Centuries are nothing but grains of sand in the infinite hourglass of our existence. Fortunately," he said, "Nashira and I were never formally joined. She wished to wait until after the Bicentenary, when she was certain of our hold on the penal colony."

"So you never—"

"Mated? No."

"Right." Heat rose up my neck. There was a tincture of amusement in his look. *Stop talking about sex, stop talking about sex.* "I . . . see you ditched the gloves."

"I may as well embrace a life of sedition."

"How daring of you. What's next? Your coat?"

Silent laughter played across his face: a softening of his features, a quick fire in his eyes. "Is it wise to torment your mentor before he begins your training?"

"Why break the habit of a lifetime?"

"Hm."

We sat together for a long time. The tension was still there, but slipping away by the moment.

"Come, then." Warden stood, towering over me. "Have you possessed anyone since coming here?"

"A bird. Jaxon saw that. And a Vigile," I said. "I made her talk into her transceiver."

"And did you hurt her?"

"She was bleeding from every orifice in her head."

"Blood is not pain. Do not fear your gift, Paige. Your spirit aches to wander," he said. "You can do more than merely force your opponents into unconsciousness. You know that very well." When I didn't answer, he glanced over his shoulder. "Possession is only dishonorable if you do deliberate harm to the host—assuming the host does not richly deserve that harm, of course. The more you practice your skills, the less likely you are to hurt."

"I just want to run through quick-fire jumping again. It's still quite hard to switch from flesh to spirit."

"You are out of practice, then."

I shrugged off my jacket. "I call it 'keeping a low profile.'"

"Good. Nashira will have very little means by which to trace you." He walked past me. "There are two fundamental problems you face when you dreamwalk. First: your breathing reflex stops. Second: your body falls to the ground. The first problem can be solved with an oxygen mask, but the second . . . not so easy."

It was the real weakness of my condition. In the scrimmage, it would be my fatal flaw. The moment I jumped, my body would be left vulnerable on the floor of the Rose Ring. One stab through the heart and I would be unable to return to it. "What do you suggest?"

"When I trained you on the meadow, your transition from flesh to spirit was clumsy, to say the least. But you are not a novice any longer." A vintage record player was balanced on a dusty old piano. He pushed open the lid. "I want to see fluidity from you. I want you to jump into the æther as if you belonged there. I want you to fly between dreamscapes."

He switched on the record player. "Where did you get that?" I said, fighting a smile.

"Somewhere or other. Like most of my belongings."

Not quite as beautiful as his gramophone, but still exquisite, set in a wooden suitcase. It was carved with the symbol of the amaranth, over and over again, petals woven through petals. "And what's it for?"

"For you." A sonorous viola played. "Maria Tănase, Romanian actress and singer of the twentieth century." He bowed to me, keeping his eyes on my face. "Let us see if dreamwalkers can dance."

A rich, soulful voice began to sing in an unfamiliar language. Without another word, we circled each other. I kept my body angled toward him, remembering the same dance on the meadow training ground. Back then I'd been shivering in that flimsy tunic, hardly understanding my gift, terrified and angry and alone. The fear reaction still ticked away inside me, an instinct burned in with the brand on my shoulder.

"What's the song?"

"This one is called 'Ciuleandra.'" He swung at me, and I ducked. "No ducking in a dance, Paige. Spin." When he tried it again, I turned to the left, avoiding his second blow. "Good. I hope there are other records to be found in this citadel, or I may lose control of my sanity more swiftly than I anticipated."

I spun again, this time to the right. "I can get more from the Garden, if you like."

"That would be kind of you." He mimicked my movements, or perhaps I mimicked his. "I want you to stay on your feet as you attack me. When you leave your body, it falls—but I think you could control that. I think you can leave a little of your consciousness in your dreamscape. Enough for you to remain standing while you inhabit another body." The look on my face must have shouted disbelief. "I told you that you had potential, Paige. It was not flattery."

"There's no way for me to stay standing. All my life functions stop."

"In your present state, yes. But we can amend that." He stepped back, breaking the routine. "Let us try a little combat. Anticipate my movements."

"How?"

"Focus. Use your skill."

I thought of an old trick Jaxon had taught me when I'd first started to dislocate my spirit. I imagined six tall vials, one for each sense, each filled with a little wine. I pictured pouring it from five of the vials into the one marked ÆTHER. When the vial was full to the brim, I opened my eyes.

The world around me was a grey haze, but it trembled with

spiritual activity. There was a field of disturbance around Warden where his aura shone.

His body moved. No, wait—his *aura* moved to the right, and *now* his body . . . I barely got out of the way before his mock punch struck the air next to my ear. I snapped back to meatspace, but he didn't wait to try again. This time, when his aura went left, I dived in the opposite direction.

"Very good," he said. "That is why sighted individuals, including Rephaim, are often better at physical combat. They see an aura shift before their opponent's muscles. You may not be able to see it, but you can sense it." The singing started again, faster. "When you see an opportunity, attack me with your spirit. Leave your body, as if you mean to possess me."

The moment he moved, I jumped.

At least, I tried to jump. Spirit and flesh strained at the seams. I exerted all my strength, struggling through each zone in my dreamscape, and hurled myself into the æther.

I didn't get far. My silver cord turned rigid, like metallic wire, and flung me back into my body.

"Up," Warden said.

I got back to my feet, already spent. "Why isn't it working?"

"Your emotions are not strong enough. You are no longer truly afraid of me, and consequently, your survival instinct is no longer forcing you from your body at the sight of me."

"Should I still be afraid of you?"

"Perhaps," he confessed, "but I would rather that you made the gift yours. You belong to yourself, not to the fear."

"Fine." Step, turn, step. "I assume you were born knowing everything about your gift."

"Never assume." He took my hand and spun me himself, so my hair whispered against his shirt, then gave me a gentle push away from him. "Now, feel the æther. Jump."

This time my spirit flew out. I leaped across the divide, ricocheted off his dreamscape like a bullet and woke to the unpleasant sensation of my skull hitting the floorboards.

"Not quite fast enough," Warden said. He stood with his hands behind his back, unmoved.

"So that's Rephaite humor." I got back to my feet, my head ringing. "*Schadenfreude.*"

"Not at all."

"Have you ever paused to reflect on how irritating you can be?"

"Once or twice," he said, eyes aflame.

I tried again, ripping myself free of my body. This time I stayed on my feet for an instant before I fell, hitting the carpet on my knees.

"Don't use anger, Paige. Imagine your spirit as a boomerang. A light throw and a quick return." He pulled me to my feet by one hand. "Remember what I taught you. Try to touch my dreamscape and return to your body before you hit the ground. And while you do it, dance."

"Dance *and* fall?"

"Of course. Remember Liss," he said. "Her act depended on dancing as she fell."

The name stung, but he was right. I thought of how Liss would climb up the multicolored silks, then untangle herself as she fell toward the stage.

"Your body is your anchor to the earth. The more your mind is forced to concentrate on it, the more difficult it will be to lift yourself free of it. Hence the trouble you encounter when you try to dreamwalk when you have been injured." He lifted my chin. "Raise yourself."

My jaw rested on his knuckle. His thumb brushed my cheek, and just for a moment—it might have been a moment—the backs of his fingers curled against my pulse. Fast. Warm.

He stepped back. I shook away the fog in my head for long enough to call on my sixth sense. I imagined moving through the æther, freeing myself from the confines of these bones.

The world dulled again. My weight tilted on to the balls of my feet. The muscles in my abdomen pulled tight. My spine straightened and my ribcage lifted. I circled him again. I was hanging on to the earth by my fingertips.

"Now," Warden said, "the song is inviting you to go faster. One, two, three!"

I spun and threw my spirit.

My journey to his dreamscape was quick and fluid. It was as if I'd been trying to throw a diving bell; now I'd flicked a pennyweight at him. I caught a glimpse of the inside of his dreamscape. Where there had once been an expanse of ash, a glimmer of bright color shone at the very center. The sight called to me: the engine of his body, tempting me to take control, to puppeteer him. But then I threw myself back out again, back into my own dreamscape, sheathing my spirit in flesh . . .

My palms hit cement. The shock jarred my arms, right to the shoulders. And my legs were trembling, but I was on my feet.

I didn't fall.

The song came to a sudden end and my knees gave way. But instead of being in pain, I was laughing, punch-drunk. Warden helped me up, cupping his hands under my elbows.

"That is the music I wanted to hear," he said. "When was the last time you laughed?"

"Have you *ever* laughed, Warden?"

"There is very little to laugh about when one is the blood-consort of Nashira Sargas."

Another song started. I hardly heard it. We stood too close to one another, my elbows still cradled by his palms, holding me against him.

"Rephaim are most vulnerable," he said, "at the points at which our bodies are most closely aligned with the physical world. Stab a Rephaite in the heel or knee or hand, and you are more likely to cause them pain than you are by striking at the head or heart."

"I'll keep it in mind," I said.

The light in his eyes was soft now, like a candle flame. I reached up and laid my palm against his cheek.

And one of his hands glided up my bare arm, over my shoulder and neck, and gently held the back of my head.

It should have been so easy to re-enact the Guildhall. There was no Nashira behind the red curtain, no Jaxon in the other room. In those moments, nothing in the world could have persuaded me to dreamwalk. Or to run. All my senses centered on the way he felt against me, and the empty space between his lips and mine; on the way our auras ran into one another, like colors on a loom. I spread my fingers over his heart, taking him in. His hand in my hair, the heat of his breath.

"You call a past lover an 'old flame.'" His apple-gold eyes were more chilling than beautiful, his face carved out of nothing earthly. "For Rephaim, it takes a long time for a flame to catch. But once it burns, it cannot go out."

It didn't take long to understand what he meant.

"But I will," I said. "I'll stop. I'll go out."

There was a long silence.

"Yes," Warden said, very softly. "You will go out."

He let go of me. With the contact broken, the night came rushing into me. "Don't talk in riddles." My chest was locked up tight, like a strongbox. "I know what you're saying. And I don't know why it happened, in the Guildhall. What I was thinking. I was afraid and you were kind to me. If you were human—"

"But I am not." His gaze burned into mine. "Your respect for the status quo continues to surprise me."

I watched his face, trying to work it out.

"Know that I am a Rephaite, and can only ever understand your world from an outsider's perspective. Know that the road walked at my side is not an easy one," he said, quiet as ever, "and that if we are discovered, you will not only lose the support you need from the Ranthen, but quite possibly your life as well. I want you to acknowledge this, Paige."

Love didn't come into this, and we both knew it. Arcturus Mesarthim was of the veil, not the world, and I was a daughter of the streets. If the Ranthen discovered anything between us, the fragile alliance we'd forged would be broken. But I could feel his warm, solid presence from here—the beating of his spirit, the tantalizing dark arc of his dreamscape, a flame wrapped up in smoke—and I realized that none of those things would change my mind. I still wanted him with me, just as I had before climbing aboard that train to my freedom.

"I didn't choose an easy life. And if I'm being paid to follow orders," I said, "then I'm just another kind of slave. Terebell should give me the money because she wants to destroy Scion and everything it stands for. Not to keep me under her control."

Warden looked at me, into me. He reached into the record player case and took out his gloves. I stiffened.

"There are always reasons," he said.

With the gloves on, he reached into the case and took out a flower. A poppy anemone with perfect scarlet petals, the flower that would scald him if he touched it. He held it out to me.

"For the scrimmage. I understand that they still use the Victorian language of flowers."

Silently, I took it.

"Paige." His voice was a gray shadow of itself. "It is not that I do not want you. Only that I might want you too much. And for too long."

Something stirred inside me.

"You can never want too much. That's how they silence us," I said. "They told us we were lucky to be in the penal colony instead of the æther. Lucky to be murdered with NiteKind, not the noose. Lucky to be alive, even if we weren't free. They told us to stop wanting more than what they gave us, because what they gave us was more than we deserved." I picked up my jacket. "You're not a prisoner any more, Arcturus."

Warden looked at me in silence. I left him in that ruined hall with the music echoing above him.

**\*\*\*\***

By the time I got back to the den, the door was still locked. The others must have given up on waiting for me to finish my "job." The gate to the courtyard was barred and chained, too. Jaxon really was making his point known.

I climbed up the building to the other side, where my window was ajar. I peeled the contacts from my aching eyes. A note lay on the nightstand, written in sleek black ink.

*I trust you enjoyed your stroll. Tell me, darling, are you a dreamwalker or a flâneuse, sauntering about the town by night? Fortunately for you, I have been called to a gathering, but we will discuss your disobedience in the morning. I am losing my patience.*

Nadine must have told him. I tossed it into the wastepaper basket. Jaxon could take his patience and shove it down the neck of a bottle. Fully clothed, I lay down on the bed and gazed into the darkness.

Warden was right. I was mortal. He wasn't.

He was Rephaite. I wasn't.

I imagined what Nick would say if I confessed to what I felt. I knew, I *knew* what he'd say. That the mental strain of captivity had forced me to develop an irrational degree of empathy toward Warden. That I was a fool for feeling like this.

I imagined what Jaxon would say. *Hearts are frivolous things, good for nothing but pickling.* He'd say it made me weak. That commitment, however small, was a fatal flaw in a mollisher.

But Warden cared if I laughed. He cared if I lived or died. He had seen me as I was, not as the world saw me.

And that meant something.

It had to. Didn't it?

Sudden resolve pushed through me, and my head was crystal-clear again. Barefoot, I stole into Jaxon's darkened office, where "Danse Macabre" was playing, and took a thick roll of paper and a candle from one of the cabinets. In the gloom, I lowered myself into my mime-lord's chair and bent my head to write my application for the scrimmage.

****

In the morning, just before sunrise, I went straight to the Garden and headed for the largest flower stall. There were already several voyants there, waiting for the stall to open so they could buy their posies for late applicants. Each kind had a label to describe its meanings in the language of flowers.

You could tell which ones were popular. Gladiolus, the warrior's flower. Cedar for strength. Begonia—a warning of a fierce fight in the ring. I walked past all those. After deliberating, I took some Bells-of-Ireland for luck, and finally, a single purple bittersweet.

*Truth*, the label said.

I threaded them all together in a single posy, tied with black ribbon: luck, truth, and Rephaite's bane, the flower that could bring down giants. Under the rising sun, I walked to the dead drop, where I laid the message down with my application.

Whatever happened next, I was not going to be the Pale Dreamer for much longer.

# Part III

## The Monarch Days

*I use this Afterword to express my fond Hope that my Research has enlightened all those Clairvoyants who have never thought to distinguish themselves from the great Mass of us that roam the Citadel. It has been an arduous Decade, but in this Pamphlet, my Wish for a more hierarchical and organized Society may yet be granted. We must fight Fire with Fire if we are to survive this Inquisition.*

—An Obscure Writer, *On the Merits of Unnaturalness*

# Interlude

## Ode to the Underworld

The monarchy had long since been dismantled, torn up from the root by blood and blade. Under cover of night, new kings and queens wore masks over their faces, gliding in the shadow of the anchor.

The violinist played a sweet sonata, lonely on a street bejeweled by rain. The voices of the dead were in her bow.

A boy without words looked up at the moon. He sang in a language he should never have known.

The man who was like snow saw the world begin to change, and his head burst with a picture of tomorrow.

*The cuckoo clock is ticking in the room.*

The lamp-eyed creatures dwelt in the bones of the citadel, their fates now bound to Paige Mahoney and the ring of roses.

*These days end with red flowers on a tomb.*

The hand without flesh lifted the silk, laying it down on the woman with two smiles and a fractured heart.

All across the citadel, the little lights stirred. Fingers skimmed a crystal ball's smooth surface, and wings beat deep within it. Wings, dark wings on the horizon, putting out the stars.

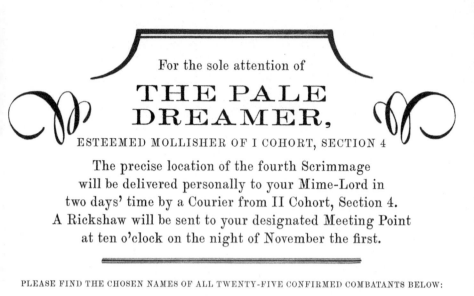

For the sole attention of

# THE PALE DREAMER,

ESTEEMED MOLLISHER OF I COHORT, SECTION 4

The precise location of the fourth Scrimmage
will be delivered personally to your Mime-Lord in
two days' time by a Courier from II Cohort, Section 4.
A Rickshaw will be sent to your designated Meeting Point
at ten o'clock on the night of November the first.

---

PLEASE FIND THE CHOSEN NAMES OF ALL TWENTY-FIVE CONFIRMED COMBATANTS BELOW:

VI COHORT: *The Hare and the Greene Manne* ❈ *Jenny Greenteeth and the May Fool*

V COHORT: *The Wretched Sylph and Bramble Briar*

IV COHORT: *Redcap and the Faerie Queene* ❈ *Faceless and the Swan Knight*

III COHORT: *The Bully-Rook and Jack Hickathrift* ❈ *The Glym Lord and the London Particular*

II COHORT: *Bloody Knuckles and Halfpenny* ❈ *The Wicked Lady and the Highwayman*
*Ark Ruffian and the Knife-Grinder*

I COHORT: *The White Binder and the Pale Dreamer*

INDEPENDENTS: *The Maverick Medium* ❈ *The Bleeding Heart* ❈ *Black Moth*

---

*Minty Wolfson.*

Secretary of the Spiritus Club, Mistress of Ceremonies

*On behalf of the Abbess,*
*Mime-Queen of I-2,*
*Interim Underqueen of the*
*Scion Citadel of London*

# 20

# Misprints

On Thursday the thirtieth of October, *The Rephaite Revelation*, the first anonymous piece of fiction to be released by Grub Street in a year and half, hit the streets of London like a firework. The Penny Post was all over the citadel, telling the macabre tale of the Rephaim and the Emim, selling booklets like freshly baked spice cakes in every corner of the underworld.

I was out in I-4 when I saw a finished copy for the first time. As the others were all busy, Jaxon had sent me out with Nick on some local errands, though we'd been instructed to stay well within Seven Dials. The bell rang as I pushed my way into Chateline's.

"Chat, I've come for your rent for next month," I said, resting my arms on the bar. "Sorry."

There was no reply. I did a double take. Chat's face was hidden behind his reading material. When I saw the title, a shiver trickled down my back.

"Chat," I repeated.

"Oh—" Looking embarrassed, he put it down and took off his reading glasses. "Sorry. What was that, love?"

"Rent. November."

"Right." A deep ruck appeared at the center of his brow. "Have you read this?"

I took it, trying not to look too interested. Grub Street usually printed in black and white, but they'd added red to this one, as they had for *On the Merits of Unnaturalness*.

"No," I said, handing it back. "What's it about?"

"Scion."

In a bewildered sort of silence, he went out to the back. I ran my fingers over the cover, a slight smile on my lips. *Thank you, Alfred.* Beneath the heavy print, a Rephaite and an Emite were locked in mortal combat. The Emite had been drawn as a hideous, melting corpse, with limbs that looked as if they'd been stretched on a rack and white orbs of eyes. Beside it, the androgynous Rephaite was a work of art, all sinew and alliciency—but terrible, too, wielding a great sword, with a shield bearing Scion's anchor.

"Here, love." Chat returned with a roll of notes in his hand. "Send Binder my regards."

I pocketed the money. "Are you doing all right, Chat? I can always wait a few more days."

"Fine. Trade's good." He flipped to the right page again. "Just imagine if this was what had really happened . . . I wouldn't put it past Scion, you know, even if all this rubbish about monsters isn't true."

"Some people think clairvoyants aren't real, in the free-world. We don't know what's out there." I lifted my silk over my mouth. "Bye, Chat."

He grunted, still staring at the pages.

I walked out of the shop, into the watery October sunshine. Nick was waiting for me outside, sitting on a bench with his face tipped up into the lukewarm rays. He looked up at me.

"Got it?" he said.

I nodded. "Let's head back."

We made our way out of the yard, walking close together. A unit of Vigiles had came marching through Seven Dials the afternoon before, asking questions at random shops and coffeehouses, forcing us to flee to Soho through the bolthole. Fortunately, they hadn't broken in to the den. "Chat's got a new penny dreadful," I said. "Anonymous authors, apparently. New to the scene."

"Oh, really? I need some new reading material," Nick said, smiling. Probably at the relative normalcy of this conversation. "What's it called?"

"*The Rephaite Revelation.*"

He stared at me. "You didn't."

"I didn't do anything."

"Pai— Dreamer! Binder will go spare if he thinks you're muscling in on his pamphleteering. He'll guess right away that it's you." His eyes were round as bottle tops. "What were you trying to achieve?"

"It tells people what they're up against. I'm tired of the world not knowing," I said coolly. "Nashira's counting on it being a secret until they choose to announce themselves. I want to hear *Rephaim* on the street and know that we've exposed them, undermined them. Even if it's just through gossip."

"Jaxon's like a lie detector. He'll know." He heaved a sigh and took the courtyard key from his pocket. "We should train before we go back in."

I followed him. Warden had armed me with a little more knowledge of my spirit, but I still needed to work on my strength and speed.

*Warden.* His name sent an odd, warm feeling through my bones. It was pointless to entertain a daydream, but I wanted to finish the conversation we'd started in the music hall.

In the courtyard behind the den, Nick dropped his coat on the bench and stretched his arms above his head. His smooth blond hair glinted in the sun. "How are you feeling about the scrimmage?"

"As good as you *can* feel, knowing you're about to fight twenty-odd people in public." I flexed my fingers. "My wrist might be a problem. I broke it in the colony."

"You can wrap your hands." He took up a defensive stance, a grin lifting his face. "Come on, then."

I pulled a face before I raised my fists.

He kept me in the courtyard for an hour, punching and dodging, feinting and ducking, making me do pull-ups on the blossom tree. At one point he pulled a spirit out of nowhere and flung it in my face, throwing me off my feet and sending both of us into fits of laughter. By the time he let me off, I was aching all over, but pleased with my progress. My arms weren't as weak as they'd been in the penal colony. I sat down on the bench to catch my breath.

"Okay, *sötnos?*"

I flexed my hand. "Fine."

"You're doing well. Remember, be quick. That's your advantage," he said, folding his arms. He'd barely broken a sweat. "And keep eating. We need you back to full strength for this fight."

"Okay." I wiped my upper lip. "Where's Zeke?"

"Doing errands, I think." He glanced up at the windows. "Go on. You should give Jax that money."

Sweat soaked my blouse. I ran up to the stairs to the bathroom and doused myself in water before changing into fresh clothes. Leaving my hair wet, I knocked on Jaxon's door.

"What?" was the tense reply.

I walked in and held up the envelope. "I got Chat's rent."

Jaxon was lying on the couch, his hands folded on his chest. He swung himself into a sitting position and hunched over, hands clasped between his knees like a bridge. For once he wasn't drunk, but in his lounging robe and striped trousers, he looked small and exhausted in a way I'd never thought possible for my mime-lord. I took out the cash—eight hundred pounds, a good chunk of Chat's monthly profit—and laid it in his bejeweled money-box.

"Take half for yourself," he said.

"It's eight hundred."

"Yes, Paige." He lit a cigarillo and held it delicately between his back teeth on one side of his mouth.

Usually he made a big show of our pay packets, and I couldn't remember the last time I'd had that much money from my work. I took half the notes and tucked them back into the envelope, then stowed it away in my jacket before he could change his mind. "Thanks, Jax."

"Anything for you, O my lovely." He held up the cigarillo, studying it. "You know I would do *anything* for you, don't you, darling?"

My back tensed.

"Yes," I said. "Of course."

"Of course. And when I have risked my neck, my section and my Seals to come to your rescue, I do not expect you to disobey my orders." His pale hand reached for his reading material. "Something was delivered to me this morning, while I was enjoying my breakfast in Neal's Yard."

I tried to look interested. "Oh?"

"Oh, yes. Oh, dear." He shook out the penny dreadful, his face stiff with disgust. "*The Rephaite Revelation,*" he read out. "*Being a true and faithful Account of the ghastly Puppet Masters behind Scion, and their Harvest of clairvoyant Peoples.*" With a flick of his wrist, he tossed it into the cold hearth. "From the quality of the writing I'd think it was one of Didion's rags, but Didion Waite is about as inventive as a sack of potatoes. And however offensively this hack forms his or her words, it certainly stretches the imagination to breaking point." In the space of three seconds he was inches from my face, his hands gripping my arms. "When did you write it?"

I stood my ground. "I didn't write it."

His nostrils flared. "Do you take me for a fool, Paige?"

"It was one of the other fugitives," I said. "She was talking about writing a pamphlet. I told her not to do it, but she must have—"

"—asked *you* to write it?"

"Jax, I couldn't write something like that to save my life. You're the pamphleteer."

He eyed me. "True." Smoke curled from his mouth. "You are still in contact with these fugitives, then."

"I've lost track of them now. Not all of them have wealthy mime-lords, Jax," I said. "They need some way to make money."

"Of course." The anger seeped out of him. "Well, there's nothing to be done about it. It will all be dismissed as fanciful nonsense, mark my words."

"Yes, Jax." I cleared my throat. "Could I have a look at it?"

Jaxon gave me a withering look.

"Next I'll be catching you reading Didion's poetry on the sly." He waved me away. "Off with you."

I fished the pamphlet from the hearth and left. He would find out about my involvement. He was probably calling Grub Street whenever he had a spare minute (which seemed to be every minute), demanding to know the identity of the author. I wanted to trust Alfred, but he'd been Jaxon's friend for a very long time, longer than I'd been alive. In the end, the secret would come out.

The first thing I noticed in my room was that several things had been moved since I'd left it. The Lanterna Magica. My box of trinkets. Someone had been snooping around in here, and I sensed it wasn't an intruder. I checked my pillowcase and found the stitches untouched. Just to be safe, I tucked the red handkerchief and the envelope of money into my boot.

Jaxon really was overstepping the mark. What did he think I was hiding? I took the penny dreadful to my bed and flicked through to the twelfth chapter, wherein Lord Palmerston was faced with his terrible choice.

*When in the morning Palmerston rose and made his way to the Octagon Hall, there the creature stood again, decked in her finery, a perfect queen in all but name. "Bright one," he said, "I fear your request will not be granted. Though I have tried to persuade the high lords of your good nature, they think my brain addled by laudanum and absinthe."*

*And the creature smiled, as beautiful as she was strange.*

*"My dear Henry," she said, "you must assure the lords that I do not come to harm your people, you who are blind to the spirit world. I come only to liberate the clairvoyants of London."*

Goose bumps broke out all over me. That hadn't been in the original. The word had been *incarcerate*, not *liberate*, and I was sure Nashira hadn't been described as *beautiful*. Had she? I didn't have the two originals now—they were with Alfred and Terebell—but why would any of us have written *beautiful*?

I read further. If it was just one mistake, it would be fine. But no, there were more and more of them, accumulating like a growth of mold on the heart of the story.

*Then the lady's shadow fell across the street, and with trembling hands the seer beheld her, and at once, her beauty soothed his wounded spirit.*

*"Come with me, poor lost soul," said she, "and I shall take you to the place beyond despair."*

*And the seer stood, and he was overjoyed.*

This time a hard jolt went through my chest. No. This was wrong. Nothing had been written about Nashira's beauty, or its soothing of anyone's wounded spirit. And no, not *overjoyed* . . . the right word was *terrified*, I remembered it clearly from the manuscript . . . I picked up my burner and dialed the number Alfred had given me, my heart pounding in my throat, my mouth dry. It rang and rang.

"Come on," I hissed.

Finally, after two more attempts, there was a crackle on the other end. "Yes, what is it?"

"I need to speak to Alfred. Tell him it's the Pale Dreamer."

"One moment."

My fingers tapped on the nightstand. Finally, a familiar voice called down the line: "Hello, dear heart! How fares *The Rephaite Revelation*?"

"It's been edited extensively." I fought to keep control of my voice. "Who did this?"

"The writers, of course. Did they not tell you?"

The bottom dropped out of my stomach. "The writers," I repeated. "Did you hear their voices, Alfred?"

"Well, I certainly heard somebody's voice. A very nice young man named Felix Coombs. He said that on reflection, he thought that there needed to be a good faction in the pamphlet as well as an evil one. As the Rephaim are the less repulsive of the two, they were chosen as the 'good guys,' to use a colloquial phrase."

"When was this?"

"Oh, just before it went to press." Pause. "Is something wrong, dear heart? Was there a typographical error?"

I sat back on the bed, my heart pounding in slow, sick throbs.

"No," I said. "Never mind."

I hung up. With heat in my eyes, I read the pamphlet again, staring at the printed letters.

Terebell's money had been used to glorify the Sargas.

The Rephaim didn't feed on humans. There was no sign of the poppy anemone. They were shown fighting the wicked Emim, protecting feeble clairvoyants. It was the beautiful myth, the one Scion's leaders had believed for two hundred years: a dark tale of the wise, omnipotent Rephaim, the gods on Earth, defending humans from the rotten giants. A black wave rose and swelled over my head.

Felix hadn't made that call of his own accord. Someone must

have got wind of the pamphlet, someone who wanted to protect the Rephaim. To give them a good reputation.

The Rag and Bone Man. It had to be. He knew about the Rephaim. If he had the fugitives . . . if he gave them to Nashira . . .

A thin film of sweat coated my body. I wiped my upper lip with my sleeve, but I couldn't stop the trembling. It wasn't Alfred's fault. He'd done his best—and besides, he wouldn't have any idea why I was upset. It was only a story, after all. Only someone else's story.

It didn't matter now. It was out there. What mattered was that the fugitives had been found. I made a grab for my coat and hat, threw them on and pushed the window open.

"Paige?" The door creaked open, and Eliza walked in. "Paige, I need to—"

She stopped dead when she saw me crouched on the windowsill, my hand gripping the frame. "I have to go out," I said, already swinging my legs over the edge. "Eliza, would you keep an ear out for the phone booth? Tell Nick I've gone to see the other fugitives."

Slowly, she closed the door behind her. "Where?"

"Camden Market."

"Oh, really?" She hitched a smile on to her face. "I wouldn't mind coming, actually. Jax needs some more white aster."

That gave me pause. "Why?"

"Just between you and me, I think he's been slipping it into his absinthe. I can't work out what's wrong with him lately. He's going to smoke and drink himself to death."

Whatever it was he wanted to forget, he wouldn't tell us. "We won't be shopping. The whole district's in lockdown," I said, then paused. "Actually, I could use your help. If you're free."

"What are we doing?"

"I'll tell you when we get there." I beckoned to her. "Bring a knife. And a gun."

\*\*\*\*

I got a local buck cabbie to drop us off at the quiet, residential northern end of Hawley Street, as near as she could get to the Stables Market. "The Rag Dolls won't let us get any closer to the markets," she said to me. "Couriers, unlicensed cabs, any under-world folk who operate from outside the district. Don't know what's got into them. You'll have some trouble getting in, I'll wager." She held out a hand. "And that'll be eight pounds forty, please."

"The White Binder will reimburse you," I said, already halfway out of the cab. "Put the bill in the I-4 dead drop."

As she drove away, I climbed up some scaffolding. Eliza followed me, but she didn't look happy.

"Paige," she said, exasperated, "do you want to explain what the blistering hell we're doing here?"

"I want to check up on the other fugitives. Something's wrong."

"And you know this how?"

I couldn't answer without letting it slip that I was involved with the penny dreadful. "I just know."

"Oh, come *on*." She hopped to the next rooftop. "Even voyants don't get to say that sort of shit, Paige."

I took off at a run across the flat rooftops. When I reached the building at the end of the street, I crouched down at the edge of the roof and examined the scene below. Chalk Farm Road was already wide awake, its shops pulsing out lights and music, the pavement awash with amaurotics and voyants. If we could cross the street without being seen and get over the wall we'd be in the Stables Market, minutes from the boutique.

Auras flickered whenever a voyant passed. There was a Rag Doll slouched against the wall, blue-haired and armed with two pistols, but she was too far away to pick up on my aura. With Eliza shadow-ing me, I climbed down the other side of the building and made a dash across the street, elbowing an amaurotic out of the way as I went. A quick jump took me to the top of the wall. Eliza scrambled after me, but her legs were shorter. I grabbed her under the arms and hauled her over to the other side.

"Are you off the cot?" she whispered to me angrily. "You heard what the cabbie said!"

"I heard." I was already walking. "And I want to know what the Rag Dolls have got to hide from the rest of us."

"Who cares what the other sections do? Your shoulders aren't big enough for the whole of London's problems, Paige . . ."

"Maybe not," I said, "but if Jaxon wants to be Underlord, his shoulders need to get a little wider." I kept a hand on my knife. "By the way, has Jax had a good rummage through your room, or is it just mine?"

She glanced at me. "I did notice a few things had been moved. You think it's Jaxon?"

"It has to be."

The market was busy at this time of the afternoon, when Scion's working day came to an end. Moribund sunlight glinted off racks of jewelry. I traversed the enclosed tunnels of the market, making my way between stalls and beneath chandeliers, keeping a constant lookout for Rag Dolls. Any of these people could be working for them. Every time I spotted a voyant, I ducked out of sight until they passed, pulling Eliza with me. By the time I reached the right place, I'd seen two large groups of Dolls and countless loitering voyants, no doubt in their employ.

Agatha's Boutique was locked up, with a CLOSED FOR RENOVA-TION sign on the door. Every piece of jewellery had vanished from the window displays. The door was guarded by a cluster of armed Rag Dolls. One of them—a bearded medium with wiry, pale green hair—had a carton of food balanced on his knee. The others were all alert, watching the nearest traders setting up their stalls.

"Eliza," I said, and she leaned in closer, "you think you can distract them?"

"You *can't* go in there," she hissed. "Imagine if someone tried to sneak into one of our buildings. Jaxon would—"

"—beat them senseless, I know." These guys wouldn't just do that; they'd kill me. "Just get them away from the shop for five minutes. I'll meet you back at the den in an hour or two."

"You'd better pay me for this, Paige. You owe me two weeks' wages. Two *years'* wages."

I just looked at her. With a few whispered curses, she crawled out from under the table. "Give me your hat," she said, holding out a hand. I took it off and tossed it to her.

If they had six guards posted to watch the shop, there must be something in there worth seeing. The fugitives might still be in the cellar, chained up like Warden had been in the catacombs.

I waited, watching the shop. Eliza had been a member of the Seven Seals for longer than I had, and a thief from her early childhood. She was a master of distraction and quick getaways, even if she hadn't done much street work since Jaxon had employed her.

After a minute, I sensed her again, approaching from my right. She came out of a shop wearing a stolen pair of cinder glasses, her ringlets crammed into my hat, looking like someone who didn't want to be seen. As soon as the Rag Dolls caught sight of her, they stiffened. One of them rose to her feet.

"Hey."

Eliza sped up, keeping her head down, and made toward the nearest passage. A Rag Doll with violet hair made a grab for her gun. "You, stay here," she said. "I don't like the look of her."

The others stood with her. The man looked up from his food for long enough to roll his eyes. "It's not like there's anything to steal in here."

"Well, if there is, and it goes missing, you'll be the one explaining things to Chiffon. And she's not in the best mood these days."

Eliza broke into a run, and the Rag Dolls took off after her. As soon as they were gone, I walked straight past the remaining guard, who didn't so much as glance at me, and made my way to the back of the shop. There had been a basement window, I recalled. After a minute of searching, I found it and kicked it in, sending glass pattering down on to the floorboards. It was a tight squeeze, but I just about got myself through the gap.

The bolthole was empty. To the outside eye, it was nothing but a cellar for an empty shop.

I stayed there for a while, crouched among the broken glass. It glistened in the dim light from outside. My first guess was that the fugitives had been taken to the Camden Catacombs, but that hiding place was compromised now. There had to be *something* here . . .

As my eyes adjusted to the gloom, my finger traced a smear of dry blood across the floorboards. It disappeared under an empty bookcase, made of dark, smooth wood.

Agatha had said that her boutique was the *bolthole* of II-4. A bolthole wasn't just a hiding spot, but a way out of the district. Ours led from Seven Dials to Soho Square. Hector's had given him a means of escaping under the fence that surrounded his slum. If they'd been trying to move the fugitives without anyone noticing, it would make sense to do it underground.

The entrance to this cellar was concealed from Vigile inspections by a curio cabinet in the shop above, and I was willing to bet that the bookcase was secret door number two. I dug my fingers in behind it and pulled with all my might, sweat standing out on my brow as my arms burned. With a hollow *click*, it finally swung open on well-oiled hinges, hardly making a sound. Beyond it was a narrow stone passage, too low for me to stand up straight. Cold, musty air drifted out, unsettling my hair.

A sensible part of me told me to wait until I had backup, but listening to that voice had never got me anywhere. I switched on my flashlight and walked inside, leaving the bookcase ajar behind me.

****

It was a long, long walk. The passageway started small and nondescript, with barely any space for me to extend my elbows beyond my ribcage, before it widened enough for me to breathe in the dank air without wheezing. I had to keep my head down and my shoulders hunched to keep from knocking myself out on the low ceiling, which looked to be made of cement.

Soon I found myself peering into the Camden Catacombs through an air vent. It was too dark to make out much, but I could see enough to know that I was looking into Warden's cell.

I was starting to suspect that Ivy's trust in her old kidsman had been misplaced. Agatha had been the gatekeeper of the Rag and Bone Man's den—and something else, from the looks of it. The passageway continued in another direction. I took a deep breath and pressed on.

Another ten minutes passed before my flashlight gave a flicker and went out, leaving me in absolute darkness. *Shit.* I tapped my watch, and the Nixie tubes inside it glowed faintly blue. I was starting to wish I'd brought Eliza with me, if only for someone to talk to. I hoped on hope that she'd escaped the Rag Dolls, or she'd be the next person to vanish without a trace. If I didn't disappear first, of course. My only comfort was that if I got lost down here, Warden would be able to sense where I was.

Using my hands to navigate, I kept going, bumping my head every few paces, until I emerged into a passage with the distinctive, rounded ceiling of the London Underground. I drew back at once, reaching for my revolver, but the tunnel was unoccupied. Another lost station, by the looks of it, like the one under the Tower.

The train waiting on the line was unusual in that it only came up to my waist, more of a cart than a carriage. The ends were painted red, the central parts in rusted black. REPUBLIC OF ENGLAND POSTAL SERVICE was stamped in gold paint along the side. I vaguely remembered something about this from school. Back in the early twentieth century, in an age before computers, a postal railway had been established to carry the new republic's secret messages across the citadel. It had long since been abandoned once mail could be sent electronically, but they must have left its skeleton to rot.

My heart thumped like a fist against my ribcage. The last thing I wanted to do was climb aboard this train to an unknown destination, but this had to be where the fugitives had been taken.

At one end of the train was a bright orange lever. There was more dried blood here, rusty fingerprints on the side of the train. A few days old, by the looks of them. I hunkered down in one of the tiny carts, swearing under my breath, and pulled the lever down with both hands. I was starting to hate trains.

With a low rumble, the train skimmed along the track, through tunnels so dark I couldn't see a thing but my watch. Nick was going to kill me when I got back.

Minutes passed. The darkness pressed on me, forcing blood into my head. I told myself over and over that this train wasn't going to the penal colony—it was too small, traveling too slowly—but it didn't stop the pounding in my ears. I kept an eye on my watch, my only source of light, cradling my wrist against my chest.

After half an hour, the train emerged in an illuminated tunnel and came to a gradual stop. Eyes burning, I climbed up on to another platform, as nondescript and narrow as the last. A single light flickered above me. Treading softly, I crept into another passage that took me up a steep, straight incline. More blood smeared the floor. I had to be a good few miles away from Camden by now, but the journey had only taken half an hour—given the size of London, I could still be in the central cohort. I climbed up a short ladder, into a tunnel that was so low I had to duckwalk. Finally, I could see light. Warm, indoor light.

There were dreamscapes nearby, fifteen of them. I recognized Ivy's, dim and quiet and broken. The fugitives must be here, but surrounded by guards. I moved on to my hands and knees to stop my boots squeaking. When I reached the end of the passage, I found myself looking through a series of thin slats, the sort you might find on a wardrobe door. Between them, I could see the back of a chair, with hands grasping its sides, and a head with short green hair.

*Agatha.*

She was sitting bolt upright, facing away from me. I didn't move.

Inside the firelit room was an enormous canopy bed, piled with shot-silk bedspreads, white sheets, monogrammed pillows and sleek cerise bolsters. Heavy curtains fell around it, glistening with delicate gold patterning. A polished nightstand held up a glass vase of pink aster flowers. High-backed velvet armchairs, a rosewood coffee table and a cheval mirror decorated the space around the fireplace, all positioned on a mint-green carpet.

When a door creaked open, Agatha's head snapped around. I withdrew into the shadows.

"There you are," she rasped. "Been waiting long enough."

It was a few moments before someone replied. "May I ask what you're doing here, Agatha?"

My gut lurched. I knew that voice, low and smoky. When I looked through the slats, even the memory of warmth drained from my body.

It was the Abbess.

**21**

# Symbiosis

*They connect with the æther by Means of their own Bodies, that of the Querent, or that of an unwilling Victim. Due to many of their Claims to use bodily Filth in their Work, they are the Pariahs of our clairvoyant Society. A large Community of Vile Augurs is known to thrive near Jacob's Island, the great Slum of II Cohort. It is my strong Advice to the Reader to avoid this Section of the Citadel, in case he or she should fall victim to their base Practices.*

—An Obscure Writer, *On the Merits of Unnaturalness*

\*\*\*\*

"I've come for my payment." Agatha's mouth was still lacquered with green. "Half of what they promised you."

"I'm aware of our agreement." The light from the slats shifted. "I suppose this is about the shop. You do understand why we had to close it, don't you?"

This had to be her night parlor. "The entrance to the tunnel is behind two hidden doors," Agatha rasped. "I made good money in that shop."

"It was a necessary precaution, my friend. The Pale Dreamer has an unfortunate habit of worming her way into hidden places."

*You have no idea*, I thought.

The Abbess tossed her jacket away, leaving her in a high-waisted skirt and a ruffled blouse, and unpinned the top hat from her scalp. Her hair cascaded down her back, thick and glossy, curled into delicate spirals at the tips. Framed by firelight, she took a seat in the upholstered armchair opposite Agatha, right in my line of sight.

"Did the Jacobite wake?"

"She did." The Abbess said, pouring two glasses of rosé wine. "We have the information we require. It took some . . . coaxing."

Agatha grunted. "Serves her right for leaving my service. Dragged her up from the gutter, I did, and she repays me by running off to work with your master."

"Be assured, I serve no master," was the cool reply.

"Then tell me, *Underqueen*, why does he never appear? Why does he hide while the little people do his dirty work?"

"Those 'little people,' Agatha"—the Abbess lifted her glass—"are all leaders of this syndicate. Your leaders. He and I have many friends. In the days to come, we will have many more."

A desiccated chuckle. "Many pawns, more like. Well, I won't be one. I might be losing my voice, but I'm no fool. If your little endeavor makes enough to keep you in those kinds of dresses, you can put some in my pocket now."

She held out a hand. The Abbess took another sip of her wine, not taking her eyes off her.

*All leaders of this syndicate. Endeavor.* I committed the words to memory, my blood racing with adrenaline. *Dirty work. Jacobite.* Whatever was going on, it went deeper than I'd ever imagined. Another dreamscape was drawing closer to the room, approaching from a lower floor.

"I spent good coin on those fugitives. Feeding them. Clothing them." Agatha's rasp was getting worse. "I had to get rid of two of them, mind. Screaming in their sleep, crying about monsters in the trees. I know broken dreamscapes when I see 'em. Useless. You don't know what I had to pay the local hirelings to dispose of them while the other four slept."

The boy and the girl, the other two survivors. Rage made me tremble. I'd taken them from one hell to another.

"We will settle your grievances soon, my friend. Ah," the Abbess said, smiling. "Turn around, Agatha. Here's your money."

"Good." The chair was pushed back with a groan of wood on wood. "There you are, boy. It's about—"

A gun went off.

The noise was so sudden, and so close to my hiding place, that I almost gave myself away with a scream. I threw myself against the floor of the wardrobe, my fist stuffed over my mouth. Through the slats, I could still see the two chairs in the gloom. Agatha's body rolled on to the floor, empty as a glove without a hand.

A shadow blocked the light. "She talked too much," a voice said, deep and male.

"She played her part." A bare foot pushed the corpse away. "You have everything ready?"

"Downstairs."

"Good." She massaged one side of her neck with her fingers. "Take my case to the car. I must . . . ready myself."

The man walked past my hiding place, his hands behind his back, and stepped over the body on the carpet. If the cowl was anything to go by, it was her mollisher, the Monk. "Do you need lithium?"

"No." His mime-queen closed her eyes, her chest expanding. "No lithium. Our symbiosis is much stronger now."

"Your body isn't getting any stronger. The last time exhausted you," her mollisher said gruffly. "They must be able to find some-one else with your gift. All this risk, for what? For *him*?"

"You know very well what it's for. Because they know my face, not his. Because I made the mistake." Her fingers flexed around the stem of her glass. "Last time it was eight armed thugs—strong, albeit drunk. This time it's a single mollisher. By tonight, Cutmouth will no longer pose a threat." She rose, empty-ing the rest of the wine on to Agatha's corpse. "I want twice the number of Rag Doll guards around Agatha's shop. Until we receive our payment, it should be sealed shut."

After a pause, the Monk said, "It will be done."

I breathed as softly as I could.

"I will need some time to . . . engage him. Knock three times on the door and wait for my order before you come in."

The light shifted again as the two of them left. I withdrew into the tunnel until their dreamscapes had retreated, then crawled forward on my elbows and pushed at the wardrobe door. Locked from the other side. I threw my weight against it, but the lock held. I rattled it in frustration before I slumped against the side of the tunnel.

If I broke the door down, she'd know someone had been here and move the fugitives somewhere else. They were here, somewhere in this building.

She was going after Cutmouth.

This was too much to take in. The implications of the interim Underqueen doing this . . . but it made no sense. She'd been Hector's friend . . . I had to work this out. *Symbiosis. Lithium.* I shook my head, my teeth clenched. *Think, Paige, think!* The Abbess was a physical medium. *Symbiosis* . . . I cursed myself again for not bringing Eliza. She would understand what it had meant.

*Think.* My brain was overheating, picking through the broken clues and words, trying to slot them together.

I could beat the Abbess to Cutmouth's hideout. Ivy had grown up with Cutmouth, she'd said—in the same community—but where? Agatha had found Ivy in the gutter in Camden. She must have been abandoned, or running from something . . .

*Wait.* My pulse was racing. There was one link between the two of them. Both of them were vile augurs: Cutmouth a haematomancer, Ivy a palmist.

And where had all the vile augurs been imprisoned after *On the Merits of Unnaturalness?* Where were they taken if syndies saw them on the streets? Where were their children born?

*Tell me where Ivy Jacob is hiding.*

I wiped the sweat from my upper lip, staring into the gloom. There was only one place they could have grown up together; one place where she could shut herself off from the outside world. One place she could have hidden from the people who had murdered her mime-lord. I launched myself back down the tunnel, back toward Camden.

Cutmouth was in Jacob's Island.

\*\*\*\*

It took me fifteen minutes to get back across the citadel on the cart—shoving the lever kicked it up a gear—then ten minutes at a dead sprint through the passages to reach the bolthole. When I wriggled through the basement window, I gulped down the fresh air like it was water, trembling all over. No time to stop, not even for breath. I sprinted across the market and back to Hawley Street, where I threw myself in front of a buck cab and slammed my hands down on the bonnet. The driver leaned out of the window, red-faced with anger.

"Hey!"

"Bermondsey." I swung myself inside, drenched in sweat. "Please, I need to go to Bermondsey. Quickly."

"You want to get yourself killed, girl?"

I had to grit my teeth to stop my spirit coming out. The effort forced a drop of blood from my nose. "If you've got a problem," I panted, "talk to the White Binder. He'll pay you for your haste."

That got him driving. I dialed the I-4 phone booth with my free thumb. It rang twice before a familiar voice answered.

"I-4."

"Muse?" Good. She'd made it back. "Muse, listen, I have to go somewhere, but—"

"Dreamer, you have to calm down and tell me what the hell is going on. You've been gone for an hour. Where are you?"

"On my way to II-6." I scraped back my damp hair. "Can you meet me in Bermondsey?"

A crackle. "Not now. Binder's curfew. Look, I'll try, but it might have to wait until he sends us somewhere."

"Fine." My throat tightened. "I have something to tell you."

On my own again. I hung up and clung to the door as the cab swung around another corner.

Jacob's Island, a cluster of streets at a bend of the river, was the worst of the SciLo slums. It was less than a mile long, written off as an irremediable dreg of the monarch days. Jaxon had discovered it as a boy. He must have thought it the perfect prison for the vile augurs, the pariahs of voyant society. With the exception of chiromancers, whose study of palms wasn't considered unsavory, they weren't a particularly popular bunch. Not when some of them were rumored to use entrails in their work.

After *On the Merits of Unnaturalness* had been distributed, forty-three vile augurs had been murdered, and the rest imprisoned here. I didn't know much about what was inside the slum, but I did know that its inhabitants were never allowed to leave. They would have had children since their imprisonment, children who had never seen the world beyond this corner of Bermondsey. Everyone who was born there took the family name *Jacob*.

Ivy hadn't had a surname on the screens. If she'd been born here, she would never have entered Scion's census. But how would she and Cutmouth have managed to leave?

If I was wrong, it would be too late.

I jumped out of the buck cab, telling him to leave the bill in the dead drop (I'd have to empty it before Jaxon noticed) and took off in the direction of the gate. My boots slithered down a muddy slope. At the bottom, a bored young syndicate guard stood at the east gate of Jacob's Island, a rifle propped against a crate beside him. Thirty-six powerful spirits surrounded the district, one from each section of the citadel. The gate itself was a grid of metal bars, set into a chain-link fence. An antique Scion plaque was nailed to the top of it.

II COHORT, SECTION 6

SUB-SECTION 10

WARNING: TYPE D RESTRICTED SECTOR

Type D was used for small construction sites that were considered too dangerous to occupy. That sign must have been there since before they decided not to repair the slum; since before Jaxon's pamphlet had forced the vile augurs into this place, beyond Scion's knowledge. As soon as he saw me, the guard drew a spool.

"Back, you. Now."

"I need access to the Island," I said. "Right away."

"You need your ears cleaned, girl? No entry except on the business of the interim Underqueen."

"I'm not the interim Underqueen, but I am the Pale Dreamer, heir of the White Binder," I bit out, "whose pamphlet is responsible for the existence of this slum. Tell the Wicked Lady and the Abbess what you like," I said, already shoving past him, "but let me in."

He shoved me back, so hard I almost went into the mud. "I don't answer to I-4. And don't think you're getting in through a hole in the fence, either. These spirits will destroy your mind."

"And I'm assuming a dutiful guard like you has some way to drive them back." I dug into my boot and threw him the envelope full of money from Chat's rent. "Is that enough for you to let me in and keep your trap shut about it?"

The guard hesitated, but the thickness of the envelope must have convinced him. He took a cloth sachet on a gold chain from his neck and tossed it to me. "Make sure you return it."

As the doorman unlocked the rusted gate, I wrapped a hand around my knife. The fragrant sachet sat in the middle of my collar, smelling faintly of sage.

"You're on your own in there," the guard warned. "I won't be coming in to get you out."

"No," I said. "You won't."

With a flick of my spirit, I knocked him unconscious, leaving him on his back in a puddle. Not even the faintest hint of a headache followed. I took the envelope of money from his hand and tucked it back into my inner pocket.

And so, alone, I walked into the most notorious slum in London. The spirits parted like a set of stage curtains.

The gate led into a tight passage. Sweat was pouring down my face, and my cheeks were burning hot.

All Jaxon's words about vile augurs rattled through my thoughts. The extispicists used animal entrails in their work. The osteomancers burned or handled bones. There were blood-loving haematomancers; drymimancers who scried with human tears; oculomancers obsessed with eyes, whether they were in the head or not. Jaxon had scared Eliza half to death when he told us about the Deflowerer, the legendary anthropomancer who prowled the sewers of this place, waiting for young women to skin and dismember before he used their entrails to predict the next one's death.

*Just a story*, I thought. *Just a story* . . . A story told in alleys and on corners, nothing more than an urban legend.

But weren't some legends true?

Turbid smoke belched from the remains of a nearby pit fire, clothing the air with a grey reek. The stench of the place turned my stomach: sulphur and wet rot and the stink of a burst sewer, mingled with charred meat. The Rookery had been a palace in comparison. Waste had built in piles around the broken doors and vomited all over the streets, which trickled with thin streams of water. I sloshed my way through translucent fish bones and the corpses of sewer rats. The silence was broken only by the caw of a raven on the nearest rooftop.

This place was like a tangle of threads. An ancient water pump stood at the end of the next one, dripping mud-brown water, with the leaking sewer only a few feet away. When a door swung open, I stopped. A woman emerged from a dwelling, thin and pale as bone. I hid behind a fence, trying to commit her aura to memory. Three years in the syndicate and I'd never laid eyes on this particular kind of augur. She pulled at the pump with a frail hand, but only a trickle of black slime rewarded her efforts. Silently, she knelt beside a deep puddle and used her palm to scoop as much of the filthy swill as she could into her pail. After licking a little off her fingers, she limped back up the steps.

The streets were narrow, squeezed between tall, roofless buildings. There was no evidence that there had ever been windows. My boots pushed through dirty water, marbled with white foam. I held my sleeve over my nose. Scion should have burned this place down a century ago.

There were dreamscapes in the houses, but they were quiet. Cutmouth had to be here somewhere. She'd be agitated and afraid, easy to sense. As the red sun sank, I emerged from an alley into the widest street I'd come across so far.

Pain exploded in my shoulder.

Something between a gasp and scream came out of my mouth, and my fingers reached automatically for the source of the agony. The thing was metal and curved, wedged right under my skin. It jerked, pulling me off my feet and into the mud.

Quick footsteps came splashing through the water. I threw out my spirit, repelling one of them, but there were six pairs of hands on me already, hauling me to my feet. A slim, quick-featured man walked out of the nearest dwelling, the other end of the fishing line wrapped around his hand. In the other was some kind of pistol, an old design with a handful of modifications.

"Looks like we've caught something. A *trespasser*," he sounded out, stroking a thick finger along the pistol. Freckles spread out across his sunburnt cheeks. "Tell me, what did you do to this one?"

He pointed to the man on all fours, who was holding his skull in both hands. I made a grab for my revolver, but the ringleader gave the line such a yank that the fish hook tore out of my shoulder, shaving off a long strip of my skin. A curse slammed against my teeth, but I swallowed it. This wouldn't end well if I antagonized them. Blood pulsed from the tear, soaking my shirt.

"We should take her to the Ship, shouldn't we?" one of the others said. "They've got rope."

*Rope?*

The ringleader seemed to consider for a moment, then nodded. "I suppose they have. Please, somebody disarm her."

My visible weapons were taken, one by one, before I was frog-marched through the narrow passageways.

After a minute of walking in silence, the ringleader pushed through a laden clothes line and emerged on to a wider street. I found myself being shoved toward a picket fence.

"What's this?"

Another stranger stood in the doorway of what looked like an old pre-Scion public house, surrounded by a wooden fence. The man was barrel-chested and bald as a teaspoon. His pale face had a semi-transparent look that reminded me of frogspawn. A discordantly beautiful sign hung from the centre of a gable above him, spelling out THE SHIP AGROUND in bold silver paint. When I didn't speak, he wiped his hands off on his shirt.

"Caught a raider, have you, lads?"

His accent was Irish, not dissimilar to mine. He was certainly from the south. "We found her sneaking around near the water pump." The ringleader threw me to the ground. "Look at this aura."

Blood seeped down my back, soaking into my blouse. I kept my fingers pressed over the wound. It didn't seem too deep, but it hurt like hell. The bald man walked down the rotten steps and crouched in front of me.

"You don't look much like a local, girl."

Saying the White Binder's name would usually get me out of a situation like this, but in this case it would be a death sentence. "I'm not," I said. "I'm looking for one of your people."

"I take it you don't work for the mime-queen, or you wouldn't be creeping around like a rat. Does the doorman know you're here, or did you break in?"

"He knows."

"We should ransom her," one of my captors said, to shouts of approval from the others. "The Assembly might let one of us out in exchange."

"Who's that?"

A new voice, quiet and high-pitched. A young woman in a pinafore had stepped out of the pub, a bucket of slop in one hand. "Go back inside, Róisín," the bald man said gruffly.

A shiver flickered through me. A tangle of distinctive scar tissue charred the left side of the woman's pallid face, jaw to temple. During the later years of Molly Riots, ScionIDE—Scion's military arm—had used an experimental nerve agent to disperse large crowds of rebels, with devastating results. I'd never learned its proper name, but the Irish had named it *an lámh ghorm*, the blue hand, after the finger-shaped indigo burns it left on those who survived it.

Other faces had appeared at the windows of the building now. Fevered eyes gaped through filthy sheets of glass. Doors and shutters creaked open in the dwellings. Footsteps slapped through the shallow water. My throat tightened as they emerged from their shacks and galleries and slowly, step by step, surrounded me. Before I knew it, I was trapped by a ring of thirty-odd vile augurs. A dull thump echoed through my ears.

Their clothes were ratty and plastered with filth. Most went barefoot or wore bits of cardboard to protect their soles. The younger ones were staring at me as if I were something gleaming and bizarre that had jumped out of the river. The older residents were wary, lingering in doorways. When I looked at them, I realized I was seeing the Rookery and its performers, huddled in their shacks. I was seeing Liss Rymore behind the curtain that had served as her front door, guarding the few frayed things in the world that were still hers.

The Irish man knocked his fist into the pub door. After ten seconds had passed in reverent silence, a woman opened it and stepped out into the dense air, wiping her hands on a dishcloth. She looked to be in her late thirties, with dark Iberian eyes and oily brown skin, spattered with freckles. Thick black hair was loosely threaded in a fishtail braid.

"What is it?" she said to the man, who nodded to me.

"We've got an intruder."

"Have we, now?" She folded her arms, looking me over. "You were clever to get in here, girl. If only it were as easy to get out."

She was from Dublin; her accent was the strongest I'd heard in a while. "Are you the leader here?" I said, trying to sound unruffled.

"This is a family, not one of your gangs," she said. "I'm Wynn Jacob, the Island's healer. Who are you?"

"A friend of Ivy," I said, hoping on hope that someone knew the name. That I wasn't wrong. "I've come here to find one of your people, someone who grew up here. She goes by the name of Cutmouth in the syndicate."

"She's talking about my Chelsea," an elderly woman shouted from another house. "Tell her to leave us alone! Hasn't the Wicked Lady taken enough of us?"

"Shut your trap, you. Get back to work." Wynn looked back at me. "We knew Ivy and Chelsea well before they left us. Raised Ivy up myself from a babe. What sort of danger is she in, pray tell?"

"What does she mean?" I said. "That the Wicked Lady's taken enough of you?"

"Don't tell her a thing," another augur spat. "If she ain't got the Jacob name, she ain't one of us."

"Wait." Róisín had picked up a flimsy bit of newspaper, so damp and wrinkled it was hard to tell how she could read it. She held up the front page, staring at me. "You're the one Scion's after."

My own face looked back at me: mangled, but still perfectly recognizable. The vile augurs fell silent, looking between the photograph and me, matching features to features.

Another hand took my sleeve, belonging to a man with blackened teeth and a glistening chunk of nose. "Her hair's different," he said, "but she's got that same look. Yes, Róisín, I think you might be right."

"We could sell her!" A woman gripped my nape. "Scion would pay us fortunes, I reckon. She's *preternatural*, this one."

The dark-haired Irish woman said nothing. My spirit was about to rupture its bonds, but these people would kill me if I hurt anyone. Suppressing the jump set off sparks in my eyes.

"Chelsea said they'd come for her." On the steps, Róisín looked terrified. "Please, don't hurt her. They said they were going to protect her."

The nearest augur's nose dripped blood. "I didn't hurt anyone. And I don't plan to." My palms tingled. "When did you meet the blue hand?"

Recognition jumped into her eyes. She lifted her fingers to her cheek. "I was ten," she said.

"Dublin?"

"Bray." The Sack of Bray, one of the most shattering defeats of the Molly Riots. She glanced at Wynn, then looked back at me with a curious expression. "Did you see the riots, too?"

"*Éire go brách,*" I said. My first language rolled off my tongue.

Wynn still said nothing, but she looked between us.

"Put her down, you two," she finally ordered, and the augurs holding my arms let go of them. "Vern, take her to Savory Dock. Quick, now, before the doorman comes looking for her."

The woman on my right bit out her next words: "You're going to let her *see* Chelsea?"

"Briefly, and with Vern beside her," Wynn said. "She'll be here because somebody from the Unnatural Assembly sent her. I won't bring down the anger of the syndicate on our heads, or they'll burn this place with us still in it."

"I want my weapons," I said.

"You can have them back on your way out."

With a hard look at the crowd, the bald man took me by the arm and marched me away from the Ship Aground. "Yeah, go on, Vern, take out the trash," the old man in the gallery shouted. "Don't come back, syndie!"

Vern walked with enormous strides, not looking at me. The stink of waste alleviated as we walked, replaced by a fug of foul water, rotten eggs, and phosphorous. A man watched from a shack with aching eyes, wrapped in clothes so filthy they were all one shade. Blood glistened on his fingertips. As soon as we rounded a corner, I jerked my arm free.

"I'm not leaving until I see Cutmouth."

"I'm taking you to Shad Thames, up Savory Dock. That's where she's staying. But I'm coming in with you," he said roughly. "You know the person who came to see her, then, do you?"

I spun to face him. "What? Who?"

"Somebody came to speak to her, somebody to make sure she's got proper protection until the scrimmage. Couldn't tell who it was, given they were in a mask," he said. "First official visit we've had since the last time the Wicked Lady deigned to check on us, which was when she took—"

I was already sprinting down the alley.

"Oi!" Vern pounded after me. "You don't know where you're going!"

"How long ago?" I shouted.

"Quarter of an hour, if that."

She was here already. The Abbess. I sprinted through the streets, ducking under clothes lines and vaulting over broken fragments of fence. The words SAVORY DOCK were printed across the grimy brick walls of the next street. Here, the slum petered out to a stretch of olive-green water, where a fleet of rotten fishing-boats rocked on the surface. Images from Cutmouth's dreamscape.

A group of mudlarks waded in the shallows on the shore, picking through wet plastic bags. When they saw me, they fled like a startled flock of birds.

"You," I shouted at one of them. "Which house is Cutmouth in?"

She pointed at a rickety dwelling with a blue door, several stories high. Only slivers of paint still clung to the wood. I didn't knock. The hinges were on their last legs.

New smells filled my nostrils. I stepped into water that came up to my shins, littered with empty bottles and bits of river debris. The tide must come up often here. Below my boots, the floorboards had a soft foundation of rot.

"Cutmouth." I waded to a rickety staircase. "Cutmouth!"

Silence.

My spine was rigid. There was a dreamscape in this building, flickering and faint. I grabbed the concealed knife in my boot, flipped it open and made my way up the stairs. As I took another step, my boot plunged through the wood and swung out over a long plummet to the basement. The rest of the staircase collapsed behind me.

With gritted teeth, I clawed myself out of the gap and kept going. My shoulder burned where the hook had torn it. Water dropped on to my face from above. At the top of the stairs, I looked down the corridor, keeping my spirit at the brink of my mind. This house was falling to bits. A wrong step could cause the floor to cave in. At the bottom of the staircase, Vern cursed.

"I'll find her," I called.

"Don't you try anything. There's another way up," he said. "I'll come around the front."

He ran back out to the street. I walked with careful steps, keeping my hands on the walls.

A door was ajar at the end of the corridor. I pushed it open, sensing the dreamscape. The room beyond the door was dark, the rotted shutters closed. Two tall red candles burned on a rickety chest of drawers. And there, sprawled across the floor, covered in blood, was Cutmouth.

I dropped to my knees and got her into my arms, the rightful Underqueen of London. Blood soaked her clothes, but she was still just about alive. Her eyelids and cheeks were hewn with the same precise V-shaped cuts as those on the rest of her gang. At her right side, close to her thigh, her fingers curled around a red handkerchief.

"D-Dreamer." She could hardly speak. "Just gone. You can—c-catch them—"

The primal urge to run whipped through my muscles. I could feel a dreamscape on the edge of the slum, moving quickly. Logic told me to follow, but I knew who it would be. And when I looked down and saw that mutilated, frightened face, wet with blood and tears, I couldn't.

"No," I said quietly. "I know who it was."

Cutmouth's skin was already freezing, as if death were breathing over her. One hand twitched to mine, and I gripped it. Her spirit guttered in her dreamscape, pulsing out signals of confusion and distress. The whole of her abdomen was awash with blood. She was still wearing the same clothes from the market night, the night Hector had died.

Footsteps thumped on the landing, so hard I thought the floor would collapse. Vern almost fell into the room.

"Chelsea!"

His fists clenched on the door frame; his face contorted with rage. Cutmouth's eyes drifted toward him, but her hand was still gripping mine. "Wasn't her," she said, and Vern clamped his mouth shut, white-faced. "Dreamer, they—they killed Hector. T-tell Ivy I didn't—I'm sorry they took her. Trusted him. She was—everything. She has to—to make it right—"

A tear ran down her cheek, smearing blood. "Why did they kill Hector?" I spoke as gently as I could. "What did he know?"

"About Rags . . . about *them* . . ." Her grip tightened on my hand until I thought my fingers would break. "Got too greedy. I told him, I told him."

Tears flooded down her face, and her bloody fingers flexed around mine. She was just like me. Same position, same age, same bizarre situation. I'd had to watch Liss die like this in the colony, powerless.

"Did so much wrong," she whispered.

"Don't worry." The backs of my fingers stroked her hair. "The æther takes us all. No matter what we've done." I met her unfocused eyes. "Tell me what they're doing. Tell me how to stop them, Chelsea."

A rasping breath. "It's—it's the gray—" Her chest rose one last time. "Gray market. Rags and . . . the Abbess, *together* . . . selling us to—" The æther trembled as her silver cord fell to pieces. "The tattoo. Saw it once. Her arm . . ."

Then she grew still. Her silver cord broke with a gentle snap, releasing her from her mortal body, and the weight of her grew heavy in my arms.

Vern crouched down beside the body and laid his hand on her wrist, checking her pulse. I stayed where I was, kneeling in the blood, too shocked by what I'd learned in the last hour to think straight.

"I suppose you think we deserve this. That *she* deserved this."

"What?" My voice was hoarse.

"What was it he said? 'Base Practices'? 'Primitive and clumsy'? And the best one: 'should properly have died out by this era.'" Vern said it between gritted teeth, and there were tears in his eyes. "Why do you have to hate us so much?"

I couldn't think of a single excuse.

"You think there are really killers in this place? You believe in the Binder's tall tales, girl?" he barked. "You think he was right to put out bitter guesswork and call it research?" He bent over Cutmouth's body, taking one limp hand between his. "This'll be the end of us. If they syndicate gets a whiff that she was killed here."

"The Binder won't know," I said.

"Oh, he'll find out."

The door swung open, and Wynn stepped into the room. She knelt beside the body and stroked Cutmouth's matted hair.

"Is nothing enough?" she murmured.

"She was from here." I wiped the sweat from my face with my sleeve. "You should bury her."

"And we will. Not that we've anything but a landfill or a river to bury her in." Vern took the handkerchief from Cutmouth's hand and covered her bloody face with it. "Now get out."

His tone made me flinch inside, but I didn't show it. I eased her body into Vern's arms and turned away from the scene, not bothering to stop my sixth sense taking over. Everything rang softly in the æther.

"Chelsea Neves"—Wynn made the sign—"be gone into the æther. All is settled. All debts are paid. You need not dwell among the living now."

Her spirit evaporated from the room, sent far away to the outer darkness. Vern buried his face in one hand. I looked at Cutmouth's body one more time—looked at it until every detail burned itself into my memory like a brand—before I went back to the landing and leaned against the wall, my hand clenched in my hair, trembling uncontrollably with anger.

Ivy was the only one left who might know why this had happened, and she was still in the Abbess's clutches. There was nothing I could say to mend this; even *sorry* sounded hollow. In life, Cutmouth had been brutal and a bully, but what had I been but that? Hadn't I used my fists and my gift to serve Jaxon? Hadn't I obeyed him without question? She must have seen everything in me I'd seen in her.

The door closed behind me. Wynn wiped the blood from her hands on a cloth. She didn't look angry. Just tired. "She wasn't a bad woman." A rough edge crept into her voice, but her eyes were dry as ashes. "She never took our name, given that she wasn't born here. Your syndies took her from the street. Stole her from her mother's side when she was only a child." She paused. "See much of the Molly Riots?"

I nodded. "My cousin was killed during the Incursion."

"I was the librarian of Trinity College at the time." She opened her collar. There was a gunshot scar between her neck and chest, like the mark left by a finger in soft clay. "What was your cousin's name?"

"Finn McCarthy."

A thread of laughter escaped her. "Oh, I remember Finn McCarthy, the troublemaker. He only ever came into my library to pull pranks. I . . . suppose he was sent to Carrickfergus with the others."

"Yes." I wanted to ask more about Finn, about how she remembered him—what pranks, what kind of trouble had he made?—but this wasn't the place. "Did you see Chelsea's killer?"

"From a distance. Couldn't see much of them. Long coat, a top hat, and some sort of mask. When I asked the doorman about it, he said this person was there on the business of the interim Underqueen and I should shut my mouth if I wanted to keep my tongue."

My fist clenched. "Did Cutmou— Chelsea say anything to you while she was here? Anything about what she saw at the Devil's Acre?"

"She got here a little while after Hector was buried, but she wouldn't say a word to anyone. Locked herself straight into this house and for all we tried she wouldn't come out. Is Ivy all right?" she asked.

"She's in trouble," I said. "And I know you have no reason to help me, Wynn."

"But you'd like my help."

I nodded. "If the Abbess wins the scrimmage, she'll have ultimate power in this syndicate. But if someone else does, they can call a trial for the deaths of Hector and Chelsea."

"If you're saying you want me to give evidence," Wynn said, "the Unnatural Assembly would never accept testimony from the mouth of a vile augur. The White Binder wouldn't allow it, for one."

"They would if there was a new Underlord. Or Underqueen. Those rules could be changed."

"Well, if that were the case, maybe all the rules could be changed. Maybe the vile augurs of Jacob's Island would no longer be obliged to stay in this small corner of Bermondsey. And if that were the case, Pale Dreamer, they'd be happy to assist whoever had over-turned the White Binder's ruling." She took off her long coat and handed it to me. "Wear that. You're covered in blood."

My trousers were steeped to the knee in slick mud, to say nothing of my boots, and blood coated my hands and chest. "I will if you take this." I lifted the gold chain from my neck and, after emptying a pinch of sage into my palm, dropped the silk sachet into her hand. "The scrimmage is being held on the first of November at midnight. This will get you past the spirits that are bound to Jacob's Island."

"Ah. The doorman's sage." She rubbed it between her fingertips. "This amount won't get more than one or two people through the barrier."

"I only need one or two."

"Then I'm glad to have been invited." With a thin smile, Wynn handed me my revolver and knives, then took me by the elbow and steered me back toward the stairs.

"I hope to be seeing you soon," she said, "Paige Mahoney. For now, hurry away. The people of this slum won't want outsiders at the burial. And please, try to help Ivy, wherever she is. This will break her heart."

# 22

# The Gray Market

There was poison in the blood of London. Cutmouth had been confused and afraid, but her last words had been chosen carefully.

I wasn't sure I could stomach what I'd learned about the Abbess. All that rubbish she'd spouted about being Hector's friend . . . and until the scrimmage, she had more power than any other voyant in London.

It was clear that she had killed both Hector and his mollisher, and if Cutmouth was right, her skin was marked with a Rag Doll tattoo— one that she had never shown in public, to my knowledge. It was possible that she'd been a Rag Doll once and left her mime-lord's service, eventually rising to lead her own section. Perhaps she'd been that first, unnamed mollisher Jaxon had mentioned, and the bitterness of her desertion was what had caused their rivalry.

Or perhaps not. What I knew for certain was that it was quick and cheap to have ink removed at a tattoo parlor. There was no reason that she should still have a tattoo she didn't want.

*A hand without living flesh, its fingers pointing to the sky. Red silk surrounds its wrist like a manacle.*

Was that the message? That the red silk handkerchiefs had been placed by the Rag and Bone Man's hand?

That the crime might just be his undoing?

I pressed my fingers to my temples, piecing the clues together. The Rag and Bone Man must have wanted Hector and Cutmouth to die so that a scrimmage would be called. Somehow he'd got the Abbess on his side, convincing her of his aims to the point that she was willing to kill for him. That he'd given the order and she had held the blade. Their public enmity must be a complete falsehood, a smokescreen to conceal their alliance.

That motive would hold up if the Rag and Bone Man wanted to be Underlord himself. It would have been necessary to get rid of the Underlord—and stop his mollisher taking his place—in order for a scrimmage to be called. But what I didn't understand was why neither the Rag and Bone Man nor the Abbess would be entering the Rose Ring. Their names hadn't been listed on the last letter as candidates. Why wouldn't they take advantage of the vacuum they'd created?

This was where the theory fell to pieces. I needed to talk to Ivy. She might be the last person alive who knew something about this, the final piece in the puzzle. I should have got it out of her that morning on the rooftop terrace, when she'd first admitted to knowing Cutmouth. Now she was locked in an unknown building at the end of a blocked tunnel. There was no chance of getting her out of there without the Abbess noticing something. I could storm the place with the Ranthen, but by the time we got past the tunnel guards, they would have alerted the Abbess and moved the fugitives elsewhere. Or just killed them.

Rain poured down on the pavement. I stayed where I was, wrapped in Wynn's long coat waiting for a buck cab, numb. After a few minutes, a rusty black car came sliding to a halt in front of me and Nick got out of the back, holding up his arm to shield his eyes.

"Paige!"

He held open the door. I clambered into the car, drenched.

"We were worried sick when Eliza said you were in Bermondsey."
Nick closed the door and wrapped an arm around my shoulders. I
leaned into him, shivering. "Whose coat is that? We've been driving
around looking for you. Where have you been?"

"Jacob's Island."

He drew in a sharp breath. "Why?"

I couldn't say it. Zeke, in the driver's seat, shot me a worried
glance before he started the engine. Beside him, Eliza sat with a
cellophane-covered painting on her lap, her hair beautifully curled,
red tint shining on her lips. She reached between the seats and
touched my shoulder.

"We're on our way to Old Spitalfields," she said quietly. "Jax wants
us to try and get a pitch there. Can this wait?"

"Not long," I said.

"We won't be long. Ognena Maria's easy to deal with."

Zeke turned on the ancient radio, switching to a music channel
before we could hear any of the news. The entrance to Jacob's Island
disappeared into the citadel as the car drove away from II-6, back to
the central cohort.

There was nothing I could do for Ivy and the others tonight.
Getting her out of that place, wherever it was, would need careful
timing. I rested my head against the window, watching the streetlamps
flash past the glass.

The car passed several units of night Vigiles. Zeke locked the doors.
They seemed to be interrogating passersby. One had his gun pointed
at an amaurotic man's head, while another man was in tears beside
him, trying to shove the Vigile's arm away. I turned to look through
the car's back window. As it rounded the corner, I just saw the Vigile's
baton coming up, and the two men crouched on the pavement with
their hands over their heads.

Zeke parked on Commercial Street, and we walked together to the covered market hall. Old Spitalfields was a far lighter space than the Garden, with a roof made of cast-iron and glass, but most of the traders were amaurotic. Cheap clothes, shoes and jewelry hung from racks, along with fashionable chatelaines for the wealthy. Ognena Maria's stall, which sold numa hidden inside hearth spaniels and vinaigrettes, was somewhere in the center of the maze. We shouldered our way through hordes of vendors and buyers, keeping an eye out for the mime-queen. Zeke stopped at a tiny stall selling trinkets from the free-world.

"I'll catch up," he said to Nick, who nodded.

I kept pace with the other two. "She'd better like this," Eliza muttered. The harsh light made her face look worn. "You know Ognena Maria, don't you, Dreamer?"

"Quite well."

"She's the one that wanted Dreamer for her section," Nick said, chuckling. "As her ID card says she lives in I-5, she's technically an I-5 denizen. Maria and Jaxon disagreed strongly over it."

Stalls that sold forbidden items were easily recognizable. They had shifty-looking owners and tended to be tucked into the darkest corners of the market halls, close to the exits. I lagged behind, sifting through the wares, hardly seeing them.

*Gray market.*

I shook myself. By the time I reached the right stall, Eliza, Nick and Ognena Maria were deep in conversation. ". . . exquisite brush-work," Maria was saying, "and the paints have clearly been selected with care—that subtle coloring is beautiful. You must have a real symbiosis with your muses to produce this sort of work, Martyred Muse. Does it affect your physiology at all?"

There was what word again. *Symbiosis.* "A little, if the muse is irritated, but I can handle it," Eliza said.

"Admirable. I think I can find room for—" She caught sight of me. "Ah, Pale Dreamer. I was just about to offer I-4 a pitch in Old Spitalfields. What do you say?"

"You won't regret it," I said, forcing a smile. "I'm happy to sell with Muse, if you don't mind fugitives on your turf."

"Oh, it's an honor to have you." Maria shook hands with all three of us. "Mind out for Vigiles on your way back. They sometimes come through on their way to the Guild."

"Thank you, Maria." Nick pulled down the brim of his hat. "Goodnight."

"I'll meet you in a minute," I said.

With a small nod, he took Eliza's arm, and they headed back towards the market's entrance. Ognena Maria placed the canvas under a table, out of sight.

"Maria," I said, "you were supposed to investigate those red handkerchiefs on Hector's body, weren't you?"

"I was, and I did. They were definitely bought from here—the maker puts a hallmark on them—but she sells plenty of them every month." She sighed. "I suppose we'll never know."

I glanced over my shoulder, then drew the hitman's red handkerchief from my boot and handed it to her. "Is this one of them?"

She turned it over, until her thumb found a tiny stitched cross near one of the corners. "It is." Her voice was low. "Where did you get this, Pale Dreamer?"

"From a Rag Doll who tried to kill me in I-4."

"To kill *you*?" When I nodded, Maria's lips pressed together, and she handed the red silk back to me. "You should burn it. I don't know a great deal about the Rag and Bone Man, but I do know that you don't want him hunting you. Have you said anything to the Unnatural Assembly?"

"No." I crammed the handkerchief back into my boot. "I . . . don't know if I trust the Abbess."

"That makes two of us." She leaned across the table on her

elbows, twisting the woven ring on her thumb. "You remember she wanted to speak to me, don't you? That day at the auction? I went to meet her at a neutral house in I-2 that night. She wanted at least five of my voyants, but not to be nightwalkers. Just said she'd pay me handsomely if I'd let them do some moonlighting."

My chest tightened. "And did you?"

"No. Moonlighting's always been illegal. I'll shut my eyes if my voyants do it of their own accord, but I won't formally allow it." Maria straightened. "A few of us still have morals."

"I see you're not going for Underqueen," I said. "Did you not think about it?"

"Wouldn't dare, sweet. I'm surprised there are as many as twenty-five combatants."

"Why?"

"I won't say Hector deserved to die in his own parlor," she said, "but he damaged this syndicate on a level that no other Underlord has managed. None of the Assembly will want to be in charge when Scion brings in Senshield. All our sections will be overrun with gutterlings and beggars and Vigiles. The last thing anyone wants is to put themselves at the prow of a sinking ship."

"Then we need someone who won't let the ship sink."

She laughed. "Like who? Name me one mime-lord or mime-queen that could turn it all around."

"I can't." Needles skittered up my sides. "I sometimes wish I could enter myself, but I'm told mollishers are ineligible."

Even insinuating this to her was a terrible risk. She'd always seemed like a decent woman, and she had no love for Jaxon, but there was no guarantee that she wouldn't go to him with that sort of information. Still, I had to see a reaction. Had to see how a member of the Unnatural Assembly would respond to the thought of a traitor mollisher as Underqueen.

Ognena Maria didn't react the way I thought she would, though she did glance up at me. "There's no specific rule against it," she said, "at least to my knowledge. And I've been a mime-queen for a decade."

"But people wouldn't like it."

"Honestly, Pale Dreamer, I don't think anyone would care. Some mollishers are far more skilled than their superiors," she said. "Look at Jack Hickathrift and the Swan Knight. Both brilliant voyants, organized and reasonably honest, and what do they do? Bow and scrape for lazy, corrupt leaders that probably maimed and swindled their way into those roles. If either of those two were to go for the crown, I'd be cheering their names."

I raised my eyebrows. "Do you think all of the Assembly feel that way?"

"Oh, no. I'd say that most of them would declare you a traitor and an ingrate. But that's only because they're afraid of you." She placed her hand over mine. "It'd be nice if we got someone competent this year."

"We can only hope," I said.

"We're running low on hope in this citadel." Her smile disappeared, and she snapped her fingers at her mollisher. "*Pobúrzaĭ.* I don't pay you to look pretty." The woman rolled her eyes.

The car was waiting outside, its headlights blazing through darts of rain. I climbed into the back with Eliza. "Are you going to tell us what's happened?" she said.

"Wait." Zeke started the engine. "We shouldn't talk here. Maria said there were Vigiles all over the place. Primrose Hill is safe enough, isn't it?"

We all looked to Nick. His eyes were smeared with shadows.

"Half an hour," he said. "I don't want to be out this late. Should Jax know about this, Paige?"

"I don't know," I said. "I've been out without permission. He might not want to hear it."

As the car navigated the streets, my mind wandered to dark places.

What if Ognena Maria *did* pass the information on to Jaxon? It might be safer to stay somewhere else until the scrimmage, but breaking away from him now would only piss him off. I might not even be allowed to take part if we were no longer an allied pair.

Primrose Hill stretched between I-4 and II-4, a rolling green space on a shallow incline. Scion had planted a vast number of oak trees and thousands of primroses here in memory of Inquisitor Mayfield, who had apparently enjoyed a spot of gardening alongside hanging, burning and beheading traitors. This close to November, there were no flowers left. Leaving the car on the street, the four of us trudged up to the crest of the hill, far away from the streetlamps and listening ears, until we reached its highest point. I looked up at the black expanse of sky, just visible between the leaves.

Warden was out there somewhere, keeping his distance. I focused on the golden cord, picturing the pattern of the stars. He could find me tonight if he knew where to look. Until then, I had some news to break.

We stopped in the shadow of a tree and stood in a circle, facing each other. "Go on," Nick said.

"The Abbess killed Hector and his gang." I spoke softly. "She just killed Cutmouth, too."

None of them spoke, but they all stared at me. In hushed tones, I told them what had happened after I'd left Eliza; how I'd found the hidden building down the mail rail, watched Agatha die, and run to Cutmouth in time to hear her last words.

"Tattoo," Eliza repeated. "Did she mean the Rag Doll mark? The skeleton's handprint?"

"That's what it's called?"

"Yeah. All of them have it put here when they join." She patted her upper right arm. "If they leave the gang, they have to let the Rag and Bone Man burn it off. They're not allowed to visit a tattoo parlor."

"So if she still has the mark, it means she's still working for him?" Zeke said, eyebrows raised. "The guy she's supposed to hate?"

"She must be," I said. "After he shot Agatha, the Monk offered the Abbess lithium for whatever she was about to do. She said didn't need it because the *symbiosis* was strong." I looked to Eliza. "What does it mean, that word?"

"Symbiosis?" She frowned. "It's the relationship between a medium and the spirit that possesses them. If you have good symbiosis, you work together well. I have good symbiosis with Rachel now that I've been working with her for a few years," she said, "but a new muse takes me a while to get used to, so I wind up being sick after the first few possessions. Once symbiosis happens, we reach an . . . understanding. If that makes sense."

Nick's face was tight. "The Abbess is a physical medium. Could she have used a spirit to kill Hector?"

Eliza hesitated before she said, "It's possible that she was possessed when she did it, which would have given her the spirit's emotions on top of hers. It might have made her faster, too. But she had to get through seven people to kill Hector, then cut off his head. The spirit doesn't give you any extra physical strength, and the Abbess doesn't look as if she could take down eight people."

"Wait, wait." Zeke held up a hand. "Even if the Abbess *did* kill Hector, why isn't she entering the scrimmage?"

"That's what I'm wondering," I said.

His eyes were full of sympathy. "You found Cutmouth. Where? Did she say anything?"

"I realized where she'd be: Jacob's Island. It took a while to get past the doorman, then the islanders held me up, and—" I took a deep breath. "I wasn't fast enough. She'd been stabbed by the time I arrived. The last thing she said was that I had to stop the *gray market*."

"What's that?"

"I don't know," I admitted. "If a black market is illegal, I guess a gray market is . . . unauthorized. Or tolerated."

"Jax has to know this," Eliza said.

"What can he do about it? He can't report the Abbess *to* the Abbess," I said, and she sighed. "She's interim Underqueen. If he lets on that he knows about it, she'll just kill him, too."

There was a short silence. Nick turned to look at the citadel, the lights caught in his eyes. "The scrimmage will decide what happens next. We know the Rag and Bone Man has some knowledge of the Rephaim," he said. "He captured Warden. So we can assume that this gray market has something to do with—"

"Whoa, what?" Zeke interrupted, staring at him.

"Sorry, *Warden's* back? As in, Paige's keeper?" Eliza let out an angry sort of laugh. "When were you going to drop that bombshell?"

"Shh." I looked over my shoulder, certain my sixth sense had flickered. "He's been back for a while. I tried telling Jax when his allies showed up on our doorstep, but he didn't want to—" I stopped. "Wait. Someone's coming."

I'd only just picked up on the presence of the dreamscape, creeping up on us from somewhere behind the tree. Almost as soon as I said it, a skinny man stepped out from behind the enormous trunk, barefoot and clad in little more than rags. I took a wide step away, hiding my face behind my hair.

"Evening, sirs and ladies, evening." He swept off his hat with a bow. "Penny for a busker?"

Nick's hand was already in his coat, on his pistol. "Bit remote for you here, isn't it?"

"Oh, no, sir." His white teeth caught the half-light of our flashlights. "Nowhere's too far for me."

"You're supposed to busk first," Eliza said, with a nervous laugh. At the same time, she took a step to the left, blocking his view of me. "I'll give you a tenner if you're good. What do you do?"

"I am but a humble rhabdomancer, milady. I give no prophecies, make no promises and play no pretty songs." He pulled a silver coin from behind his ear. "But I can take you to treasure, sure as there's a nose on my face. We rhabdomancers are like a compass when it comes to treasure. Take a walk with me, and you shall share it, milady."

"Don't," I said, hardly moving my lips.

"He might have overheard us," she whispered. "I've got some white aster in my bag. We can make sure."

Every fine hair on my arms was standing on end. He'd been close enough to listen in us. Nick looked wary, too, but he didn't argue. The rhabdomancer looped his arm through Eliza's and led us down the hill, joking and telling tales as he went. Zeke ran after them, giving Nick a worried look. I kept my cravat over my face, wondering if I should just hightail it in the other direction.

The rhabdomancer weaved his way down to the trees. I stayed well behind. When he led us toward a dense thicket, I put on my English accent and called to the rhabdomancer, "You're not taking us in there, are you?"

"Just a little way, ma'am, I promise."

"He could murder us," I hissed at Nick.

"Agreed. I don't like it." He cupped his hands around his mouth. "Muse! Diamond! Wait a minute!"

But she was already following the busker into the trees, and his words were snatched away by the wind.

Nick switched on his flashlight and followed, keeping hold of my arm. My heartbeat came in heavy thumps. My boots crunched on dry leaves. Or a skull ... Adrenaline came shooting through my veins. Suddenly I was back in my pink tunic, bundled in a jacket and staring at the trees of No Man's Land, waiting for the monster to emerge. My fingers dug into Nick's arm.

"You okay?"

I nodded, trying to keep my breathing steady.

The rhabdomancer had led them deep into the trees. Glass-like teardrops hung from the leaves, and each was fringed with crystals. Sheets of clear ice coated the branches, making them creak. A spider's web, strung among the foliage, had been transformed to a silver lacery. Its creator hung from a thread, petrified. Nick's flashlight beam fell on the others' footprints, but they were already beginning to freeze over. My breath billowed in dense white clouds.

"Can you feel any spirits?" Nick murmured.

"No."

We quickened our pace. Zeke was crouching near a small body of frozen water and Eliza was kneeling beside it. I stopped dead. Bluish fog lingered a few inches from the ground. Behind them, the busker was talking with animated gestures: ". . . for years, you know, sir, and I always said there was treasure underneath it. Now, if you'd be so kind as to take this and try to break the ice."

"Looks like a perfect circle." Zeke ran his finger around the edge. "How likely is that?"

It didn't just look like one. It *was* a perfect circle.

"Diamond, are you all right?" Nick said.

"I'm fine. Have you seen this? It's incredible . . ."

Zeke took the coin from the rhabdomancer and brought it down on the ice. "Twice more, sir." The rhabdomancer looked over his shoulder. "Twice more."

My sixth sense was ringing like a set of bells. I'd seen this before, with Warden. The woods. The cold. The absence of spirits. As Zeke tapped the coin against the ice a second time, a wave surged through the æther. The realization punched the breath from my lungs.

He was knocking on a door that shouldn't be opened.

"Get away from it." I ran towards them. "Diamond, stop!"

Eliza started. "It's just ice, Dreamer. Relax."

"It's a cold spot." There was a rough edge to my voice. "A portal to the Netherworld."

At once, Nick hooked his arms under hers and pulled her to her feet, away from the ice. Zeke retreated too, swearing, but the rhabdomancer punched him hard in the jaw, making him stagger and fall. The coin slipped from between his fingers and rolled toward the ice. Without hesitating, I snatched one of my knives and hurled it at the rhabdomancer's head, missing by an inch. He grabbed the coin and cradled it to his chest with one hand, scrambling toward the cold spot with the other.

"They're coming," he said. His eyes were unfocused, his lips tilted. "To give me my treasure."

"Stop!" My revolver was already in my hands. "Don't do it. You won't find any treasure there."

"You're a dead woman," he said, and raised the coin.

This time, the impact cracked the ice. The cold spot exploded. A million shards burst up from the ground, blinding me with diamond dust—and with a scream that echoed all over II-4, a Buzzer crawled out of the gateway, into London.

****

With impossible speed, the creature was on top of us. It leaped on the rhabdomancer, clapped its jaws over his head and, with a jerk of muscle, ripped it away. The body slumped, twitching as if it had been shocked. Dark blood pulsed from what remained, spilling on to the cold spot.

It was looking at me. The creature generated its own darkness—a cloud of black static on my vision—but for the first time, I could just about see the rotten giant. It was muscled and grotesque, with a blunt head, and its skin had a shiny, bloated look. Everything about it was too long, as if it had been stretched: its arms, its legs, its neck. A spine pressed through its skin like a knife edge. Its eyes were pure white orbs, slightly luminous, like moons.

The sound of flies filled the air. Sweat ran down my neck. This creature was far larger than the one I'd faced in the woods.

There was a pouch of salt in my trouser pocket. Making no sudden movements, I drew it into my palm and looped the golden string over two of my fingers, showing it to the creature. I didn't know how much it could understand, but it might sense what was inside.

The Buzzer stretched its neck with a wet clicking sound, then shook its head so fast it blurred. It sank its blunt fingers into the earth, freezing it, and crawled towards us.

I tried to focus on the auras of the other three. They registered like bad signals on my radar. The Buzzer was turning the æther to a dense, congealed mass, incapable of supporting spirits. Clots surrounded it, like blobs of oil in water. Nick tried to make a spool, but the spirits pulled against him so violently that he had to let them go.

There was no strength left in my knees. My vision shorted out for a moment. If I didn't do something, we'd all go into spirit shock. I waited for the creature to get a few feet closer before I tipped a handful of salt into my hand and hurled it. It collided with the Buzzer with a sizzling burst of smoke, making a sound like a firecracker.

When it opened its mouth, showing its abyssal throat, a terrible scream emerged from inside it. Not just one scream, but a thousand tortured cries, moans and sobs, all held in one mouth. The sound pulled up every hair on my body and chilled the blood beneath my skin.

"Run," I shouted.

We pounded through the trees, down the steep incline, toward the bottom of the hill and the car. Branches slashed at my face and snared in my hair. Ice skidded under my boots. I pulled frantically on the golden cord, blinking away the darkness in my vision. Warden might be our only chance to live. The ground seemed to pull at my ankles, dragging my limbs and eyelids downward. *So tired.* I kept going. *Just stop.* I kept going. When we reached another clearing, Zeke's knees gave way. He fell as if his bones had disappeared.

Nick went down next. I staggered to a stop and grabbed his shoulders, trying to pull him back up, but my arms were running water and I collapsed beside him, shuddering. My aura constricted, flinching away from the creature, shortening my link to the æther. Suddenly I couldn't feel Zeke, who was farthest away. With a blink, he vanished from my perception.

*Stop I need it stop stop it's like dying can't breathe can't breathe stop*

My aura was like a vital organ squeezed in a fist, hampering its function. My eyes watered with the effort of staying conscious. Spirit shock was creeping up on me. My fingers were tipped with gray, my nails with a sickly white. I could breathe, but I was drowning. I could see, but I was blind.

*Can't focus stop can't think stop stop*

Eliza was ahead of us, a few feet away from Nick. She pushed herself up on her arms, gasping out curses, but the heels of her hands were slipping on ice and she couldn't seem to get back to her feet. I couldn't feel her dreamscape or her aura. Half-blind, I opened the pouch of salt again.

"Circle," I wheezed at Nick.

That noise erupted again, the screams of the damned in a rotting cavern of mouth. Gritting his teeth, Nick dragged Eliza toward him, his strength doubled by adrenaline.

"Give me the salt!"

I thrust it into his hands. The Buzzer loped toward us, blurring with the darkness, white eyes and shadow and raw-boned rage. Too fast. Nick's hands were shaking.

"Zeke!" His voice was hoarse. "*Zeke!*"

The creature was too close, bearing down on Zeke's shivering body. I hurled my spirit across the clearing.

When I collided with the dreamscape, it was just like it had been in Sheol I: a blistering point of impact, sending sparks through my spirit. A force was festering in this dreamscape, deep within the innards of its mind. With all the effort I could muster, I cut through its first line of defence, into its hadal zone.

The pain was catastrophic.

My spirit fell into what felt like a quagmire. I was on fire, a tongue of fire, burning inside out. This was no dreamscape.

This was a nightmare.

The hadal zone of this creature was excruciatingly dark, but I could just about see what my dream-form was standing in: a rotten mass of dead tissue. Blood bubbled through a slick of melted flesh. The sludge gripped my ankles and pulled me down, down, down until I'd sunk up to my waist in it. A skeletal hand gripped my nape, bending my body toward it. I threw my weight backward, trying to escape, to fly back to my body, but it was too late. Layers of decay closed over my head.

\*\*\*\*

No air, no thought, no pain, no brain.

Evanescence.

Dissolution.

The loop of endless nothing, nothing, *nothing.*

In the void, there was one last inkling of thought: that this was hell. The absence of æther, of anything at all. This was what we feared, we voyants. Not death, but *non-existence.* The total destruction of spirit and self. Faces slipped away. In here there was no Nick and no Warden and no Eliza and no Jaxon and no Liss and everything was fading and Paige was going, *going* . . .

\*\*\*\*

My silver cord tightened, like a harness, and unearthed my dream-form from the rot. I surfaced in the terrible dreamscape, gasping for air that didn't exist, beating at the hands that grasped me. Voices screamed in languages I didn't understand. They wouldn't let me go. I was going to die in here, inside the Buzzer's dreamscape. Not sinking and suffocating. I broke a putrid arm in two, and with a last wrench, the cord threw me back across the æther, into my own body.

My lids lifted.

I took a breath.

The salt circle was sealed. Nick dropped the empty pouch and collapsed on his side as if he'd been shot.

The æther rippled, creating a kind of ethereal barrier around us, like the fences that had held us in the penal colony. The creature reeled back as though the salt had transformed to molten lava, throwing out more of its strange static. Was that an aura, horribly corrupted? It let out one last death-howl before it lumbered away, leaving its darkness to hang like smoke in the æther.

The four of us lay beneath the frozen branches of the trees. "Zeke," Nick choked out, shaking him with one hand.

I couldn't so much as turn my head. Eliza was closest to me. Her eyes were glassy with shock, her lips almost as dark as mine.

For a while, I lay on the ground, my body racked with twitches. My pulse was feeble, my hearing muffled. There was a long period of darkness and silence before footsteps came through the leaves. A silhouette stood over us, just beyond the circle. The next thing I made out was a low female voice: "Dreamwalker. Hearken to me."

Then a word I didn't understand, a Gloss word. Something else was calling me back. The golden cord wrenched—the strongest pull I'd ever felt from it—and my eyes opened.

"Are you injured?" The voice belonged to Pleione Sualocin. "Speak to me, or I can offer no cure."

"Aura," I said, but my voice sounded faint even to my own ears. Still, Pleione heard me. She took a vial of amaranth, and with a gloved finger, placed a single drop below my nose. As I breathed the ambrosial smell deep into my lungs, my aura began to regenerate. I rolled over and retched. Pain collided with the front of my skull and pulsed outward in ripples.

Pleione got back to her feet. She was dressed as a denizen again, with her long black curls swept to one side of her neck. "The Emite is gone, but it will return in time. Nashira has placed a high price on your life, dreamwalker."

I couldn't stop shaking. "Is she ever going to show her face?"

"She will not dirty her hands." She wiped her blade with a cloth, staining it with what looked like oil. "Get up."

The edges of my vision were blurred, but I forced myself back to my feet. I hated how weak these sarx-creatures made me, how useless my years on the street seemed when I faced them. It made me realize that I'd only ever been a scrapper, not a true fighter. On the edge of the clearing, Eliza was curled against a tree trunk, her hands over her ears. I made toward her.

"Paige!"

The panic in Nick's voice set my heart thumping. I ran to where he was crouched at the base of another tree. Zeke was lying in his lap, unconscious.

"What happened?" I knelt beside him, jolting another bolt of pain into my eye.

"I don't know. I don't know." Nick's hands, usually so steady, were shaking. "What do we do? Paige, please—you must know how to help him . . ."

"Shh. Don't worry. There were plenty of voyants in the colony who'd been bitten or scratched," I said, but he didn't stop trembling. "We'll get help from the Rephaim. You don't know how to—"

"We have to do *something*, Paige, now!"

His voice cracked. I squeezed his shoulder. "Pleione," I shouted across the clearing. "Errai!"

Errai ignored me, but Pleione came back for us. Kneeling, she held one gloved hand to Zeke's forehead, the other to his cheek. "Quickly, dreamwalker," she said. "You must bear him to a safer place than this."

Nick's face crumpled. He framed Zeke's face between his palms, murmuring to him.

Eliza had been close to unconsciousness, but when she looked up and saw Pleione crouched nearby, she screamed as though she'd seen her own death. I ran to her and clapped a hand over her mouth.

"Still think it's a flux flash?"

She shook her head.

When I sensed Warden again, I stood, pulling Eliza up with me. He pushed through the foliage, his eyes scorching like torches. He took it all in: the salt circle, the wounded human.

"There are no others." He walked through the clearing. "What are you doing here, Paige?"

Eliza swallowed. "We were talking," I said. How sad that something so normal could sound so stupid, so thoughtless.

"I see." He walked past us. "There is a decapitated corpse beside the cold spot."

"It was a rhabdomancer." A sharp pain in my side made it difficult to talk. Or breathe, for that matter. "He must have followed us from the market."

"A thrall of the Sargas," Pleione said to Warden. "Paid to ensure that she failed to attend the scrimmage, perhaps."

"I think not. It is unlikely that they know a great deal about the syndicate's workings. In any case, they seem to want Paige alive." He paused. "The cold spot must be sealed, or more of them will come through. Where is the nearest safe house, Paige?"

I glanced at Eliza. "Any ideas?"

"One." She wiped her upper lip with a shaking hand. "Someone needs to get the car."

"You go, medium." Pleione nodded toward the trees. "Make haste."

The color left Eliza's cheeks. "What if there are more of those things?"

"Then run, very fast, and try not to succumb to death too swiftly."

The remaining color seeped from her face. I pressed my revolver into her hand, along with what was left of the salt. She groaned, took a deep breath, and took off into the trees.

Behind me, Warden kept watch. In the circle, Nick eased Zeke's head into his lap and stroked his hair, talking to him in Swedish. Pleione and Errai stood guard on either side of the clearing.

We waited.

****

Nick's nerves were frayed by the time Eliza returned. We drove back to I-4, leaving the Rephaim to stand guard around the cold spot, and got out of the car. As we ran down a cobblestoned alley, dimly lit by gas lamps and flanked on both sides by shops with bay windows, I glanced at Eliza. She was riffling through her pockets, breathing hard.

"Goodwin's Court?"

"We're going to Leon's," she bit out.

"Who?"

"Leon Wax. The screever. You know him."

Vaguely, in the way most people in the syndicate knew *of* each other. Leon Wax was a good friend of Jaxon's, a specialist in producing fake paperwork for voyants: travel papers, birth certificates, proof of Scion background, anything that made it easier to put blind spots in our government's eyes. He was the one who had forged documents for Zeke and Nadine, stating that they were legal settlers in case they should ever be stopped on the street. Like many amaurotic traders with syndicate links, he lived in a tumbledown dwelling in this tiny lane.

The front of the little shop was painted black, with a variety of dusty objects cluttering the shelves beyond the window. Snuffers, trick candles, matchboxes, candlesticks made of silver and brass, even an old metal candle clock. Silver letters spelled out WAX AND CANDLE, the legal face of Leon's trade. The bay window looked as if it hadn't been cleaned in weeks.

Eliza pulled a key from her pocket and opened the door. Why she had a key for Leon Wax's chandlery, I had no idea. Nick carried Zeke down the steps and into the tiny living room, where we laid him on the couch and lowered his head on to a cushion. I pushed at a light switch, to no avail.

"Eliza?"

"Leon doesn't believe in electric lighting." Eliza snatched a box of matches from an alcove. "Put some coal in the grate."

For Nick's sake, I didn't argue. I shucked Wynn's heavy coat and threw it over the banister, revealing the dried blood and filth on my clothes. Eliza stared.

"Paige—"

"It's not mine." I took the matches. "Cutmouth."

The wait for help was agonizing. Nick refused to leave Zeke's side, and every few minutes he tried to coax water past his lips. I ran up to the bedrooms to get blankets while Eliza lit every candle in the house.

Warden came through the door just as I got back downstairs, my arms full of crocheted blankets. Without a word, I led him into the living room. A coal fire glowed in the hearth, giving Zeke's skin a misleading warmth. Nick held his wrist in one hand, measuring his pulse.

In the corner, Eliza recoiled from the towering, lamp-eyed stranger. Warden paid her no attention.

"Where is the bite?"

"Left side," I said.

Zeke's shirt was slick with dark blood. With tight lips, Nick peeled it away from the wound, which Warden examined for some time. My stomach was strong, but the spread of the marks—from Zeke's upper chest to the lower half of his waist—was more than enough to turn it. The punctures looked deep, and the skin surrounding it was a milky gray, but the blood had already clotted.

"He will be all right," he concluded. "There is no need for treatment."

"What?" Nick sounded strangled. "Look at him!"

"Unless his bloodstream has been altered, he will recover. Does he drink alcohol or use recreational drugs?"

"No."

"Then he is immune." Warden fixed a hard gaze on Nick. "His condition may appear grave, Dr. Nygård, but his body and dreamscape will fight the pollution. Bathe the wounds in saline and sew them. Let him sleep. Those are the only remedies he needs."

With a weak groan, Nick sank into an armchair with his face in his hands. All of us looked at Zeke. His breathing was shallow, his cheeks were tinged with grey, and his fingertips looked as if he'd dipped them in soot, but he didn't look as if he was getting any worse.

"It isn't fair." Nick sounded exhausted. "He needs a proper hospital."

"Yes, and we all know what the prognosis would be then," I said. "Nitrogen asphyxiation."

"Paige!" Eliza scolded.

"He does not need a hospital," Warden said. "He will recover of his own accord—and in any case, no Scion hospital would understand his symptoms. Keep him warm and hydrated."

There was silence for a long time, scattered with the crackle in the hearth. "Should we tell Nadine?" I said to the others.

"No. She'd lose her mind over this." Eliza finally got up from the chair. "I'll get you all some fresh clothes. You can sleep here tonight. Leon's away until tomorrow." She cleared her throat, looked a long way up at Warden. "Do you . . . want to stay, too?"

"I will not stay long," Warden said.

"The attic's free, if you want it."

"Thank you. I will consider it."

When she was gone, the space felt even smaller. With a glance at Warden, I sidled into the hallway.

In the utility room, I turned on the boiler, dug an empty jam jar from the back of a dusty cupboard, and filled it with water and salt. My knees were close to giving way. Had it really been this morning that I'd found Chat reading *The Rephaite Revelation*? It seemed like weeks ago.

As I stirred the solution, I tried to get a handle on my breathing. Zeke was fine this time, but without the penal colony, more Emim would appear in the citadel before long.

I shoved the thought aside. Nick needed me now. I took a few rolls of gauze and a suture kit from the cupboard and went straight back to the living room, where he'd moved to a footstool beside the low fire. Zeke's hand was wrapped in his. I sat down on the floor beside him and curled an arm around my knees. The heat of the fire didn't reach my core, but it was enough to warm my fingers.

"Did I ever tell you about my sister?" he said hoarsely.

"You've mentioned her."

Only once. Karolina Nygård, a voyant whose gift had never had a chance to surface.

"I keep remembering how she looked." His voice was dull. "When I found them in the forest."

"Don't." I turned his cheek, so he had to look at me. "Zeke isn't going to die. I promise. Warden knows what he's talking about."

I shouldn't make these promises. After all, I hadn't saved Seb or Liss from their fates.

"Scion can't take anyone else from me. This is their fault," he murmured. "They were spineless. They gave in when they could have fought the Rephaim with everything they had. Maybe they were afraid at the beginning. Now they're thriving off the system they've created. If you become Underqueen," he said, "I'm leaving Scion. I'll take everything I can and destroy them with it."

"And if I don't?"

"I'll do it anyway. Jaxon doesn't need my blood money to waste on his cigars." It was rare to see Nick's face so cold. "I joined them because I wanted to learn everything I could about the enemy. I've learned enough, Paige. I've seen enough. All I want to do now is bring them down."

"We're on the same page, then." The fire crackled. "Jax will be wondering where we are."

"Eliza's gone back to the den. She's saying we've stayed out late training in I-6." He took the jar from my hand with a thin smile, but his face was wan. "You get some sleep, *sötnos*. You've seen enough today."

He unpacked the suture kit with steady fingers. I left, pulling the door to, but something made me stop. Zeke's eyes flickered open, and seeing Nick, he smiled and murmured "hey." Nick leaned down and kissed him, first on the forehead, then on the lips. I smiled. And there it was: a final, clean snip inside me, as if a thread had been cut.

Then it was gone. Quietly, I closed the door.

The chandlery had three floors, including the attic. It was a narrow building, packed with tiny rooms. The bathroom was about as wide as I was tall, tiled with cracked ceramic. I lit the stub of candle on the sink. The mirror confirmed that I wouldn't look out of place among mudlarks. Dark blood plastered my clothes to my body and the skin around my lips was smudged with grey.

A deep chill held fast to my bones. I would have done anything for a hot bath at that moment. I peeled off the clothes and bundled them into the corner. Water rattled through the pipes when I turned the aging shower's dial, bursting out in a lukewarm sputter. Once I'd stood under the drizzle for a few minutes and scrubbed away the smell of salted Emite, I leaned close to the mirror to peel off my contacts. One of my pupils was dilated, taking up most of my iris. I blinked and looked at the candle, but my left pupil refused to react.

There was a spare room on this floor, where Eliza had left a clean nightshirt on one of two identical beds. I buttoned the shirt and breathed in its delicate, floral smell. It was all I could do not to collapse, but I wouldn't sleep for long in this room. A bed-warmer might shake the chill.

I brushed out my wet hair and walked back to the landing, trying to ignore the dull ache in my side. As I headed for the stairs, Warden came up them. He stopped when he saw me.

"Paige."

My arms were still covered in gooseflesh. Part of me wanted to go to him, but something warned me away.

"Warden," I said, too softly to be heard from downstairs.

"You tried to possess the Emite."

I raised my eyebrows. "Did you steal another memory?"

"This time I am innocent of that." Warden studied the painting on the wall. It was one of Eliza's favorite pieces of art, something she'd worked on without spirits over the course of a year. "Your pupils are unequally sized. It is a sign that your silver cord has been shaken. Had the creature succeeded in trapping you, it would have devoured your spirit."

"If you'd let me in on that one," I said, "I probably wouldn't have tried walking in its dreamscape."

"Hindsight has given me wisdom on that matter." He laid his hands on the banister. "I take it you were on the hill to talk in secret."

My voice was hoarse, but I made myself tell the story again. He listened without changing his expression.

"A 'gray market,'" he repeated. "I have not heard the term."

"That makes two of us."

"Then it seems a great deal hinges on your victory in the scrimmage." His eyes burned away the gloom. "The man who lured you to the cold spot may have something to do with this operation."

I had to wonder how many people were involved. How many people were willing to kill and to die to protect whatever the Abbess and the Rag and Bone Man were plotting. "Will the Emim keep coming through?"

"Oh, yes." His hands tightened on the banister. "Now the penal colony has been abandoned, the Emim will no longer be attracted towards the spiritual activity there. No matter what the costs of that colony, it served well as a beacon. Now they will be tempted by the great hive of spirits in London. Cold spots to their realm can be closed, but the art is difficult."

"Their realm?"

"A large part of the Netherworld is overrun with Emim. You may have noticed that that cold spot repelled spirits, rather than attracting them, for even spirits fear their side."

This must have been what Ognena Maria had meant all those weeks ago, when she'd said that spirits were disappearing from her section.

"We can't let them come here," I said.

Neither of us moved for a long time. Words kept stumbling to my lips and retreating again. He watched me now as he had once in a crowded room, always indecipherable. There was nothing that gave away how he felt—*if* he felt—when he looked at me.

What had happened in the clearing, along with everything else, had left an ache behind my ribs. I'd learned too much in one day. With the smallest of movements, I shifted myself closer to him, resting my head against his arm. Warmth radiated from inside him, as if his chest was stacked with hot coals. His hands grasped the banister on either side of me, not quite touching my hips. The low sound he made sent a chain of tremors along my abdomen.

When I lifted my chin, his nose listed against mine. My fingers traced the hard line of his jaw and the shell of his ear as I listened to his breathing and his heartbeat. They were just rhythms to him— not countdowns, like they were for me. That burning started in my dreamscape again, as it had once in the Guildhall.

I had no name for what he made me feel. I had no real sense of what it was; only that it was blood-deep, like some long-forgotten instinct. Only that I wanted it to let it take me over.

"I have thought about what you said," he said. "In the music hall."

I waited. His finger followed the line that arced from the side of my palm, above my thumb, down to just above my wrist.

"You are right. It is how they silence us. I will not be silenced, Paige, but nor will I lie to you. Our lifelines will meet only when the æther sees fit. That may not be often. It can never be *always*."

I linked his fingers through mine.

"I know," was all I said.

# 23

## Liminal

As soon as I closed the door to the attic, Warden took my face between his callused palms. All I could hear was my own breathing, my own heartbeat. My fingers found the key and turned it, locking myself into the darkness with a Rephaite. He was a creature of the limen; any false impression of humanity was gone. I smoothed my hands over his shoulders, up the slope of his neck, and at last, when my heart was pounding, his mouth took hold of mine.

In the darkness, I was nothing but feeling. Fingers pushing through my hair, climbing up the column of my spine. I pulled him closer, draping one arm around his neck, winding my fingers into rough-spun hair. He tasted of red wine and something else, something earthen and rich and just faintly amaroidal.

A callused palm came to rest against my bare stomach, where my breaths came quick and shallow. Until now, I hadn't understood how much I'd wanted him to hold me, to touch me. Intimacy had no place in either of our worlds.

Warden lifted me, swinging the floor from under my feet. His hand cupped my cheek, and we broke the silence with our breathing. He held me so our foreheads touched, as if he were reassuring me that this was all right. As if that wasn't a lie. I pressed my mouth against his jaw, savoring the warmth of his skin and the low-pitched notes of Gloss that trembled in his throat.

His dreamscape sent a tongue of fire across my flowers. There was still that voice in my head as I kissed him, as I whispered his name into his mouth. *Stop, Paige, stop.* An innate warning. The Ranthen could walk in and discover us, like Nashira had. But with this nocturne playing, the voice of reason was easy to ignore. He was right: this wouldn't last forever. He would never be a steady presence in my life. But how much could a moment matter?

We sank on to what felt like a buttoned couch, with my legs on either side of him and his arm wrapped around my hips. My fingers strayed to the welts that criss-crossed his back, the scars left for his treachery. Scars he'd received when a human traitor had fed information to Nashira.

Warden grew still. I caught his gaze before I followed the branching scar tissue from his back, over his ribs, round to his abdomen. Their texture was almost waxen. Cold to the touch, like the ones on my hand.

These were the prints of a poltergeist. Warden watched my face as I drew away, tracing a vicious mark along his ribcage.

"Whose spirit was it?"

"One of her fallen angels. The poltergeist." His finger followed my jaw. "Naturally, its name is a closely guarded secret. Perhaps time has forgotten it."

I could envision no better way to control him than to ration out drops of amaranth for the pain. Nashira Sargas had more imagination than I'd given her credit for.

We stayed there in the dark of the attic, sprawled in slats of moonlight. Adrenaline pulsed through my veins. The others wouldn't pick up on our dreamscapes from the lower floor, but they might if they came upstairs.

"I'll still go out."

"That was an observation," he said. "A selfish one. It has no bearing on my choices."

"It isn't just that. It's every reason under the sun."

"True enough." He traced a sliver of moonlight across my waist. "A good thing, then, that we are not under the sun."

I smiled into his shoulder. Downstairs, someone was playing a piano. Not a whisperer. No spirits stirred to the rhythm. I looked up at Warden.

"Cécile Chaminade. An elegy."

"Do you keep a jukebox in your head?"

"Hm." He pushed a curl from my eyes. "That would make a fine addition to my dreamscape."

There was a nervous tremor in my core, the same feeling I got when I discovered some rare ornament or instrument on the black market. The sense that my fingers would slip on its surface. That it would break before it saw the light of day. I laid a hand on his abdomen, so I felt it rise with each steady breath.

"If you want this," he said, very softly, "even if it does not last, it must be kept from the Ranthen."

Or they would destroy me. And him, and the alliance, all so we could touch and kiss and hold each other if we wanted. It was pure, reckless feeling, the sort Jaxon would scoff at.

Warden's gaze roved over my face. I was about to answer with a lie—*it doesn't matter*—but it caught in my throat. He knew it mattered, and it hadn't been a question. I turned over, so my back was against his chest, and looked up at the window.

"I've been so blind," I said. " About the syndicate . . ."

"I find that hard to believe."

"I've always known it was corrupt, but not like this. The Abbess and the Rag and Bone Man are doing something terrible, something to do with the Rephaim. And I can't work out what it is, but I feel like the answer's staring me in the face." I traced the scars along his knuckles. "The traitor from the first rebellion. Did you ever see their face?"

"If I did, I may never know. I was never told which human had betrayed us."

It must have eaten away at him for years, not knowing who had done this to him. His muscles tensed as he spoke.

I took my hand from his stomach. "I'm going to have to enter Jaxon's dreamscape at the scrimmage. I haven't been in anyone else's mind for a while."

He studied me for a while. "Do you intend to kill Jaxon?"

The question gnawed at me. "I don't want to," I said. "If I can control him for long enough to make him surrender, I might still be able to win."

"An honourable choice," he remarked. "More honorable than any the White Binder himself will make, I imagine."

"He risked everything to get me out of Sheol. He wouldn't kill me."

"Let us assume, for safety's sake, that he will try."

"Wasn't it you who said 'never assume'?"

"I make some exceptions." Warden sat back against the cushions. "It will be easy for you to enter my dreamscape now. By the time you face Jaxon, you will be exhausted and injured. You will need the last of your strength to make the jump."

"Let me try, then. Without the mask."

It was no small thing to let me in again, yet he didn't raise a word of objection. I reached up to his nape and held him there, taking deep, slow breaths. I was already beginning to feel drowsy; slipping out of my body was easy.

When I stepped into his dreamscape, I found myself in his

hadal zone, where the silence pressed against me like a wall. Red velvet drapes swirled down from high above and vanished into bonfire smoke. My footsteps echoed as if I were walking through a cathedral, but this dreamscape remained a floating island in the æther, taking no clear form. It just *was*. Maybe the Netherworld was like this, a desolate realm with no life left in it. I pushed past the swathes of velvet, through each ring of his consciousness until I reached the very heart of Arcturus Mesarthim's mind. His dream-form stood with its hands behind its back. A hollow, washed-out thing.

"Welcome back, Paige."

The drapes surrounded us. "You've gone for a minimalist look, I see."

"I was never one for mental clutter."

But something had changed in this part of his mind. A flower had grown from the dust, with petals of a warm and unnameable color, sealed under the bell jar like a preserved specimen. "The amaranth." I crouched down and touched the glass surface. "What's it doing here?"

"I do not claim to know how dreamscapes choose their shape," he said, walking around it, "but it seems I am no longer an 'empty shell,' as you put it."

"Do you have defenses?"

"Only those which my nature has gifted me. Jaxon will not have walls as strong as mine, but he may have manifestations of memory."

"Specters," I recalled. I'd read about them in an early draft of *On the Machinations of the Itinerant Dead*, and seen them for myself when I'd glimpsed the insides of other dreamscapes. Silent, spidery figures that crawled in the hadal zone. Most people had at least one. Some people, like Nadine, had a dreamscape overrun with them. "Those are memories?"

"In a manner of speaking. They are projections of one's regrets or anxieties. When something 'plays on your mind,' as you say, it is the specters at work."

I stood. "Do you have any?"

His head turned toward the drapes. Twelve specters had gathered at the edges of his twilight zone, held back by the light in the center of his dreamscape. They had no discernible faces, though their shape was loosely human. They were somewhere between solid and gas, with skin that seemed to slip and slide around smoke.

"They cannot hurt your dream-form," he said, "but they may attempt to block your path. You must not tarry, nor let them hold you."

I studied his collection. "Do you know which memory is which?"

"Yes." Warden watched them. "I know."

His profile was much harsher in his dreamscape, all the softness leached out of his features.

I'd never touched another person's dream-form. Entering a dreamscape was already an invasion of privacy, and it had always struck me as too cruel to contemplate, handling the image they held of their own nature. Leaving fingerprints on that image could do irrevocable damage: burst or bolster an inflated ego, shatter a last inch of hope. But my wanderlust had turned to lust and wonder. A thirst for knowledge, no matter how dangerous. So when Warden's ember-eyes looked down at me, I reached up and laid my hand against his cheek.

Cold against my fingers. Vibrations through my dream-form. His vision of me, in direct contact with his vision of himself. I had to remember that they weren't my fingers, though they looked exactly like the ones I knew. These were my hands only as Warden perceived them. I let them rest against his face for a long while, tracing the firm lips and carved jaw.

"Take heed, dreamwalker." He lifted a hand to cover mine. "Self-portraits are as fragile as mirrors."

His resonant voice shook me to the core, snapping me out of it. When I returned to my body, I swung my legs over the edge of the couch, my chest heaving. Doing this without the mask was still difficult, teaching my body how to hold out without its most basic functions. Warden watched me from a distance until I got a handle on it.

"You—" I caught my breath, one hand against my chest. "Why do you see yourself like that?"

"I cannot see my own dream-form. I confess myself intrigued."

"It's like a statue, but scarred, like someone's taken a chisel to it. To you." A frown creased my brow. "Is that how you see yourself?"

"In a sense. Years as a blood-consort to Nashira Sargas certainly eroded my sanity, if nothing else." He touched his thumb to my cheekbone. "You will not need to break from your body entirely during the scrimmage. Remember what I taught you. Leave enough of yourself behind to keep your life functions working."

I didn't miss his avoidance, but I'd already invaded his privacy. "I don't understand how." I rested my head against his shoulder. "I can't split my spirit between two bodies."

"You did it in the music hall. Do not think of it as splitting yourself," he said, "but leaving a shadow behind."

In the moonlight, we watched one another for a while. One of us should have gone, but neither of us did. His fingers grazed a line from my temple to my neck, stroking downward to where the collar of my shirt fell open above my breasts. Emotion pulsed through the cord, too complex to pull apart.

"You look exhausted." The words rumbled through his chest.

"It's been a long day." I held his gaze. "Warden, I need you to promise me something."

He only looked at me. I'd asked him for a favor once before, facing death at the hands of his fiancée.

*If she kills me, you have to let the others know. You have to lead them.*

*I will not need to lead them.*

"If I lose the scrimmage," I said, "make sure the gray market ends. Whatever it is."

It was a while before he answered. "I will do what I can, Paige. I will always do what I can."

That was all I could ask. His touch strayed to the brand on my shoulder, the six digits that had been my name.

"You were a slave once," he said. "Do not be a slave to fear, Paige Mahoney. Make the gift your own."

****

That night was a first. I'd never slept at someone's side, with their aura wrapped around mine like a second skin. It took a while for my sixth sense to adjust to his proximity. My defenses kept rising, set on edge by his dreamscape. I imagined that this was what it would be like to sleep on a ship, adrift on a surface that never quite stopped shifting. More than once I woke disoriented, hearing another heartbeat near my ear, warmer than I would have been alone.

The first time I panicked, and his eyes gave me such a fierce reminder of Sheol I that I rolled off the couch and made a grab for my knife. Warden watched in silence, waiting for me to remember. Afterward, he let me lie with my back against his chest, making no attempt to hold me there.

When I woke for good, it was just past four in the morning. Warden was still asleep, his arm around my middle. The smell of hot metal lingered on his skin.

A chill worked its way down my sides. The others would wonder where I'd been all night.

This time he didn't wake with me. I'd never seen him look as human as he did now. Softer, as if all the heavy memories had slipped out of his dreamscape.

I unlocked the door and crept out of the attic. On the landing, I leaned against the banister and crossed my arms tightly. Trusting Warden was one thing, but by touching his dream-form, I'd turned this into something else. Something far more dangerous.

I knew that I could never spend a single night with him, as Jaxon's rules permitted. There was too much of him I wanted to learn.

I also knew that it couldn't last. Whatever this was, it was too much of a risk. Why was I doing it? Like it or not, I would need the Ranthens' support in the days to come. And if they even suspected . . .

I gripped the banister with both hands, listening to the footsteps downstairs. I'd stayed under Scion's radar since I'd joined Jaxon's fold. For ten years I'd concealed a vast part of my life from my father. Warden was a master at veiling his intentions—he had orchestrated two rebellions behind his own fiancée's back.

I wanted this. To stop running, just once. For all the darkness and the cold in him, there was warmth that made me feel alive and strong. It was so different from how it had been with Nick—and this couldn't be like it had been with Nick. With him, it had been like dying. A long yielding of myself to the idea that he could want to be with me. I'd depended on that idea for too long. With Warden, it was like having two heartbeats rather than half of one.

I padded down the stairs, barefoot, and opened the kitchen door. Nick was already at the table, reading the *Daily Descendant* and picking at a basket of hot bread from the cookshop.

"Morning."

"Not quite yet." I sat down. "Was that you on the piano last night?"

"It was. Only piece I ever learned," he said. "I thought it might help Zeke sleep. He was a whisperer before he became unreadable."

"How is he?"

He laid down his newspaper and rubbed his eyes with one hand. "I'm going to let him rest for a while longer, but we'll have to clear out in a few hours. Leon will be home soon."

"You should ask them to keep him here for a while." I pulled the paper toward me. "Jax will only ask questions."

"He'll ask questions anyway."

There was a piercing clarity to his gaze that hadn't been there yesterday. Ignoring it, I scanned the paper. Scion was encouraging denizens to increase their vigilance in the hunt for Paige Mahoney and her allies, stressing that the fugitives were likely to have altered their appearances to avoid detection. They were to look out for other clues, such as accents, dyed hair, masks, or the scars of recent backstreet surgery. Examples of the latter were shown: seams of purpled stitching through raw skin, often located on the cheeks, near the hairline, or behind the ears.

"I need to tell the others what I'm planning for the scrimmage." I poured us both a coffee. "And find out who they'd side with if I won."

"Are you going to tell them about Warden?"

A pendulum clock ticked above the sink. I put down my coffee cup. "What?"

"Paige, I've known you for ten years. I know when something's different."

"Nothing's different." When I saw his face, I framed my temples with my fingers. "Everything's different."

"I know it's none of my business."

I stirred my coffee.

"I'm not going to lecture or patronize you," he murmured, "but I want you to remember what he did. Even if he's changed, even if he never meant to hurt you by keeping you there, and even if he wasn't the one who captured you in the first place, you have to remember that he used you. Promise me, *sötnos*."

"Nick, I don't *want* to forget what he did. He could have let me go the first day he took me in. I know that. That doesn't mean I can stop feeling like this. And I know you think I've started to sympathize with him," I said, holding his gaze. "I haven't. I don't sympathize with what he did to me—I have no compassion for it—but I understand why he did it. Does that make sense?"

He didn't reply for a short while. "Yes," he finally said. "It makes sense. But he's so cold, Paige. Does he make you happy?"

"I don't know yet." I took a deep sip of coffee, and it warmed me. "I just know that he sees me."

He sighed.

"What?" I said, more gently.

"I don't want you to be Underqueen. Look at what happened to Hector and Cutmouth."

"That won't happen," I said, but the thought still made me cold. Even if Jaxon had remembered to report those hitmen to the Abbess, I knew now that she would have ignored it. "Seen any more visions?"

"Yes." He rubbed his temples. "They come every few days now. There's so much packed into them, I can't explain it . . ."

"Don't think about them." I squeezed his hand, then eased mine out of his grip. "I have to do it, Nick. Someone has to try."

"It doesn't have to be *you*. I have a bad feeling about it."

"We're clairvoyant. We're supposed to have bad feelings about things."

He gave me a flat look. The kitchen door swung open then, and Eliza sat down opposite us.

"Hi," she said.

Nick frowned. "I thought you were at the den?"

"Jaxon sent me back to find you. He wants us all at Dials in an hour." She poured herself a coffee. "We should have gone straight back last night."

"I don't think any of us were expecting a monster on the hill," Nick said. "But why are we at Leon Wax's chandlery?"

"Because he's like family to me."

It was rare for any of us to mention the word *family*. Jaxon liked to forget the concept existed, as if we'd all hatched from miraculous Fabergé eggs. Nick laid his newspaper to one side. "Like family?"

"When I was a baby I was dumped on a doorstep and raised by a bunch of traders. They hated me. Made me fetch packages from Soho and carry them two miles back to Cheapside on my own, past Vigiles and gangsters. Four miles a day from the minute I could walk. When I was seventeen, I finally got my own job at the penny gaff. That was where I met Bea Cissé. She was brilliant, the best actress in the Cut. She was the first voyant I'd ever met who didn't spit on me."

Nick and I listened in silence. The corners of her mouth tightened.

"Bea's a physical medium. She used to let all sorts of spirits possess her for performances. Escape artists, contortionists, dancers. It wore her dreamscape down after twenty years of it." Her voice shook. "Bea and Leon are my closest friends outside the gang. Half the reason I applied for the job with Jax was so I could help pay for her medicine."

I couldn't quite believe it. Eliza's loyalty and commitment to Jaxon had always seemed impeccable.

"What are you treating her with?" Nick said quietly.

"Purple aster. He's taken her away to the country for a few days to try and find new herbs."

"That's where you kept going," I said. "On market night."

"She was bad that day. I thought we'd lose her." She dabbed her raw eyes with her sleeve. "They use this place as a shelter for beggars when they're here, just to get them fed and on their feet. Now they're struggling to keep it going." Her shoulders slumped. "Sorry. It's just been a stressful few months."

"You should have told us," Nick murmured.

"I couldn't. You might have told Jax."

"You're kidding." He wrapped an arm around her, and she let out a weak hiccup of laughter. "You used to tell me everything when we were the first two Seals. We're always here for you."

We were all silent for a long time, picking at bread and honey. On the floor above, Warden's dreamscape stirred as he woke.

"I was going to tell you yesterday," I said to her. "I've decided to go against Jaxon in the scrimmage."

Eliza's eyes widened. She turned to Nick, as if he could snap me out of this moment of madness, but all he did was sigh.

"No." When I didn't laugh, she shook her head. "Paige, don't. You can't. Jaxon will—"

"—kill me." I finished my coffee. "He's welcome to try."

"Jaxon is twice your age and the citadel's resident expert on clairvoyance. And if you go against him, it's over. The gang is over."

There was no denying it. Like it or not, he was the linchpin that had drawn us all together. "And if I don't go against him," I said, "everything else is over. You know what we're up against. If the Abbess *is* the one behind all this, then we can't trust the syndicate to do anything about it. We have to take charge of it ourselves, before it crumbles."

She didn't speak again.

"You mustn't tell Nadine. You know she'd go straight to Jax. Dani might join me, but we can't tell Zeke. We don't know who he'll side with." I looked at Nick, who clasped his hands. "Do we?"

It took him a while to answer. "No," he finally said. "He wants to fight the Rephaim, and he knows I'll always side with you, but he loves his sister. I don't know who he'd choose."

Still Eliza sat in silence, her mouth a narrow line of worry.

"Paige," she said, "did . . . Jaxon really say he wouldn't do anything about the Rephaim?"

"All he cares about is the syndicate," I said.

"Now I've seen them, I don't understand it." She pinched the skin between her eyebrows. "I know what you're doing is right. I know we have to get rid of those things. But Jax took me in when I had nothing, even though I was a lower order. I know he's . . . difficult, but I've been with him for such a long time. And I have the same problem as Nadine. I need money."

"You'll have it. I promise you, Eliza, you'll have it." I spoke gently. "It's your choice. But if I win, I'd like you to be on my side."

Eliza looked up at me. "Really?"

"Really."

As I spoke, the golden cord gave a shiver. His dreamscape was outside the door. I put down the newspaper.

"One minute," I said. Nick watched me go.

In the hallway, Warden was taking his coat from the stand by the door. When he caught sight of me, his eyes burned.

"Good morning, Paige."

"Hi." I cleared my throat. "You're welcome to stay for breakfast, but you might need a cleaver to cut through the tension."

I sounded too brisk. How were you supposed to talk to someone you'd just spent the night with? I didn't have a wealth of personal experience in the subject.

"Tempting though it is," Warden said, "the Ranthen are waiting for me outside. They will want to speak with you before the scrimmage." He flicked his gaze over my face. "On that note, you would do well to survive this trial, Paige Mahoney. For all our sakes."

"I intend to."

There was no smile on his mouth, but I could see it in his gaze, warm and lambent. I raised my hands to his back, so I could feel the slow rhythm of his breathing. Heat reached out from behind my ribs and trailed along my arms, right to my fingertips.

And I had a strange sense that I belonged. Not in the material sense, as I belonged to Jaxon, as I'd once belonged to the Rephaim. This was belonging of a different sort, as things that are alike belong with one another.

I had never felt like this, and it scared the living daylights out of me.

"Did you sleep well?" he asked.

"Fine. Apart from the knife incident." I took Nick's jacket from the door. "Will the Ranthen know?"

"They may have their suspicions. Nothing more."

Our auras were still pulling apart as he opened the door, letting in the chill wind from outside. I pulled on my boots and followed him from the chandlery, into a crisp fog. The Ranthen were waiting at the other end of Goodwin's Court, gathered under the only streetlamp. At the sound of our footsteps, they turned in unison to look at us, and Pleione said, "How fares the human?"

"Great." I raised an eyebrow. "Thanks for asking."

"Not you. The boy."

A Rephaite asking after an injured human. I never thought I'd see the day. "Zeke's fine," I said. "Warden kept an eye on him."

The bones of Terebell Sheratan's face stood out in the electric-blue light, casting shadows under her cheekbones. My fists tightened in my pockets.

"I hope," she said, "that you slept well. We bring word that Situla Mesarthim, Nashira's mercenary, has been sighted in this section of the citadel. I am sure you remember her." I remembered Situla very well, a relative of Warden's whose only resemblance to him was her physical appearance. "We must leave for our safe house in the East End to await your success in the scrimmage."

"About that," I said. "I have a favour to ask."

"Explain," Terebell said.

"The last four survivors of the Bone Season were captured by the mime-lord who had Warden. One of them has valuable information I need. Her name's Ivy Jacob."

"Thuban's plaything."

The word made me flinch. "He was her keeper," I said. "Without her, there might still be voyants who doubt my ability to run the syndicate. The fugitives have been imprisoned in a night parlour somewhere in I-2. I don't know where, but I know a way into the—"

"You *dare* to imply that we should fetch them for you," Errai sneered. "We are not your thralls, to be ordered about at will."

"You don't scare me, Rephaite. You think I wasn't beaten hard enough in the colony?" I wrenched down my shirt, showing him the brand. "You think I don't remember this?"

"I do not think you remember it well enough."

"Errai, peace." To his right, Lucida held up a hand. "Arcturus, is this a rational course of action?"

Warden's eyes were full of fire. "I believe so," he said. "This Rag and Bone Man was able to capture and imprison me without a great deal of difficulty. He is ruthless, cruel and knowledgeable about the Rephaim. His 'gray market' must be stopped, lest he continue to mock us from the shadows."

"What is the meaning of 'gray market,' dreamwalker?" Terebell's patience sounded as if it was wearing thin.

"I don't know," I said. "But Ivy will."

"You know for certain that this Ivy is imprisoned in the night parlor, then."

"I didn't see her, but I felt her dreamscape. I know she's there."

"You expect us to risk our lives," Pleione said, "for a feeling."

"Yes, Pleione, just like I risked my life when Warden asked me to help him with your rebellion, even though the first one crashed and burned," I said coldly. Immediately I regretted saying it, but Warden didn't react. "Everyone will be distracted on the night of the scrimmage. Win or lose, I need Ivy to talk."

Terebell's features were hard. "The Ranthen do not generally interfere in such things. The Mothallath belief was that we should never act against the natural events of the corporeal world," she said. "We must not stop their deaths if they were ordained by the æther."

"That's ridiculous," I said, appalled. "Nobody's death is *ordained*."

"So you say."

"They fought to survive. They fought to get out of your colony. If you want me to get you an army, you have to get me Ivy."

They didn't speak for some time. I stared them out, shaking with anger. Terebell gave me a last look before she led them away down the alley.

"Was that a 'yes'?" I said to Warden.

"I suppose it was not a 'no.' In any case, I will persuade them."

"Warden"—I caught his arm—"I'm sorry for saying that. About the first rebellion."

"The truth requires no apology." The light in his eyes dwindled to a low, beating flame. "Good luck."

The weight of his gaze made my skin prickle. That, and the stillness of our bodies. When I didn't move, he touched his lips to my hair.

"I am no soothsayer, nor oracle," Warden said to me, his voice a low rumble, "but I have every confidence in you."

"You're mad," I said into his neck.

"Madness is a matter of perspective, little dreamer."

The last I saw of him was his back disappearing into the fog. Somewhere in the citadel, a bell began to ring.

****

Jaxon Hall was locked into his office when we got back to the den, playing "Danse Macabre" so loudly we could hear it from the downstairs hallway. Eliza and I parted on the landing and tiptoed to our rooms. I waited for a bang on the wall, but there was nothing.

Trying not to make too much noise, I prepared myself for the scrimmage. I took a hot shower to loosen my muscles. Laid out the clothes Eliza had made for me. Sat on the bed and practiced possessing a spider that had strung a spangled web across my window. After two humans, a bird, and a deer, such a small creature was easy to control. Inside its dreamscape I found a delicate maze of silk.

After five attempts, I was able to control the spider without abandoning my own body entirely. I left a tiny drop of perception in my dreamscape, just the barest shadow of awareness. Enough to keep my body upright for a few seconds while I scuttled along the windowsill, until I teetered off my feet and whacked my head against the nearest wall. Spewing profanities, I clapped the oxygen mask over my mouth and drew in shuddering breaths.

If I couldn't do this at the scrimmage, I had no chance. Every time I jumped, my body would be vulnerable to attack. I'd be killed in the first few minutes. My injuries from Primrose Hill weren't serious, but I needed a good night's sleep under my belt for my dreamscape to recover. I switched off the lamp and curled up in my bed, listening to Jaxon's record player. "A Bird in a Gilded Cage" drifted through the wall, rustling with static.

I didn't know where I'd be the day after tomorrow. Certainly not here, in my little room at Seven Dials. I could be on the streets, a pariah and a traitor. I could be Underqueen, ruling the syndicate.

I could be in the æther.

Just beyond the window was a solitary dreamscape. I looked past my curtains, down into the courtyard, where Jaxon Hall sat alone under the red sky. He wore his lounging robe and trousers with polished shoes, and his cane lay on the bench beside him.

Our eyes met. He crooked a finger.

Outside, I joined him on the bench. His eyes were on the stars above our den. Their light was trapped in the crypts and furrows of his irises, so they seemed to sparkle with the knowledge of some private joke.

"Hello, darling," he said.

"Hi." I gave him a sidelong look. "I thought you were calling a meeting?"

"I shall. Soon." He clasped his hands. "Do your glad rags fit?"

"They're beautiful."

"They are. My medium has talent to rival half of London's dressmakers." Jaxon's eyes were full of starlight. "Do you know that today is the anniversary of the day I made you mollisher?"

So it was. October the thirty-first. I hadn't even thought about it.

"It was the very first time I let you do a job at street level, wasn't it? Before that day you were the tea girl, the lowly researcher. And getting quite cross with it, too, I'd imagine."

"Very." I couldn't help but smile. "I'd never met someone who drank so much tea."

"I was testing your patience! Yes, it was when those dratted poltergeists were loose in I-4. Sarah Metyard and her daughter, the murderous milliners," he recalled. "You and Dr. Nygård spent the best part of the morning tracking those two down. And what did I say to you, darling, when you came back with your prize for me to bind? I took you to the pillar and pointed out the sundial facing this side of Monmouth Street, and I said to you—"

"'You see this, O my lovely? This is yours. This street, this path, is yours to walk,'" I finished.

It had been the best day of my life. Earning Jaxon Hall's approval, along with the right to call myself his protégée, had filled me with such joy that I couldn't have imagined a world without him in it.

"Precisely. Precisely that." He paused. "I've never been much of a gambler; I never had much faith in chance, my dear. I know we have our differences, but we are the Seven Seals. Brought together across oceans and fault lines by the mysterious wiles of the æther. It wasn't chance. It was fate. And we shall bring about a day of reckoning in London."

With that image in his mind, Jaxon closed his eyes and smiled. I craned my neck to look up at the stars, breathing in the thickness of the night. Roasted chestnuts, smoky coffee, and extinguished fires. It was the smell of fire and life and renewal. The smell of ash and death and ending.

"Yes," I said. *Or a day of change.*

# 24

## The Rose Ring

### November 1, 2059

The clocks of London chimed eleven. Inside the Interchange building in II-4, every light had been extinguished. But beneath the brick warehouse, in the secret labyrinth of the Camden Catacombs, the fourth scrimmage in the history of the London syndicate was about to begin.

Jaxon and I arrived in the buck cab and disembarked in the yard. Participants traditionally displayed the colors of their auras, with the mollishers adopting their mime-lord's hue, but Jaxon and I were haughtily monochrome ("Darling, I would sooner be caught waltzing with Didion Waite than dressed from head to toe in orange").

My hair had been pinned with a fascinator, woven together from swan feathers and ribbon. My lips were black and my eyes painted with kohl, expertly applied by Eliza. Jaxon's hair shone with oil, and his irises were blanched by white contacts, as were mine. On his head was a top hat with a white silk band around it. During the scrimmage, the matching outfits would show that we were a mime-lord and mollisher pair, permitted to fight together whenever we chose.

"Well." Jaxon brushed down his lapels. "It seems the hour is upon us."

The rest of the Seven Seals disembarked from their car, all in black and white. Twenty more specially selected voyants from I-4 were waiting, all supporting the White Binder's claim to the crown. They kept a respectful distance from us, talking among themselves.

"We're with you, Jax," Nadine said.

"Absolutely." Her brother's brow was damp with sweat, but he smiled. "All the way."

"You are too kind, my darlings." Jaxon clapped his hands. "We've talked enough about this night. To battle, then. May the æther smile upon I-4."

Together, the party walked down the steps to the door of the Camden Catacombs. The dog was nowhere to be seen, but the unreadable guard was there, dressed in black.

"What a show this will be," Jaxon said against my ear. "The citadel will talk about it for decades, darling, you mark my words."

His voice stippled my neck with gooseflesh. The guard looked us over. When she gave us a nod, we filed through the door in pairs.

As we walked down the winding steps, my ribcage seemed to grow smaller. I strained to look over my shoulder, but the exit was already out of sight. If there was one place I didn't want to be going, it was back into the Rag and Bone Man's lair, where manacles and chains hung from the walls; where people could be swallowed up, never to be found. If he had his way, I would never walk out of here alive. I took in deep breaths, but they weren't reaching my lungs. Jaxon patted my hand.

"Don't be nervous, my Paige. I have every intention of winning tonight."

"I know."

Inside the Camden Catacombs, the tunnels were no longer decrepit. All the junk and rubble had been cleared, and in the place of broken bulbs there were strings of stained-glass lanterns, each the color of an aura.

The central vault looked nothing like it had when I'd last been here. Grand crimson drapes hung from every wall, turning the vast space into a theatre of war. A painting of Edward VII looked down on us all, holding up the sceptre of a king. Music was played by a line of whisperers: luxuriant, sepulchral soundscapes that played all kinds of havoc with the æther. Two hundred upholstered chairs had been placed near the entrance, some turned to face round tables, each of which was marked with a section number.

Golden bowls glinted here and there, brimming with red wine. Plates of lavish food steamed on burgundy tablecloths. Vast meat pies, drizzled with thick gravy; sandwiches with vintage cheese and walnuts; brisket of beef, boiled with onions and spices. Sponge cakes, as light as you please, layered with whipped cream and strawberry jam. Clearly someone had a cookshop waitron on their side. People were already finding seats, stuffing their faces with plum pudding and flummery and fragile brandy snaps.

"This is grotesque," Nick said as we walked toward our table. "There are buskers starving out there, and we've found money to waste on a party."

"Thanks, Nick," Danica said.

"What?"

"I've been searching for a long time for someone who is more boring than me. I'm so glad to have found you."

We stopped at the drinks table. While most of the others chose wine, I scooped my glass through a bowl of blood mecks. Real alcohol could get me killed tonight. I sipped the spiced fruit syrup, scanning the vault.

A wide chalk line separated the seating area from where the fight would begin. And there was the Rose Ring, the old symbol of unnaturalness. Dark crimson rose-heads, one for each participant, had been carefully arranged in a circle that spanned thirty feet. Ash had been poured into it to soak up any blood we spilled. We wouldn't have to fight within its confines for the whole event, but the Rose Ring would hold all of us at close quarters at the beginning, giving us a chance to strike a devastating first blow.

Eliza came to stand beside me, carrying a glass. "Are you ready?" she said softly.

"No."

"What are you going to do if—?"

"Let's cross that bridge when we come to it," I said.

Voyants were everywhere. All the dominant gangs and more. Some were trailing guardian angels or wisps; there was even a single brooding psychopomp in one corner of the vault. Jaxon returned and whispered in my ear: "Do you see the spirit?" He pointed with his cane. "That is a rare thing: a psychopomp. It has been present at every scrimmage since the first."

"Where did it come from?"

"No one knows. After the final round, it escorts the vanquished candidate's spirit to the last light. A final kindness from the syndicate. Isn't that delicious?"

I looked at the place where the spirit was floating and wondered if it had once served the Rephaim. Why it had chosen to serve the syndicate now.

"And there's Didion." Jaxon had the look of a lion sizing up prey. "Do excuse me."

He kissed my hand and strode away. My sixth sense was jostled by the endless crackle of people and spirits. Warden's emotions came across the cord as relatively calm; clearly nothing had changed on his end yet. As I took a seat at the I-4 table with the others, Danica tapped my shoulder and leaned in close.

"I finished the mask." She took a slim pouch from her pocket and tugged out a coil of tubing, so delicate it was hardly visible. Uncoiling the tube with her thumb, she grasped my wrist and wrapped it in a bulky cuff. "The tank is concealed in here, but it also monitors your pulse. Feed the tube through your sleeve and over your ear, so it's right by your mouth. The second you leave your body, your heart will stop and this will start."

"Danica," I said, "you're a genius."

"You say that like I don't know." She sat back and folded her arms. "The tank is small, so don't go overboard."

I pushed the tube past my wrist and hooked it over my right ear, then pulled my sleeve over the cuff. If anyone noticed the tube, it would pass as an unusual earpiece.

It took time for them all to arrive: the mime-lords, mime-queens, mollishers and mobsters of the Scion Citadel of London. These people weren't particularly concerned about timekeeping.

After what seemed like hours, the seats were filled and rivers of illegal alcohol were flowing. A petite psychographer walked into the middle of the ring, her collar pale against her intensely dark skin. Her coiled black hair was pinned up with a fountain pen.

"Good evening, mime-lords and mime-queens, mollishers and mobsters," she called over the noise. "I am Minty Wolfson, your mistress of ceremonies for the evening." She touched three fingers to her forehead. "Welcome to the Camden Catacombs. We extend our thanks to the Rag and Bone Man for allowing us to use this space for our proceedings."

She motioned to the silent figure on her right, dressed in a great-coat. A cautious patter of applause welcomed the mime-lord of II-4. He wore a yellowed mask of cloth over his face, with a thin slot for him to see through, and a flat brown cap on top. The Abbess turned her head away as if the very sight of him repelled her.

I sensed he was watching me through that mask. Not taking my eyes off him, I raised my glass.

*Soon, you faceless coward.*

He looked back toward Minty. It was then that I realized why he chilled me: I couldn't read him.

Panic flickered through my gut. I glanced at a nearby voyant, reading them at once: soothsayer, specifically a cyathomancer. But the Rag and Bone Man . . . I could feel his dreamscape—a guarded one—but the most I could say about his aura was that he had one.

He wasn't a Rephaite. The hollowness reminded me of a Buzzer, but he couldn't be one of those, either. Apart from that, I couldn't say a thing about his gift.

Minty gave a tinny cough. "As a long-standing patron of Grub Street, I am delighted to tell you that pamphlets will be provided when you leave tonight, free of charge—including the popular and ghastly new penny dreadful, *The Rephaite Revelation*. If you haven't yet read this story, prepare to be charmed by the tale of the Rephaim and the Emim." Cheers. "We have also been granted a glimpse of the first pages of the long-awaited new pamphlet from the White Binder, *On the Machinations of the Itinerant Dead*, which we all look forward to perusing."

There was a tumult of applause, and a few voyants clapped Jaxon on the back. He winked at me. I forced a smile.

"I'll now hand you over to the Abbess, who has acted as interim Underqueen during this time of crisis."

Minty took a respectful step away from the floor. There she was. The Abbess cut an imposing figure against the stage curtains, dressed in a black crepe suit with white cuffs and high boots. It was only now that I realised both she and Minty were in mourning attire.

"Good evening, one and all," the Abbess said. Her smile was just visible below her birdcage veil. "It has been a pleasure to serve as your Underqueen following my dear friend Hector's death. We were deeply saddened, three days past, to hear of his mollisher Cutmouth's demise. She was discovered in a squalid hut in Jacob's Island, her throat cut from ear to ear."

Murmuring from the crowd.

"Ostensibly, she was murdered at the hand of the vile augurs of Savory Dock. We mourn her loss. We mourn for a competent, intelligent young woman and what could have been her prosperous reign as Underqueen. And we condemn, with one voice, the actions of her murderers."

What an actress. The woman could give Scarlett Burnish a run for her money.

"I will now read out the names of all participants who have put their names forward for the scrimmage; as I say each one, the named participant should step forward and take their place in the Rose Ring. I call for silence from the present company at this time." She opened the scroll. "From VI Cohort: the Hare, of VI-2, and his esteemed mollisher, the Greene Manne."

Jaxon chuckled as the two of them went forward. One wore a hideous hare mask, complete with ears; the other had painted himself green from head to toe. "What's funny?" Eliza's smile was nervous.

"Every mime-lord outside the central cohort, my lovely. Suburban amateurs."

The Rag and Bone Man had detached himself from the crowd. I stood. Jaxon looked at me with raised eyebrows.

"Are you going somewhere, Dreamer?"

Nadine watched me over the rim of her glass. "Don't be long. You're up in a minute."

"Good thing I'll only be a minute, then."

Leaving them to watch the parade of combatants, I followed the masked man into the corridor. There would be enough pomp and ceremony for a quick word with him.

The route to the labyrinth had been blocked with wire fences, and each one had a Rag Doll guard. As I passed the foul-smelling alcove that served as a lavatory, a gloved hand grabbed my arm and shoved me against the wall.

My muscles seized up. The Rag and Bone Man loomed over me, his mask fluttering against his breath. It fell down to his upper chest, disguising his face and neck.

"Go back, Pale Dreamer."

The stench of sweat and blood was on his coat. His voice sounded strange, too deep, as if it had been mechanically altered. "Who are you?" I asked softly. A muffled *thud* hammered at my ears. "Are you going to confess that you had Hector and Cutmouth killed, or let someone else take the blame for it?"

"Do not interfere. I will cut your throat, as a pig's for the slaughter."

"You, or one of your puppets?"

"We are all but puppets in the anchor's shadow."

He let go of my wrist and turned his back on me. "I'm going to stop you," I said as he walked away, into the darkness of the tunnel. "And your gray market. You may think you've won this, Rag and Bone Man, but you won't be the one wearing the crown." When I tried to follow, two Rag Dolls blocked my path. One of them shoved me away.

"Don't try it."

"What's he hiding in there?"

"Do you want me to deck you, brogue?"

"If you don't mind me decking you back."

She took a revolver and leveled it at my forehead. "Can't shoot me back, though, can you?"

I gave her a heavy nosebleed before I turned away.

By the time I got back to the table, it was almost our turn to stand. Jaxon seemed deathly calm. As he smoked, he grasped a heavy ebony cane with a solid silver pommel at the top, shaped like a disfigured, scarred head. Danica had modified it with a mechanism that enabled the blade to be fully withdrawn or shot out of the end, delivering a lethal, spring-loaded stab before it retracted.

"From II Cohort: the Wicked Lady, and her esteemed mollisher, the Highwayman, of II-6."

Cheering. The Wicked Lady was a favorite among gamblers. With a dismissive wave of her hand, she took her position behind one of the roses.

"Remember, Paige," Jaxon said, "this is a show. I know you could kill them in a heartbeat, darling, but don't. You must *grandstand*. You are a debutante at your very first ball. Show them the whole spectrum of a dreamwalker's talents."

Then the Abbess was calling us to the ring: "Our favorites from I Cohort: the White Binder, and his esteemed mollisher, the Pale Dreamer, of I-4."

There was thunderous applause and stamping from the I Cohort tables, even from some of the others. Nick touched a hand to my back. I stood and followed Jaxon to the ring. The joints in my legs felt motorized. I took my place on Jaxon's left side, keeping the rose between my boots.

"And lastly," the Abbess said, "the three independent candidates. First, the Maverick Medium. Second, the Bleeding Heart." Both the newcomers took their places, to a smattering of applause. "And last, but by no means least, the Black Moth."

Silence. The Abbess turned to the crowd.

"Black Moth, please step forward."

The silence continued. One rose remained.

"Oh, dear. Perhaps the moth has flown away." Murmurs from the audience. A Grub Street hireling darted out to get rid of the last rose. "Now that we have our candidates, twenty-four in all, I formally open the fourth scrimmage in the history of the London syndicate."

She took hold of a heavy golden hourglass and turned it on its head. "When the hourglass is empty, I will call out 'begin.' Until you hear this command, please do not move."

Every pair of eyes in the room settled on the hourglass.

Directly opposite me was the Bully-Rook, Nell's mime-lord, who wore a rudimentary plastic mask with holes punched out for his eyes and mouth. Automatically, my body pulled into the posture Warden had taught me. I imagined myself on a string, being lifted, unshackled, throwing off the quick flesh that enclosed me. But my body was distracting me tonight: heart clapping, ears ringing, every inch of bare skin chilled with fear.

Which of these combatants did the Rag and Bone Man and the Abbess want to win?

Most of the competitors were soothsayers and augurs, dependent on a numen. They wouldn't be too difficult to overcome. But there were six, Jaxon included, that could pose a real challenge.

Five seconds. I imagined the vials pouring. My vision flattened and diluted as the æther took over.

Three seconds.

One second.

"Begin," the Abbess roared.

\*\*\*\*

As soon as the last grain of sand had slipped through the hourglass, I ran toward the Bully-Rook. The audience roared their approval as the first few combatants clashed. At last, the mime-lords and mime-queens had emerged from their dens to do battle in the heart of Scion's empire. My spirit was like an enraged animal in a cage, but I had to control it. There would be nothing noble, admirable, or entertaining about an Underqueen who'd killed her opponents with a flick of her spirit.

The Bully-Rook was a good six feet tall, lean and powerful. All he carried was a silver chain. I thrust my fist straight toward his throat, but he caught it in his hand and twisted me around, like he was spinning me in a waltz. A heavy boot kicked me in the back, and I went sprawling. I rolled back to my feet and turned to face him again, my fists raised. The audience's focus wasn't solely on me, but the nearest voyants jeered.

It wasn't a good start. Compared to some of these combatants, I was frail. The urge to use my spirit on the lot of them was overwhelming, but I had to show that I was strong.

My radar was alert to other dreamscapes. I sensed someone behind me and leapt out of the way. The Knife-Grinder stumbled as he missed his mark. An enormous machete glinted in his hand, big enough to cut through my neck in one swing. *Macharomancer.* That was his numen, the one that made him lethal.

His head tilted, making the light shine on his silver mask. As soon as he regained his balance, he flicked two stilettos from his sleeve and tossed them at me with one hand. They went whipping past my right ear, one after the other, nicking my face as they went. He came at me with the machete again, slashing and stabbing in equal measure, trying to wear me down. I threw out a hand to protect myself, and he sliced across all four of my fingers, leaving shallow cuts. I pushed with my spirit, just enough to disorient him, before I took a running dive into a roll and kicked him in the stomach as hard as I could, shoving him into the Maverick Medium.

Someone else took hold of me before I could so much as take a breath. Arms wrapped around my waist, pinning my elbows to my sides. I knew from the smell of clove and orange that this was Halfpenny, Bloody Knuckles's mollisher and an excellent sniffer. He often rubbed oils on to his wrists to keep the stink of spirits from his nostrils. I cut the side of my hand into his groin again and again until he released me, then smashed the back of my skull into his face. Twisting at the waist, I punched him between the eyes, breaking his nose. The impact sent a shock from my knuckles to my elbow, but it knocked him down hard enough to daze him.

The Bleeding Heart was there next, one of the independent candidates, with veins tattooed all over his face. I felt his aura shift to the right and avoided his fist with a neat spin, as Warden had taught me to do. He sent a feeble spool toward me, woven together from wisps, so frail I didn't know why he'd bothered. They didn't even make it to my dreamscape. I spooled a few of my own—stronger spirits, plucked from the farthest corners of the vault—and launched all six at him. With no sound, he flopped like a boneless fish on to the ash. Definitely playing dead. He was too afraid to fight, and with killers in the ring, I didn't blame him.

A muscular arm locked across my chest. With a snarl, I gripped the Bully-Rock's elbow and shoved it upward, trying to writhe my way free of his hold. My spirit burst into his dreamscape like a firework. As soon as he let go of me, I drove my right elbow into his solar plexus, pulled his arm out as far as I could and struck the back of the joint. There was a crack of bone, and he lurched away.

"Go on, Dreamer," Eliza shouted, clapping.

My knuckles gave a throb, but the pain rushed away on a wave of adrenaline. This competition wasn't about strength. Speed and skill could overcome muscle. I spun on my heel and deflected one of the Knife-Grinder's spools, sending it straight back into his dreamscape. The force of it knocked him over. Bloody Knuckles leapt over him and hurled a complex string of spools at me, each made from several kinds of spirit. I threw myself into a roll under his arm and scissored my legs around the Knife-Grinder's ankles when he got back up. I forced pressure from my dreamscape to deflect the spools, making the nearest ten people's noses bleed. As he sprinted past us, Jack Hickathrift delivered a swift blow to the Knife-Grinder's nape, finishing him off before he had the chance to grind a single knife. He grinned at me before he took on Bloody Knuckles.

At my feet, Halfpenny was rising again. I slashed with my spirit, shoving him into his midnight zone. Pain gripped my skull, but I could control it. Some of the audience must have seen the tell-tale flicker of my spirit in the æther—they shouted out "Pale Dreamer!," and Jimmy O'Goblin threw a rose at me. I picked it up and curtseyed low, and the volume of the shouting jolted higher. More roses flew from Ognena Maria and a group of I-4 footpads.

My moment of glory was cut short when Jenny Greenteeth grabbed my shoulders. Her teeth sank into my shoulder, puncturing skin, and a choking scream escaped me. At the same time, the Hare took hold of my ankles. They were pulling me in opposite directions. Did they want to rip me in half? The crowd's cheers were for Jenny now. Taking a chunk out of I-4's famous mollisher—who wouldn't be impressed with such a shocking tactic? With a growl, I kicked out at the Hare. The toe of my boot caught his chin, snapping his head back. A glimpse of throat flashed beneath the mask. When he grasped my knees, my heels pushed against his chest, forcing Jenny Greenteeth backward, right off her feet. I rolled free of her arms and hurled my dagger at the Hare with one hand. He caught it in one hand and lumbered towards me, panting out vile threats through the thin slot in his mask.

I didn't have time to think before his fist closed around my collar. As he angled the blade towards my face, a slither of steel came flashing from behind him. It sliced downward, ripping muscle from muscle, rending bone. Half a pallid arm flopped to the ground.

The Hare curled over with a howl of agony, staring at the blunted limb. Blood disgorged from the clean stump at his elbow. Behind me, a collective breath was drawn.

"Binder, you—what have you *done*—?"

"Hush, foul hare," Jaxon sneered, and stabbed him through the eyehole of his mask.

I made an involuntary sound of disgust as the mime-lord slumped on to his front. Blood leaked through the eyehole and pooled around his head. His spirit fled without waiting for the threnody.

Jaxon twirled his cane, laughing. The VI Cohort tables booed and bellowed at him, but they were drowned out by the united roar of approval from the centrals. The first real blood of the night had been spilled, and it was all over my boots. At the front, Nadine was standing with her fellow Covent Garden buskers, cheering for him at the top of her lungs. It was Jaxon's turn to take a bow.

I couldn't watch for long. Jenny Greenteeth was back with red on her pearly whites, clawing and scratching at my legs. She was a hydromancer, but there was no water here for her to use against me. She was only as good as physical combat. I held her back with my bare hands, my teeth clenched with the effort, but she was gaining a few inches with every passing moment. VI Cohort's crowd were screaming for her to rip out my gullet. They couldn't stand centrals like me. Spittle dripped from Jenny's cracked lips, frothing like suds between her teeth as she screamed obscenities in my face. Drenched in sweat, I forced her back with my arms, farther and farther, until I could wedge my heel against her chest.

I couldn't be rescued by Jaxon again. Once was acceptable, a display of loyalty between mime-lord and mollisher, but twice would be unforgivably weak. I booted Jenny Greenteeth in the abdomen, hard enough to wind her. As soon as she was on the floor, I jumped out of my body.

It was harder to be quick this time. I fought with her dream-form in her sunlit zone, which took the form of a bog in the mist that fastened itself to my ankles like quicksand. When I finally forced her into a darker ring of sanity, I returned to my body—only to find myself falling toward the ashes in the ring. My palms swung out just in time, and oxygen hissed from my tank. Beside me, Jenny gave a twitch.

The clumsy end to my jump didn't seem to daunt the crowd. They'd never seen the White Binder's dreamwalker in action before. His best-keep secret and his greatest weapon, she would be the brightest jewel in the Underlord's crown. A chorus of buskers started to chant.

> *Pale Dreamer, the jumper, just look at her leap!*
> *The wrath of the dreamwalker will make you weep*
> *She's got poor sweet Jenny and Halfpenny, too*
> *Watch out for her, Bully, she's coming for you!*

The chant ended in a cheer that reverberated through the vault. A few more roses soared toward me. This time I took a sweeping bow. They wouldn't follow someone who didn't play into their charade. Nick was clapping along with them, wearing a reluctant smile. Behind him, Eliza punched the air with a shout of "PALE DREAMER!," joined by the rest of I Cohort. I found myself smiling back as I straightened, electrified by the spectacle. For once, these voyants, divided for so many years by the hierarchy and by gang wars, were *united*—in their love for the syndicate, in their passion for the wonders of the æther; even in their bloodlust.

As I caught my breath, I scanned the vault. There were still a good number of participants fighting. Redcap, the youngest of the mime-queens, was standing nearby. Her aura was restless and unstable, impossible to miss—a fury's aura. Beneath her crimson beret, her eyes were obscured by shadow. Her adversary was the Swan Knight, a mollisher with a head of brilliantly white hair, wearing a purple cloak over her black attire.

"Don't think I won't kill you, brat."

"Please," Redcap said, "try."

The Swan Knight raised her sword. Redcap took a deep breath, filling her lungs, and screamed.

The scream was so unearthly that glasses and bottles burst on the tables. In a whirl of rage, Redcap clawed her foe across the face. Her own face was flushed and contorted, and the screams pouring from her mouth were appalling. Spirits were reeling around her, lifting her limbs, snapping them into impossibly fast moves. The Swan Knight stood no chance.

As soon as her opponent was out of action, Redcap flew toward the next opponent, giving no sign that she might slow down. "Cool off," someone bellowed at her from the ring. "Control it, Red, *control* it!" But she kept going, hitting and clawing and howling out that awful noise, her cheeks turning puce. Her eyes rolled back into her head. Half the combatants stopped to watch as she fought with Jack Hickathrift, all fists and grinding teeth—but she was staggering now, drunk on æther, out of control. She knocked him off his feet with a single blow to his knee. He flung up his arms to shield his face, his eyes squeezed shut above his mask.

Then, quite without warning, Redcap fell to the floor. Her head smacked against the ring, but her limbs began to tremble violently. Jack Hickathrift scrambled out of the way. A footpad rushed to her side and held her skull between his spade-sized hands. Once she stopped twitching, he carried her from the floor.

Boos and cheers jarred against each other. The initial performance had been impressive, but she had no staying power. I'd never seen clairvoyance manifest itself like that before. She must have overstepped her bounds. I couldn't do that. I wouldn't do that.

Redcap's display had halted the fighting, but two mime-lords were exchanging blows a few feet away. The brawl was short: both buffeted each other about with spools for a while, swearing and snarling, then the London Particular knocked his opponent flat with a massive fist. Groaning and booing ensued. *Boring*, they were saying.

"Behind you, darling," Jaxon shouted at me, and spun to meet the fallen mime-lord's mollisher.

The Wicked Lady was closest, with no one attacking her. I spun a throwing knife into my hand and held it by the blade. She caught sight of me and grinned, holding out her arms. The sight made me hesitate, but I hurled the knife a moment later, aiming for her forearm. A non-lethal injury, just enough to put her in pain so I could knock her senseless with my spirit.

In a blur, someone else threw themselves between me and the Wicked Lady. Bramble Briar was my next rival, an axinomancer with roses threaded through her golden hair. The knife buried itself in her shoulder. She screamed in pain before she tore it out, throwing it into the audience. A courier caught it. Before I could register what had happened, she swung back her arms, and with incredible strength, hurled her broad-axe across the ring. I pulled to the right and threw myself backward, my feet sweeping over my head, my knees tucked against my chest. Cheers rose from the crowd. As soon as I landed, I found myself face-to-mask with Faceless. Dressed in silks that blazed with sunset colors, she wore a shell of porcelain that wiped out all her features. No eyeholes, or even a gap to breathe through.

On my right, Bramble Briar was closing in on her axe. And there was the Bully-Rook, charging toward me yet again, and Bloody Knuckles on my left. I took up a defensive position, my throat clenched like a fist.

All of them were closing in on *me*. With a quick movement, I pulled out another knife and threw it at the Wicked Lady. Bloody Knuckles swung out his arm, knocking it out of the way.

Were they *protecting* her?

Jaxon was fending off a single mollisher with his cane, hardly breaking a sweat, while I was fighting a mime-queen, two mime-lords and a mollisher. When Jaxon saw them all converging on me, his pale eyes widened. Once they killed me, they would probably target him.

I twisted to look over my shoulder. The Rag and Bone Man was watching from the corner of the vault.

He wanted to see me die, here in this eddy of hot blood and adrenaline, where my death would be applauded, not investigated or questioned.

Murmuring names under her breath, Faceless began to gather spirits to her sides. She was a summoner. Her palms turned inward, forming a cup. I stayed absolutely still, waiting for her to let go of the spool that formed between her hands. She was a living lodestone, drawing spirits from all over the citadel and into the pocket of æther between her palms. The Bully-Rook swung his blood-slick chain like a pendulum. Bramble Briar retrieved her broad-axe and lifted it. Bloody Knuckles raised his fists. Knuckledusters were hooked over his fingers, each topped with a lethal spike.

They all struck together. Faceless hurled her spool at me. One of them was a breacher: an archangel or a poltergeist, hard to tell. The pendant deflected it back at her with such force that I stumbled. She was lifted off her feet, into the audience, in a flurry of orange silk. Two of her spirits shot into my dreamscape, but I catapulted them straight back out. My defenses had grown stronger. I ducked a hard punch from Bloody Knuckles and whipped my spirit across his dreamscape.

Blinking away images, I ran toward Bramble Briar. Her expression slid from murderous to shocked when I ducked under her arm, but her broad-axe was already swinging, too heavy to stop. It struck the Bully-Rook instead. The blade lodged in his upper chest with a meaty *whack*. As soon as I heard it, I snatched the rope from his hand and slung it around Bramble Briar's neck, pulling her towards the floor. She let go of the axe and scrabbled at her throat, wide-eyed. The Bully-Rook fell to his knees and took hold of its haft, his mouth open in a silent scream, but his clothes were already smothered in vital blood. No amount of wrenching would exhume that blade. The audience were cheering and shouting, baying for it, like amaurotics did in front of their TVs. Like they must have cheered when my cousin was hanged at Carrickfergus.

When had we made a show of death?

"Rotten ploy, girl," Bramble Briar retched out.

"This isn't," I said into her ear. I nudged her into her twilight zone and she keeled over, unconscious.

The Bully-Rook wouldn't last much longer. Bloody Knuckles was crawling, clutching his head. The Maverick Medium danced past and rammed a blade through his skull.

Lights punched at the edges of my vision, but I shook them away. Fifteen combatants were either dead or out of action, leaving eight with a chance of winning, including Jaxon and me. Jaxon himself unzipped the hapless London Particular's stomach, to howls of appreciation from the crowd and a scream of horror from a woman near the front. He beckoned to me, and I ran to him.

"Back to back, darling."

I turned to face the audience, the bloody knife held out in front of me. "What's the story?"

"Only five to go. The crown's in the bag! Perhaps we should take down this miserable imbecile."

I flinched when I saw who he meant. The Glym Lord walked with a shuffling gait as he hauled a screeching mollisher across the ash. "Why is he walking like that?" I shouted over the clashing of weapons and the screaming of the audience.

"He's a physical medium, darling. He's let some angry spirit take his body and puppeteer it." He pointed his cane. "I will dislocate the intruding spirit with my boundlings. You will cast out his."

Having crushed his opponent's windpipe, Glym was staring at us with clouded eyes. His mouth hung open; he panted like a bellows. "Come back to yourself, you old bastard," Tom the Rhymer roared at him. I thought of how Eliza looked when she was possessed.

"We don't have to kill him," I said to Jaxon.

"Do, or he'll be back to haunt us. Every person in this ring left alive will challenge us for that crown."

A rope of saliva hung from Glym's lips. The spirit inside him was waiting, poised to attack. With a sneer, Jaxon called one of his boundlings with his left hand. His fingers bent into claw-like arches, and the veins along his arm snaked with hot blood. His lips moved, commanding the boundling. Glym fell to his knees and clapped his hands over his ears. There was a struggle—Jaxon's teeth gritted, and a vessel ruptured in his eye—before he seized my wrist and swung me toward his victim.

"Now!"

I pitched my spirit toward him.

The intruder and Jaxon's boundling were already at the edge of Glym's dreamscape, and they tumbled out when I came soaring in. Outside, his body would be crumpling. I passed through the landscape of his mind in one sprint. My dream-form threw out a hand and grasped Glym's spirit, tossing it gently into his twilight zone. I burst out of him and flew back to my own body.

Silence had fallen over the audience. The only people left in the ring were me, Jaxon, the Wicked Lady and the Wretched Sylph. The latter looked as wretched as her name. One of her fingers hung by a thick tress of skin, and tears shone in her eyes, but she didn't run.

"You take the Sylph," Jaxon murmured.

"No," I said. "I'll take the Lady."

The Wicked Lady had set her sights on him first, but now she turned her attention to me. She wore no mask over her face. Jaxon twirled his cane, gravitating toward the Wretched Sylph. I walked around my opponent: the woman who controlled the poorest slums, who had kept them in a cycle of poverty and misery. The back of her hand swiped across her upper lip.

"Hello, Pale Dreamer," she called. "Do we have a feud I missed?"

I circled her, as Jaxon circled his foe. Both of our opponents' mollishers lay unconscious or dead on the ash. We were the only allied pair that remained. The audience began to shout the names of their favorites, or whoever they'd put money on. *White Binder* was the loudest of them all.

"No," I said, "but I wouldn't mind starting one."

We were too far from the crowd to be heard now, close to the spotlight cart. The Wicked Lady held out her cutlass. "Any particular reason," she said, "or are you as mindlessly violent as everyone seems to think you are?"

"You've left half of your voyants to rot in a slum."

"The vile augurs? They're nothing. And are you so virtuous? Murderer and madwoman, Scion calls you."

"Do you listen to Scion?"

"When they talk sense."

She slashed at me with her cutlass, and I stepped back.

"You know, it's good that Cutmouth's dead. She got a cut too far above her station. A lowly Jacob's Islander at the side of the Underlord . . . I should have got rid of her before she could cross my fence." I struck at her with my knife, but she avoided me neatly. "As for the Jacobite, as she calls herself, she won't last long. He sent her away for betraying him—poetic justice, he called it—but this time he'll cut her throat and be done with it."

"Poetic justice? What the hell are you talking about?"

"You must have at least *guessed*, Pale Dreamer. Or are you too noble to have thought of it?"

She was in league with them, too. Whoever they were. The Abbess was watching us from the dais, smiling. I kicked the Wicked Lady in the ribs, doubling her over.

"We almost asked you to join us, you know. Until you started meddling." She wheezed a laugh. "It does seem like a shame to have to kill you, honey, but I have my orders."

She lunged toward me and swung with the cutlass, aiming for my throat. It was such a quick motion, I could only whip my head to one side to avoid it. The blade opened a cut from my earlobe to my jaw, almost to my chin. Pain blinded me, white-hot and screeching. My hand jerked up to the wound automatically, and another hard jolt of agony flared from my fingertips.

The tear along my face began to pound. Still reeling from the blow, I threw out pressure from my dreamscape. My temples throbbed, but I pushed until her eyes and nose leaked blood. She let go of the cutlass. I wrested it from her hand and threw it out of the ring. It clattered across the floor and spun to a halt under the nearest table. A courier picked it up and cheered.

My fingertips were wet with blood. The Rag and Bone Man had his hands on the back of a chair. Like the Abbess, he was waiting. The Wicked Lady looked across the room at him, and her grin widened, giving me a flash of a silver canine. Another rich mime-queen.

And I understood.

The Rag and Bone Man and the Abbess hadn't entered because they planned to put someone else on the throne. A figurehead to control from the shadows. A face for whatever dirty work they were doing. How many people in this ring had been conspirators, helping the Wicked Lady to win? How many of these corpses wore bones on their skin?

Now it wasn't just important that I won. It was *imperative*. And I had to trust that I could do it; that I was more than just the Pale Dreamer, the White Binder's protégée, the rebel slave, the dreamwalker.

I had to trust in myself to knock this pawn off the board.

We circled each other, gazes locked. Jaxon had been cruel to put voyants into a hierarchy, but he'd been right about one thing: the three lowest orders had fairly passive gifts. The Wicked Lady was some kind of augur. Without a numen, she couldn't use her gift in battle. At least, that was what I believed about augurs until she whirled a spool together and threw it not at me, but at the candelabra hanging from the ceiling.

And the spool *caught fire*.

It was as if they were made of flammable gas. Five burning spirits came soaring towards me like comets, leaving tails of blue flame in their wake. The combustion took me so completely by surprise, I almost didn't duck at all. At the last second I rolled to avoid them, but two seared across my upper arm, burning away my sleeve. The pain wrenched a scream from the back of my throat. Above me, the spool broke apart like a firework, leaving a shadow in its wake, before all five spirits extinguished themselves. In the audience, screams for the Wicked Lady doubled.

My arm scorched. The livid skin was already blistering. The Wicked Lady had to be a pyromancer. I'd always thought they were hypothetical, but there was no doubt about it: her numen was fire.

"Done?" She wiped her bloody hands on her trousers. "If you play dead, I might let you off lightly."

"If you like," I said, through gritted teeth.

My empty body buckled and collapsed. In the instant she was surprised, I bowled myself straight through the junkyard of her mind, knocking her spirit out into the æther. Her silver cord snapped, as easily as if I'd cut through string with scissors. I killed her for Vern and Wynn, for Cutmouth, and for Ivy. She stayed upright for a moment, a look of mild shock on her face, before she tipped off her heels and collapsed on the ash. Her hair lay around her head like a wreath.

Almost in chorus, Jaxon struck the Wretched Sylph with a

boundling. Her head snapped to the side, and she collided with the floor.

And just like that, Jaxon Hall and I had won the fourth scrimmage in the history of London.

The audience stood as one and broke into thunderous applause. It rattled the tables. "White Binder," they roared. "WHITE BINDER. WHITE BINDER." They stamped their feet so loudly I thought they would raise the warehouse from on top of us; that Scion would discover the nest of sedition hidden beneath. They were calling my name and Jaxon's name, calling and calling. Roses came flying at us, skidding through the ash and the blood of our opponents. Jaxon grabbed my hand and lifted it with a laugh, intoxicated by his first, sweet taste of victory.

The boy they'd once called gutterling was king of the whole citadel.

His arms spread wide, embracing the applause. The cane—held aloft, like a scepter—was glossy with blood. I couldn't even smile. My wrist was limp in the grasp of his hand.

Over our heads, Edward VII, the Bloody King, looked down with frozen eyes. The hint of lip beneath his beard seemed to smile.

*But with a leader like Jaxon Hall, I foresee only blood and revelry—and in the end, destruction.*

He was the King of Wands, the one Liss had predicted.

He was lord over London, and he had to be stopped.

Two psychographers ran out from behind the curtains. One carried a large book; the other, a small cushion, made from deepest purple velvet. On that cushion was the symbol of the Underlord's power. A few more voyants stepped out and began to remove the bodies from the ring.

Supposedly stolen from the Tower by a loyal servant when the monarchy fell, Edward VII's crown had been stripped of its jewels and reworked into a corolla with many types of soothsayers' numa: keys, needles, shards of crystal and mirror, animal bones, dice, and tiny ceramic images of the tarot, all woven with wire into something like a wreath. Light was thrown off it from all angles. On this special occasion, it was strung with the perishable numa of augury: flowers, mistletoe, even slivers of ice. Minty Wolfson took it from the cushion and walked towards us.

"It is with great pleasure that I announce that the White Binder has won the scrimmage—and that his mollisher, the Pale Dreamer, still stands beside him. In the tradition of our syndicate, I will now crown him Underlord of the Scion Citadel of London." She turned to the audience. "Does anyone know of any reason why this man should not hold such a title? Why this man should not rule the syndicate for as long as he lives?"

"Actually," I said, "I do."

As Jaxon turned to face me, his hand tightened around his cane. The clatter from the audience died down, leaving a backcloth of creased brows in its wake.

"I'm Black Moth." With a heavy heart, I stepped away from him. "And I challenge you, White Binder."

Not so much as a whisper broke the silence.

A few feet away, Minty handed the crown back to one of her hirelings. The room was so quiet, I heard their fingers grazing across the velvet.

Across the ring, the Abbess rose from her seat with suitable elegance, but a flush swept into her cheeks. Her lips parted as she walked toward the ring, heeled boots ticking on the stone.

"What?" Jaxon said, very softly.

I didn't repeat myself. He'd heard me. With one quick motion, he snatched my wrist and wrenched me closer.

"If I'm not mistaken," he breathed, "you just publicly *challenged* me." His eyes bored into mine. "I saved you from a life of servitude. I mobilized the Seven Seals to get you out of that colony. Had any of them been seen, twenty years of my life's work could have been undone in a heartbeat—but I was willing to risk it. Stop now, Paige, and I will forget your ingratitude."

"You saved my life. I will always be grateful, Jaxon." I stared him out. "That doesn't mean you own it."

"Oh, but I still know your secret." His fingers dug into my forearm. "Did you forget, darling?"

I smiled. "Secret, Jax?"

Jaxon stared at me, his nostrils flared. I gave him a glimpse of the skin beneath my sleeve, just enough to show him that the Monster's parting gift was gone.

And oh, it was glorious, watching Jaxon Hall put two and two together. Watching him understand, inch by agonizing inch, that he could no longer blackmail me into submission. That words, for all their worth, would not protect him this time. His eyes turned to glass fixtures in his skull. For once in his life, he would have to play by someone else's rules.

Slowly, he drew away from me. I stepped back, pulling my wrist free of his hand.

"You see," he said quietly. Then, in a shout: "Do you see, my dear friends? I predicted this betrayal. You saw it yourself, mistress of ceremonies, when you received my message of flowers. Did I not place monkshood at its very center—the flower of treachery, of warning? But did you expect my very own mollisher to turn on me? I think not. I think that this has shocked you all."

Murmuring.

"Is this permissible?" the Abbess asked Minty. A smile crept along her mouth. "Surely she can't declare herself this late, under a separate identity."

"There's no rule against it," Minty said, watching me. "To my knowledge."

"She is a wanted *fugitive*," Jaxon bit out. "Tell me, how is she to lead us when Scion knows her face, her name? And do you really want to allow this backstabber to partake in these proceedings, Miss Wolfson? If she can challenge her own mime-lord, what will she do to her subjects?"

"Coward," I said.

Jaxon turned to face me. There were a few jeers from the audience, but other than that, silence reigned. "Say that again, little traitor." He cupped a hand around his ear. "I didn't quite catch it."

The crowd was hungry for this kind of drama. I sensed it in their dreamscapes, in their auras, in their faces. This was a first in syndicate history, a real-life revenge tragedy that could only end in death. A mime-lord and a mollisher at war. I stepped through the ash and the blood.

"I said you were a coward." I held up my blade, letting it catch the candlelight. "Prove me wrong, White Binder, or I'll send you to the æther tonight."

There it was. The beast lurking in Jaxon Hall. The film of ice that spread across his eyes: the look I'd seen before, when he struck a pleading beggar with his cane or told Eliza he would fire her from the job that was her lifeline. The look in his eyes when he'd told me I was his, that I was property. An asset. A slave. His lips tilted, and he bowed to me.

"With pleasure," he said, "O my dearest traitor."

# 25

## Danse Macabre

Jaxon Hall wasn't one to waste time when he wanted something done, and it was clear that he'd had no absinthe today. The blade came singing toward me in a flash of silver and a gust of dark wood, almost too fast to avoid, but I was ready for him to strike. I'd sensed his aura move to the right a split second before he had.

He was as easy to read as a book to a bibliomancer. For the first time in my life, I could predict my mime-lord's intentions. With two quick turns, I avoided the stab and stopped myself dead, like a wind-up dancer in a music box.

With arched eyebrows, Jaxon took a second swing, this time with the blunt end. It hit the flagstones with a heavy, gong-like chime, but the blast of air soon came again. The chunk of metal caught the front of my shoulder, knocking me back a few steps. My hands came straight back up.

Jaxon herded me toward the crowd. Their auras registered like a wall of heat on my back. I cartwheeled past him and spun on the spot, back in the middle of the ring. A smattering of cautious applause broke out from the I-4 supporters. Jaxon's head turned toward the audience. If he won this battle, they would pay for their treachery.

He stayed where he was, with his back facing me. An open invitation to strike. It would have been irresistible to most participants, but I knew him too well to take the bait.

"Rotten ploys, Jaxon," I said. "Last I checked, no voyant used a cane to touch the æther."

"Yet you seem to be dancing out of its way, O my lovely." The cane's blade dragged across the flagstones, sharp enough to leave sparks in its wake. "If I didn't know you better, I'd say that was a sign of fear. Now, tell me—where did you learn these pretty pirouettes?"

"From a friend."

"Oh, I'm quite sure you did. Tall sort of fellow, is he?" His footsteps matched my heartbeat. "Variable eye color?"

He didn't swing for me; instead, he stabbed with the spring-loaded blade. Its reach was much farther than I'd anticipated, forcing me into an awkward step backward. "In a manner of speaking," I said, ignoring the laughs in the audience. "Are you seeing him behind my back?"

"I know more than you might think about the sort of company you keep. More than I care to know, my sweet traitor."

It sounded like banter to the watching crowd, who expected a good show for this unprecedented finale, but there was meaning underneath the mockery. He knew about Warden, but what else did he know? When I looked at him now, with the raw clarity of adrenaline, I saw a mask with empty eyes, soulless as a mannequin.

"Of course, this is a duel," Jaxon said, "much like the duels of the monarch days, when honor was settled with blood and steel. Whose honor are we settling today, I wonder?" Swing, spin. "You know very well that your reign will never be accepted by these good people.

Even if you win this fight, you will always be remembered as the Underqueen who murdered her own mime-lord. And, as rumor has it, the Underlord." Spin, clash, an arc of sparks. "I don't think we've yet thought of a name for someone so callous, so ungrateful, that she turns on the man who kept her safe for years. Who fed her and taught her and put silk on her precious back."

"Call me whatever you want," I said. "London is what matters. London and her people."

That got a fair few cheers from the spectators, enough to ratchet up my confidence.

"As if you care for people." His voice was too soft for the crowd to hear. "You're lost to them, Paige, and London does not forget a traitor. It will suck you down, O my lovely. Into the tunnels and the plague pits. Into its dark heart, where all the traitors' bodies sink."

The cane arced over his head this time, hitting home an inch from my right foot. Had it met its mark, it would have broken every toe. He spun it in his hands and took a step back.

"I think we've both established that we excel in good old-fashioned *mêlée*," he said, "but perhaps we ought to show the world what sort of gifts we hide beneath these simple exteriors. The first act should be yours, I think. After all, only I have ever known the true extent of your abilities. You ought to have your chance to shine."

Jaxon was going to take my head off if I didn't get hold of a sturdy barrier to block him. I pushed my spirit to the edge of my dreamscape.

Veins swelled in Jaxon's temples. He tried to hide it, but he gritted his teeth against the sudden influx of pressure that hammered at his dreamscape. My eyes ached, but I kept pushing until I felt something crack inside his mind. Blood wept from his nose, a shock of red against his waxy skin. He lifted a hand to touch it, staining the white silk fingers of his gloves.

"Blood," he said. "Blood! Is she no stronger than a haemato-mancer, this so-called dreamwalker?"

Their laughs seemed distant now. My ears closed as my sixth sense took control. Jaxon thought I'd fall when I left my body, and it was entirely possible that he was right. I'd not yet mastered the art of staying on my feet. I should have practiced more often with Warden. Like a fool, I'd allowed myself to be distracted by him.

I snapped my attention back to meatspace when Jaxon attacked with his cane again, swinging and stabbing with vicious accuracy. When he aimed at my side, so hard the air whistled in its wake, I brought my blade to meet it. The metal deflected the force before it could shatter one side of my ribcage.

My feet carried me away from the next onslaught. A spring of laughter welled up inside me. Some swings I met with the blade, others with evasion. I thought I heard a growl of frustration from Jaxon. Amused by the chase, the julkers took up another chant:

*Ring a ring o' roses, Binder's got a nosebleed.*
*Defeat her, the Dreamer! She won't fall down!*

"How appropriate," Jaxon called to them. "Some say that song is linked to the Black Death. My first strike will be with a dear friend, who died of bubonic plague in 1349."

I soon worked out what he meant. One of his boundlings hurled itself from the corner and crashed into my dreamscape.

At once, a hideous slideshow of images went ripping past my eyes. Blackened fingers. Buboes swelling under my skin, bursting under the weight of a hen's feather. Most spooled spirits were easy to force out, but this one was under Jaxon's control, carrying his willpower into its attacks. I staggered, fighting to see past the horror: mass graves, red crosses barring doors, leeches growing fat on blood, all growing out of my poppy anemones. Through his boundlings, Jaxon could manipulate the appearance of my dreams-cape. My defenses expelled the spirit just in time to throw myself out of the way.

Not quite fast enough. As my arm came up, the cane-blade tore down my left side, leaving a shallow wound from underarm to hip. The base of my spine hit the stone with a force that jarred what felt like every nerve. I rolled to avoid the second slash. My blade lay a few feet away.

*Imagine your spirit as a boomerang. A light throw and a quick return.*

I needed a few seconds to reach the blade. My spirit lashed into his dreamscape. Jaxon reeled back with a shout of anger. As soon as I made impact, I returned to my body, drenched in sweat, and crawled toward the knife. Behind me, he swung blindly with his cane. Another surge of blood flowed from his nostrils, past his lips and chin.

"Dislocation," Jaxon said, pointing at me. "You see, friends—the dreamwalker can leave the confines of her own body. She is the high-est of all seven orders." When I launched myself at him, he blocked my offensive with the cane, holding both ends. "But she forgets herself. She forgets that without flesh, there is no anchor to the earth. To one's autonomy."

With a sudden shove and a deft hack, he knocked my legs out from under me and pitched me on to my back. My left side was soaked, the white silk of my blouse tarnished with red. I could feel it trickling from my gashed collar, oozing down my chest to my stomach.

"Now," he said, "I do believe it's my turn. Say hello to another friend of mine."

Sweat ran down my neck. I readied myself, snapping up every defense, imagining my dreamscape with walls as dense as those of an unreadable.

The spirit hit me.

Oxygen ignited in my throat.

Stakes pinned my clothes to the earth. All around me, my flowers were withering away as easily as paper. The boundling took the form of a shadow-figure in my hadal zone, laughing from afar. I recognized that laugh.

The London Monster, back to get me.

From out of the earth of my mind, new flowers rose and bloomed, shaking blood from their petals. Artificial flowers, wrapped into posies with lengths of barbed wire. Spikes burst from between their silken petals. In meatspace, my hands hit the floor of the Rose Ring. The pendant was burning on my chest, trying to force the creature's pictures from my mind, but Jaxon was fighting to keep it rooted. In meatspace, Jaxon raised his cane to strike. One blow to my head, and all of this would stop.

*No.*

It wasn't just my life that hung in the balance. If I didn't defeat this enemy, others would rise up and seize the syndicate. Everything would be lost. Liss's and Seb's deaths, Julian's sacrifice, Warden's scars—all of it would have been for nothing. I swung my head under Jaxon's cane. I willed the Monster gone, willed it until my dream-form screamed with the effort. The earth trembled beneath me, and a rolling wave turned the artificial flowers on their heads, burying their spikes in the earth. The London Monster screamed as my poppies bloomed around him. My defenses slammed back up, and he was pitched into the æther.

When my vision cleared, Jaxon was perfectly still, both hands folded on the top of his cane. A strand of hair had worked its way loose from the oil, and his breathing was heavy with the effort of keeping control. Still, a smile was playing on his lips.

"Very good," he said.

My blade was in one of his hands, the cane in the other. Fury swelled from the darkest parts of me. I seized a candlestick from a terrified libanomancer and used it to block the cane. When he struck with the knife, I used the candlestick to knock it from his hand and into mine. As soon as my fist closed around it, my wrist flicked up. A scarlet line appeared above Jaxon's eyebrow. A smear of paint on a blank canvas.

"Ah. More blood." His gloves were more red than white. "There are pints of it in my veins, O my lovely."

"Is it blood or absinthe?" I caught his cane in my hands when he thrust it toward me. Fire blazed along my left side. "Not that it matters," I said softly. "I can spill it all either way."

"I'm afraid I can't let you do that," he said. My hands were slick, hardly gripping the ebony. "I need a little more of it, you see. I have one more trick before the grand finale."

I kicked out with the side of my boot, catching his knee. Jaxon's grip loosened. And somehow, I wrenched the cane against his throat.

Both of us grew still. His pupils were tiny dots of hatred.

"Go on," he whispered.

The blade of the cane pressed against his neck, where his jugular pulsed with blood. My hands trembled. *Do it, Paige, just do it.* But he'd saved my life, my sanity. *He'll come back to haunt you if you don't.* But he'd been like my father, taught me and sheltered me, saved me from a life lived without knowledge of my gift. *You're an item of his property. That's why he saved you. He doesn't care, he never cared.* He had given me a world in Seven Dials. *He wouldn't listen when it mattered.*

My hesitation cost me. His right fist punched up and caught the underside of my chin, right where the Wicked Lady had cut me open. I staggered back, almost retching at the pain, before the same fist crashed into my ribcage. The crack of bone resonated through my body, and I fell to my knees with a cry of agony. The audience shouted out: some cheering, some booing. Whistling, Jaxon drew the full sword from inside the hollowed cane.

This was it, then. He was going to take my head off and be done with it.

But Jaxon didn't turn the sword on me. Instead, he pushed up his own sleeve and set to work. White score marks had scarred the underside of his right arm. When I saw the letters that he carved there, my heart jolted into my throat.

*Paige*

I stared at him, frozen. His eyes shone with the arch delight I'd once admired in him.

Once that name was finished, I would be unable to use my gift without putting myself in terrible danger.

In the æther, as a spirit, I was vulnerable to Jaxon's binding. He could trap me for as long as he liked. Clever, clever Jaxon, always thinking . . . turning my own gift against me . . .

The knife slid through his skin, creating the next letter. Forcing the last of my strength into the jump, I leaped out of my body and into his dreamscape, aiming for the heart.

Jaxon had immense defenses. Not quite as tough as a Rephaite's or an unreadable's, but stronger than any other I'd ever seen. They threw me out at once, as if I'd hit a wall. My body buckled and collapsed again. Fresh blood dampened my side, and my skin glinted with mingled blood and sweat. Raucous jeering boomed from every corner of the vault.

"Look at the little dreamwalker! She's *tired*!"

"Put her to sleep, Binder!"

But there were some cries for me. I couldn't tell whose voices they were, but I heard a distinct shout of "Go on, Dreamer!" My legs were like straw. It didn't feel as if I could lift a single coin from the gutter, let alone dislocate my spirit again.

"Dreamer! Dreamer!"

"Come on! Give him what for!"

*Blood is not pain.*

"Get up, girl," shouted one of the mime-queens. "Get up!"

My hand pressed to my injured side, wetting my fingers. I could survive this. I could survive Jaxon Hall.

The balls of my feet pushed against the floor. I lunged for the fallen candlestick and ran at him, ignoring the screaming burn in my shoulders. Jaxon laughed. I attacked again and again, but he blocked each blow with ease—and worse, he only used one arm to wield his cane. The other was behind his back. He was so much stronger than I was, this man that never raised a finger. *Don't use anger*, Warden called from my memory. *Dance and fall.*

But the anger was already there, overflowing from all the parts of myself I'd locked away: anger at Jaxon, at Nashira, at the Abbess and the Rag and Bone Man and everyone else who had corrupted the syndicate. The syndicate I loved, in spite of everything. I hit him an eighth time. A split second later, his fist collided with my stomach. I doubled over, gasping for air as my diaphragm went into spasm.

"Sorry about that, darling." He turned the blade on his arm again. "You mustn't interrupt. This is delicate work."

Every muscle in my abdomen was reacting to the blow, but there was only a small window of opportunity to stop him. I dragged in oxygen. The tank must be empty.

The pommel of his cane struck my forearm. I didn't scream. I didn't have the breath left in my lungs. Weak, but still fighting, I picked up a chair and hurled it. Jaxon let out a shout of anger and fell, dropping his cane. It rolled. I made a grab for it. He clawed it back into his hand. The blade swung over my head. We were spitting and snarling like animals now; any pretense of a duel had dissolved. The cane came flying at me again, striking my elbow. Crackling agony burst from the point of impact, sending prickles to my fingertips.

I was running out of time. Gathering my strength, I shucked my battered flesh and shot through the æther, right into his dreamscape. My dream-form's feet fell on frost and grass. Jaxon's midnight zone.

In meatspace, the window of opportunity slammed shut. Outside his dreamscape, the æther trembled. I launched myself back out and into my body.

And couldn't breathe.

My fingers went straight to my neck. A creak of sound escaped me, edged with panic. This had only happened to me two or three times before. Nick had called it *laryngospasm*, a sudden constriction in the larynx when I dislocated. It always resolved itself within half a minute, but I was already starving for oxygen after the jump. Eyes watering, I looked up at Jaxon.

Too late.

The name was carved.

The oxygen tank had run too low to help. While I drowned without water, Jaxon smiled down at me. Blood seeped from his cut eyebrow. He added a little curl to the "y" at the end of my surname, just for good measure, but it was done. It had been finished while I was still in spirit form. His influence was already gripping my limbs, keeping my knees locked and my head held stiffly upright. Sweat dripped into my eyes. He held out his arm for all to see, and the letters glistened in the candlelight.

*Paige Eva Mahoney*

All I heard was my own thin breaths, the air whistling through a tiny space between my vocal cords.

"Stand, Paige," he said.

I stood.

"Come to me."

I went to him.

The mime-lords and mime-queens were chuckling. This was a first. No binder had ever snared a living person's spirit. The dreamwalker was a sleepwalker now, defeated by her own pride, by someone two orders lower than she was. Jaxon took my arm and turned me to face the audience. I was limp and pliant. A puppet.

"There, now. I believe this counts as unconsciousness, mistress of ceremonies." He curled his fingers into my hair. "What do you say, my boundling?"

I touched my finger to his arm, letting my lips part a little, as if I were mindlessly fascinated.

"Yes, my lovely, that's *your* name."

Howls of laughter.

I didn't say a word. All I did was jump, thanking every star that my father had changed my birth name.

His defenses were weakened by vanity and premature thoughts of triumph. They snapped up just an instant too late.

Inside his dreamscape, I stumbled over snarls of weeds and twisted tree roots, whipping branches out of my way. Each branch dripped bloodred leaves. As I sprinted, I caught glimpses of the lichen-covered slabs that surrounded me. They radiated out from the center, right into the depths of his hadal zone, embossed with numbers that blurred as I passed them. Jaxon's dreamscape was an enormous graveyard. Nunhead Cemetery, perhaps, where he'd mastered his gift for the very first time.

I didn't stop. He could correct my middle name, if he didn't mind making a mess of his arm. It wasn't too tough to guess its Irish counterpart. But as I sprinted towards the very heart of his dreamscape, I strained my dream-eyes to see the names on the graves, but there were none.

Specters were scuttling from his hadal zone, tall and translucent, creatures made from memory. Their fingers reached for me.

"Back," I shouted.

My voice echoed endlessly through Jaxon's mind. One of them gripped my dream-form in its arms, and for the first time in my life, I looked into a specter's eyes. Two yawning pits gaped back at me, full to the brim with fire.

In another person's dreamscape, they determined what my dream-form looked like—but only if they were focused. Just as I had with Nashira, I imagined myself growing larger, too large for the specter to hold. Its arms fell apart, and I tumbled free. My dream-form fell into his twilight zone, where the grass was thick and living and the smell of lilies hung on the air. The specters gave chase, but I was faster. I jumped over another grave and ran toward the light.

At the center of Jaxon's sunlight zone was a statue. Carved into the shape of an angel, it was slumped over a burial vault as if in grief. As soon as I was close enough, one of its hands lifted the lid of the tomb. Jaxon's dream-form was inside it. Its eyes opened, and it climbed out.

"There you are," he said. "Do you like my angel, honeybee?"

He put his hands behind his back. The dream-form's face wasn't quite Jaxon's; it was softer, older, almost plain. Cold black eyes stared at me with odium. The curling hair that grew from his scalp was like beaten copper, and strands of silver fingered out from his parting.

"You look different," I said.

"So do you. But you'll never know what *my* Paige looks like." He looked up. "Or will you?"

An X-shaped shadow hovered over my head. When I tried to move my wrists, I realized they were bound, as were my ankles.

"Poor puppet," he said. "You have no idea of anything, do you?"

"Neither do you." I pulled my wrists downward, and the strings evaporated. "Good thing I never told you my name, or that trick might have worked."

A smile touched his lips. "I see that you can change the natural state of your dream-form within my dreamscape. Your talents continue to impress."

I paced around him. His dream-form stood with its hands behind its back. Black eyes watched me.

"What are you going to do now? Make me dance around the ring? Make me cry and beg and whimper, just to show how powerful you are? Or perhaps you mean to force my spirit out, though I doubt you have the strength to do that now."

"I'm not going to kill you, Jaxon," I said.

"It would make a grand denouement. What a show it would be," he said. "Prove them right. Prove you're a destroyer, darling."

"I'm not your darling, or your lovely, or your honeybee. But I'm not going to kill you. I'm going to take your crown."

That was when I ran.

He was slow. The specters couldn't breach his sunlit zone, and his injuries had weakened his focus on his dream-form. I threw myself into the burial vault, and the lid slammed down on top of me.

My vision was sucked into Jaxon's sighted eyes. Colors flared up everywhere, each like an electric storm. Nerve systems in the æther, outstretched for any spiritual activity. The faces of the audience blurred and spun. My vision—Jaxon's vision—slid in and out of focus. Everything felt oddly light, as if I hadn't quite possessed him. Like his body was too loose. Like I wasn't quite filling it.

Then I saw why. My body was still standing, straight-backed. A thin line of blood had seeped from my nose, and my eyes looked vacant, but I was upright. The silver cord was holding me in both dreamscapes.

I could still do this.

Jaxon's body fell to its knees. I reached out a hand and saw a white silk glove. "In the name of the æther," I started in his voice, and this time I didn't slur.

*Wait.* His dream-form's voice was a whisper in my ear. *Stop.*

465

"—I, the White Binder, mime-lord of I Cohort, Section 4—"

*Stop. No, no, get out, GET OUT!*

"—yield—"

*STOP IT! SHUT MY MOUTH!* Jaxon's suppressed spirit was fighting me, kicking and screaming, banging on the lid of the burial vault. His body's hand slapped against the floor. *Damn you to hell! I fed you! I clothed you! I took you in! You would be dead if not for me. You would be nothing. Do you hear me, Paige Mahoney? YOU WILL BE THEIRS IF YOU ARE NOT MINE—*

"—to my mollisher," I finished, gasping the last words, "the Pale Dreamer."

Rigid fingers seized my consciousness. My vision flickered back to Jaxon's dreamscape, where the statue of the angel had me in its grasp. Jaxon's dream-form was on its knees, howling with rage. With a crunch of ancient stone, it pitched me into the darkness. I went hurtling into the æther and back into my own flesh, just in time to hear Jaxon regain control. I raised my arms, but the cane was blocked by another pair of hands. Eliza was standing over me, pushing Jaxon back, but his hands clawed at my throat.

"Stop it, Jaxon, stop!"

"The scrimmage is over." Minty Wolfson stepped into the ring. "Unhand her, White Binder!"

His hands were wrenched away. My knees folded beneath my weight. A pair of arms came around my waist, lifting me back to my feet. Nick. I gripped his forearm with white knuckles, heaving.

"You did it," he whispered in my ear. "You did it, Paige."

It took six people to restrain Jaxon. His nostrils were flared, his eyes wide with rage, and blood dripped from his chin. The I-4 tables were divided. Some were booing, but they were drowned out by clapping hands and stamping feet and roars of "Black Moth! BLACK MOTH!"

But the undercurrent of murmuring still set my nerves on edge. I let Nick and Danica pull my arms around their necks and help me to the other side of the ring. The other two had gone to hold Jaxon back. Eliza joined us at the edge and clamped a padded dressing over my side.

My ears rang. I couldn't think straight. It seemed impossible that I'd just defeated Jaxon Hall.

"Order," Minty called. "Order!"

She clapped her hands, but it took a long time for the audience to settle down. Jaxon stood with Nadine, who was offering him a handkerchief for his bloody nose, and Zeke. He stayed close to his sister, but his throat bobbed as he looked at Nick, who said nothing as he pressed a pot of fibrin gel into my hand. I daubed a generous amount on to my ribcage, but my front was already soaked with blood. They'd be calling me the Bloody Queen by sunrise at this rate.

Eliza came back with adrenaline. I caught Nadine's eye across the room. She didn't smile, but she gripped Jaxon's shoulder to steady him.

"Bring forth the crown," Minty commanded, to deafening cheers. "We have a winner!"

"Wait." The Abbess strode through the ash and blood. "What is the meaning of this?"

"The White Binder has yielded to his mollisher."

"Mime-lords do not yield to their mollishers."

"This is a first, then."

"It is clear," the Abbess said, with a stare at me, "that the great mime-lord of I-4 did not yield out of choice. The girl is a cheat."

"She is a dreamwalker. The scrimmage allows for *unlimited* use of an individual's clairvoyance. If the æther has gifted the Pale Dreamer with any ability, then it was, and is, her right to use it."

"And what of her blatant treachery? What of her contempt for the love and authority of her mime-lord?"

"There is a *lex non scripta* regarding a mollisher's loyalty, but no written laws about the nature of combat. You'd know that if you'd read a single book about this syndicate and its history. And if we cared about morals, I doubt you'd be a mime-queen, Abbess."

"You dare. You're in league with this turncoat, aren't you?" the Abbess sneered. "You and your hacks."

"I am the mistress of ceremonies. And my decision is final."

Beneath her golden veil, the Abbess's face drained of emotion. She was stripped of the interim Underqueen's power now, power she'd stolen from Hector and Cutmouth. Her head turned as she scanned the vault, no doubt for her partner in crime, but the Rag and Bone Man was nowhere to be seen. Her lace-clad hand pulled into a fist over her heart.

Commotion broke out on the other side of the Rose Ring. With a growl, Jaxon shoved away a hireling who had been tending to his wounds. "Get back," he barked. "I may not be Underlord by Grub Street's corrupt standards, but I *will* have my due from this day. Get out of my sight."

The hireling scarpered out of the way of his cane, whimpering apologies. The spectators fell silent, waiting for the defeated mime-lord's traditional speech.

"The Seven Seals are broken," was all he said, in a voice almost too soft to hear. But I heard it.

I heard it.

Jaxon Hall was far too proud to watch his former mollisher be crowned Underqueen, but he wouldn't leave without having the last word. He walked toward the audience, his cane making soft *clinks* against the floor.

"Do you know, my Paige . . . I find that I'm altogether quite proud of you. I truly believed you would stay your hand in the Rose Ring, like the weakling you were when you first came into my service, and walk away without a single death on your conscience." He stopped in front of me, his face inches from mine. "But no. You have learned, O my lovely, to be just like me." He caught my wrist, squeezing so tightly I felt the blood pumping in my veins, and whispered against my ear, "I will find other allies. Be warned: you have not seen the last of me."

I didn't answer. I wouldn't play his games, not any more. With a smile on his lips, Jaxon drew away.

"So the queen will fight for freedom, and her subjects for survival. But in the end, my Paige, those who seek freedom will only ever find it in the æther." He touched the blade of his cane to my bleeding cheek. "So enjoy your freedom, when the ashes fall. The theatre of war opens tonight."

"I look forward to it," I said.

His smile widened.

They parted to let him through. Not even the most foolhardy mobster dared taunt him as he left: the White Binder, mime-lord of I-4, the man who was almost Underlord. The man to whom I owed so much, who'd been my mentor and my friend; who could have been the man to lead us, if only he'd opened his eyes to the threat in the shadows. I'd never known it was possible to feel so much pain from the bruises and still hurt more inside. Nadine took his coat from his seat and went after him.

At the doorway, Jaxon stopped. He was waiting, I realized. Waiting to see which of his Seven Seals would go with him.

Danica stayed sitting on her chair, arms folded. When I raised my eyebrows at her, she shrugged. She would stay.

Beside me, Nick was hard-faced. Tears swelled into Eliza's eyes, and she took a shuddering breath, but she didn't follow him.

They would stay.

But Zeke took a step forward. Then another. He swallowed, hard, and closed his eyes. With no expression, he took his jacket and pulled it over his shoulders. Nick reached for his hand, and he squeezed it once before his fingers slipped away. He gave me a quick, remorseful look, then walked out of the vault after his sister and

Jaxon. Nadine took his arm as they rounded the corner. Several of the most loyal I-4 footpads and buskers went after him.

Now the adrenaline was wearing off, all sorts of pains were flooding through my body. The sight of Nick's face broke my heart, but this night wasn't over. Not by a long shot.

With a gentle hand, Nick pushed me forward. I walked into the center of the Rose Ring. Minty lifted the crown from the velvet cushion.

"Ready?" she said.

My throat was aching, stopping anything I might have said in return. Carefully, Minty lowered the crown on to my head.

"In the name of Thomas Ebon Merritt, he who founded this syndicate, I crown you Black Moth, Underqueen of the Scion Citadel of London, mime-lord of mime-lords, mime-queen of mime-queens, and resident supreme of I Cohort and the Devil's Acre. Long may you reign."

The silence went on. I stood tall, raising my chin.

"Thank you, Minty." My voice came out too soft.

"Who is your mollisher?"

"I have two. The Red Vision," I said, "and the Martyred Muse."

Eliza looked at me, startled. I raised my bloody hands, removed the crown and threw it on to the ash.

Murmurs of confusion followed. Minty looked as if she might say something, but her mouth clamped shut.

"As you can see"—I indicated my blood-stained clothes—"I'm not really in a fit state to be talking for too long. But I owe you an explanation for why I turned on my mime-lord and broke the unwritten rule of this syndicate. Why I risked everything for the opportunity to speak without hindrance. And it wasn't for a crown, or a throne. It was so that I would have a voice."

I focused on Nick's face, and he nodded.

"This syndicate—the SciLo syndicate," I said, lifting up my voice, "is facing threats from the outside, and we've ignored them for long enough. We all know that Haymarket Hector ignored them. In a month's time, Scion aims to have Senshield installed all over the citadel. Walking the streets freely and invisibly, as we always have, will be a thing of the past. If we don't fight back," I continued, "we'll be crushed beneath the anchor. We've already been pushed into an underworld, hated and despised, blamed even for *breathing*—but if this continues, if Scion takes another step, there will be no syndicate left by the new decade."

"Senshield is a Scion-made fabrication, vomited from the bowels of the Archon. Not only is this Underqueen a liar and a cheat," the Abbess shouted, "but she is also the prime suspect in the murder of our last Underlord. My own glym jack saw her leave the Devil's Acre with Hector Grinslathe's blood on her hands!"

The crowd descended into chaos. Some were already on their feet, screaming for my head; others for hard evidence, for proof, for the glym jack himself to come forward and speak.

"You have no evidence of this, Abbess," the Pearl Queen called out in a withering tone. "The word of an amaurotic, without good evidence to prove their veracity, is rotten. And if you knew that the Pale Dreamer had killed Hector, why have you shielded her for all this time?"

"I believe the claims of those I employ."

"I ask again. Why did you shield her, when there was ample opportunity to have her convicted at the last meeting of the Assembly?"

"The White Binder convinced me that she was simply in the wrong place at the wrong time," she said, spitting out the words. Her smokescreen of soft charm was breaking down. "It seems even his faith in her was misplaced. She is a backstabber and a murderess. I see now that if she could turn on her mime-lord, if she has so little respect for this syndicate's time-honored traditions, then she *must* be Hector's murderer. How sad that I overlooked it."

"You believe the claims of your employees, Abbess," I interrupted her, "but I believe in what I've seen with my own eyes. And what I've seen is tyranny built on a lie: the lie that clairvoyant people are unnatural and dangerous. That we should despise ourselves enough to will ourselves into extinction. They ask us to hand ourselves over to be tortured and executed, and they call it clemency!" I shouted at the crowd, turning to face them. "But Scion itself is the greatest lie in history. A two-hundred-year-old façade for the true government of England. The true inquisitors of clairvoyance."

"Of whom do you speak, Underqueen?" the Heathen Philosopher asked.

"She speaks of us."

Every head turned toward the entrance to the vault, and a clamor of shouting and gasping ensued. In the doorway was Arcturus Mesarthim, and at his back were his allies.

"Rephaim," Ognena Maria murmured.

Courage came rushing back.

"No," I said. "Ranthen."

# 26

## Thaumaturge

Eight of them had come. Some of them I hadn't seen before, all in heavy black silks and velvets and leathers, regally magnificent. Terebell was there, but there were others, too: silver and gold, brass and copper, all with the same chartreuse eyes. In the dim, confined space of the vault, they seemed enormous. And deeply threatening. The crowd surged away from the ring.

"That *is* a Rephaite," someone said.

"Just like the pamphlet . . ."

"They've come to save us . . ."

At least they knew what they were looking at. Warden stepped forward with Terebell. The others formed a semicircle on either side of them.

"You have heard of us"—Warden's gaze swept along the rows of voyants—"in the pages of a penny dreadful. But we are no work of fiction. For two centuries we have controlled the arm of Scion, let down the anchor in whichever cities we desired and transformed this Citadel into a feeding ground. Your world is not your own, voyants of London."

"What is this, Underqueen?" a hireling shouted. "A joke?"

"Clearly," Didion said, though his eyes were popping, "these are costumes. And this is an elaborate jest."

"You're an elaborate jest, Didion," Jimmy said.

"It's no jest," I said.

The group of Rephaim walked toward the dais, parting the voyants. Ivy was with them, trailing behind Pleione, her wrists and ankles blistered with the shadows of restraints. The other three fugitives brought up the rear with Lucida and Errai. Relief surged up inside me. They looked shaken, but they were alive and walking. I stepped down to meet Warden. His gaze darted over me, measuring my injuries.

"They were being held captive at the night parlor, as you suspected," he murmured. "Ivy insisted on being brought here at once to address the Unnatural Assembly." His eyebrows lifted as he noticed the Rose Ring, littered with corpses and limbs. "Or . . . what is left of them, in any case."

I nodded. Warden turned to face the crowd, and the other Ranthen stood on either side of him. In the long silence that followed, I stepped back on to the dais.

Whatever the reason behind the pamphlet being doctored, it had worked to my advantage in the end. There was fear of the Ranthen all around me, but it was mingled with curiosity, even wonder, rather than hostility.

"These are the Rephaim," I said, "or one faction of them. Their race are the true inquisitors of Scion. They have controlled our government for the last two centuries, directing Weaver and his puppets to suppress and destroy us. This small group of them"—I indicated the eight—"are willing to help us survive. They respect our gifts and our autonomy." Not quite true. "But there are other Rephaim in the Archon that care nothing for humans. They will enslave all voyants if we let them."

"This is shameful," the Abbess said, trying her best to sound disappointed. "Do you take us all for fools?"

"Hortensia," Ivy spat, her face contorted, "if anything in this room is shameful, it's *you*. You and your lies. Our lies."

The Abbess fell silent.

Under the eyes of every voyant of note in the Scion Citadel of London, Ivy stepped toward the dais. She stood before the spotlight in her dirty clothes and bare feet, her head tilted away from the glare. Dark hair was growing back, but the shape of her scalp was still clearly visible.

"Announce yourself, child," the Pearl Queen said.

"Divya Jacob. Ivy." Her gaze dropped. "Most of you won't know my real face, but I used to go by the name of the Jacobite. Until January this year, I was mollisher for the Rag and Bone Man."

Some of the II-4 voyants looked shocked; others, outright aggressive. Ivy gripped her right arm with her left hand.

"When I was seventeen, I ran away from Jacob's Island and worked for a kidsman called Agatha for three years. The Rag and Bone Man watched me for all that time. When I was twenty, he made me his mollisher and asked me to join him on an . . . 'endeavor,' as he called it. Said his people were suffering—people like me—and he wanted to make it better."

I listened in silence. Ivy stood perfectly still, her slender arms folded.

"He was selling voyants to Scion," she said.

Uproar. I stood.

"Let her speak," I called.

When there was enough quiet for her to continue, Ivy spoke again. I listened, cold all over.

It couldn't be. Of all the things I'd imagined, it was the only one that made perfect sense, but my syndicate could not be *that* corrupt. The Unnatural Assembly were lazy, yes, and cruel, but surely not this . . .

"He called it the gray market. He said we were recruiting them into the Rag Dolls." She drew in sharp breaths, looking wildly around at the audience. "But the people I sent to him . . . I never saw them again. I went to Cutmouth, Hector's mollisher, and reported it to her. She came to see him with a group of bodyguards and asked to see the catacombs, and she found someone in chains." Her hands dug into her arm, as if she was only just holding herself together. "She said she had to tell Hector. That an operation like that couldn't go on without his knowledge."

The Pearl Queen gripped her cane. "Did he do anything to stop it? Was that why he was killed?"

"No. He didn't stop it. He joined in with it."

This time the commotion lasted for a full minute before Ivy could speak again. Now I understood what Cutmouth had meant. *Selling us.* As Scion had sold us to the Rephaim, our own leaders had sold us to Scion.

"Cutmouth and I didn't know exactly what was happening. All we knew was that voyants were disappearing and we were making money. I was terrified of him," she said. "The only thing that got me through it was choosing the voyants we'd sell."

"How did you choose?" I said quietly.

Ivy shook her head. "What do you—?"

"How did you *choose* which voyants to sell, Ivy?"

To her credit, she didn't flinch. "When Cutmouth and I picked, we sent murderers and kidsmen. Violent thieves and thugs. People who'd hurt others for pleasure or coin."

"What about the Abbess?" I said, nodding to her. "Did you ever see this woman with them?"

"Yes. She often visited. Her night parlor is just a cover," Ivy said, staring her out. "She lures them into her den and pumps them full of pink aster and wine before she *sells* them to—"

"Lies!" the Abbess barked at once, over the shouts of outrage.

"But the Rag and Bone Man wasn't finished with me," Ivy shouted back, her skin tinged with a flush of rage. "One night, he called me to these catacombs and stuck me in the neck with a syringe full of flux. When I woke up, I was in the Tower. He must have guessed it was me that reported him." She managed a grim smile. "Poetic justice."

My vision was beginning to darken. The girl who'd been beaten and broken and tortured in the colony had most likely helped to send a good portion of the prisoners to the same place.

"So you were in London when the Underlord died." There was a deep crease across Ognena Maria's forehead. "Were you privy to any details?"

"No. A few days after Hector was killed, I found Cutmouth and she told me it was the Abbess who did it. Cutmouth saw her in the Devil's Acre, cutting up Magtooth's face with a butcher's knife."

Cries of horror. "How do you suppose that I killed eight people, alone?" the Abbess sneered. "How very convenient that the Jacobite gives her testimony with only a dead witness to prove it."

Ivy looked up. "What?"

"Yes, Jacobite. Your fellow vile augur, Cutmouth, is *dead*."

Grief wrote itself in small print on Ivy. She gripped her arms until her fingertips bruised marks into her skin.

"Her name was Chelsea Neves," she said, "and without her, I can't prove a word of this."

"Perhaps I can."

If the nerves of the audience were half-frayed by the presence of the Rephaim, they would be in pieces now. They surged toward the walls as Wynn and Vern of Jacob's Island walked into the vault, Wynn with the sachet of sage around her neck. Ivy let out a weak groan before she threw her arms around Vern, who held her to his chest without a word.

Wynn kept striding until she reached the middle of the ring. She looked down at the Wicked Lady with disgust and kicked her corpse's arm out of the way.

"If the Underqueen will accept another vile augur's testimony," she said, inclining her head to me, "I shall give it."

"Another vile augur? No resident of Jacob's Island shall give testimony before the Unnatural Assembly," Didion spluttered. "None but the palmists may speak before us. This cannot be allowed, Underqueen!"

"Go ahead, Wynn." I beckoned her. "Tell us what you know."

"A masked assassin arrived in Savory Dock, where Chelsea Neves was hiding from the syndicate, on the morning that she died. The guard said to me that the interim Underqueen had sent this person on her business. Apparently," she shouted over the rising protests, "her business was to cut open Chelsea's throat and slice her poor face apart!"

"These accusations are grotesque. Hector was my dearest friend, and although I had no idea *whatsoever* of this supposed betrayal, I could never have killed his mollisher. If you'll excuse me, good people of London, I'll be returning to my parlor to mourn in peace." The Abbess swept around and started to leave with two of her voyants in tow. "I have suffered enough of this false queen and her ravings."

"No, Abbess," I said softly. "You haven't." All that could be heard was the ring of my footfalls on the dais. The Ranthen parted to let me stand between them. "Under the First Code of this syndicate, I'm charging you with the murders of Hector Grinslathe, Chelsea Neves, and their seven associates: Magtooth, Slabnose, Bloatface, Slipfinger, Roundhead, the Underhand, and the Undertaker." Another few steps. "I'm also charging you with abduction, voyant trafficking, sending hitmen to a rival section, and high treason. You'll be placed under house arrest in your parlor to await trial by the Unnatural Assembly."

There were shocked faces all around the vault.

The Abbess laughed into the silence. "And with what authority do you charge me? We are the lawless of London. What prison cell will you throw me in? Or will you kill me now and throw my corpse into Flower and Dean Street? What kind of Underqueen will you be?"

"I hope I can be a just one," I said.

"Just? Where is the justice here? Where is your *evidence*, bantam queen?"

"You, Abbess. You're the evidence. You," I said to a courier, who jumped to attention, "could you check the Wicked Lady's right arm?"

"Yes, Underqueen."

Trembling, he knelt beside the body, unbuttoned her right cuff and pushed up the sleeve. I watched the color drain out of the Abbess's face, the tilting of her hand toward her arm. As soon as the Wicked Lady's shoulder was exposed, a grim smile touched my lips.

A tattoo of a skeletal hand, rendered in simple black and white. The courier swallowed. Ognena Maria stepped forward, crouching down to look closer.

"That's a Rag Doll mark," she concluded.

"Yes," I said. "The same ink that's on her, and on him"—I pointed to Bramble Briar and Hangman's corpses—"and on every other mime-lord, mime-queen and mollisher who was helping her in the ring, because all of them were working for the Rag and Bone Man. All of them were in on this . . . gray market." I looked up at the Abbess, now so pale she looked half a skeleton herself. "Let's see that arm, Abbess."

Her teeth were clenched. She took a step backward, away from the crowd and the evidence in the ring. Faces were darkening. Eyes hardening.

"Arrest her," I said.

And they obeyed. Jimmy O'Goblin, Jack Hickathrift, and Ognena Maria reacted at once, as did every remaining courier, footpad, and hireling from I-4.

The Abbess stared at them, then looked over her shoulder. There were no Rag Dolls left in the crowd. Even her own associates had vanished. The Rag and Bone Man had abandoned his assassin.

It took a moment for the Abbess to realize that she was on her own. In an instant of strange clarity, I saw the tiny, shifting details of her features as if under a microscope. Her lips pulling back over her teeth. Wisps of hair across her face, strangely delicate against the backdrop of volcanic rage.

And a monster rose up from the floor at her feet.

It was a poltergeist I didn't know, and one I didn't want to know. That was my last thought before it hit me.

"Here," the Abbess called, "is Hector's *true* murderer."

An explosion in the æther blew me backward off my feet, right back on to the dais. The air was slammed from my lungs, freezing on its way out of my body. A white cloud burst from my lips. I was pinned against the stage curtains, held up by an unseen hand.

Panic closed my throat and racked my limbs. I was the little girl on the field again. This poltergeist's apport took no clear form; it manifested as a wall of weight against my body.

The poltergeist circled the vault once, as though it were taking a good look at the crowd. It soared past the chandelier, extinguishing every candle. Lanterns guttered. Chairs and tables rattled. Spirits and guardian angels cowered in its wake. Below me, several of the Ranthen had seized up, letting out keens of agony that sent goose bumps rippling down my back. Warden was among them. Pain broke through the mask of his features, pain that I felt in my own chest. The Abbess stood with her hand aimed toward me, her face contorted with the effort of controlling the thing.

Then it was as if a wire had snapped. She slid to the floor, catching herself on her hands. Above us, the poltergeist melted into the ceiling. The grip relaxed, and I fell, landing in a crouch on the dais.

The spotlight cart flickered. In the guttering light, I climbed back to my feet. Across my neckline, faint silver marks were branching out like veins from where the pendant glowed like an ember.

The golden cord vibrated so harshly that I felt it in my bones. Warden was gripping his shoulder, his right hand flexing in and out of a fist. Just from the look on his face, I knew he was in agony. Four of the other Ranthen were in the same state, including Terebell.

I stood tall.

The Abbess stared at me, and I saw her lips form the word "impossible." With a snarl, she took a revolver from her jacket and aimed it at my heart.

My vision tunnelled; my reactions failed me. All I did was half-raise my hands. The gun went off. The bullet missed me by a hair's breadth.

The Abbess kept on shooting as she backed out of the vault, but the Ranthen shielded me with their bodies. Warden took three in quick succession and fell back against the stage, his hand clamped over his chest. Turning wildly, like a cornered animal, the Abbess blasted back fifteen voyants with spools and fired her gun twice more, detaching a curtain rail from the ceiling. Red drapes billowed down on the top of the nearest voyants' heads.

The next bullet hit Ivy, throwing her against the floor. I heard myself shout. The Abbess started to laugh.

And a gun went off, but it wasn't hers.

The bullet hit her just under the ribcage. Two more shots finished her off, one each from Tom the Rhymer and Ognena Maria, head and heart. The Abbess collapsed into the red velvet, dead.

I took in a deep, gulping breath. Blood seeped from the hole in the Abbess's temple. Nick's knuckles were white on the pistol.

My ears rang with the sound of the three gunshots. At my side, Nick seemed to come to his senses. He grasped my arm, helping me to my feet. "Paige." He held my head between his hands, bone-pale. "Paige, that poltergeist . . . I've never felt anything like it . . ."

"I don't know." I shook my head, drained. "Please, just . . . get Ivy and Warden and the others patched up."

He squeezed my elbow and made his way to Warden, who was pushing himself up on his arms. The remaining members of the Unnatural Assembly, along with their mollishers and mobsters, were looking to me to make sense of this madness, but words failed me. Jaxon would have known how to explain, but I'd never been much of a storyteller. And this was one hell of a strange story.

This was the cream of London's crop. There could be hundreds, if not thousands more with loyalty to these leaders.

"So, Underqueen," Ognena Maria finally said, "here we are. You seem to have won the day. And cleared your name."

"What will you do with this one?" A masked trader nodded to Ivy, who didn't so much as raise her head.

"There won't be any punishment without a trial. A full investigation needs to be conducted, starting with a thorough search of the Abbess's night parlor," I said. "Any volunteers?"

"I'll take my people," Ognena Maria said. "I know where it is." She whistled to her hirelings, and they followed her from the vault.

"Underqueen," said a footpad, sweeping off his hat, "the penny dreadful told a great tale of these creatures, but are they to be feared or worshipped?"

"Feared," Errai rumbled.

Lucida tilted her head. "Or worshipped. We will not reject tribute."

"Feared," I said, giving her a hard look, "and certainly not worshipped." Black crept into my vision. "Scion can have their natural order. The White Binder can keep his Seven Orders of Clairvoyance. And because our actions will speak loud and clear to Scion, who would never listen to our words . . . ours will be the Mime Order."

With those words, my vision failed me.

After that, I've no idea what happened.

****

I was no longer the Pale Dreamer, mollisher of I-4. No longer a songbird in Jaxon's gilded cage. Now I was Black Moth, Underqueen, and still the most wanted person in Scion. Safe inside my dreamscape, I curled up in the poppy anemones, drenched in the warm blood of rebirth.

The damage to my dreamscape wasn't so bad this time. A few chinks in my mental armor. My body had endured far more than my dreamscape.

When I broke from the shadows, I was lying on a rug, my head pillowed by a coat. My blood-stained clothes had been peeled off. A kerosene lamp sat to my right. The warmth stopped me from shivering, but my bruises ached in a draft.

I coughed.

A searing pain ripped through my ribs and shot bolts into the back of my head. Other pains flared up all over the place, erupting from my knuckles and my legs and the point where my neck met my shoulder. A scream shot up my throat and came out as a weak groan. When the throbbing stopped, I didn't dare move again.

Jaxon wouldn't wake up in much pain. A light headache. A bruise or two. He'd already be making plans to pull the syndicate out from under me.

Let him try.

Outside, London would be rippling with the repercussions of my victory. I sensed the Rag and Bone Man wouldn't just accept defeat. He would be preparing for vengeance now.

They must have wanted one of their own to lead the syndicate. Probably the Wicked Lady, given what she'd seemed to know. A handful of mime-lords and mime-queens had been employed to get rid of me, to ensure that she won. She'd been nothing but a pawn in his plan. By killing her, and not dying myself, I'd flung a spanner into their plans. The Rag and Bone Man would want retribution. He'd left his lackey to die alone.

After a while, which could have been an hour or a minute, a silhouette emerged from the stage curtains. I tensed, reaching for a knife that wasn't there, but it was Warden who came into the light of the kerosene lamp.

"Good evening, Underqueen," he said, eyes burning.

I sank back into the coat. "Not feeling that regal."

As soon as I spoke, a line of fire jumped from my jaw to my ear.

"I must confess," Warden said, "that you do not look particularly majestic at this time. Nonetheless, you are Underqueen of the Mime Order." He sat down beside me and clasped his hands. "An interesting name."

"What time is it?" I touched my hand to the side of my face. "Are you all right?"

"Bullets do no lasting harm to Rephaim. It has been two hours since the scrimmage ended," he said. "Dr. Nygård will not be pleased that you are awake."

"Let's not tell him, then." With difficulty, I drank from the canteen of water he handed me. It tasted of blood. "Tell me you have amaranth."

"Sadly not. Dr. Nygård has gone to Seven Dials to collect your possessions, and I quote, 'before Jaxon can sell them.' They plan to join Ognena Maria and search the Abbess's parlor for any evidence of the Rag and Bone Man's involvement."

Nick had good sense, and the foresight I should have expected from an oracle. "They won't find anything," I said. "The Abbess was just a vessel for his poltergeist. He'll be back."

"And you will be ready."

I looked up at him. "It was *that* poltergeist, wasn't it?"

"Yes." His hands clasped a little more tightly. "An old enemy."

"Then how could the Abbess have controlled it?"

"That creature obeys Nashira alone. She would have had to command it to comply with the orders of another."

The implication settled over me. That the gray market might not be between the syndicate and Scion. That it might be a direct pipeline to the Rephaim. The world was suddenly too big for the cramped little cup of pain inside my skull, and I closed my eyes to block it out. I could think about this when I was clear-headed. If I thought about it now, I'd crack.

I risked a glance into the antique mirror propped against the nearest wall, framed with gilt. My face looked awful—grazes and bruises, swollen lip—but the wound along my jaw was the worst by far, worse than anything Jaxon had left. Black darts shot through a red and swollen cut.

"It was a clean wound," Warden said. "It may not scar."

I found I didn't care either way. If this came to war, scars of all kinds were on the horizon.

Farther down the aisle, three sleeping shapes were curled under blankets. Nell, Felix, and Jos, huddled together, the way people had slept in the Rookery to ward off the cold. "They were whitewashed," Warden said. "They remember nothing of what happened at the parlor."

"No chance of knowing how the Rag and Bone Man got them to change the pamphlet, then." I looked past them. Ivy sat on the stage, her thin arms bare, staring up at the ceiling. "How is she?"

Warden looked at her, too. "The bullet had been extracted. Dr. Nygård said that the true pain is in her heart."

"Cutmouth." I sighed, making my ribs ache. "I know she's been through hell, but I don't know if I can forgive her for what she did."

"You ought not to be hard on her for acting out of fear."

It was true. Ivy might have sent countless people to the penal colony, but adding to her guilt would never undo her actions. I took another sip from the canteen. "Where are the Ranthen?"

"They have retreated to a safe house close to the Old Nichol. They leave to spread the word of your victory tomorrow." He paused. "Several voyants were whispering that you are a . . . thaumaturge. They can see no other explanation for how you withstood the poltergeist."

Jaxon had used that word for me before, always in jest. It was whispered by the handful of voyants that worshipped what they called the *zeitgeist*, the spirit that had supposedly created the æther. The faithful didn't use *thaumaturge* lightly. It referred to someone touched by the zeitgeist itself, someone with unprecedented mastery of the æther's secrets.

"They don't know about this." I picked open the top of my shirt. The pendant was cool, but the vein-like marks still spread out from beneath it. "This is the thaumaturge."

"And how well it suits you."

"I don't want them to believe I'm some sort of miracle-worker, Warden. My achievement here is wearing a necklace."

"You are free to correct them later. For now, there is no harm in letting them talk. Your job is to heal."

We sat in silence for a while, with the lantern between us. How far we'd come in the space of a few weeks. "I have a question for you," Warden said. "If I may."

I drank again. "If it won't make my head hurt."

"Hm." He paused. "When Jaxon employed you, he seemed willing to pay you any sum of money you desired for your services. Yet you cannot be the wealthy mollisher I once believed you to be, else you would not have been forced to solicit the Ranthen's patronage. What did you do with your contract money?"

I'd wondered when he might ask me that.

"There was no money. Jaxon doesn't even have a bank account," I said. "All his money comes from our work and goes into a little jewel-box in his office to be shared between us. That's our payment. After that, I don't know where it goes."

"Then why continue to work for him?" He watched me. "He lied to you."

A husk of laughter came out of me. "Because I was naïve enough to be loyal to Jaxon Hall."

"That was not naïveté, Paige. You cared enough for Jaxon to continue working for him. You understood that he was necessary for your survival." His gloved hand lifted my chin. "You will not need Terebell's money forever. In the end, loyalty will outweigh greed. When they have hope."

"Isn't hope just another kind of naïveté?"

"Hope is the lifeblood of revolution. Without it, we are nothing but ash, waiting for the wind to take us."

I wished I could believe it. I *had* to believe it—that hope alone would be enough to get us through this. But hope couldn't control a syndicate. Hope wouldn't bring down the Westminster Archon, which had stood strong for two hundred years. It wouldn't destroy the creatures inside it, who had watched the world for far longer than that.

Warden dimmed the kerosene lamp. "You ought to rest," he said. "You have a long reign ahead of you, Black Moth."

Across the hall, Ivy was still sitting on the stage, motionless. "I need to talk to her first," I said.

"I will find Nick's medical kit. He left another dose of scimorphine for you."

He made to stand, but I touched his arm, keeping him there. Wordlessly, I leaned into him, so my brow rested against his. Gentle blue fire started in my dreamscape, illuminating it. We stayed like that for a long time, silent and still, Rephaite and human. I could have stayed like that for hours, just breathing him in.

"Warden," I said, so quietly he had to lean closer to hear me, "I don't—I don't know if . . ."

Fire played in his eyes. "You are under no obligation to decide tonight." After a moment, his lips grazed my forehead. "Go."

Seeing that he understood lifted a weight from my shoulders. I was a different person now than I'd been before the scrimmage, still in metamorphosis, uncertain of who I might become tomorrow. But I sensed that whatever I decided, he would still be with me. On a whim, I kissed his cheek. He gathered me to his chest, his arms crossed tightly over my back.

"Go," he repeated, softer.

Leaving him to find Nick's case, I got myself across the auditorium and on to the stage. Pains shot through me, but the medicine held some of it at bay. Ivy didn't move when I sat beside her.

"It was brave of you to tell the truth."

Her raw hands gripped the edge of the stage. On her right upper arm was the twisted mess of scar tissue where her tattoo had once been, a shock of pink and scarlet that plowed through the undamaged skin.

"Brave," she repeated, as though it were a word she didn't know. "I'm a yellow-jacket."

A code understood only by those who had lived through the first nightmare. Her fingernails dug into the burnt flesh.

"I used to beg Thuban to kill me, you know." She shook her head. "When I heard about your plan to break out of there, I considered not getting on the train. I had no right to it, after what I'd done. And I was so sure Chelsea had betrayed me."

"You thought she told Rags it was you who reported him?"

"That's what I thought until I found her. After you told me she was looking for me, I bribed the doorman outside Jacob's Island. She told me she'd passed my report to Hector and let slip that it was me. And then he told Rags." There was nothing left in her voice but grief. "She always tried to see the best in Hector. Always trusted him. It killed her, in the end. Wanting a better life than what we had as kids in that slum. I left her and went back to Agatha, thinking she'd be safe . . ."

Tears choked her. "You got on the train, Ivy," I said. "You must have hoped you could still have that life."

"I got on the train because I'm too much of a coward to die." A smile trembled on her lips. "Weird, isn't it? Even though we're voyant, even though we know there's something more, we're still afraid to die."

I shook my head. "We don't know what waits in the last light. Even dreamwalkers don't know that." Ivy chewed on her knuckles, still stroking her scar. "When the Unnatural Assembly gets back on its feet, you'll be given a fair hearing and a trial by jury. And I promise you this: the Rag and Bone Man will be charged for his crimes."

Her face twitched. "That's all I can ask. Justice." She finally met my gaze. "I want to see his face, Paige. Before the end."

"I'd be curious to see it myself." Every muscle ached as I pushed myself off the stage. "Chelsea died in my arms. Do you know what she said to tell you?" Silence from behind me. "That you were everything to her, and that you had to make it right." I walked away. "So make it right."

Still Ivy didn't move or speak. When I got back to the kerosene lamp, I lay down on the coat and rested my hand on the crown—the symbol of the syndicate, the weapon I would use to bring down Scion.

Warden closed my hand around the syringe. I pushed it into my hip and pressed down on the plunger.

****

With the help of scimorphine and the steady presence of Warden's aura, I slipped into a fitful doze. It didn't last long. As the first light of dawn crept into the hall, a cool hand shook me back to life.

"I'm sorry, sweetheart." It was Nick, and he looked shattered. "You need to see this. Now."

# 27

# The Mutual Friend

Danica's Scion-made laptop sat on the floor in front of me, a clear glass screen with a delicate silver keypad. I pushed my weight on to my elbow, unsteady. Scimorphine was still slithering through my bloodstream.

"What is it?"

Nobody answered. I rubbed my temple, trying to focus. Nick, Eliza and Danica were all around me, surrounded by bags and suitcases. They must have just returned from Seven Dials. Behind me, Warden was leaning toward the screen, his eyes scorching in the gloom.

"It started about half an hour ago," Eliza said. "It's been on repeat since then. All over the citadel."

My gaze focused on the screen.

The broadcast was silent, with no commentary from ScionEye, though its symbol rotated at the corner of the screen. A line of small text gave the camera's location as I Cohort, Section 5, in the district of Lychgate Hill. This was the inner courtyard of Old Paul's, where unnaturals were traditionally executed. The condemned stood alongside each other on a long scaffold, each an arm's length apart from the next, their bare feet planted on scarlet trapdoors. Their faces had been left uncovered.

A tight knot worked its way up my throat. I recognised the woman in the middle. Lotte, one of the last Bone Season survivors, dressed in the black shift of a convicted unnatural. A deep cut crossed her forehead. Her hair was bound in a knot at the side of her neck, which was stippled with fresh bruises, like her forearms. I pressed a finger to the screen, zooming in on them. Charles was on her right, bruised and bleeding—Charles, who had guided other voyants to the train—and on her left was Ella, whose shift was caked with dry vomit.

"Paige." I heard Warden say it, but I couldn't take my eyes off the screen. His voice was far, far away, somewhere I wasn't. "You must not obey the summons. This is a message to you, and you alone. To lure you out of hiding."

As if to confirm it, the screen switched to a white background. The anchor kept rotating in the corner. A mocking little spinning-top.

PAIGE EVA MAHONEY, SURRENDER YOURSELF TO THE CUSTODY OF THE ARCHON. YOU HAVE ONE HOUR.

The broadcast returned a moment later, panning over the whole courtyard. I said, "You say this started half an hour ago?"

Eliza exchanged a glance with Nick before she nodded. "We got here as fast as we could."

Pressure radiated from my dreamscape, reaching out through the æther for the others. A drop of red slipped from Eliza's nostril, and Nick shouted something through the deafening explosion in my skull. I reigned it in with a scream of effort, gathering it inward, cramming it down until blood ran from my nose and flooded my mouth with the taste of metal.

Someone must have told them I was Underqueen, that I posed a real threat to them at last. That was why they'd been so quiet, why Nashira hadn't thrown her iron fist down on I-4 the minute I'd escaped her colony with my head on my shoulders. She'd wanted me to think there was hope, to believe that I could raise an army, before she broke me.

If I entered the Westminster Archon, I would never come out. If I didn't, the voyants on the screen would die, and every voyant in London would believe that I had done nothing to save them.

"Paige," Jos said, "we can't let them die."

"Shh." Nell gathered him into her arms. "Nobody's going to die. Paige won't let them. She saved us, didn't she?"

"You want Paige to hand herself in?" Eliza shook her head. "That's exactly what they want."

"They won't hurt her. She's a dreamwalker."

"That," Warden said, "is precisely why they will hurt her."

"You stay out of this, Rephaite," she snarled. "Those are *human* lives, and if you think they're less important than yours, you can go fu—"

"He's right," Nick said quietly. "If we lose Paige, we lose any influence we have over the syndicate. We lose the war before it's started."

Nell choked out a scream of frustration. Tears filled Jos's eyes, and he clung to her shirt like a child of half his age.

A high-pitched whistle filled my ears, a shriek inside my skull. A hand shook my arm. "Paige," Eliza said, her voice harder than usual, "you can't go. You're Underqueen." Her grip tightened. "I left Jaxon because I believed you could do this. Don't make me regret it."

"You have to try, Paige," Nell said. "For the others."

"No." Tears shone in Jos's eyes. "Lotte wouldn't want Paige to die."

"She wouldn't want to die herself, either!" Her tone made Jos cringe. Nell turned her glistening eyes on me, her cheeks pink with anger. "Look, I was friends with Lotte in the colony. You weren't a harlie. Your keeper was good to you. Don't treat us the way they did. Like fodder."

They were looking to their Underqueen to make the call. I gazed at the screen. All three of the prisoners' mouths were sealed with dermal adhesive.

I said, "I'll go to the Archon."

"Paige, *no*," Nick said hotly, echoed by Eliza. "You know they won't let you walk out of there alive."

"Nashira will be counting upon your altruism." Warden's voice was soft. "If you present yourself at the Archon, you play into her hands."

"I said I was going," I said. "Not that I was going in person."

There was a short silence. Nell and Jos looked at each other, but the remaining Seals understood.

"It's too far," Nick murmured. "More than a mile. You did too much at the scrimmage. If you overstretch yourself—"

"You can drive me closer to the Archon. Keep my body in the back of the car."

Nick looked at me for a long while. Finally, he closed his eyes. "I don't see another choice." He took a deep breath. "Danica, Warden, both of you come with us. Eliza, stay here and look after the others."

"But Paige is hurt," Jos said.

"She's fine." Nell just watched. "She knows what she's doing."

I pushed myself on to my arms, my teeth gritted. Sickening pain punched a fist through my skull, poured fire down my side and branched out across my ribcage, breaking the loose grip of scimorphine.

Without complaining, Danica picked up her backpack of equipment and slung it over her shoulders. Nick lifted me into his arms, supporting my head with one hand, and followed her out of the music hall to the car, with Warden bringing up the rear. He sat in the back on my left side. On my other side, Danica took out my oxygen mask and made her adjustments. Nick locked the doors before he started the engine.

This was their declaration of power, the promise that Scion would bring down the full might of their empire on the heads of my fellow clairvoyants. Even if I turned back now, the gears of war would still be turning.

The rusted car raced toward I-1, its engine clattering. There were Vigiles everywhere, but Nick avoided them, taking the narrowest streets at high speed. My wounds throbbed, and a headache pounded like a drum between my eyes.

"I'll park under the Hungerford Bridge, near the floating restaurants," Nick said. "You have to be quick, Paige."

I had to try. For Lotte and Charles, who had helped me in the colony. For every voyant who had been killed in our escape. For every Bone Season in history.

The theatre of war would open tonight. I was Underqueen now, with the might of the syndicate at my back, as I'd promised Nashira that day on the stage. They had poisoned the syndicate from the inside, leaving it to rot while they ruled over our citadel.

There had to be something better than this. Something worth the price we would pay. Not just these endless trials, these harrowed days. Beggars crawling in the gutters, crying for mercy to a world that didn't hear. Quaking in the shadow of the anchor. Fighting for survival in the shadows—every minute, every hour, every day of our short lives.

We already existed on a level of hell. And we would have to walk right through this hell to leave it.

Nick braked hard under the bridge and parked on the pavement, close to where a pleasure-barge twinkled with blue lanterns, full of amaurotics drinking mecks and laughing. Behind them, on a screen no one was watching, the prisoners stood on their scaffold, waiting for me.

Danica tied the mask's straps at the back of my head. "You've got ten minutes before this thing runs dry," she said. "I'll shake your body, but it might not work when you're so far away. Watch the clock."

There were no Vigiles nearby. I looked at Warden, sitting in silence beside me. His would be the last face I saw, the last face in my mind, before I stepped into the nest of the enemy. He inclined his head, just slightly. Not visible enough to be seen by the others. Just enough to give me strength.

The mask lit up, pushing oxygen into my body. I took one last breath of my own before my spirit twisted free of its restraints and rose into the night.

In my purest spirit form, where my vision was no longer fixed to insufficient eyes, London was an infinite cosmos of its own. A vast galaxy of tiny lights, each emitting a unique color. All the millions of minds, bound by one underlying current of energy, strung together by a web of thoughts, of emotions, of knowledge and of information. Each spirit was a lantern in the glass orb of a dreamscape. It was the highest form of bioluminescence, one that transcended the physical aspects of color and crossed into a spectrum no naked eye could see.

Identifying single buildings was difficult in the æther, but I knew the Westminster Archon when I saw it. The whole place had the look of death and fear, and its insides were crowded with hundreds of dreamscapes. I passed into the first person I saw. When I opened my eyes, I was tucked inside another person's flesh.

I could feel difference in my body. Shorter legs, wider waist, an aching right elbow. But behind these new eyes, and this Vigile's visor, I was utterly myself.

All around me were sleek walls and gleaming floors and lights too bright for these new eyes. The stranger's heart pounded. Even though I was disoriented and afraid, the feeling was invigorating. Like I'd shucked a threadbare set of clothes and pulled on a luxurious dress.

With effort, I moved the woman's legs. It was something like moving a puppet, and when I caught sight of myself in a gilded mirror, I could see that she was walking like one: jerky, drunken, completely graceless. The sight entranced me. I was myself. I was not myself. The woman looking back at me was perhaps thirty, and a thread of blood was leaking from her nostril. My suit of armor.

I was ready.

****

The Westminster Archon loomed above me, a palace of black granite and wrought-iron. The clock was red.

Whichever Vigile I'd possessed commanded the rest of the unit. Their guns snapped up when I turned on my heel. They marched after me like a wake, flanking me on all sides: six, twelve, twenty of them. I didn't know if it was my heartbeat I could hear, or the footfalls of my guard.

My boots fell on the red marble floor of the Octagon Hall, the lobby of the Archon. Twisting pillars rose high above me, stretching to the great star-shaped ceiling, where gilt shone in the light of a beautiful chandelier.

*I will destroy the doctrine of tyranny.*

This was the very center of Scion. Heart of the heartland. All around me, the walls were encased by vast arches, carved with the likenesses of every leader of the republic since 1859. They looked down from their lofty heights, their faces full of shadow and judgment. Above them were the eight tympana, painted with richly imagined scenes from Scion's history.

I stood in the light for what seemed like forever, a grain of dust between the stars: one above, one below.

*I will cut the strings from the limbs of the puppets.*

Above me, the tower pealed out six o'clock.

I walked up a flight of steps and down a long corridor, where the eyes of granite busts watched from all sides. The paintings melted into waves of dark oil and gold.

"Wait," I said.

My guard stopped at the threshold. Alone, I walked under the archway.

*I will rip the anchor from the heart of London.*

Four figures stood at the other end of the vast gallery. On the far left was Scarlett Burnish. Her hair was the red of the carpet, and a red smile tipped her lips. Not like blood. Too bright, too false. Stage blood.

On the far right, Gomeisa Sargas towered in his high-collared robes, a chain of woven gold and topaz strung between his shoulders. There was hunger in his stare. In a moment of sheer madness, I had the urge to congratulate him on such an admirably human expression of malice.

Frank Weaver was beside him, stiff and gaunt as a corpse. It was as if they'd switched species.

And there she was. Nashira Sargas, blood-sovereign and butcher. Argentate and beautiful. Ravenous and terrible. Standing between humans as if they were equals—as if they were her friends, these mindless mannequins.

"You have not been summoned, Vigile," she said. "I hope you have the fugitive, or I will have your eyes put out."

Her voice called to me from a dark part of my memory.

"Hello, Nashira," I said, in a voice that wasn't mine. "It's been a while."

To her credit, she didn't look surprised. Not so much as a flicker of curiosity.

"Wise of you to come in another's body, 40," she said, "but we have no use for an errant spirit in a stranger's skin."

"We were willing to show clemency," Scarlett Burnish said. She looked exactly as she did on the screen, as though she'd been moulded from polished vinyl, but her tone was cooler. "If you had surrendered yourself to the custody of the Archon in person, we would gladly have freed them all."

I stood perfectly still, looking up at the enormous Scion anchor behind the four seats. "Don't you tell enough lies, Scarlett?"

She fell silent.

High on the platform, the Grand Inquisitor, Frank Weaver, said nothing at all. He was no more than a mannequin after all. Nashira walked down the steps, her long black dress spilling behind her.

"Perhaps I misjudged you after all." She touched a gloved finger to my host's cheek. "Have you not the courage to give me your life in exchange for theirs, Underqueen?"

So she knew.

"You'll spare theirs," I said, "or I'll take his."

In a single movement, the Vigile's pistol was in my hand and aimed at Frank Weaver's heart. His body gave the briefest start, but he still made no sound as a red dot hovered on his chest. Scarlett Burnish moved toward him, but I fired the pistol between them. She froze.

"To prevent London slipping back into human control," Weaver said, robotic, "I am willing to lay down this mortal life."

Gomeisa laughed, a sound like grinding metal. "It seems you were wrong, Nashira. 40 is willing to take a fellow human's life for her own ends."

"I am," I said. "For all the lives he's taken in your name."

The Sargas made no attempt to shield their Grand Inquisitor. "Even if you topple this pawn where he stands, you will not stop what is coming," Gomeisa said. "Not if you cleave your mountains and raze your cities. Not if you lay down your life in pursuit of our downfall. Our influence is buried deep in the mortal coil, rooting us like an anchor to this earth."

"I'm a dreamwalker, Gomeisa," I said. "I recognize no anchor to this earth."

But I'd lost. They didn't care if I shot Frank Weaver; all they'd do was find another willing servant.

I had no leverage.

"If it helps to ease your guilt"—Gomeisa watched the screen with no emotion—"we were always going to do this, whether you presented yourself or not. These lives will pay for the one of ours that you took in the colony, and even that is not enough for the loss of the blood-heir."

Kraz Sargas. The Rephaite I had killed with a bullet and a flower. Scarlett Burnish touched her earpiece.

"Lower the anchor," she said.

On the screen, the Grand Executioner walked to the switch that had murdered so many of my people. As his gloved hand reached toward it, Lotte wrenched her arms from behind her back—someone must have smuggled her a blade—and cut right through the binding on her lips. Blood unfurled from her mouth, but her eyes were sparkling with wild triumph.

"BLACK MOTH RULES IN LONDON," she screamed at the camera. "VOYANTS, DO YOU HEAR ME? BLACK MOTH RULES IN—"

The broadcast cut off. Something small and vital fractured into pieces. I was a live wire, a lit fuse, an exploding star on the verge of supernova. My spirit crested against the inside of my dreamscape, rearing up to meet the storm that gathered in my mind. Iridescent colors framed my vision. They blinded me, like splinters of the sun.

"This is the fate that will befall them all." Nashira watched me with that mockery of a smile. "It can end tomorrow if you turn back now."

A hollow sound clattered from my host's throat, something that might have passed for a laugh.

*Voyants, do you hear me?*

"It will end," I said, "when there are no Rephaim left on this side of the veil. When you rot with the rest of your world. The moths are out of the box, Nashira. Tomorrow, we will be at war."

A word that most syndicate voyants would never use. Even *gang war* didn't have quite the same weight as that word when it stood alone.

*Do you hear me?*

"War." Nashira's face was blank. "You have threatened us with your thieves and thugs before, yet still we have seen nothing. Your threats are empty." She paced past me with silent footsteps, back to the windows that looked over Westminster Bridge. "I would almost believe that this syndicate of yours did not exist, were it not for the steady stream of voyants we have received from the Unnatural Assembly over the years."

*Do you hear me?*

"The gray market was never supposed to exist," the enemy continued, "but I confess, it has had its uses over the years. The voyants we received through that channel were always far more powerful than those that Scion plucked from the street. The Rag and Bone Man has been our ally for many years, along with the Abbess, Haymarket Hector, and the Wicked Lady."

"Three of those four are dead." My vision flickered. "Looks like you'll have to make some new friends."

"Oh, but I have an old one." Nashira didn't smile. "A very old ally. One who returned to me at two o'clock this morning, after twenty long years of estrangement. One who does not recognize you as Underqueen, despite your . . . association." She turned away, looking out of the windows. "Miss Burnish, summon him. 40 ought to meet our mutual friend in person."

Scarlett Burnish walked across the room, as swift and poised as she was in the studio, and opened the double doors. A sound echoed through the hallway beyond. The clink of metal against marble.

And when he arrived, I knew his face.

Yes, I knew it very well.

*Words, my walker . . . words are everything. Words give wings even to those who have been stamped upon, broken beyond all hope of repair . . .*

No words. No wings.

*Dance and fall.*

Like a puppet. All those years of dancing.

The doors swung open. I looked up, knowing the mistake I'd made, knowing what a fool I'd been to trust, to care, to let him live.

"You," I whispered.

"Yes." His hands were gloved in silk. "Me, O my lovely."

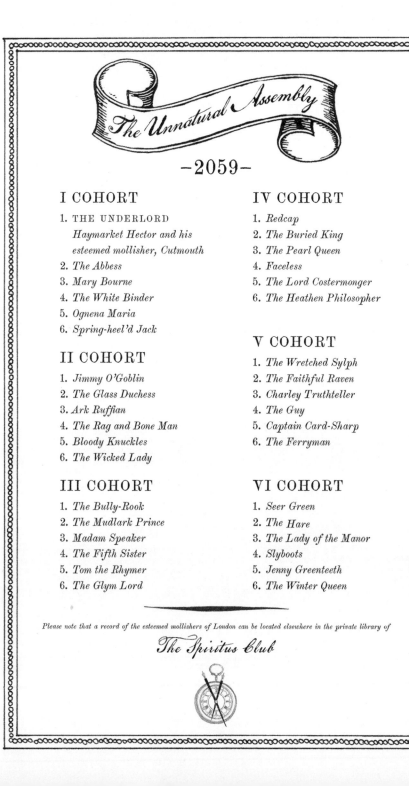

# The Unnatural Assembly

## –2059–

### I COHORT

1. THE UNDERLORD
   Haymarket Hector and his
   esteemed mollisher, Cutmouth
2. *The Abbess*
3. *Mary Bourne*
4. *The White Binder*
5. *Ognena Maria*
6. *Spring-heel'd Jack*

### II COHORT

1. *Jimmy O'Goblin*
2. *The Glass Duchess*
3. *Ark Ruffian*
4. *The Rag and Bone Man*
5. *Bloody Knuckles*
6. *The Wicked Lady*

### III COHORT

1. *The Bully-Rook*
2. *The Mudlark Prince*
3. *Madam Speaker*
4. *The Fifth Sister*
5. *Tom the Rhymer*
6. *The Glym Lord*

### IV COHORT

1. *Redcap*
2. *The Buried King*
3. *The Pearl Queen*
4. *Faceless*
5. *The Lord Costermonger*
6. *The Heathen Philosopher*

### V COHORT

1. *The Wretched Sylph*
2. *The Faithful Raven*
3. *Charley Truthteller*
4. *The Guy*
5. *Captain Card-Sharp*
6. *The Ferryman*

### VI COHORT

1. *Seer Green*
2. *The Hare*
3. *The Lady of the Manor*
4. *Slyboots*
5. *Jenny Greenteeth*
6. *The Winter Queen*

*Please note that a record of the esteemed mollishers of London can be located elsewhere in the private library of*

## The Spiritus Club

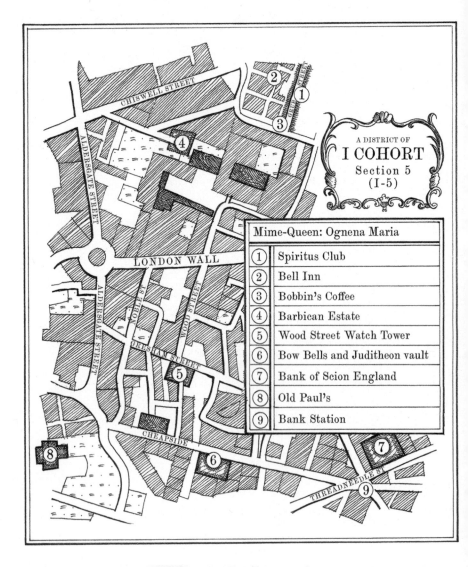

A DISTRICT OF
## I COHORT
Section 5
(I-5)

Mime-Queen: Ognena Maria

| | |
|---|---|
| ① | Spiritus Club |
| ② | Bell Inn |
| ③ | Bobbin's Coffee |
| ④ | Barbican Estate |
| ⑤ | Wood Street Watch Tower |
| ⑥ | Bow Bells and Juditheon vault |
| ⑦ | Bank of Scion England |
| ⑧ | Old Paul's |
| ⑨ | Bank Station |

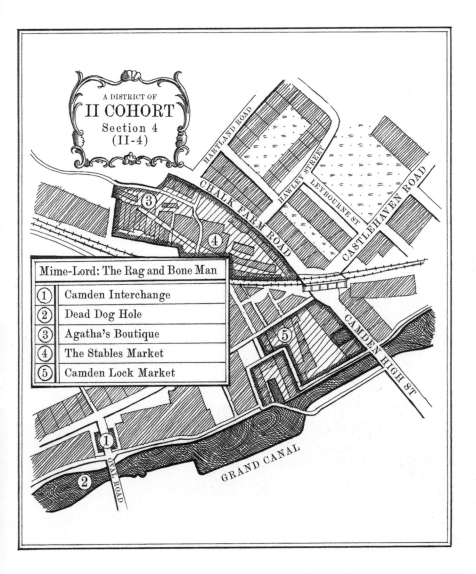

A DISTRICT OF
**II COHORT**
Section 4
(II-4)

HARTLAND ROAD

HAWLEY STREET

LEYBOURNE ST

CASTLEHAVEN ROAD

CHALK FARM ROAD

Mime-Lord: The Rag and Bone Man

| | |
|---|---|
| ① | Camden Interchange |
| ② | Dead Dog Hole |
| ③ | Agatha's Boutique |
| ④ | The Stables Market |
| ⑤ | Camden Lock Market |

CAMDEN HIGH ST

OVAL ROAD

GRAND CANAL

# THE SEVEN ORDERS OF CLAIRVOYANCE
## —According to *On The Merits of Unnaturalness*—

### ✳ I. SOOTHSAYERS ✳
*—purple—*

Require ritual objects (numa) to connect with the æther. Most often used to predict the future.

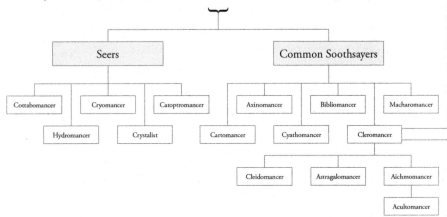

| Seers | Common Soothsayers |
|---|---|

Cottabomancer | Cryomancer | Catoptromancer | Axinomancer | Bibliomancer | Macharomancer

Hydromancer | Crystalist | Cartomancer | Cyathomancer | Cleromancer

Cleidomancer | Astragalomancer | Aichmomancer

Acultomancer

### ✳ III. MEDIUMS ✳
*—green—*

Connect with the æther through spiritual possession. Subject to some degree of control by spirits.

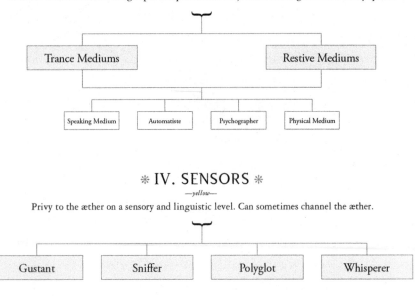

| Trance Mediums | Restive Mediums |
|---|---|

Speaking Medium | Automatiste | Psychographer | Physical Medium

### ✳ IV. SENSORS ✳
*—yellow—*

Privy to the æther on a sensory and linguistic level. Can sometimes channel the æther.

Gustant | Sniffer | Polyglot | Whisperer

## ✳ II. AUGURS ✳
*—blue—*

Use organic matter, or elements, to connect with the æther. Most often used to predict the future.

**Vile Augurs**  **Common Augurs**

Osteomancer | Haematomancer | Drymimancer | Chiromancer | Oculomancer | Anthropomancer | Extispicist

Rhabdomancer | Pyromancer | Halomancer | Tasseographer | Botanomancer | Theriomancer | Spodomancer | Capnomancer

Anthomancer | Sycomancer | Dendromancer | Daphnomancer

Libanomancer

## ✳ V. GUARDIANS ✳
*—orange—*

Have a higher degree of control over spirits than average and can bend ordinary ethereo-spatial limits.

Binder | Summoner | Necromancer | Exorcist

## ✳ VI. FURIES ✳
*—orange-red—*

Subject to internal change when connecting with the æther, typically to the dreamscape

Sibyl | Unreadable | Berserker

## ✳ VII. JUMPERS ✳
*—red—*

Able to affect the æther outside their own physical limits. Greater than average sensitivity to the æther.

Dreamwalker | Oracle

# Glossary

The slang used by clairvoyants in *The Mime Order* is loosely based on words used in the criminal underworld of London in the nineteenth century, with some amendments to meaning or usage. Other words have been invented by the author or taken from modern English or transliterated Hebrew.

**Æther:** [noun] The spirit realm, accessible by clairvoyants.

**Amaranth:** [noun] A flower that grows in the Netherworld. Its essence helps to heal spiritual injuries.

**Amaurotic:** [noun *or* adjective] Non-clairvoyant.

**Bone Season:** [noun] The decadal harvest of clairvoyant humans, organised by Scion in order to appease the Rephaim.

**Boundling:** [noun] A spirit that obeys a binder.

**Brogue:** [noun] An ethnic slur for an Irish person. Generally agreed to have originated from the name for an Irish accent, but may also be a result of an anti-Scion rebellion in Belfast; from "Belfast rogue."

**Buck cab:** [noun] A cab that accepts voyant clients. Many buck cabbies are employed by the syndicate.

**Busking:** [noun] Cash-in-hand clairvoyance. Most buskers offer to read fortunes for money. Not permitted within the clairvoyant crime syndicate unless the busker pays the local mime-lord or mime-queen a certain percentage of their earnings.

**Chair-warmer:** [noun] A useless, vapid person whose job is to look attractive.

**Charlatanism:** [noun] The practice of pretending to be clairvoyant in order to earn money. Strictly forbidden by the Unnatural Assembly.

**Chin music:** [noun] Talk nonsense.

**Chol-bird:** [noun] A winged *sarx-creature*. They are companions of the Rephaim and can travel to Earth in spirit form as *psychopomps*.

**Cookshop:** [noun] An establishment that sells hot food to be taken away.

**Costermonger:** [noun] A street vendor. Also called *hawker*.

**Dream-form:** [noun] The form a spirit takes within the confines of a dreamscape.

**Dreamscape:** [noun] The interior of the mind, where memories are stored. Split into five zones or "rings" of sanity: sunlight, twilight, midnight, lower midnight, and hadal. Clairvoyants can consciously access their own dreamscapes, while amaurotics may catch glimpses when they sleep.

**Ectoplasm:** [noun] Also *ecto*. Rephaite blood. Chartreuse yellow, luminous and slightly gelatinous. Can be used to open cold spots.

**Emim, the:** [noun] [singular *Emite*] Also *Buzzers*. The purported enemies of the Rephaim; "the dreaded ones." Described by Nashira Sargas as carnivorous and bestial, with a taste for human flesh. Their blood can be used to mask the nature of a clairvoyant's gift.

**Fluxion:** [noun] Also *flux*. A psychotic drug causing pain and disorientation in clairvoyants.

**Glossolalia:** [noun] Also *Gloss*. The language of spirits and Rephaim. Among clairvoyant humans, only polyglots can speak it.

**Glym jack**: [noun] From *glym*, meaning "lantern" or "light." A street bodyguard, rented to protect denizens from unnaturals at night. Identified by a distinctive green light.

**Golden cord**: [noun] A link between two spirits. Can be used to call for aid and transmit emotions. Little else is known about it.

**Gutterling**: [noun] [a] A homeless person; [b] someone who lives with, and works for, a *kidsman*. Like buskers and beggars, they are not considered fully fledged members of the syndicate, but may go on to become *hirelings* when their kidsman releases them from service.

**Hireling**: [noun] The lowest class of syndicate voyant, employed to run general errands for the dominant gang in a section. When the mime-lord or mime-queen deems it best, they will be promoted to a higher rank, e.g. *kidsman* or courier.

**Kidsman**: [noun] A class of syndicate voyant. They specialize in training young gutterlings in the arts of the syndicate.

**Meatspace**: [noun] The corporeal world; Earth.

**Mime-lord or mime-queen**: [noun] A gang leader in the clairvoyant syndicate; a specialist in mime-crime. Generally has a close group of five to ten followers, known as a section's *dominant gang*, but maintains overall command over all clairvoyants in one section within a cohort.

**Mollisher**: [noun] A clairvoyant associated with a mime-lord or mime-queen, sometimes shortened to "moll." Usually presumed to be [a] the mime-lord or mime-queen's lover, and [b] heir to his or her section, though the former may not always be the case. The Underlord's heir is known as *mollisher supreme* and is the only mollisher permitted to be a member of the Unnatural Assembly.

**Mort**: [noun] Woman. A mildly offensive term.

**Netherworld**: [noun] Also known as *She'ol* or *the half-realm*, the Netherworld is the original domain of the Rephaim. It acts as a middle ground between Earth and the æther, but has not served its original purpose since the Waning of the Veils, during which it fell into decay.

**Neutral house**: [noun] An establishment in which voyants from different sections can gather within a rival section.

**Nightwalker**: [noun] One who sells his or her clairvoyant knowledge as part of a sexual bargain. They may work independently or within a group in a *night parlor.*

**Novembertide**: [noun] The annual celebration of Scion London's official foundation in November 1929.

**Numen**: [noun] [plural *numa*, originally *numina*] An object or material used by a soothsayer or augur to connect with the æther, e.g. fire, cards, blood.

**Off the cot**: [adjective] Insane; reckless.

**Penny dreadful**: [noun] An illegal horror story, usually printed on cheap paper and sold for a low price by the *Penny Post.*

**Penny hangover**: [noun] A shelter for the homeless, open in Scion citadels from September to February. Clients are able to sleep on, or "hang over," a rope placed in front of a bench.

**Penny Post**: [noun] Grub Street's mobile bookshop. Post messengers carry illegal literature around the citadel and sell it to clairvoyants.

**Rainbow ruse**: [noun] A situation in which a clairvoyant busker cheats a client, usually by giving vague readings that cover all possible outcomes. Strictly prohibited by the Unnatural Assembly.

**Ranthen, the**: [noun] Also known as *the scarred ones.* An alliance of Rephaim who oppose the rule of the Sargas family and believe in the eventual restoration of the Netherworld.

**Raven**: [noun] A member of the Guard Extraordinary. The name originates from the ravens that traditionally lived in the Tower of London in the monarch days.

**Red zone**: [noun] The second highest level of security in a Scion citadel, followed only by Martial Law.

**Rephaite**: [noun] [plural *Rephaim*] [a] A biologically immortal, humanoid inhabitant of the Netherworld. Rephaim are known to feed on the aura of clairvoyant humans. [adjective] [b] The state of being a Rephaite; *to be Rephaite.*

**Rotmonger**: [noun] One of the gravest insults in Rephaite culture. It implies a conscious attempt to contribute to the decay of the Netherworld.

**Rottie**: [noun *or* adjective] Amaurotic.

**Saloop**: [noun] A hot, starchy drink made from orchid root, seasoned with rosewater or orange blossom.

**Sarx**: [noun] The incorruptible flesh of Rephaim and other creatures of the Netherworld (called *sarx-beings* or *sarx-creatures*). It has a slightly metallic sheen.

**Séance**: [noun] [a] For voyants, a group communion with the æther; [b] for Rephaim, transmitting a message between members of a group via a *psychopomp.*

**She'ol**: [noun] The true name of the Netherworld.

**Silver cord**: [noun] A permanent link between the body and the spirit. It allows a person to dwell for many years in one physical form. Particularly important to dreamwalkers, who use the cord to leave their bodies temporarily. The silver cord wears down over the years, and once broken cannot be repaired.

**Specter:** [noun] A manifestation of a person's fears or anxieties. Specters dwell in the hadal zone of the dreamscape.

**Star-sovereign:** [noun] An outdated term for the leader of the Rephaim. Used during the rule of the Mothallath family, after which it was replaced with *blood-sovereign*.

**Syndicate:** [noun] A criminal organization of clairvoyants, based in the Scion Citadel of London. Active since the early 1960s. Governed by the Underlord and the Unnatural Assembly. Members specialize in mime-crime for financial profit.

**Syndie:** [noun] Member of the clairvoyant crime syndicate.

**Thaumaturge:** [noun] Miracle-worker. Used among some voyants to praise someone who is particularly close to the *æther*, or touched by the zeitgeist.

**Threnody:** [noun] A series of words used to banish spirits to the outer darkness, a part of the æther that lies beyond the reach of clairvoyants.

**Underlord or Underqueen:** [noun] Head of the Unnatural Assembly and mob boss of the clairvoyant syndicate. Traditionally resides in the Devil's Acre in I Cohort, Section 1.

**Vigiles:** [noun] Also *Gillies*. Scion's police force, split into two main divisions: the clairvoyant Night Vigilance Division (NVD) and the amaurotic Sunlight Vigilance Division (SVD).

**Voyant:** [noun] Clairvoyant.

**Wisp:** [noun] From *will o' the wisp*, referring to a spirit that has been bound to a specific person or section of the citadel. The most common kind of drifter.

# Acknowledgments

This is my love song to the city of London.

My first and biggest thanks goes to those of you that have finished this book, which probably means you finished *The Bone Season* as well. Thank you for coming back to this world and these characters.

Thank you to David Godwin and all the staff at David Godwin Associates for their constant belief in my writing, and for always being a phone call away.

To Alexa von Hirschberg, thank you for being the most patient and enthusiastic editor I could ask for. To Alexandra Pringle, that formidable mime-queen of Bedford Square, for being such a fierce supporter of my books and an all-round inspiration to me.

Thank you to Justine Taylor and Lindeth Vasey for hunting down all the devils in the details.

To everyone at Bloomsbury, especially Amanda Shipp, Anna Bowen, Anurima Roy, Brendan Fredericks, Cassie Marsden, Cristina Gilbert, David Foy, Diya Kar Hazra, George Gibson, Ianthe Cox-Willmott, Isabel Blake, Jennifer Kelaher, Jude Drake, Kate Cubitt, Kathleen Farrar, Laura Keefe, Madeleine Feeny, Marie Coolman, Nancy Miller, Oliver Holden-Rea, Rachel Mannheimer, Sara Mercurio, and Trâm-Anh Doan. These books couldn't be in better hands.

To Anna Watkins, Caitlin Ingham, Bethia Thomas, and Katie Bond, who have since moved on to pastures new. It has been such a privilege to work with all of you.

To Hattie Adam-Smith and Eleanor Weil at Think Jam—thank you for your incredible enthusiasm for all things *Bone Season*.

515

The beautiful maps at the front of *The Mime Order* were drawn by Emily Faccini, and the cover was designed by the ever-brilliant David Mann. Thank you both for making this book so beautiful.

Thank you to the fantastic team at the Imaginarium Studios—Will Tennant, Chloe Sizer, Andy Serkis, Jonathan Cavendish, and Catherine Slater—for your continued passion for the *Bone Season* series. Will and Chloe, an especially big thanks to you for being such dedicated and responsive readers.

Thank you to my publishers, editors, and translators around the world for getting *The Bone Season* and *The Mime Order* to so many readers. A particularly big thank you to Ioana Schiau and Miruna Meirosu at Curtea Veche for introducing me to the music of Maria Tănase.

Thank you to Alana Kerr for being such a wonderful Paige for the audiobooks.

I'm very grateful to Sara Bergmark Elfgren, Ciarán Collins, and Maria Naydenova for letting me pester them with questions about languages, and to Melissa Harrison for her help with the starling part.

Thank you to my friends for continuing to put up with the long absences from the real world—most of all to Ilana Fernandes-Lassman, Victoria Morrish, Leiana Leatutufu, and Claire Donnelly, who have been my rocks this year. I never thought I'd be lucky enough to find friends like you.

And lastly, thank you to my family for your love, support, and hours of laughter. I couldn't have started this journey without you.

# Even a Dreamer Can Start a Revolution

Don't miss any of the books in the epic series from Samantha Shannon

### THE BONE SEASON

### THE MIME ORDER

### THE SONG RISING
Coming November 2016 . . .

"A great imagination at work." —*People*
"Shannon creates vividly dilapidated, macabre, and mysterious worlds." —*Booklist* **(starred review)**
"An intoxicating urban-fantasy series." —**NPR.org**